THE GREAT HC

BY

Stanley John Weyn

THE GREAT HOUSE

Published by Silver Scroll Publishing

New York City, NY

First published circa 1928

Copyright © Silver Scroll Publishing, 2015

All rights reserved

ABOUT SILVER SCROLL PUBLISHING

Silver Scroll Publishing is a digital publisher that brings the best historical fiction ever written to modern readers. Our comprehensive catalogue contains everything from historical novels about Rome to works about World War I.

CHAPTER I: THE HÔTEL LAMBERT--UPSTAIRS

On an evening in March in the 'forties of last century a girl looked down on the Seine from an attic window on the Ile St. Louis. The room behind her--or beside her, for she sat on the window-ledge, with her back against one side of the opening and her feet against the other--was long, whitewashed from floor to ceiling, lighted by five gaunt windows, and as cold to the eye as charity to the recipient. Along each side of the chamber ran ten pallet beds. A black door broke the wall at one end, and above the door hung a crucifix. A painting of a Station of the Cross adorned the wall at the other end. Beyond this picture the room had no ornament; it is almost true to say that beyond what has been named it had no furniture. One bed--the bed beside the window at which the girl sat--was screened by a thin curtain which did not reach the floor. This was her bed.

But in early spring no window in Paris looked on a scene more cheerful than this window; which as from an eyrie commanded a shining reach of the Seine bordered by the lawns and foliage of the King's Garden, and closed by the graceful arches of the Bridge of Austerlitz. On the water boats shot to and fro. The quays were gay with the red trousers of soldiers and the coquettish caps of soubrettes, with students in strange cloaks, and the twin kling wheels of yellow cabriolets. The first swallows were hawking hither and thither above the water, and a pleasant hum rose from the Boulevard Bourdon.

Yet the girl sighed. For it was her birthday, she was twenty this twenty-fifth of March, and there was not a soul in the world to know this and to wish her joy. A life of dependence, toned to the key of the whitewashed room and the thin pallets, lay before her; and though she had good reason to be thankful for the safety which dependence bought, still she was only twenty, and springtime, viewed from prison windows, beckons to its cousin, youth. She saw family groups walking the quays, and father, mother, children, all, seen from a distance, were happy. She saw lovers loitering in the garden or pacing to and fro, and romance walked with every one of them; none came late, or fell to words. She sighed more deeply; and on the sound the door opened.

"Hola!" cried a shrill voice, speaking in French, fluent, but oddly accented. "Who is here? The Princess desires that the English Mademoiselle will descend this evening."

"Very good," the girl in the window replied pleasantly. "At the same hour, Joséphine?"

"Why not, Mademoiselle?" A trim maid, with a plain face and the faultless figure of a Pole, came a few steps into the room. "But you are alone?"

"The children are walking. I stayed at home."

"To be alone? As if I did not understand that! To be alone--it is the luxury of the rich."

The girl nodded. "None but a Pole would have thought of that," she said.

"Ah, the crafty English Miss!" the maid retorted. "How she flatters! Perhaps she needs a touch of the tongs to-night? Or the loan of a pair of red-heeled shoes, worn no more than thrice by the Princess--and with the black which is convenable for Mademoiselle, oh, so neat! Of the ancien régime, absolutely!"

The other laughed. "The ancien régime, Joséphine--and this!" she replied, with a gesture that embraced the room, the pallets, her own bed. "A curled head--and this! You are truly a cabbage----"

"But Mademoiselle descends!"

"A cabbage of--foolishness!"

"Ah, well, if I descended, you would see," the maid retorted. "I am but the Princess's second maid, and I know nothing! But if I descended it would not be to this dormitory I should return! Nor to the tartines! Nor to the daughters of Poland! Trust me for that--and I know but my prayers. While Mademoiselle, she is an artist's daughter."

"There spoke the Pole again," the girl struck in with a smile.

"The English Miss knows how to flatter," Joséphine laughed. "That is one for the touch of the tongs," she continued, ticking them off on her fingers. "And one for the red-heeled shoes. And-- but no more! Let me begone before I am bankrupt!" She turned about with a flirt of her short petticoats, but paused and looked back, with her hand on the door. "None the less, mark you well, Mademoiselle, from the whitewash to the ceiling of Lebrun, from the dortoir of the Jeunes Filles to the Gallery of Hercules, there are but twenty stairs, and easy, oh, so easy to descend! If Mademoiselle instead of flattering Joséphine, the Cracovienne, flattered some pretty gentleman-- who knows? Not I! I know but my prayers!" And with a light laugh the maid clapped to the door and was gone.

The girl in the window had not throughout the parley changed her pose or moved more than her head, and this was characteristic of her. For even in her playfulness there was gravity, and a measure of stillness. Now, left alone, she dropped her feet to the floor, turned, and knelt on the sill with her brow pressed against the glass. The sun had set, mists were rising from the river, the quays were gray and cold. Here and there a lamp began to shine through the twilight. But the girl's thoughts were no longer on the scene beneath her eyes.

"There goes the third who has been good to me," she pondered. "First the Polish lodger who lived on the floor below, and saved me from that woman. Then the Princess's daughter. Now Joséphine. There are still kind people in the world--God grant that I may not forget it! But how much better to give than to take, to be strong than to be weak, to be the mistress and not the puppet of fortune! How much better--and, were I a man, how easy!"

But on that there came into her remembrance one to whom it had not been easy, one who had signally failed to master fortune, or to grapple with circumstances. "Poor father!" she whispered.

CHAPTER II: THE HÔTEL LAMBERT--DOWNSTAIRS

When ladies were at home to their intimates in the Paris of the 'forties, they seated their guests about large round tables with a view to that common exchange of wit and fancy which is the French ideal. The mode crossed to England, and in many houses these round tables, fallen to the uses of the dining-room or the nursery, may still be seen. But when the Princess Czartoriski entertained in the Hôtel Lambert, under the ceiling painted by Lebrun, which had looked down on the arm-chair of Madame de Châtelet and the tabouret of Voltaire, she was, as became a Pole, a law to herself. In that beautiful room, softly lit by wax candles, her guests were free to follow their bent, to fall into groups, or to admire at their ease the Watteaus and Bouchers which the Princess's father-in-law, old Prince Adam, had restored to their native panels.

Thanks to his taste and under her rule the gallery of Hercules presented on this evening a scene not unworthy of its past. The silks and satins of the old régime were indeed replaced by the high-shouldered coats, the stocks, the pins and velvet vests of the dandies; and Thiers beaming through his glasses, or Lamartine, though beauty, melted by the woes of Poland, hung upon his lips, might have been thought by some unequal to the dead. But they were now what those had been; and the women peacocked it as of old. At any rate the effect was good, and a guest who came late, and paused a moment on the threshold to observe the scene, thought that he had never before done the room full justice. Presently the Princess saw him and he went forward. The man who was talking to her made his bow, and she pointed with her fan to the vacant place. "Felicitations, my lord," she said. She held out her gloved hand.

"A thousands thanks," he said, as he bent over it. "But on what, Princess?"

"On the success of a friend. On what we have all seen in the Journal. Is it not true that you have won your suit?"

"I won, yes." He shrugged his shoulders. "But what, Madame? A bare title, an empty rent-roll."

"For shame!" she answered. "But I suppose that this is your English phlegm. Is it not a thing to be proud of--an old title? That which money cannot buy and the wisest would fain wear? M. Guizot, what would he not give to be Chien de Race? Your Peel, also?"

"And your Thiers?" he returned, with a sly glance at the little man in the shining glasses.

"He, too! But he has the passion of humanity, which is a title in itself. Whereas you English, turning in your unending circle, one out, one in, one in, one out, are but playing a game--marking time! You have not a desire to go forward!"

"Surely, Princess, you forget our Reform Bill, scarce ten years old."

"Which bought off your cotton lords and your fat bourgeois, and left the people without leaders and more helpless than before. No, my lord, if your Russell--Lord John, do you call him?--had one jot of M. Thiers' enthusiasm! Or your Peel--but I look for nothing there!"

He shrugged his shoulders. "I admit," he said, "that M. Thiers has an enthusiasm beyond the ordinary."

"You do? Wonderful!"

"But," with a smile, "it is, I fancy, an enthusiasm of which the object is--M. Thiers!"

"Ah!" she cried, fanning herself more quickly. "Now there spoke not Mr. Audley, the attaché--he had not been so imprudent! But--how do you call yourself now?"

"On days of ceremony," he replied, "Lord Audley of Beaudelays."

"There spoke my lord, unattached! Oh, you English, you have no enthusiasm. You have only traditions. Poor were Poland if her fate hung on you!"

"There are still bright spots," he said slyly. And his glance returned to the little statesman in spectacles on whom the Princess rested the hopes of Poland.

"No!" she cried vividly. "Don't say it again or I shall be displeased. Turn your eyes elsewhere. There is one here about whom I wish to consult you. Do you see the tall girl in black who is engaged with the miniatures?"

"I saw her some time ago."

"I suppose so. You are a man. I dare say you would call her handsome?"

"I think it possible, were she not in this company. What of her, Princess?"

"Do you notice anything beyond her looks?"

"The picture is plain--for the frame in which I see her. Is she one of the staff of your school?"

"Yes, but with an air----"

"Certainly--an air!" He nodded.

"Well, she is a countrywoman of yours and has a history. Her father, a journalist, artist, no matter what, came to live in Paris years ago. He went down, down, always down; six months ago he died. There was enough to bury him, no more. She says, I don't know"--the Princess indicated doubt with a movement of her fan--"that she wrote to friends in England. Perhaps she did not write; how do I know? She was at the last sou, the street before her, a hag of a concierge behind, and withal--as you see her."

"Not wearing that dress, I presume?" he said with a faint smile.

"No. She had passed everything to the Mont de Piété; she had what she stood up in--yet herself! Then a Polish family on the floor below, to whom my daughter carried alms, told Cécile of her. They pitied her, spoke well of her, she had done--no matter what for them--perhaps nothing. Probably nothing. But Cécile ascended, saw her, became enamoured, enragée! You know Cécile--for her all that wears feathers is of the angels! Nothing would do but she must bring her here and set her to teach English to the daughters during her own absence."

"The Princess is away?"

"For four weeks. But in three days she returns, and you see where I am. How do I know who this is? She may be this, or that. If she were French, if she were Polish, I should know! But she is English and of a calm, a reticence--ah!"

"And of a pride too," he replied thoughtfully, "if I mistake not. Yet it is a good face, Princess." She fluttered her fan. "It is a handsome one. For a man that is the same."

"With all this you permit her to appear?"

"To be of use. And a little that she may be seen by some English friend, who may tell me."

"Shall I talk to her?"

"If you will be so good. Learn, if you please, what she is."

"Your wishes are law," he rejoined. "Will you present me?"

"It is not necessary," the Princess answered. She beckoned to a stout gentleman who wore whiskers trimmed à la mode du Roi, and had laurel leaves on his coat collar. "A thousand thanks."

He lingered a moment to take part in the Princess's reception of the Academician. Then he joined a group about old Prince Adam Czartoriski, who was describing a recent visit to Cracow, that last morsel of free Poland, soon to pass into the maw of Austria. A little apart, the girl in black bent over the case of miniatures, comparing some with a list, and polishing others with a square of silk. Presently he found himself beside her. Their eyes met.

"I am told," he said, bowing, "that you are my countrywoman. The Princess thought that I might be of use to you."

The girl had read his errand before he spoke and a shade flitted across her face. She knew, only too well, that her hold on this rock of safety to which chance had lifted her--out of a gulf of peril and misery of which she trembled to think--was of the slightest. Early, almost from the first, she had discovered that the Princess's benevolence found vent rather in schemes for the good of many than in tenderness for one. But hitherto she had relied on the daughter's affection, and a little on her own usefulness. Then, too, she was young and hopeful, and the depths from which she had escaped were such that she could not believe that Providence would return her to them.

But she was quick-witted, and his opening frightened her. She guessed at once that she was not to be allowed to await Cécile's return, that her fate hung on what this Englishman, so big and bland and forceful, reported of her.

She braced herself to meet the danger. "I am obliged to the Princess," she said. "But my ties with England are slight. I came to France with my father when I was ten years old."

"I think you lost him recently?" He found his task less easy than it should have been.

"He died six months ago," she replied, regarding him gravely. "His illness left me without means. I was penniless, when the young Princess befriended me and gave me a respite here. I am no part of this," with a glance at the salon and the groups about them. "I teach upstairs. I am thankful for the privilege of doing so."

"The Princess told me as much," he said frankly. "She thought that, being English, I might advise you better than she could; that possibly I might put you in touch with your relations?"

She shook her head.

"Or your friends? You must have friends?"

"Doubtless my father had--once," she said in a low voice. "But as his means diminished, he saw less and less of those who had known him. For the last two years I do not think that he saw an Englishman at home. Before that time I was in a convent school, and I do not know."

"You are a Roman Catholic, then?"

"No. And for that reason--and for another, that my account was not paid"--her color rose painfully to her face--"I could not apply to the Sisters. I am very frank," she added, her lip trembling.

"And I encroach," he answered, bowing. "Forgive me! Your father was an artist, I believe?"

"He drew for an Atelier de Porcelaine--for the journals when he could. But he was not very successful," she continued reluctantly. "The china factory which had employed him since he came to Paris, failed. When I returned from school he was alone and poor, living in the little street in the Quartier, where he died."

"But forgive me, you must have some relations in England?"

"Only one of whom I know," she replied. "My father's brother. My father had quarrelled with him--bitterly, I fear; but when he was dying he bade me write to my uncle and tell him how we were placed. I did so. No answer came. Then after my father's death I wrote again. I told my uncle that I was alone, that I was without money, that in a short time I should be homeless, that if I could return to England I could live by teaching French. He did not reply. I could do no more."

"That was outrageous," he answered, flushing darkly. Though well under thirty he was a tall man and portly, with one of those large faces that easily become injected. "Do you know--is your uncle also in narrow circumstances?"

"I know no more than his name," she said. "My father never spoke of him. They had quarrelled. Indeed, my father spoke little of his past."

"But when you did not hear from your uncle, did you not tell your father?"

"It could do no good," she said. "And he was dying."

He was not sentimental, this big man, whose entrance into a room carried with it a sense of power. Nor was he one to be lightly moved, but her simplicity and the picture her words drew for him of the daughter and the dying man touched him. Already his mind was made up that the Czartoriski should not turn her adrift for lack of a word. Aloud, "The Princess did not tell me your name," he said. "May I know it?"

"Audley," she said. "Mary Audley."

He stared at her. She supposed that he had not caught the name. She repeated it.

"Audley? Do you really mean that?"

"Why not?" she asked, surprised in her turn. "Is it so uncommon a name?"

"No," he replied slowly. "No, but it is a coincidence. The Princess did not tell me that your name was Audley."

The girl shook her head. "I doubt if she knows," she said. "To her I am only 'the English girl.'"

"And your father was an artist, resident in Paris? And his name?"

"Peter Audley."

He nodded. "Peter Audley," he repeated. His eyes looked through her at something far away. His lips were more firmly set. His face was grave. "Peter Audley," he repeated softly. "An artist resident in Paris!"

"But did you know him?" she cried.

He brought his thoughts and his eyes back to her. "No, I did not know him," he said. "But I have heard of him." And again it was plain that his thoughts took wing. "John Audley's brother, the artist!" he muttered.

In her impatience she could have taken him by the sleeve and shaken him. "Then you do know John Audley?" she said. "My uncle?"

Again he brought himself back with an effort. "A thousand pardons!" he said. "You see the Princess did not tell me that you were an Audley. Yes, I know John Audley--of the Gatehouse. I suppose it was to him you wrote?"

"Yes."

"And he did not reply?"

She nodded.

He laughed, as at something whimsical. It was not a kindly laugh, it jarred a little on his listener. But the next moment his face softened, he smiled at her, and the smile of such a man had its importance, for in repose his eyes were hard. It was clear to her that he was a man of position, that he belonged of right to this keen polished world at which she was stealing a glance. His air was distinguished, and his dress, though quiet, struck the last note of fashion.

"But I am keeping you in suspense," he said. "I must tell you, Miss Audley, why it surprised me to learn your name. Because I, too, am an Audley."

"You!" she cried.

"Yes, I," he replied. "What is more, I am akin to you. The kinship is remote, but it happens that your father's name, in its place in a pedigree, has been familiar to me of late, and I could set down the precise degree of cousinship in which you stand to me. I think your father was my fourth cousin."

She colored charmingly. "Is it possible?" she exclaimed.

"It is a fact, proved indeed, recently, in a court of law," he answered lightly. "Perhaps it is as well that we have that warrant for a conversation which I can see that the Princess thinks long. After this she will expect to hear the whole of your history."

"I fear that she may be displeased," the girl said, wincing a little. "You have been very kind----"

"Who should be kind," he replied, "if not the head of your family? But have no fear, I will deal with the Princess. I shall be able to satisfy her, I have no doubt."

"And you"--she looked at him with appeal in her eyes--"will you be good enough to tell me who you are?"

"I am Lord Audley. To distinguish me from another of the same name, I am called Audley of Beaudelays."

"Of Beaudelays?" she repeated. He thought her face, her whole bearing, singularly composed in view of his announcement. "Beaudelays?" she repeated thoughtfully. "I have heard the name more than once. Perhaps from my father."

"It were odd if you had not," he said. "It is the name of my house, and your uncle, John Audley, lives within a mile of it."

"Oh," she said. The name of the uncle who had ignored her appeals fell on her like a cold douche.

"I will not say more now," Lord Audley continued. "But you shall hear from me. To--morrow I quit Paris for three or four days, but when I return have no fear. You may leave the matter in my hands in full confidence that I shall not fail--my cousin."

He held out his hand and she laid hers in it. She looked him frankly in the face. "Thank you," she said. "I little thought when I descended this evening that I should meet a kinsman."

"And a friend," he answered, holding her hand a little longer than was needful.

"And a friend," she repeated. "But there--I must go now. I should have disappeared ten minutes ago. This is my way." She inclined her head, and turning from him she pushed open a small door masked by a picture. She passed at once into a dark corridor, and threading its windings gained the great staircase.

As she flitted upwards from floor to floor, skirting a long procession of shadowy forms, and now ogled by a Leda whose only veil was the dusk, now threatened by the tusks of the great boar at bay, she was not conscious of thought or surprise. It was not until she had lighted her taper outside the dormitory door, and, passing between the rows of sleeping children, had gained her screened corner, that she found it possible to think. Then she set the light in her tiny washing-basin--such was the rule--and seated herself on her bed. For some minutes she stared before her, motionless and unwinking, her hands clasped about her knees, her mind at work.

Was it true, or a dream? Had this really happened to her since she had viewed herself in the blurred mirror, had set a curl right and, satisfied, had turned to go down? The danger and the delivery from it, the fear and the friend in need? Or was it a Cinderella's treat, which no fairy godmother would recall to her, with which no lost slipper would connect her? She could almost believe this. For no Cinderella, in the ashes of the hearth, could have seemed more remote from the gay ball-room than she crouching on her thin mattress, with the breathing of the children in her ears, from the luxury of the famous salon.

Or, if it was true, if it had happened, would anything come of it? Would Lord Audley remember her? Or would he think no more of her, ignoring to-morrow the poor relation whom it had been the whim of the moment to own? That would be cruel! That would be base! But if Mary had fallen in with some good people since her father's death, she had also met many callous, and a few cruel people. He might be one. And then, how strange it was that her father had never named this great kinsman, never referred to him, never even, when dying, disclosed his name!

The light wavered in the draught that stole through the bald, undraped window. A child whimpered in its sleep, awoke, began to sob. It was the youngest of the daughters of Poland. The girl rose, and going on tip-toe to the child, bent over it, kissed it, warmed it in her bosom, soothed it. Presently the little waif slept again, and Mary Audley began to make ready for bed.

But so much turned for her on what had happened, so much hung in the balance, that it was not unnatural that as she let down her hair and plaited it in two long tails for the night, she should see her new kinsman's face in the mirror. Nor strange that as she lay sleepless and thought-ridden in her bed the same face should present itself anew relieved against the background of darkness.

CHAPTER III: THE LAWYER ABROAD

Half an hour later Lord Audley paused in the hall at Meurice's, and having given his cloak and hat to a servant went thoughtfully up the wide staircase. He opened the door of a room on the first floor. A stout man with a bald head, who had been for some time yawning over the dying fire, rose to his feet and remained standing.

Audley nodded. "Hallo, Stubbs!" he said carelessly, "not in bed yet?"

"No, my lord," the other answered. "I waited to learn if your lordship had any orders for England."

"Well, sit down now. I've something to tell you." My lord stooped as he spoke and warmed his hands at the embers; then rising, he stood with his back to the hearth. The stout man sat forward on his chair with an air of deference. His double chin rested on the ample folds of a soft white stock secured by a gold pin in the shape of a wheat-sheaf. He wore black knee-breeches and stockings, and his dress, though plain, bore the stamp of neatness and prosperity.

For a minute or two Audley continued to look thoughtfully before him. At length, "May I take it that this claim is really at an end now?" he said. "Is the decision final, I mean?"

"Unless new evidence crops up," Stubbs answered--he was a lawyer--"the decision is certainly final. With your lordship's signature to the papers I brought over----"

"But the claimant might try again?"

"Mr. John Audley might do anything," Stubbs returned. "I believe him to be mad upon the point, and therefore capable of much. But he could only move on new evidence of the most cogent nature. I do not believe that such evidence exists."

His employer weighed this for some time. At length, "Then if you were in my place," he said, "you would not be tempted to hedge?"

"To hedge?" the lawyer exclaimed, as if he had never heard the word before. "I am afraid I don't understand."

"I will explain. But first, tell me this. If anything happens to me before I have a child, John Audley succeeds to the peerage? That is clear?"

"Certainly! Mr. John Audley, the claimant, is also your heir-at-law."

"To title and estates--such as they are?"

"To both, my lord."

"Then follow me another step, Stubbs. Failing John Audley, who is the next heir?"

"Mr. Peter Audley," Stubbs replied, "his only brother, would succeed, if he were alive. But it is common ground that he is dead. I knew Mr. Peter, and, if I may say it of an Audley, my lord, a more shiftless, weak, improvident gentleman never lived. And obstinate as the devil! He married into trade, and Mr. John never forgave it--never forgave it, my lord. Never spoke of his brother or to his brother from that time. It was before the Reform Bill," the lawyer continued with a sigh. "There were no railways then and things were different. Dear, dear, how the world changes! Mr. Peter must have gone abroad ten years ago, but until he was mentioned in the suit I don't think that I had heard his name ten times in as many years. And he an Audley!"

"He had a child?"

"Only one, a daughter."

"Would she come in after Mr. John?"

"Yes, my lord, she would--if living."

"I've been talking to her this evening."

"Ah!" The lawyer was not so simple as he seemed, and for a minute or two he had foreseen the dénouement. "Ah!" he repeated, thoughtfully rubbing his plump calf. "I see, my lord. Mr. Peter Audley's daughter? Really! And if I may venture to ask, what is she like?"

Audley paused before he answered. Then, "If you have painted the father aright, Stubbs, I should say that she was his opposite in all but his obstinacy. A calm and self-reliant young woman, if I am any judge."

"And handsome?"

"Yes, with a look of breeding. At the same time she is penniless and dependent, teaching English in a kind of charity school, cheek by jowl with a princess!"

"God bless my soul!" cried the lawyer, astonished at last. "A princess!"

"Who is a good creature as women go, but as likely as not to send her adrift to-morrow."

"Tut-tut-tut!" muttered the other.

"However, I'll tell you the story," Audley concluded. And he did so.

When he had done, "Well," Stubbs exclaimed, "for a coincidence----"

"Ah, there," the young man broke in, "I fancy, all's not said. I take it the Princess noted the name, but was too polite to question me. Anyway, the girl is there. She is dependent, friendless; attractive, and well-bred. For a moment it did occur to me--she is John Audley's heiress--that I might make all safe by----" His voice dropped. His last words were inaudible.

"The chance is so very remote," said the lawyer, aware that he was on delicate ground, and that the other was rather following out his own thoughts than consulting him.

"It is. The idea crossed my mind only for a moment--of course it's absurd for a man as poor as I am. There is hardly a poorer peer out of Ireland--you know that. Fourteenth baron without a roof to my house or a pane of glass in my windows! And a rent-roll when all is told of----"

"A little short of three thousand," the lawyer muttered.

"Two thousand five hundred, by God, and not a penny more! If any man ought to marry money, I am that man, Stubbs!"

Mr. Stubbs, staring at the fire with a hand on each knee, assented respectfully. "I've always hoped that you would, my lord," he said, "though I've not ventured to say it."

"Yes! Well--putting that aside," the other resumed, "what is to be done about her? I've been thinking it over, and I fancy that I've hit on the right line. John Audley's given me trouble enough. I'll give him some. I'll make him provide for her, d--n him, or I don't know my man!"

"I'd like to know, my lord," Stubbs ventured thoughtfully, "why he didn't answer her letters. He hated her father, but it is not like Mr. John to let the young lady drift. He's crazy about the family, and she is his next heir. He's a lonely man, too, and there is room at the Gatehouse."

Audley paused, half-way across the room. "I wish we had never leased the Gatehouse to him!"

"It's not everybody's house, my lord. It's lonely and----"

"It's too near Beaudelays!"

"If your lordship were living at the Great House, quite so," the lawyer agreed. "But, as it is, the rent is useful, and the lease was made before our time, so that we have no choice."

"I shall always believe that he had a reason for going there!"

"He had an idea that it strengthened his claim," the lawyer said indulgently. "Nothing beyond that, my lord."

"Well, I've made up my mind to increase his family by a niece!" the other replied. "He shall have the girl whether he likes it or not. Take a pen, man, and sit down. He's spoiled my breakfast many a time with his confounded Writs of Error, or whatever you call them, and for once I'll be even with him. Say--yes, Stubbs, say this:

"'I am directed by Lord Audley to inform you that a young lady, believed to be a daughter of the late Mr. Peter Audley, and recently living in poverty in an obscure'--yes, Stubbs, say obscure--'part of Paris, has been rescued by the benevolence of a Polish lady. For the present she is in the lady's house in a menial capacity, and is dependent on her charity. Lord Audley is informed that the young lady made application to you without result, but this report his lordship discredits. Still, he feels himself concerned; and if those to whom she naturally looks decline to aid her, it is his lordship's intention to make such provision as may enable her to live respectably. I am to inform you that Miss Audley's address is the Hôtel Lambert, He St. Louis, Paris. Letters should be addressed "Care of the Housekeeper."'"

"He won't like the last touch!" the young man continued, with a quiet chuckle. "If that does not touch him on the raw, I'll yield up the title to-morrow. And now, Stubbs, good-night."

But Stubbs did not take the hint. "I want to say one word, my lord, about the borough--about Riddsley," he said. "We put in Mr. Mottisfont at the last election, your lordship's interest just tipping the scale. We think, therefore, that a word from you may set right what is going wrong."

"What is it?"

"There's a strong feeling," the lawyer answered, his face serious, "that the party is not being led aright. And that Mr. Mottisfont, who is old----"

"Is willing to go with the party, eh, Stubbs?"

"No, my lord, with the party leaders. Which is a different thing. Sir Robert Peel--the land put him in, but, d--n me, my lord"--the lawyer's manner lost much of its deference and he spoke bluntly and strongly--"it looks as if he were going to put the land out! An income-tax in peace time, we've taken that. And less protection for the farmer, very good--if it must be. But all this taking off of duties, this letting in of Canadian corn--I tell you, my lord, there's an ugly feeling abroad! There are a good many in Riddsley say that he is going to repeal the Corn Laws altogether; that he's sold us to the League, and won't be long before he delivers us!"

The big man sitting back in his chair smiled. "It seems to me," he said, "that you are travelling rather fast and rather far, Stubbs!"

"That's just what we fear Sir Robert is doing!" the lawyer retorted smartly, the other's rank forgotten. "And you may take it from me the borough won't stand it, my lord, and the sooner Mr.

Mottisfont has a hint the better. If he follows Peel too far, the bottom will fall out of his seat. There's no Corn Law leaguer will ever sit for Riddsley!"

"With your help, anyway, Stubbs," my lord said with a smile. The lawyer's excitement amused him.

"No, my lord! Never with my help! I believe that on the landed interest rests the stability of the country! It was the landed interest that supported Pitt and beat Bony, and brought us through the long war. It was the landed interest that kept us from revolution in the dark days after the war. And now because the men that turn cotton and iron and clay into money by the help of the devil's breath--because they want to pay lower wages----"

"The ark of the covenant is to be overthrown, eh?" the young man laughed. "Why, to listen to you, Stubbs, one would think that you were the largest landowner in the county!"

"No, my lord," the lawyer answered. "But it's the landowners have made me what I am. And it's the landowners and the farmers that Riddsley lives by and is going to stand by! And the sooner Mr. Mottisfont knows that the better. He was elected as a Tory, and a Tory he must stop, whether Sir Robert turns his coat or not!"

"You want me to speak to Mottisfont?"

"We do, my lord. Just a word. I was at the Ordinary last fair day, and there was nothing else talked of. Free Canadian corn was too like free French corn and free Belgian corn for Stafford wits to see much difference. And Peel is too like repeal, my lord. We are beginning to see that."

Audley shrugged his shoulders. "The party is satisfied," he said. "And Mottisfont? I can't drive the man."

"No, but a word from you----"

"Well, I'll think about it. But I fancy you're overrunning the scent."

"Then the line is not straight!" the lawyer retorted shrewdly. "However, if I have been too warm, I beg pardon, my lord."

"I'll bear it in mind," Audley answered. "Very good. And now, good-night, Stubbs. Don't forget to send the letter to John Audley as soon as you reach London."

Stubbs replied that he would, and took his leave. He had said his say on the borough question, lord or no lord; which to a Briton--and he was a typical Briton--was a satisfaction.

But half an hour later, when he had drawn his nightcap down to his ears and stood, the extinguisher in his hand, he paused. "He's a sober hand for a young man," he thought, "a very sober hand. I warrant he will never run his ship on the rocks for lack of a good look-out!"

CHAPTER IV: HOMEWARD BOUND

In the corner of the light diligence, seating six inside, which had brought her from Montreuil, Mary Audley leant forward, looking out through the dingy panes for the windmills of Calais. Joséphine slept in the corner facing her, as she had slept for two hours past. Their companions, a French shopkeeper and her child, and an English bagman, sighed and fidgeted, as travellers had cause to sigh and fidget in days when he was lucky who covered the distance from Paris to Calais in twenty-five hours. The coach rumbled on. The sun had set, a small rain was falling. The fading light tinged the plain of the Pas de Calais with a melancholy which little by little dyed the girl's thoughts.

She was on her way to her own country, to those on whom she might be dependent without shame. And common sense, of which she had a large share, told her that she had cause, great cause to be thankful. But the flush of relief, to which the opening prospect had given rise, was ebbing. The life before her was new, those amongst whom she must lead that life were strange; nor did the cold phrases of her uncle's invitation, which ignored both her father and the letters that she had written, promise an over-warm welcome.

Still, "Courage!" Mary murmured to herself, "Courage!" And she recalled a saying which she had learned from the maid, "At the worst, ten fingers!" Then, seeing that at last they were entering the streets of the town and that the weary journey was over--she had left Paris the day before--she touched Joséphine. "We are there," she said.

The maid awoke with her eyes on the bagman, who was stout. "Ah!" she muttered. "In England they are like that! No wonder that they travel seeing that their bones are so padded! But, for me I am one ache."

They jolted over the uneven pavement, crossed a bridge, lumbered through streets scarcely wider than the swaying diligence, at last with a great cracking of whips they swerved to the left and drew up amid the babel of the quay. In a twinkling they were part of it. Porters dragged down, fought for, snatched up their baggage. English-speaking touts shook dirty cards in their faces. Tide-waiters bawled questions in their ears. The postilion, the conductor, all the world stretched greedy palms under their noses. Other travellers ran into them, and they ran into other travellers. All this, in the dusk, in the rain, while the bell on the deck overhead clanged above the roar of the escaping steam, and a man shouted without ceasing, "Tower steamer! Tower steamer! Any more for England?"

Joséphine, after one bitter exchange of words with a lad who had seized her handbag, thrust her fingers into her ears and resigned herself. Even Mary for a moment was aghast. She was dragged this way and that, she lost one article and recovered it, lost another and recovered that, she lost her ticket and rescued it from a man's hand. At last, her baggage on board, she found herself breathless at the foot of the ladder, with three passengers imploring her to ascend, and six touts clinging to her skirts and crying for drink-money. She had barely time to make her little gift to the kind-hearted maid--who was returning to Paris by the night coach--and no time to thank her, before they were parted. Mary was pushed up the ladder. In a moment she was looking down from the deck on the wet, squalid quay, the pale up-turned faces, the bustling crowd.

She picked out the one face which she knew, and which it pained her to lose. By gestures and smiles, with a tear in the eye, she tried to make amends to Joséphine for the hasty parting, the half-spoken words. The maid on her side was in tears, and after the French fashion was proud of them. So the last minute came. The paddles were already turning, the ship was going slowly astern, when a man pushed his way through the crowd. He clutched the ladder as it was unhooked, and at some risk and much loss of dignity he was bundled on board. There was a lamp amidships, and, as he regained his balance, Mary, smiling in spite of herself, saw that he was an Englishman, a man about thirty, and plainly dressed. Then in her anxiety to see the last of Joséphine she crossed the deck as the ship went about, and she lost sight of him.

She continued to look back and to wave her handkerchief, until nothing remained but a light or two in a bank of shadow. That was the last she was to see of the land which had been her home for ten years; and chilled and lonely she turned about and did what, had she been an older traveller, she would have done before. She sought the after-cabin. Alas, a glance from the foot of the companion was enough! Every place was taken, every couch occupied, and the air, already close, repelled her. She climbed to the deck again, and was seeking some corner where she could sit, sheltered from the wind and rain, when the captain saw her and fell foul of her.

"Now, young lady," he said, "no woman's allowed on deck at night!"

"Oh, but," she protested, "there's no room downstairs!"

"Won't do," he answered roughly. "Lost a woman overboard once, and as much trouble about her as about all the men, drunk or sober, I've ever carried. All women below, all women below, is the order! Besides," more amicably, as he saw by a ray of lantern-light that she was young and comely, "it's wet, my dear, and going to be d--d wet, and as dark as Wapping!"

"But I've a cloak," she petitioned, "if I sit quite still, and----"

A tall form loomed up at the captain's elbow. "This is the lady I am looking for," the new-comer said. "It will be all right, Captain Jones."

The captain turned sharply. "Oh, my lord," he said, "I didn't know; but with petticoats and a dark night, blest if you know where you are! I'm sure I beg the young lady's pardon. Quite right, my lord, quite right!" With a rough salute he went forward and the darkness swallowed him.

"Lord Audley?" Mary said. She spoke quietly, but to do so she had to steady her voice.

"Yes," he replied. "I knew that you were crossing to-night, and as I had to go over this week I chose this evening. I've reserved a cabin for you."

"Oh, but," she remonstrated, "I don't think you should have done that! I don't know that I can----"

"Afford it?" he said coolly. "Then--as it is a matter of some shillings--your kinsman will presume to pay for it."

It was a small thing, and she let it pass. "But who told you," she asked, "that I was crossing to-night?"

"The Princess. You don't feel, I suppose, that as you are crossing, it was my duty to stay in France?"

"Oh no!" she protested.

"But you are not sure whether you are more pleased or more vexed? Well, let me show you where your cabin is--it is the size of a milliner's box, but by morning you will be glad of it, and that may turn the scale. Moreover," as he led the way across the deck, "the steward's boy, when he is not serving gin below, will serve tea above, and at sea tea is not to be scorned. That's your number--7. And there is the boy. Boy!" he called in a voice that ensured obedience, "Tea and bread and butter for this lady in number 7 in an hour. See it is there, my lad!"

She smiled. "I think the tea and bread and butter may turn the scale," she said.

"Right," he replied. "Then, as it is only eight o'clock, why should we not sit in the shelter of this tarpaulin? I see that there are two seats. They might have been put for us."

"Is it possible that they were?" she asked shrewdly. "Well, why not?"

She had no reason to give--and the temptation was great. Five minutes before she had been the most lonely creature in the world. The parting from Joséphine, the discomfort of the boat, the dark sea and the darker horizon, the captain's rough words, had brought the tears to her eyes. And then, in a moment, to be thought of, provided for, kindly entreated, to be lapped in attentions as in a cloak--in very fact, in another second a warm cloak was about her--who could expect her to refuse this? Moreover, he was her kinsman; probably she owed it to him that she was here.

At any rate she thought that it would be prudish to demur, and she took one of the seats in the lee of the screen. Audley tucked the cloak about her, and took the other. The light of a lantern fell on their faces and the few passengers who still tramped the windy deck could see the pair, and doubtless envied him their shelter. "Are you comfortable?" he inquired--but before she could answer he whistled softly.

"What is it?" Mary asked.

"Not much." He laughed to himself.

Then she saw coming along the deck towards them a man who had not found his sea-legs. As he approached he took little runs, and now brought up against the rail, now clutched at a stay. Mary knew the man again. "He nearly missed the boat," she whispered.

"Did he?" her companion answered in the same tone. "Well, if he had quite missed it, I'd have forgiven him. He is going to be ill, I'll wager!"

When the man was close to them he reeled, and to save himself he grasped the end of their screen. His eyes met theirs. He was past much show of emotion, but his voice rose as he exclaimed, "Audley. Is that you?"

"It is. We are in for a rough night, I'm afraid."

"And--pardon me," the stranger hesitated, peering at them, "is that Miss Audley with you?"

"Yes," Mary said, much surprised.

"Oh!"

"This is Mr. Basset," Audley explained. Mary stared at the stranger. The name conveyed nothing to her.

"I came to meet you," he said, speaking with difficulty, and now and again casting a wild eye abroad as the deck heaved under him. "But I expected to find you at the hotel, and I waited there until I nearly missed the boat. Even then I felt that I ought to learn if you were on board, and I came up to see."

"I am very much obliged to you," Mary answered politely, "but I am quite comfortable, thank you. It is close below, and Lord Audley found this seat for me. And I have a cabin."

"Oh yes!" he answered. "I think I will go down then if you--if you are sure you want nothing."

"Nothing, thank you," Mary answered with decision.

"I think I--I'll go, then. Good-night!"

With that he went, making desperate tacks in the direction of the companion. Unfortunately what he gained in speed he lost in dignity, and before he reached the hatch Lord Audley gave way to laughter.

"Oh, don't!" Mary cried. "He will hear you. And it was kind of him to look for me when he was not well."

But Audley only laughed the more. "You don't catch the full flavor of it," he said. "He's come three hundred miles to meet you, and he's too ill to do anything now he's here!"

"Three hundred miles to meet me!" she cried in astonishment.

"Every yard of it! Don't you know who he is? He's Peter Basset, your uncle's nephew by marriage, who lives with him. He's come, or rather your uncle has sent him, all the way from Stafford to meet you--and he's gone to lie down! He's gone to lie down! There's a squire of dames for you! Upon my honor, I never knew anything richer!"

And my lord's laughter broke out anew.

CHAPTER V: THE LONDON PACKET

Mary laughed with him, but she was not comfortable. What she had seen of the stranger, a man plain in feature and ordinary in figure, one whom the eye would not have remarked in a crowd, did not especially commend him. And certainly he had not shown himself equal to a difficult situation. But the effort he had made to come to her help appealed to her generosity, and she was not sure how far she formed a part of the comedy. So her laughter was from the lips only, and brief. Then, "My uncle's nephew?" she asked thoughtfully.

"His wife's nephew. Your uncle married a Basset."

"But why did he send him to meet me?"

"For a simple reason--I should say that he had no one else to send. Your uncle is not a man of many friends."

"I understood that some one would meet the boat in London," she said. "But I expected a woman."

"I fancy the woman would be to seek," he replied. "And Basset is a kind of tame cat at the Gatehouse. He lives there a part of the year, though he has an old place of his own up the country. He's a Staffordshire man born and bred, and I dare say a good fellow in his way, but a dull dog! a dull dog! Are you sure that the wind does not catch you?"

She said that she was very comfortable, and they were silent awhile, listening to the monotonous slapping of a rope against the mast and the wash of the waves as they surged past the beam. A single light at the end of the breakwater shone in the darkness behind them. She marked the light grow smaller and more distant, and her thoughts went back to the convent school, to her father, to the third-floor where for a time they had been together, to his care for her--feeble and inefficient, to his illness. And a lump rose in her throat, her hands gripped one another as she strove to hide her feelings. In her heart she whispered a farewell. She was turning her back on her father's grave. The last tendril which bound her to the old life was breaking.

The light vanished, and gradually the girl's reflections sought a new channel. They turned from the past to the present, and dwelt on the man beside her, who had not only thought of her comfort, who had not only saved her from some hours of loneliness, but had probably wrought this change in her life. This was the third time only that she had seen him. Once, some days after that memorable evening, he had called at the Hôtel Lambert, and her employer had sent for her. He had greeted her courteously in the Princess's presence, had asked her kindly if she had heard from England, and had led her to believe that she would hear. And she remembered with a blush that the Princess had looked from one to the other with a smile, and afterwards had had another manner for her.

Meanwhile the man wondered what she was thinking, and waited for her to give him the clue. But she was so long silent that his patience wore thin. It was not for this, it was not to sit silent beside her, that he had taken a night journey and secured these cosey seats.

"Well?" he said at last.

She turned to him, her eyes wet with tears. "It seems so strange," she murmured, "to be leaving all and going into a world in which I know no one."

"Except the head of your family."

"Except you! I suppose that I owe it to you that I am here?"

"I should be happy if I thought so," he replied, with careful reticence. "But we set a stone rolling, we do not know where it falls. You will soon learn--Basset will tell you, if I don't--that your uncle and I are not on good terms. Therefore it is unlikely that he was moved by what I said."

"But you said something?"

"If I did," he answered, smiling, "it was against the grain--who likes to put his finger between the door and the jamb? And let me caution you. Your uncle will not suffer meddling on my part, still less a reminder of it. Therefore, as you are going to owe all to him, you will do well to be silent about me."

She was sure that she owed all to him, and she might have said so, but at that moment the boat changed its course and the full force of the wind struck them. The salt spray whipped and stung their faces. Her cloak flew out like a balloon, her scarf pennon-wise, the tarpaulin flapped like some huge bird. He had to spring to the screen, to adjust it to the new course, to secure and tuck in her cloak--and all in haste, with exclamations and laughter, while Mary, sharing the joy of the struggle, and braced by the sting of the salt wind, felt her heart rise. How kind he was, and how strong. How he towered above ordinary men. How safe she felt in his care.

When they were settled anew, she asked him to tell her something about the Gatehouse.

"It's a lonely place," he said. "It is quite out of the world. I don't know, indeed, how you will exist after the life you have led."

"The life I have led!" she protested. "But that is absurd! Though you saw me in the Princess's salon, you know that my life had nothing in common with hers. I was downstairs no more than three or four times, and then merely to interpret. My life was spent between whitewashed walls, on bare floors. I slept in a room with twenty children, ate with forty--onion soup and thick tartines. The evening I saw you I wore shoes which the maid lent me. And with all that I was thankful, most thankful, to have such a refuge. The great people who met at the Princess's----"

"And who thought that they were making history!" he laughed. "Did you know that? Did you know that the Princess was looking to them to save the last morsel of Poland?"

"No," she said. "I did not know. I am very ignorant. But if I were a man, I should love to do things like that."

"I believe you would!" he replied. "Well, there are crusades in England. Only I fear that you will not be in the way of them."

"And I am not a princess! But tell me, please, what are they?"

"You will not be long before you come upon one," he replied, a hint of derision in his tone. "You will see a placard in the streets, 'Shall the people's bread be taxed?' Not quite so romantic as the independence of Poland? But I can tell you that heads are quite as likely to be broken over it."

"Surely," she said, "there can be only one answer to that."

"Just so," he replied dryly. "But what is the answer? The land claims high prices that it may thrive; the towns claim cheap bread that they may live. Each says that the country depends upon it. 'England self-supporting!' says one. 'England the workshop of the world!' says the other."

"I begin to see."

"'The land is the strength of the country,' argues the squire. 'Down with monopoly,' cries the cotton lord. Then each arms himself with a sword lately forged and called 'Philanthropy,' and with that he searches for chinks in the other's armor. 'See how factories work the babes, drive the women underground, ruin the race,' shout the squires. 'Vote for the land and starvation wages,' shout the mill-owners."

"But does no one try to find the answer?" she asked timidly. "Try to find out what is best for the people?"

"Ah!" he rejoined, "if by the people you mean the lower classes, they cry, 'Give us not bread, but votes!' And the squires say that that is what the traders who have just got votes don't mean to give them; and so, to divert their attention, dangle cheap bread before their noses!"

Mary sighed. "I am afraid that I must give it up," she said. "I am so ignorant."

"Well," he replied thoughtfully. "Many are puzzled which side to take, and are waiting to see how the cat jumps. In the meantime every fence is placarded with 'Speed the Plough!' on one side, and 'The Big Loaf!' on the other. The first man you meet thinks the landlord a devourer of widows' houses; to the next the mill-owner is an ogre grinding men's bones to make his bread. Even at the Gatehouse I doubt if you will escape the excitement, though there is not a field of wheat within a mile of it!"

"To me it is like a new world," she said.

"Then, when you are in the new world," he replied, smiling as he rose, "do not forget Columbus! But here is the lad to tell you that your tea is ready."

He repented when Mary had left him that he had not made better use of his time. It had been his purpose to make such an impression on the girl as might be of use in the future, and he wondered why he had not devoted himself more singly to this; why he had allowed minutes which might have been given to intimate subjects to be wasted in a dry discussion. But there was a quality in Mary that did not lightly invite to gallantry--a gravity and a balance that, had he looked closely into the matter, might have explained his laches.

And in fact he had builded better than he knew, for while he reproached himself, Mary, safe within the tiny bathing machine which the packet company called a cabin, was giving much thought to him. The dip-candle, set within a horn lantern, threw its light on the one comfortable object, the tea-tray, seated beside which she reviewed what had happened, and found it all interesting; his meeting with her, his thought for her, the glimpses he had given her of things beyond the horizon of the convent school, even his diversion into politics. He was not on good terms with her uncle, and it was unlikely that she would see more of him. But she was sure that she would always remember his appearance on the threshold of her new life, that she would always recall with gratitude this crossing and the kindness which had lapped her about and saved her from loneliness.

In her eyes he figured as one of the brilliant circle of the Hôtel Lambert. For her he played a part in great movements and high enterprises such as those which he had revealed to her. His light treatment of them, his air of detachment, had, indeed, chilled her at times; but these were perhaps natural in one who viewed from above and from a distance the ills which it was his task to treat. How ignorant he must think her! How remote from the plane on which he lived, the standards by which he judged, the objects at which he aimed! Yet he had stooped to explain things to her and to make them clear.

She spent an hour deep in thought, and, strange as the life of the ship was to her, she was deaf to the creaking of the timbers, and the surge of the waves as they swept past the beam. At intervals hoarse orders, a rush of feet across the deck, the more regular tramp of rare passengers, caught her attention, only to lose it as quickly. It was late when she roused herself. She saw that the candle was burning low, and she began to make her arrangements for the night.

Midway in them she paused, and colored, aware that she knew his tread from the many that had passed. The footstep ceased. A hand tapped at her door. "Yes?" she said.

"We shall be in the river by daybreak," Audley announced. "I thought that you might like to come on deck early. You ought not to miss the river from the Nore to the Pool."

"Thank you," she answered.

"You shouldn't miss it," he persisted. "Greenwich especially!"

"I shall be there," she replied. "It is very good of you. Good-night."

He went away. After all, he was the only man on board shod like a gentleman; it had been odd if she had not known his step! And for going on deck early, why should she not? Was she to miss Greenwich because Lord Audley went to a good bootmaker?

So when Peter Basset, still pale and qualmish, came on deck in the early morning, a little below the Pool, the first person he saw was the girl whom he had come to escort. She was standing high above him on the captain's bridge, her hands clasping the rail, her hair blown about and shining golden in the sunshine. Lord Audley's stately form towered above her. He was pointing out this and that, and they were talking gaily; and now and again the captain spoke to them, and many were looking at them. She did not see Basset; he was on the deck below, standing amid the common crowd, and so he was free to look at her as he pleased. He might be said not to have seen her before, and what he saw now bewildered, nay, staggered him. Unwillingly, and to please his uncle, he had come to meet a girl of whom they knew no more than this, that, rescued from some backwater of Paris life, into which a weak and shiftless father had plunged her, she had earned her living, if she had earned it at all, in a dependent capacity. He had looked to find her one of two things; either flashy and underbred, with every fault an Englishman might consider French, or a nice mixture of craft and servility. He had not been able to decide which he would prefer.

Instead he saw a girl tall, slender, and slow of movement, with eyes set under a fine width of brow and grave when they smiled, a chin fuller than perfect beauty required, a mouth a little large, a perfect nose. Auburn hair, thick and waving, drooped over each temple, and framed a face as calm as it was fair. "Surely a pearl found on a midden!" he thought. And as the thought passed through his mind, Mary looked down. Her eyes roved for a moment over the crowded deck, where some, like Basset, returned her gaze with interest, while others sought their baggage or bawled for missing companions. He was not a man, it has been said, to stand out in a crowd, and her eyes travelled over him without seeing him. Audley spoke to her, she lifted her eyes, she looked ashore again. But the unheeding glance which had not deigned to know him stung Basset! He dubbed her, with all her beauty, proud and hard. Still--to be such and to have sprung from such a life! It was marvellous.

He knew nothing of the convent school with its hourly discipline lasting through years. He did not guess that the obstinacy which had been weakness in the father was strength in the child. Much less could he divine that the improvidence of that father had become a beacon, warning the daughter off the rocks which had been fatal to him! Mary was no miracle, but neither was she proud or hard.

They had passed Erith, and Greenwich with its stately pile and formal gardens glittering in the sunshine of an April morning. The ripple of a westerly wind, meeting the flood, silvered the turbid surface. A hundred wherries skimmed like water-flies hither and thither, long lines of colliers fringed the wharves, tall China clippers forged slowly up under a scrap of foresail, dumb barges deep laden with hay or Barclay's Entire, moved mysteriously with the tide. On all sides hoarse voices bawled orders or objurgations. Charmed with the gayety, the movement, the color, Mary could not take her eyes from the scene. The sunshine, the leap of life, the pulse of spring, moved in her blood and put to flight the fears that had weighed on her at nightfall. She told herself with elation that this was England, this was her native land, this was her home.

Meanwhile Audley's mind took another direction. He reflected that in a few minutes he must part from the girl, and must trust henceforth to the impression he had made. For some hours he had scarcely given a thought to Basset, but he recalled him now, and he searched for him in the throng below. He found him at last, pressed against the rail between a fat woman with a basket and a crying child. Their eyes met. My lord glanced away, but he could not refrain from a smile as he pictured the poor affair the other had made of his errand. And Basset saw the smile and read its meaning, and though he was not self--assertive, though he was, indeed, backward to a fault, anger ran through his veins. To have travelled three hundred miles in order to meet this girl, to have found her happy in another's company, and to have accepted the second place--the position had vexed him even under the qualms of illness. This morning, and since he had seen her, it stirred in him an unwonted resentment. He d--d Audley under his breath, disengaged himself from the basket which the fat woman was thrusting into his ribs, lifted the child aside. He escaped below to collect his effects.

But in a short time he recovered his temper. When the boat began to go about in the crowded Pool and Mary reluctantly withdrew her eyes from the White Tower, darkened by the smoke and the tragedies of twenty generations, she found him awaiting them at the foot of the ladder. He was still pale, and the girl's conscience smote her. For many hours she had not given him a thought. "I hope you are better," she said gently.

"Horrid thing, mal de mer!" remarked my lord, with a gleam of humor in his eye.

"Thank you, I am quite right this morning," Basset answered.

"You go from Euston Grove, I suppose?"

"Yes. The morning train starts in a little over an hour."

No more was said, and they went ashore together. Audley, an old traveller, and one whose height and presence gave weight to his orders, saw to Mary's safety in the crowd, shielded her from touts and tide-waiters, took the upper hand. He watched the aproned porters disappearing with the baggage in the direction of the Custom House, and a thought struck him. "I am sorry that my servant is not here," he said. "He would see our things through without troubling us." His eyes met Basset's.

Basset disdained to refuse. "I will do it," he said. He received the keys and followed the baggage.

Audley looked at Mary and laughed. "I think you'll find him useful," he said. "Takes a hint and is not too forward."

"For shame!" she cried. "It is very good of him to go." But she could not refrain from a smile.

"Well trained," Audley continued in a whimsical tone, "fetches and carries, barks at the name of Peel and growls at the name of Cobden, gives up a stick when required, could be taught to beg--by the right person."

She laughed--she could not resist his manner. "But you are not very kind," she said. "Please to call a--whatever we need. He shall not do everything."

"Everything?" Lord Audley echoed. "He should do nothing," in a lower tone, "if I had my way."

Mary blushed.

CHAPTER VI: FIELD AND FORGE

The window of the clumsy carriage was narrow, but Mary gazed through it as if she could never see enough of the flying landscape, the fields, the woods, the ivy-clad homes and red-roofed towns that passed in procession before her. The emotions of those who journeyed for the first time on a railway at a speed four times as great as that of the swiftest High-flier that ever devoured the road are forgotten by this generation. But they were vivid. The thing was a miracle. And though by this time men had ceased to believe that he who passed through the air at sixty miles an hour must of necessity cease to breathe, the novice still felt that he could never tire of the panorama so swiftly unrolled before him.

And it was not only wonder, it was admiration that held Mary chained to the window. Her infancy had been spent in a drab London street, her early youth in the heart of a Paris which was still gloomy and mediæval. Some beautiful things she had seen on fête days, the bend of the river at Meudon or St. Germain, and once the Forest of Fontainebleau; on Sundays the Bois. But the smiling English meadows, the gray towers of village churches, the parks and lawns of manor-houses, the canals with their lines of painted barges, and here and there a gay packet boat--she drank in the beauty of these, and more than once her eyes grew dim. For a time Basset, seated in the opposite corner, did not exist for her; while he, behind the Morning Chronicle, made his observations and took note of her at his leisure. The longer he looked the more he marvelled.

He asked himself with amusement what John Audley would think of her when he, too, should see her. He anticipated the old man's surprise on finding her so remote from their preconceived ideas of her. He wondered what she would think of John Audley.

And while he pondered, and now scanned his paper without reading it, and now stole another glance at her, he steeled himself against her. She might not have been to blame, it might not have been her fault; but, between them, the two on the boat had put him in his place and he could not forget it. He had cut a poor figure, and he resented it. He foresaw that in the future she would be dependent on him for society, and he would be a fool if he then forgot the lesson he had learned. She had a good face, but probably her up-bringing had been anything but good. Probably it had taught her to make the most of the moment and of the man of the moment, and he would be foolish if he let her amuse herself with him. He had seen in what light she viewed him when other game was afoot, and he would deserve the worst if he did not remember this.

Presently an embankment cut off the view, and she withdrew her eyes from the window. In her turn she took the measure of her companion. It seemed to her that his face was too thoughtful for his years, and that his figure was insignificant. The eye which had accustomed itself to Lord Audley's port and air found Basset slight and almost mean. She smiled as she recalled the skill with which my lord had set him aside and made use of him.

Still, he was a part of the life to which she was hastening, and curiosity stirred in her. He was in possession, he was in close relations with her uncle, he knew many things which she was anxious to know. Much of her comfort might depend on him. Presently she asked him what her uncle was like.

"You will see for yourself in a few hours," he replied, his tone cold and almost ungracious. "Did not Lord Audley describe him?"

"No. And you seem," with a faint smile, "to be equally on your guard, Mr. Basset."

"Not at all," he retorted. "But I think it better to leave you to judge for yourself. I have lived too near to Mr. Audley to--to criticise him."

She colored.

"Let me give you one hint, however," he continued in the same dry tone; "you will be wise not to mention Lord Audley to him. They are not on good terms."

"I am sorry."

He shrugged his shoulders. "It cannot be said to be unnatural, after what has happened."

She considered this. "What has happened?" she asked after a pause.

"Well, the claim to the peerage, if nothing else----"

"What claim?" she asked. "Whose claim? What peerage? I am quite in the dark."

He stared. He did not believe her. "Your uncle's claim," he said curtly. Then as she still looked a question, "You must know," he continued, "that your uncle claimed the title which Lord Audley bears, and the property which goes with it. And that the decision was only given against him three months ago."

"I know nothing of it," she said. "I never heard of the claim."

"Really?" he replied. He hardly deigned to veil his incredulity. "Yet if your uncle had succeeded you were the next heir."

"I?"

"Yes, you."

Then her face shook his unbelief. She turned slowly and painfully red. "Is it possible?" she said. "You are not playing with me?"

"Certainly I am not. Do you mean that Lord Audley never told you that? Never told you that you were interested?"

"Never! He only told me that he was not on good terms with my uncle, and that for that reason he would leave me to learn the rest at the Gatehouse."

"Well, that was right," Basset answered. "It is as well, since you have to live with Mr. Audley, that you should not be prejudiced against him."

"No doubt," she said dryly. "But I do not understand why he did not answer my letters."

"Did you write to him?"

"Twice." She was going to explain the circumstances, but she refrained. Why appeal to the sympathies of one who seemed so cold, so distant, so indifferent?

"He cannot have had the letters," Basset decided after a pause.

"Then how did he come to write to me at last?"

"Lord Audley sent your address to him."

"Ah!" she said. "I supposed so." With an air of finality she turned to the window, and for some time she was silent. Her mind had much upon which to work.

She was silent for so long that before more was said they were running through the outskirts of

Birmingham, and Mary awoke with a shock to another and sadder side of England. In place of parks and homesteads she saw the England of the workers--workers at that time exploited to the utmost in pursuance of a theory of economy that heeded only the wealth of nations, and placed on that wealth the narrowest meaning. They passed across squalid streets, built in haste to meet the needs of new factories, under tall chimneys the smoke of which darkened the sky without hindrance, by vile courts, airless and almost sunless. They looked down on sallow children whose only playground was the street and whose only school-bell was the whistle that summoned them at dawn to premature toil. Haggard women sat on doorsteps with puling babes in their arms. Lines of men, whose pallor peered through the grime, propped the walls, or gazed with apathy at the train. For a few minutes Mary forgot not only her own hopes and fears, but the aloofness and even the presence of her companion. When they came to a standstill in the station, where they had to change on to the Grand Junction Railway, Basset had to speak twice before she understood that he wished her to leave the carriage.

"What a dreadful place!" she exclaimed.

"Well, it is not beautiful," Basset admitted. "One does not look for beauty in Birmingham and the Black Country."

He got her some tea, and marshalled her carefully to the upper line. But his answer had jarred upon her, and when they were again seated, Mary kept her thoughts to herself. Beyond Birmingham their route skirted towns rather than passed through them, but she saw enough to deepen the impression which the lanes and alleys of that place had made upon her. The sun had set and the cold evening light revealed in all their meanness the rows of naked cottages, the heaps of slag and cinders, the starveling horses that stood with hanging heads on the dreary lands. As darkness fell, fires shone out here and there, and threw into Dantesque relief the dark forms of half-naked men toiling with fury to feed the flames. The change which an hour had made in all she saw seemed appalling to the girl; it filled her with awe and sadness. Here, so near the paradise of the country and the plough, was the Inferno of the town, the forge, the pit! Here, in place of the thatched cottage and the ruddy faces, were squalor and sunken cheeks and misery and dearth.

She thought of the question which Lord Audley had raised twenty-four hours before, and which he had told her was racking the minds of men--should food be taxed? And she fancied that there was, there could be, but one answer. These toiling masses, these slaves of the hammer and the pick, must be fed, and, surely, so fed that a margin, however small, however meagre, might be saved out of which to better their sordid lot.

"We call this the Black Country," Basset explained, feeling the silence irksome. After all, she was in his charge, in a way she was his guest. He ought to amuse her.

"It is well named," she answered. "Is there anything in England worse than this?"

"Well, round Hales Owen and Dudley," he rejoined, "it may be worse. And at Cradley Heath it may be rougher. More women and children are employed in the pits; and where women make chains--well, it's pretty bad."

She had spoken dryly to hide her feelings. He replied in a tone as matter-of-fact, through lack of feeling. For this he was not so much to blame as she fancied, for that which horrified her was to him an everyday matter, one of the facts of life with which he had been familiar from boyhood. But she did not understand this. She judged him and condemned him. She did not speak again.

By and by, "We shall be at Penkridge in twenty minutes," he said. "After that a nine-miles drive will take us to the Gatehouse, and your journey will be over. But I fear that you will find the life quiet after Paris."

"I was very quiet in Paris."

"But you were in a large house."

"I was at the Princess Czartoriski's."

"Of course. I suppose it was there that you met Lord Audley?"

"Yes."

"Well, after that kind of life, I am afraid that the Gatehouse will have few charms for you. It is very remote, very lonely."

She cut him short with impatience, the color rising to her face. "I thought you understood," she said, "that I was in the Princess's house as a governess? It was my business to take care of a number of children, to eat with them, to sleep with them, to see that they washed their hands and kept their hair clean. That was my position, Mr. Basset. I do not wish it to be misunderstood."

"But if that were so," he stammered, "how did you----"

"Meet Lord Audley," she replied. "Very simply. Once or twice the Princess ordered me to descend to the salon to interpret. On one of these occasions Lord Audley saw me and learned-- who I was."

"Indeed," he said. "I see." Perhaps he had had it in his mind to test her and the truth of Audley's letter, which nothing in her or in my lord's conduct seemed to confirm. He did not know if this had been in his mind, but in any case the result silenced him. She was either very honest or very clever. Many girls, he knew, would have slurred over the facts, and not a few would have boasted of the Princess's friendship and the Princess's society, and the Princess's hôtel, and brought up her name a dozen times a day.

She is very clever, he thought, or she is--good. But for the moment he steeled himself against the latter opinion.

No other travellers alighted at Penkridge, and he went away to claim the baggage, while she waited, cold and depressed, on the little platform which, lit by a single oil lamp, looked down on a dim churchyard. Dusk was passing into night, and the wind, sweeping across the flat, whipped her skirts and chilled her blood. Her courage sank. A light or two betrayed the nearness of the town, but in every other direction dull lines of willows or pale stretches of water ran into the night.

Five minutes before she had resented Basset's company, now she was glad to see him return. He led the way to the road in silence. "The carriage is late," he muttered, but even as he spoke the quick tramp of a pair of horses pushed to speed broke on them, lights appeared, a moment later a fly pulled up beside them and turned. "You are late," Basset said.

"There!" the man replied. "Minutes might be guineas since trains came in, dang 'em! Give me the days when five minutes made neither man nor mouse, and gentry kept their own time."

"Well, let us get off now."

"I ask no better, Squire. Please yourself and you'll please me."

When they were shut in, Basset laughed. "Stafford manners!" he said. "You'll become used to them!"

"Is this my uncle's carriage?" she asked.

"No," he replied, smiling in the darkness. "He does not keep one."

She said no more. Though she could not see him, her shoulder touched his, and his nearness and the darkness in which they sat troubled her, though she was not timid. They rode thus for a minute or two, then trundled through a narrow street, dimly lit by shop windows; again they were in the dark and the country. Presently the pace dropped to a walk as they began to ascend.

She fancied, peering out on her side, that they were winding up through woods. Branches swept the sides of the carriage. They jolted into ruts and jolted out of them. By and by they were clear of the trees and the road seemed to be better. The moon, newly risen, showed her a dreary upland, bare and endless, here dotted with the dark stumps of trees, there of a deeper black as if fire had swept over it and scarred it. They met no one, saw no sign of habitation. To the girl, accustomed all her life to streets and towns, the place seemed infinitely desolate--a place of solitude and witches and terror and midnight murder.

"What is this?" she asked, shivering.

"This is the Great Chase," he said. "Riddsley, on the farther side, is our nearest town, but since the railway was opened we use Penkridge Station."

His practical tone steadied her, but she was tired, and the loneliness which she had felt while she waited on the bleak platform weighed heavily on her. To what was she going? How would her uncle receive her? This dreary landscape, the gaunt signpost that looked like a gibbet and might have been one, the skeleton trees that raised bare arms to heaven, the scream of a dying rabbit, all added to the depression of the moment. She was glad when at last the carriage stopped at a gate. Basset alighted and opened the gate. He stepped in again, they went on. There were now shadowy trees about them, sparsely set. They jolted unevenly over turf.

"Are we there?" she asked, a tremor in her voice.

"Very nearly," he said. "Another mile and we shall be there. This is Beaudelays Park."

She called pride to her aid, and he did not guess--for all day he had marked her self-possession--that she was trembling. Vainly she told herself that she was foolish, that nothing could happen to her, nothing that mattered. What, after all, was a cold reception, what was her uncle's frown beside the poverty and the hazards from which she had escaped? Vainly she reassured herself; she could not still the rapid beating of her heart.

He might have said a word to cheer her. But he did not know that she was suffering, and he said no word. She came near to hating him for his stolidity and his silence. He was inhuman! A block!

She peered through the misty glass, striving to see what was before them. But she could make out no more than the dark limbs of trees, and now and then a trunk, which shone as the light of the lamp slipped over it, and as quickly vanished. Suddenly they shot from turf to hard road, passed through an open gateway, for an instant the lamp on her side showed a grotesque pillar-- they wheeled, they stopped. Within a few feet of her a door stood open, and in the doorway a girl held a lantern aloft in one hand, and with the other screened her eyes from the light.

CHAPTER VII: MR. JOHN AUDLEY

An hour later Basset was seated on one side of a wide hearth, on the other John Audley faced him. The library in which they sat was the room which Basset loved best in the world. It was a room of silence and large spaces, and except where four windows, tall and narrow, broke one wall, it was lined high with the companions of silence--books. The ceiling was of black oak, adorned at the crossings of the joists and beams with emblems, butterflies, and Stafford knots and the like, once bright with color, and still soberly rich. A five-sided bay enlarged each of the two inner corners of the room and broke the outlines. One of these bays shrined a window, four-mullioned, the other a spiral staircase. An air of comfort and stateliness pervaded the whole; here the great scutcheon over the mantel, there the smaller coats on the chair-backs blended their or and gules with the hues of old rugs and the dun bindings of old folios. There were books on the four or five tables, and books on the Cromwell chairs; and charts and deeds, antique weapons and silver pieces, all the tools and toys of the antiquary, lay broadcast. Against the door hung a blazoned pedigree of the Audleys of Beaudelays. It was six feet long and dull with age.

But Basset, as he faced his companion, was not thinking of the room, or of the pursuits with which it was connected in his mind, and which, more than affection and habit, bound him to John Audley. He moved restlessly in his chair, then stretched his legs to meet the glow of the wood fire. "All the same," he said, "I think you would have done well to see her to-night, sir."

"Pooh! pooh!" John Audley answered with lazy good humor. "Why? It doesn't matter what I think of her or she thinks of me. It's what Peter thinks of Mary and Mary thinks of Peter that matters. That's what matters!" He chuckled as he marked the other's annoyance. "She is a beauty, is she?"

"I didn't say so."

"But you think it. You don't deceive me at this time of day. And stand-off, is she? That's for the marines and innocent young fellows like you who think women angels. I'll be bound that she's her mother's daughter, and knows her value and will see that she fetches it! Trading blood will out!"

To the eye that looked and glanced away John Audley, lolling in his chair, in a quilted dressing-gown with silk facings, was a plump and pleasant figure. His face was fresh-colored, and would have been comely if the cheeks had not been a little pendulous. His hair was fine and white and he wore it long, and his hands were shapely and well cared for. As he said his last word he poured a little brandy into a glass and filled it up with water. "Here's to the wooing that's not long adoing!" he said, his eyes twinkling. He seemed to take a pleasure in annoying the other.

He was so far successful that Basset swore softly. "It's silly to talk like that," he said, "when I have hardly known the girl twenty-four hours and have scarcely said ten times as many words to her."

"But you're going to say a good many more words to her!" Audley retorted, grinning. "Sweet, pretty words, my boy! But there, there," he continued, veering between an elfish desire to tease and a desire equally strong to bring the other to his way of thinking. "I'm only joking. I know you'll never let that devil have his way! You'll never leave the course open for him! I know that. But there's no hurry! There's no hurry. Though, lord, how I sweated when I read his letter! I had never a wink of sleep the night after."

"I don't suppose that he's given a thought to her in that way," Basset answered. "Why should he?"

John Audley leant forward, and his face underwent a remarkable change. It became a pale, heavy mask, out of which his eyes gleamed, small and malevolent. "Don't talk like a fool!" he said harshly. "Of course he means it. And if she's fool enough all my plans, all my pains, all my rights--and once you come to your senses and help me I shall have my rights--all, all, all will go for nothing. For nothing!" He sank back in his chair. "There! now you've excited me. You've excited me, and you know that I can't bear excitement!" His hand groped feebly for his glass, and he raised it to his lips. He gasped once or twice. The color came back to his face.

"I am sorry," Basset said.

"Ay, ay. But be a good lad. Be a good lad. Make up your mind to help me at the Great House." Basset shook his head.

"To help me, and twenty-four hours--only twenty-four hours, man--may make all the difference! All the difference in the world to me."

"I have told you my views about it," Basset said doggedly. He shifted uneasily in his chair. "I cannot do it, sir, and I won't."

John Audley groaned. "Well, well!" he answered. "I'll say no more now. I'll say no more now. When you and she have made it up"--in vain Basset shook his head--"you'll see the question in another light. Ay, believe me, you will. It'll be your business then, and your interest, and nothing venture, nothing win! You'll see it differently. You'll help the old man to his rights then."

Basset shrugged his shoulders, but thought it useless to protest. The other sighed once or twice and was silent also. At length, "You never told me that you had heard from her," Basset said.

"That I'd----" John Audley broke off. "What is it, Toft?" he asked over his shoulder.

A man-servant, tall, thin, lantern-jawed, had entered unseen. "I came to see if you wanted anything more, sir?" he said.

"Nothing, nothing, Toft. Good-night!" He spoke impatiently, and he watched the man out before he went on. Then, "Perhaps I heard from her, perhaps I didn't," he said. "It's some time ago. What of it?"

"She was in great distress when she wrote."

John Audley raised his eyebrows. "What of it!" he repeated. "She was that woman's daughter. When Peter married a tradesman's daughter--married a----" He did not continue. His thoughts trickled away into silence. The matter was not worthy of his attention.

But by and by he roused himself. "You've ridiculous scruples," he said. "Absurd scruples. But," briskly, "there's that much of good in this girl that I think she'll put an end to them. You must brighten up, my lad, and spark it a little! You're too grave."

"Damn!" said Basset. "For God's sake, don't begin it all again. I've told you that I've not the least intention----"

"She'll see to that if she's what I think her," John Audley retorted cheerfully. "If she's her mother's daughter! But very well, very well! We'll change the subject. I've been working at the Feathers--the Prince's Feathers."

"Have you gone any farther?" Basset asked, forcing an interest which would have been ready enough at another time.

"I might have, but I had a visitor."

Visitors were rare at the Gatehouse, and Basset wondered. "Who was it?" he asked.

"Bagenal the maltster from Riddsley. He came about some political rubbish. Some trouble they are having with Mottisfont. D--n Mottisfont! What do I care about him? They think he isn't running straight--that he's going in for corn-law repeal. And Bagenal and the other fools think that that will be the ruin of the town."

"But Mottisfont is a Tory," Basset objected.

"So is Peel. They are both in Bagenal's bad books. Bagenal is sure that Peel is going back to the cotton people he came from. Spinning Jenny spinning round again!"

"I see."

"I asked him," Audley continued, rubbing his knees with sly enjoyment, "what Stubbs the lawyer was doing about it. He's the party manager. Why didn't he come to me?"

Basset smiled. "What did he say to that?"

"Hummed and hawed. At last he said that owing to Stubbs's connection with--you know who-- it was thought that he was not the right person to come to me. So I asked him what Stubbs's employer was going to do about it."

"Ah!"

"He didn't know what to say to that, the ass! Thought I should go the other way, you see. So I told him"--John Audley laughed maliciously as he spoke--"that, for the landed interest, the law had taken away my land, and, for politics, I would not give a d--n for either party in a country where men did not get their rights! Lord! how he looked!"

"Well, you didn't hide your feelings."

"Why should I?" John Audley asked cheerfully. "What will they do for me? Nothing. Will they move a finger to right me? No. Then a plague on both their houses!" He snapped his fingers in schoolboy fashion and rose to his feet. He lit a candle, taking a light from the fire with a spill. "I am going to bed now, Peter. Unless----" he paused, the candlestick in his hand, and gazed fixedly at his companion. "Lord, man, what we could do in two or three hours! In two or three hours. This very night!"

"I've told you that I will have nothing to do with it!" Basset repeated.

John Audley sighed, and removing his eyes, poked the wick of the candle with the snuffers. "Well," he said, "good-night. We must look to bright eyes and red lips to convert you. What a man won't do for another he will do for himself, Peter. Good-night."

Left alone, Basset stared fretfully at the fire. It was not the first time by scores that John Audley had tried him and driven him almost beyond bearing. But habit is a strong tie, and a common taste is a bond even stronger. In this room, and from the elder man, Basset had learned to trace a genealogy, to read a coat, to know a bar from a bend, to discourse of badges and collars under the guidance of the learned Anstie or the ingenious Le Neve. There he had spent hours flitting from book to book and chart to chart in the pursuit, as thrilling while it lasted as any fox-chase, of some family link, the origin of this, the end of that, a thing of value only to those who sought it, but to them all-important. He could recall many a day so spent while rain lashed the tall mullioned windows or sunlight flooded the window-seat in the bay; and these days had endeared to him every nook in the library from the folio shelves in the shadowy corner under the staircase to the cosey table near the hearth which was called "Mr. Basset's," and enshrined in a long drawer a tree of the Bassets of Blore.

For he as well as Audley came of an ancient and shrunken stock. He also could count among his forbears men who had fought at Blore Heath and Towton, or had escaped by a neck from the ruin of the Gunpowder Plot. So he had fallen early under the spell of the elder man's pursuits, and, still young, had learned from him to live in the past. Later the romantic solitude of the Gatehouse, where he had spent more of the last six years than in his own house at Blore, had confirmed him in the habit.

Under the surface, however, the two men remained singularly unlike. While a fixed idea had narrowed John Audley's vision to the inhuman, the younger man, under a dry and reserved exterior--he was shy, and his undrained acres, his twelve hundred a year, poorly supported an ancient name--was not only human, but in his way was something of an idealist. He dreamed dreams, he had his secret aspirations, at times ambition of the higher kind stirred in him, he planned plans and another life than this. But always--this was a thing inbred in him--he put forward the commonplace, as the cuttle-fish sheds ink, and hid nothing so shyly as the visions which he had done nothing to make real. On those about him he made no deep impression, though from one border of Staffordshire to the other his birth won respect. Politics viewed as a game, and a selfish game, had no attraction for him. Quarter Sessions and the Bench struck no spark from him. At the Races and the County Ball richer men outshone him. But given something to touch his heart and fire his ambition, he had qualities. He might still show himself in another light.

Something of this, for no reason that he could imagine, some feeling of regret for past opportunities, passed through his mind as he sat fretting over John Audley's folly. But after a time he roused himself and became aware that he was tired; and he rose and lit a candle. He pushed back the smouldering logs and slowly and methodically he put out the lights. He gave a last thought to John Audley. "There was always one maggot in his head," he muttered, "now there's a second. What I would not do to please him, he thinks I shall do to please another! Well, he does not know her yet!"

He went to bed.

CHAPTER VIII: THE GATEHOUSE

It is within the bounds of imagination that death may make no greater change in our inner selves than is wrought at times by a new mood or another outlook. When Mary, an hour before the world was astir on the morning after her arrival, let herself out of the Gatehouse, and from its threshold as from a ledge saw the broad valley of the Trent stretched before her in all the beauty of a May morning, her alarm of the past night seemed incredible. At her feet a sharp slope, clothed in gorse and shrub, fell away to meet the plain. It sank no more than a couple of hundred feet, but this was enough to enable her to follow the silver streak of the river winding afar between park and coppice and under many a church tower. Away to the right she could see the three graceful spires of Lichfield, and southward, where an opal haze closed the prospect, she could imagine the fringe of the Black Country, made beautiful by distance.

In sober fact few parts of England are less inviting than the low lands of Staffordshire, when the spring floods cover them or the fogs of autumn cling to the cold soil. But in spring, when larks soar above them and tall, lop-sided elms outline the fields, they have their beauty; and Mary gazed long at the fair prospect before she turned her back on it and looked at the house that was fated to be her home.

It was what its name signified, a gatehouse; yet by turns it could be a sombre and a charming thing. Some Audley of noble ideas, a man long dead, had built it to be the entrance to his demesne. The park wall, overhung by trees, still ran right and left from it, but the road which had once passed through the archway now slid humbly aside and entered the park by a field gate. A wide-latticed Tudor tower, rising two stories above the arch and turreted at the four corners, formed the middle. It was buttressed on either hand by a lower building, flush with it and of about the same width. The tower was of yellowish stone, the wings were faced with stained stucco. Right and left of the whole a plot of shrubs masked on the one hand the stables, on the other the kitchens--modern blocks set back to such a distance that each touched the old part at a corner only.

He who had planned the building had set it cunningly on the brow of the Great Chase, so that, viewed from the vale, it rose against the skyline. On dark days it broke the fringe of woodland and stood up, gloomy and forbidding, the portal of a Doubting Castle. On bright days, with its hundred diamond panes a-glitter in the sunshine, it seemed to be the porch of a fairy palace, the silent home of some Sleeping Beauty. At all times it imposed itself upon men below and spoke of something beyond, something unseen, greater, mysterious.

To Mary Audley, who saw it at its best, the very stains of the plaster glorified by the morning light, it was a thing of joy. She fancied that to live behind those ancient mullioned windows, to look out morning and evening on that spacious landscape, to feel the bustle of the world so remote, must in itself be happiness. For a time she could not turn from it.

But presently the desire to explore her new surroundings seized her and she re-entered the house. A glance at the groined roof of the hall--many a gallant horseman had ridden under it in his time--proved that it was merely the archway closed and fitted with a small door and window at either end. She unlocked the farther door and passed into a paved court, in which the grass grew between the worn flags. In the stables on the left a dog whined. The kitchens were on the other hand, and before her an opening flanked by tall heraldic beasts broke a low wall, built of moss-grown brick. She ventured through it and uttered a cry of delight.

Near at hand, under cover of a vast chestnut tree, were traces of domestic labor: a grindstone, a saw-pit, a woodpile, coops with clucking hens. But beyond these the sward, faintly lined at first with ruts, stretched away into forest glades, bordered here by giant oaks brown in bud, there by the yellowish-green of beech trees. In the foreground lay patches of gorse, and in places an ancient thorn, riven and half prostrate, crowned the russet of last year's bracken with a splash of cream. Heedless of the spectator, rabbits sat making their toilet, and from every brake birds filled the air with a riot of song.

To one who had seen little but the streets of Paris, more sordid then than now, the scene was charming. Mary's eyes filled, her heart swelled. Ah, what a home was here! She had espied on her journey many a nook and sheltered dell, but nothing that could vie with this! Heedless of her thin shoes, with no more than a handkerchief on her head, she strayed on and on. By and by a track, faintly marked, led her to the left. A little farther, and old trees fell into line on either hand, as if in days long gone, before age thinned their ranks, they had formed an avenue.

For a time she sat musing on a fallen trunk, then the hawthorn that a few paces away perfumed the spring air moved her to gather an armful of it. She forgot that time was passing, almost she forgot that she had not breakfasted, and she might have been nearly a mile from the Gatehouse when she was startled by a faint hail that seemed to come from behind her. She looked back and saw Basset coming after her.

He, too, was hatless--he had set off in haste--and he was out of breath. She turned with concern to meet him. "Am I very late, Mr. Basset?" she asked, her conscience pricking her. What if this first morning she had broken the rules?

"Oh no," he said. And then, "You've not been farther than this?"

"No. I am afraid my uncle is waiting?"

"Oh no. He breakfasts in his own room. But Etruria told me that you had gone this way, and I followed. I see that you are not empty-handed."

"No." And she thrust the great bunch of may under his nose--who would not have been gay, who would not have lost her reserve in such a scene, on such a morning? "Isn't it fresh? Isn't it delicious?"

As he stooped to the flowers his eyes met hers smiling through the hawthorn sprays, and he saw her as he had not seen her before. Her gravity had left her. Spring laughed in her eyes, youth fluttered in the tendrils of her hair, she was the soul of May. And what she had found of beauty in the woodland, of music in the larks' songs, of perfume in the blossoms, of freshness in the morning, the man found in her; and a shock, never to be forgotten, ran through him. He did not speak. He smelled the hawthorn in silence.

But a few seconds later--as men reckon time--he took note of his feelings, and he was startled. He had not been prepared to like her, we know; many things had armed him against her. But before the witchery of her morning face, the challenge of her laughing eyes, he awoke to the fact that he was in danger. He had to own that if he must live beside her day by day and would maintain his indifference, he must steel himself. He must keep his first impressions of her always before him, and be careful. And be very careful--if even that might avail.

For a hundred paces he walked at her side, listening without knowing what she said. Then his coolness returned, and when she asked him why he had come after her without his hat he was ready.

"I had better tell you," he answered, "this path is little used. It leads to the Great House, and your uncle, owing to his quarrel with Lord Audley, does not like any one to go farther in that direction than the Yew Tree Walk. You can see the Walk from here--the yews mark the entrance to the gardens. I thought that it would be unfortunate if you began by displeasing him, and I came after you."

"It was very good of you," she said. Her face was not gay now. "Does Lord Audley live there-- when he is at home?"

"No one lives there," he explained soberly. "No one has lived there for three generations. It's a ruin--I was going to say, a nightmare. The greater part of the house was burnt down in a carouse held to celebrate the accession of George the Third. The Audley of that day rebuilt it on a great scale, but before it was finished he gave a housewarming, at which his only son quarrelled with a guest. The two fought at daybreak, and the son was killed beside the old Butterfly in the Yew Walk--you will see the spot some day. The father sent away the builders and never looked up again. He diverted much of his property, and a cousin came into the remainder and the title, but the house was never finished, the windows in the new part were never glazed. In the old part some furniture and tapestry decay; in the new are only bats and dust and owls. So it has stood for eighty years, vacant in the midst of neglected gardens. In the sunlight it is one of the most dreary things you can imagine. By moonlight it is better, but unspeakably melancholy."

"How dreadful," she said in a low voice. "I almost wish, Mr. Basset, that you had not told me. They say in France that if you see the dead without touching them, you dream of them. I feel like that about the house."

It crossed his mind that she was talking for effect. "It is only a house after all," he said.

"But our house," with a touch of pride. Then, "What are those?" she asked, pointing to the gray shapeless beasts, time-worn and weather-stained, that flanked the entrance to the courtyard.

"They are, or once were, Butterflies, the badge of the Audleys. These hold shields. You will see the Butterflies in many places in the Gatehouse. You will find them with men's faces and sometimes with a fret on the wings. Your uncle says that they are not butterflies, but moths, that have eaten the Audley fortunes."

It was a thought that matched the picture he had drawn of the deserted house, and Mary felt that the morning had lost its brightness. But not for long. Basset led her into a room on the right of the hall, and the sight drew from her a cry of pleasure. On three sides the dark wainscot rose eight feet from the floor; above, the walls were whitewashed to the ceiling and broken by dim portraits, on stretchers and without frames. On the fourth side where the panelling divided the room from a serving-room, once part of it, it rose to the ceiling. The stone hearth, the iron dogs, the matted floor, the heavy chairs and oak table, all were dark and plain and increased the austerity of the room.

At the end of the table places were laid for three, and Toft, who had set on the breakfast, was fixing the kettle amid the burning logs.

"Is Mr. Audley coming down?" Basset asked.

"He bade me lay for him," Toft replied dryly. "I doubt if he will come. You had better begin, sir. The young lady," with a searching look at her, "must want her breakfast."

"I am afraid I do," Mary confessed.

"Yes, we will begin," Basset said. He invited her to make the tea.

When they were seated, "You like the room?"

"I love it," she answered.

"So do I," he rejoined, more soberly. "The panelling is linen--pattern of the fifteenth century-- you see the folds? It was saved from the old house. I am glad you like it."

"I love it," she said again. But after that she grew thoughtful, and during the rest of the meal she said little. She was thinking of what was before her; of the unknown uncle, whose bread she was eating, and upon whom she was going to be dependent. What would he be like? How would he receive her? And why was every one so reticent about him--so reticent that he was beginning to be something of an ogre to her? When Toft presently appeared and said that Mr. Audley was in the library and would see her when she was ready, she lost color. But she answered the man with self-possession, asked quietly where the library was, and had not Basset's eyes been on her face he would have had no notion that she was troubled.

As it was, he waited for her to avow her misgiving--he was prepared to encourage her. But she said nothing.

None the less, at the last moment, with her hand on the door of the library, she hesitated. It was not so much fear of the unknown relative whom she was going to see that drove the blood from her cheek, as the knowledge that for her everything depended upon him. Her new home, its peace, its age, its woodland surroundings, fascinated her. It promised her not only content, but happiness. But as her stay in it hung upon John Audley's will, so her pleasure in it, and her enjoyment of it, depended upon the relations between them. What would they be? How would he receive her? What would he be like? At last she called up her courage, turned the handle, and entered the library.

For a moment she saw no one. The great room, with its distances and its harmonious litter, appeared to be empty. Then, "Mary, my dear," said a pleasant voice, "welcome to the Gatehouse!" And John Audley rose from his seat at a distant table and came towards her.

The notion which she had formed of him vanished in a twinkling, and with it her fears. She saw before her an elderly gentleman, plump and kindly, who walked with a short tripping step, and wore the swallow-tailed coat with gilt buttons which the frock-coat had displaced. He took her hand with a smile, kissed her on the forehead, and led her to a chair placed beside his own. He sat for a moment holding her hand and looking at her.

"Yes, I see the likeness," he said, after a moment's contemplation. "But, my dear, how is this? There are tears in your eyes, and you tremble."

"I think," she said, "I was a little afraid of you, sir."

"Well, you are not afraid now," he replied cheerfully. "And you won't be again. You won't be again. My dear, welcome once more to the Gatehouse. I hope that it may be your home until another is offered you. Things came between your father and me--I shall never mention them again, and don't you, my dear!"--this a little hurriedly--"don't you; all that is buried now, and I must make it up to you. Your letters?" he continued, patting her hand. "Yes, Peter told me that you wrote to me. I need not say that I never had them. No, never had them--Toft, what is it?"

The change in his voice struck her. The servant had come in quietly. "Mr. Basset, sir, has lost----"

"Another time!" John Audley replied curtly. "Another time! I am engaged now. Go!" Then when the door had closed behind the servant, "No, my dear," he continued, "I need not say that I never had them, so that I first heard of your troubles through a channel upon which I will not dwell. However, many good things come by bad ways, Mary. I hope you like the Gatehouse?"

"It is charming!" she cried with enthusiasm.

"It has only one drawback," he said.

She was clever enough to understand that he referred to its owner, and to escape from the subject. "This room," she said, "is perfection. I have never seen anything like it, sir."

"It is a pleasant room," he said, looking round him. "There is our coat over the mantel, gules, a fret or; like all old coats, very simple. Some think it is the Lacy Knot; the Audley of Edward the First's time married a Lacy. But we bore our old coat of three Butterflies later than that, for before the fall of Roger Mortimer, who was hung at Tyburn, he married his daughter to an Audley, and the escheaters found the wedding chamber in his house furnished with our Butterflies. Later the Butterfly survived as our badge. You see it there!" he continued, pointing it out among the mouldings of the ceiling. "There is the Stafford Knot, the badge of the great Dukes of Buckingham, the noblest of English families; it is said that the last of the line, a cobbler, died at Newport, not twenty miles from here. We intermarried with them, and through them with Peter's people, the Bassets. That is the Lovel Wolf, and there is the White Wolf of the Mortimers--all badges. But you do not know, I suppose, what a badge is?"

"I am afraid not," she said, smiling. "But I am as proud of our Butterfly, and as proud to be an Audley, sir, as if I knew more."

"Peter must give you some lessons in heraldry," he answered. "We live in the past here, my dear, and we must indoctrinate you with a love of our pursuits or you will be dull." He paused to consider. "I am afraid that we cannot allot you a drawing-room, but you must make your room upstairs as comfortable as you can. Etruria will see to that. And Peter shall arrange a table for you in the south bay here, and it shall be your table and your bay. That is his table; this is mine. We are orderly, and so we do not get in one another's way."

She thanked him gratefully, and with tears in her eyes, she said something to which he would not listen--he only patted her hand--as to his kindness, his great kindness, in receiving her. She could not, indeed, put her relief into words, so deep was it. Nowhere, she felt, could life be more peaceful or more calm than in this room which no sounds of the outer world except the songs of birds, no sights save the swaying of branches disturbed; where the blazoned panes cast their azure and argent on lines of russet books, where an aged hound sprawled before the embers, and the measured tick of the clock alone vied with the scratching of the pen. She saw herself seated there during drowsy summer days, or when firelight cheered the winter evenings. She saw herself sewing beside the hearth while her companions worked, each within his circle of light.

Then, she also was an Audley. She also had her share in the race which had lived long on this spot. Already she was fired with the desire to know more of them, and that flame John Audley was well fitted to fan. For he was not of the school of dry-as-dust antiquaries. He had the knack of choosing the picturesque in story, he could make it stand out for others, he could impart life to the actors in it. And, anxious to captivate Mary, he bent himself for nearly an hour to the display of his knowledge. Taking for his text one or other of the objects about him, he told her of great castles, from which England had been ruled, and through which the choicest life of the country had passed, that now were piles of sherds clothed with nettles. He told her of that woodland country on the borders of three counties, where the papists had long lived undisturbed and where the Gunpowder Plot had had its centre. He told her of the fashion which came in with Richard the Second, of adorning the clothes with initials, reading and writing having become for the first time courtly accomplishments; and to illustrate this he showed her the Westminster portrait of Richard in a robe embroidered with letters of R. He quoted Chaucer:

And thereon hung a broch of gold ful schene
On which was first i-written a crowned A
And after that, Amor vincit omnia.

Then, turning his back on her, he produced from some secret place a key, and opening a masked cupboard in the wall, he held out for her inspection a small bowl, bent and mis-shapen by use, and supported by two fragile butterflies. The whole was of silver so thin that to modern eyes it seemed trivial. Traces of gilding lingered about some parts of it, and on each of the wings of the butterflies was a capital A.

She was charmed. "Of all your illustrations," she cried, "I prefer this one! It is very old, I suppose?"

"It is of the fifteenth century," he said, turning it about. "We believe that it was made for the Audley who fell early in the Wars of the Roses. Pages and knights, maids and matrons, gloves of silk and gloves of mail, wrinkled palms and babies' fingers, the men, the women, the children of twelve generations of our race, my dear, have handled this. Once, according to an old inventory, there were six; this one alone remains."

"It must be very rare?" she said, her eyes sparkling.

"It is very rare," he said, and he handled it as if he loved it. He had not once allowed it to go out of his fingers. "Very rare. I doubt if, apart from the City Companies, there is another in the hands of the original owners."

"And it came to you by descent, sir?"

He paused in the act of returning it to its hiding-place. "Yes, that is how it came to me," he said in a muffled tone. But he seemed to be a long time putting it away; and when he turned with the key in his hand his face was altered, and he looked at her--well, had she done anything to anger him, she would have thought he was angry. "To whom besides me could it descend!" he asked, his voice raised a tone. "But there, I must not grow excited. I think--I think you had better go now. Go, my dear, now. But come back presently."

Mary went. But the change in tone and face had been such as to startle her and to dash the happy mood of a few moments earlier. She wondered what she had said to annoy him.

CHAPTER IX: OLD THINGS

The Gatehouse, placed on the verge of the upland, was very solitary. Cut off from the vale by an ascent which the coachmen of the great deemed too rough for their horses, it was isolated on the other three sides by Beaudelays Park and by the Great Chase, which flung its barren moors over many miles of table-land. In the course of the famous suit John Audley had added to the solitude of the house by a smiling aloofness which gave no quarter to those who agreed with his rival. The result was that when Mary came to live there, few young people would have found the Gatehouse a lively abode.

But to Mary during the quiet weeks that followed her arrival it seemed a paradise. She spent long hours in the open air, now seated on a fallen trunk in some glade of the park, now watching the squirrels in the clear gloom of the beech-wood, or again, lying at length on the carpet of thyme and heather that clothed the moor. She came to know by heart every path through the park--except that which led to the Great House; she discovered where the foxgloves clustered, where the meadow-sweet fringed the runlet, where the rare bog-bean warned the traveller to look to his footing. Even the Great Chase she came to know, and almost daily she walked to a point beyond the park whence she could see the distant smoke of a mining village. That was the one sign of life on the Chase; elsewhere it stretched vast and unpeopled, sombre under a livid sky, smiling in sunshine, here purple with ling, there scarred by fire--always wide under a wide heaven, raised high above the common world. Now and again she met a shepherd or saw a gig, lessened by distance, making its slow way along a moorland track. But for days together she might wander there without seeing a human being.

The wide horizon became as dear to her as the greenwood. Pent as she had been in cities, straitened in mean rooms where sight and smell had alike been outraged, she revelled in this sweet and open life. The hum of bees, the scent of pines, the flight of the ousel down the water, the whistle of the curlew, all were to her pleasures as vivid as they were new.

Meantime Basset made no attempt to share her excursions. He was fighting a battle with himself, and he knew better than to go out of his way to aid the enemy. And for her part she did not miss him. She did not dislike him, but the interest he excited in her was feeble. The thought of comparing him with Lord Audley, with the man to whose intervention she owed this home, this peace, this content, never occurred to her. Of Audley she did think as much perhaps as was prudent, sometimes with pensive gratitude, more rarely with a smile and a blush at her folly in dwelling on him. For always she thought of him as one, high and remote, whom it was not probable that she would ever see again, one whose course through life lay far from hers.

Presently, it is not to be denied, Basset began to grow upon her. He was there. He was part of her life. Morning and evening she had to do with him. Often she read or sewed in the same room with him, and in many small ways he added to her comfort. Sometimes he suggested things which would please her uncle; sometimes he warned her of things which she would do well to avoid. Once or twice he diverted to himself a spirt of John Audley's uncertain temper; and though Mary did not always detect the manœuvre, though she was far from suspecting the extent of his vigilance or the care which he cast about her, it would have been odd if she had not come to think more kindly of him, and to see merits in him which had escaped her at first.

Meanwhile he thought of her with mingled feelings. At first with doubt--it was never out of his mind that she had made much of Lord Audley and little of him. Then with admiration which he withstood more feebly as time went on, and the cloven hoof failed to appear. Later, with tenderness, which, hating the scheme John Audley had formed, he masked even from himself, and which he was sure that he would never have the courage to express in her presence.

For Basset was conscious that, aspire as he might, he was not a hero. The clash of life, the shock of battle, had no attraction for him. The library at the Gatehouse was, he owned it frankly, his true sphere. She, on the other hand, had had experiences. She had sailed through unknown seas, she had led a life strange to him. She had seen much, done much, suffered much, had held her own among strangers. Before her calmness and self-possession he humbled himself. He veiled his head.

He did not attempt, therefore, to accompany her abroad, but at home he had no choice save to see much of her. There was only one living room for all, and she glided with surprising ease into the current of the men's occupations. At first she was astray on the sea of books. Her knowledge was not sufficient to supply chart or compass, and it fell to Basset to point the way, to choose her reading, to set in a proper light John Audley's vivid pictures of the past, to teach her the elements of heraldry and genealogy. She proved, however, an apt scholar, and very soon she dropped into the position of her uncle's secretary. Sometimes she copied his notes, at other times he set her on the track of a fact, a relationship, a quotation, and she would spend hours in a corner, embedded in huge tomes of the county histories. Dugdale, Leland, Hall, even Polydore Vergil, became her friends. She pored over the Paston Letters, probed the false pedigrees of Banks, and could soon work out for herself the famous discovery respecting the last Lovel.

For a young girl it was an odd pursuit. But the past was in the atmosphere of the house, it went with the fortunes of a race whose importance lay in days long gone. Then all was new to her, enthusiasm is easily caught, and Mary, eager to please her uncle, was glad to be of use. She found the work restful after the suspense of the past year. It sufficed for the present, and she asked no more.

She never forgot the lamplit evenings of that summer; the spacious room, the fluttering of the moths that entered by the open windows, the flop of the old dog as it sought a cooler spot, the whisper of leaves turned ceaselessly in the pursuit of a fact or a fancy. In the retrospect all became less a picture than a frame containing a past world, a fifteenth-century world of color and movement, of rooms stifled in hangings and tapestries, of lines of spear-points and rows of knights in surcoats, of tolling bells and praying monks, of travellers kneeling before wayside shrines, of strange changes of fortune. For says the chronicler:

"I saw one of them, who was Duke of Exeter (but he concealed his name) following the Duke of Burgundy's train barefoot and bare-legged, begging his bread from door to door--this person was the next of the House of Lancaster and had married King Edward's sister."

And of dark sayings:

"Thys sayde Edward, Duke of Somerset, had herde a fantastyk prophecy that he sholde dy under a Castelle, wherefore he, as meche as in him was, he lete the King that he sholde not come in the Castelle of Wynsore, dredynge the sayde prophecy; but at Seint Albonys there was an hostelry havyng the sygne of a Castelle, and before that hostelry he was slayne."

"His badge was a Portcullis," her uncle said, when she read this to him, "so it was natural that he should fall before a castle. He used the Beanstalk, too, and if his name had been John, a pretty thing might have been raised upon it. But you're divagating, my dear," he continued, smiling-- and seldom had Mary seen him in a better humor--"you're divagating, whereas I--I believe that I have solved the problem of the Feathers."

"The Prince of Wales's? No!"

"I believe so. Of course there is no truth in the story which traces them to the blind King of Bohemia, killed at Crécy. His crest was two vulture wings."

"But what of Arderne, who was the Prince's surgeon?" Basset objected. "He says clearly that the Prince gained it from the King of Bohemia."

"Not at all!" John Audley replied arrogantly--at this moment he was an antiquary and nothing more. "Where is the Arderne extract? Listen. 'Edward, son of Edward the King, used to wear such a feather, and gained that feather from the King of Bohemia, whom he slew at Crécy, and so assumed to himself that feather which is called an ostrich feather which the first-named most illustrious King, used to wear on his crest.' Now who was the first-named most illustrious King, who before that used to wear it?"

"The King of Bohemia."

"Rubbish! Arderne means his own King, 'Edward the King.' He means that the Black Prince, after winning his spurs by his victory over the Bohemian, took his father's insignia. He had only been knighted six weeks and waited to wear his father's crest until he had earned it."

"By Jove, sir!" Basset exclaimed, "I believe you are right!"

"Of course I am! The evidence is all that way. The Black Prince's brothers wore it; surely not because their brother had done something, but because it was their father's crest, probably derived from their mother, Philippa of Hainault? If you will look in the inventory of jewels made on the usurpation of Henry the Fourth you will see this item, 'A collar of the livery of the Queen, on whom God have mercy, with an ostrich.'"

"But that," Basset interposed, "was Queen Anne of Bohemia--she died seven years before. There you get Bohemia again!"

"Compare this other entry," replied the antiquary, unmoved: "'A collar of the livery of Queen Anne, of branches of rosemary.' Now either Queen Anne of Bohemia had two liveries--which is unlikely--or the inventory made by order of Henry IV. quotes verbatim from lists made during the lifetime of Queen Anne; if this be the case, the last deceased Queen, on whom God have mercy, would be Philippa of Hainault; and we have here a clear statement that her livery was an ostrich, of which ostrich her husband wore a feather on his crest."

Basset clapped his hands. Mary beat applause on the table. "Hurrah!" she cried. "Audley for ever!"

"Miss Audley," Basset said, "Toft shall bring in hot water, and we will have punch!"

"Miss Audley!" her uncle exclaimed, with a wrinkling nose. "Why don't you call her Mary? And why, child, don't you call him Peter?"

Mary curtseyed. "Why not, my lord?" she said. "Peter it shall be--Peter who keeps the keys that you discover!"

And Peter laughed. But he saw that she used his name without a blush or a tremor, whereas he knew that if he could force his lips to frame her name, the word would betray him. For by this time, from his seat at his remote table, and from the ambush of his book, he had watched her too often for his peace, and too closely not to know that she was indifferent to him. He knew that at the best she felt a liking for him, the growth of habit, and tinged, he feared, with contempt.

He was so far right that there were three persons in the house who had a larger share of the girl's thoughts than he had. The first was John Audley. He puzzled her. There were times when she could not doubt his affection, times when he seemed all that she could desire, kind, good-humored, frank, engaged with the simplicity of a child in innocent pursuits, and without one thought beyond them. But touch a certain spot, approach with steps ever so delicate a certain subject--Lord Audley and his title--and his manner changed, the very man changed, he became secretive, suspicious, menacing. Nor, however quickly she might withdraw from the danger-line, could the harm be undone at once. He would remain for hours gloomy and thoughtful, would eye her covertly and with suspicion, would sit silent through meals, and at times mutter to himself. More rarely he would turn on her with a face which rage made inhuman, a face that she did not know, and with a shaking hand he would bid her go--go, and leave the room!

The first time that this happened she feared that he might follow up his words by sending her away. But nothing ensued, then or later. For a while after each outburst he would appear ill at ease. He would avoid her eyes, and look away from her in a manner almost as unpleasant as his violence; later, in a shamefaced way, he would tell her that she must not excite him, she must not excite him, it was bad for him. And the man-servant meeting her in the hall, would take the liberty of giving her the same advice.

Toft, indeed, was the second who puzzled her. He was civil, with the civility of the trained servant, but always there was in his manner a reserve. And she fancied that he watched her. If she left the house and glanced back she was certain to see his face at a window, or his figure in a doorway. Within doors it was the same. He slept out, living with his wife in the kitchen wing, which had a separate entrance from the courtyard. But he was everywhere at all hours. Even his master appeared uneasy in his presence, and either broke off what he was saying when the man entered, or continued the talk on another note. More rarely he turned on Toft and without rhyme or reason would ask him harshly what he wanted.

The third person to share Mary's thoughts, but after a more pleasant fashion, was Toft's daughter, Etruria. "I hope you will like her, my dear," John Audley had said. "She will give you such attendance as you require, and will share the south wing with you at night. The two bedrooms there are on a separate staircase. I sleep above the library in this wing, and Peter in the tower room--we have our own staircase. I have brought her into the house because I thought you might not like to sleep alone in that wing."

Mary had thanked him, and had said how much she liked the girl. And she had liked her, but for a time she had not understood her. Etruria was all that was good and almost all that was beautiful. She was simple, kindly, helpful, having the wide low brow, the placid eyes, and perfect complexion of a Quaker girl--and to add to these attractions she was finely shaped, though rather plump than slender; and she was incredibly neat. Nor could any Quaker girl have been more gentle or more demure.

But she might have had no tongue, she was so loth to use it; and a hundred times Mary wondered what was behind that reticence. Sometimes she thought that the girl was merely stupid. Sometimes she yoked her with her father in the suspicions she entertained of him. More often, moved by the girl's meek eyes, she felt only a vague irritation. She was herself calm by nature, and reserved by training, the last to gossip with a servant, even with one whose refinement appeared innate. But Etruria's dumbness was beyond her.

One day in a research which she was making she fancied that she had hit on a discovery. It happened that Etruria came into the room at the moment, and in the fulness of her heart Mary told her of it. "Etruria," she said, "I've made a discovery all by myself."

"Yes, Miss."

"Something that no one has known for hundreds of years! Think of that!"

"Indeed, Miss."

Provoked, Mary took a new line. "Etruria," she asked, "are you happy?"

The girl did not answer.

"Don't you hear me? I asked if you were happy."

"I am content, Miss."

"I did not ask that. Are you happy?"

And then, moved on her side, perhaps, by an impulse towards confidence, Etruria yielded. "I don't think that we can any of us be happy, Miss," she said, "with so much sorrow about us."

"You strange girl!" Mary cried, taken aback. "What do you mean?"

But Etruria was silent.

"Come," Mary insisted. "You must tell me what you mean."

"Well, Miss," the girl answered reluctantly, "I'm sad and loth to think of all the suffering in the world. It's natural that you should not think of it, but I'm of the people, and I'm sad for them."

Balaam when the ass spoke was scarcely more surprised than Mary. "Why?" she asked.

The girl pointed to the open window. "We've all we could ask, Miss--light and air and birds' songs and sunshine. We've all we need, and more. But I come of those who have neither light nor air, nor songs nor sunshine, who've no milk for children nor food for mothers! Who, if they've work, work every hour of the day in dust and noise and heat. Who are half clemmed from year's end to year's end, and see no close to it, no hope, no finish but the pauper's deals! It's for them I'm sad, Miss."

"Etruria!"

"They've no teachers and no time to care," Etruria continued in desperate earnest now that the floodgates were raised. "They're just tools to make money, and, like the tools, they wear out and are cast aside! For there are always more to do their work, to begin where they began, and to be worn out as they were worn out!"

"Don't!" Mary cried.

Etruria was silent, but two large tears rolled down her face. And Mary marvelled. So this mild, patient girl, going about her daily tasks, could think, could feel, could speak, and upon a plane so high that the listener was sensible of humiliation as well as surprise! For a moment this was the only effect made upon her. Then reflection did its part--and memory. She recalled that glimpse of the under-world which she had had on her journey from London. She remembered the noisome alleys, the cinder wastes, the men toiling half-naked at the furnaces, the pinched faces of the women; and she remembered also the account which Lord Audley had given her of the fierce contest between town and country, plough and forge, land-lord and cotton-lord, which had struck her so much at the time.

In the charms of her new life, in her new interests, these things had faded from her mind. They recurred now, and she did not again ask Etruria what she meant. "Is it as bad as that?" she asked.

"It is not as bad as it has been," Etruria answered. "Three years ago there were hundreds of thousands out of work. There are thousands, scores of thousands, still; and thousands have no food but what's given them. And charity is bitter to many," she added, "and the poorhouse is bitter to all."

"But what has caused things to be so bad?"

"Some say one thing and some another. But most that machines lower wages, Miss, and the bread-tax raises food."

"Ah!" Mary said. And she looked more closely at the girl who knew so much that was at odds with her station.

"Others," Etruria continued, a faint color in her cheeks, "think that it is selfishness, that every one is for himself and no one for one another, and----"

"Yes?" Mary said, seeing that she hesitated.

"And that if every one thought as much of his neighbor as of himself, or even of his neighbor as well as of himself, it would not be machines nor corn-taxes nor poorhouses would be strong enough to take the bread out of the children's mouths or the work out of men's hands!"

Mary had an inspiration. "Etruria," she cried, "some one has been teaching you this."

The girl blushed. "Well, Miss," she said simply, "it was at church I learned most of it."

"At church? What church? Not Riddsley?" For it was to Riddsley, to a service as dull as it was long, that they proceeded on Sundays in a chaise as slow as the reader.

"No, Miss, not Riddsley," Etruria answered. "It's at Brown Heath on the Chase. But it's not a real church, Miss. It's a room."

"Oh!" Mary replied. "A meeting-house!"

For some reason Etruria's eyes gleamed. "No, Miss," she said. "It's the curate at Riddsley has a service in a room at Brown Heath on Thursdays."

"And you go?"

"When I can, Miss."

The idea of attending church on a week-day was strange to Mary; as strange as to that generation was the zeal that passed beyond the common channel to refresh those whom migrations of population or changes in industry had left high and dry. The Tractarian movement was giving vigor not only to those who supported it, but to those who withstood it.

"And you've a sermon?" Mary said. "What was the text last Thursday, Etruria?"

The girl hesitated, considered, then looked with appeal at her mistress. She clasped her hands. "'Two are better than one,'" she replied, "'because they have good reward for their labor. For if they fall, one will lift up his fellow, but woe to him that is alone when he falleth, for he hath not another to lift him up.'"

"Gracious, Etruria!" Mary cried. "Is that in the Bible?"

Etruria nodded.

"And what did your preacher say about it?"

"That the employer and the workman were fellows, and if they worked together and each thought for the other they would have a good reward for their labor; that if one fell, it was the duty of the other to help him up. And again, that the land and the mill were fellows--the town and the country--and if they worked together in love they would have a good return, and if trouble came to one the other should bear with him. But all the same," Etruria added timidly, "that the bread-taxes were wrong."

"Etruria," Mary said. "To-morrow is Thursday. I shall go with you to Brown Heath."

CHAPTER X: NEW THINGS

Mary Audley, crossing the moor to a week-day service, was but one of many who in the 'forties were venturing on new courses. In religion there were those who fancied that by a return to primitive forms they might recapture the primitive fervor; and those again who, like the curate whom Mary was going to hear, were bent on pursuing the beaten path into new places. Some thought that they had found a panacea for the evils of the day in education, and put their faith in workmen's institutes and night schools. Others were satisfied with philanthropy, and proclaimed that infants of seven ought not to toil for their living, that coal-pits were not fit places for women, and that what paid was not the only standard of life. A few dreamt of a new England in which gentle and simple were to mix on new-old terms; and a multitude, shrewd and hard-headed, believed in the Corn Law League, whose speakers travelled from Manchester to carry the claims of cheap bread to butter crosses and market towns, and there bearded the very landlord's agent.

The truth was that the country was lying sick with new evils, and had perforce to find a cure, whether that cure lay in faith, or in the primer, or in the Golden Rule, or in Adam Smith. For two generations men had been quitting the field for the mill, the farm for the coal-pit. They had followed their work into towns built haphazard, that grew presently into cities. There, short of light, of air, of water, lacking decency, lacking even votes--for the Reform Bill, that was to give everything to everybody, had stopped at the masters--lacking everything but wages, they swarmed in numbers stupendous and alarming to the mind of that day. And then the wages failed. Machines pushed out hands, though

Tools were made, and born were hands,
Every farmer understands.

Machines lowered wages, machines glutted the markets. Men could get no work, masters could sell no goods. On the top of this came bad seasons and dear bread. Presently hundreds of thousands were living on public charity, long lists of masters were in the Gazette. In the gloomy cities of the North, masses of men heaved and moaned as the sea when the south-west wind falls upon it.

All but the most thoughtless saw danger as well as unhappiness in this, and called on their gods. The Chartists proclaimed that safety lay in votes. The landed interest thought that a little more protection might mend matters. The Golden Rulers were for shorter hours. But the men who were the loudest and the most confident cried that cheap bread would mend all. The poor, they said, would have to eat and to spend. They would buy goods, the glut would cease. The wheels would turn again, there would be work and wages. The Golden Age would return. So preached the Manchester men.

In the meantime the doctors wrangled, and the patient grew a little, not much, better. And Mary Audley and Etruria walked across the moorland in the evening sunshine, with a light breeze stirring the bracken, and waves of shadow moving athwart the stretches of purple ling. They seemed very far, very remote from the struggle for life and work and bread that was passing in the world below.

Presently they dropped into a fern-clad dingle and saw below them, beside the rivulet that made music in its bottom, a house or two. Descending farther, they came on more houses, crawling up the hill slopes, and on a few potato patches and ash-heaps. As the sides of the valley rose higher and closed in above the walkers cottages fell into lines on either side of the brook, and began to show one behind the other in rough terraces, with middens that slid from the upper to the lower level. The valley bent to the left, and quickly tall chimneys became visible, springing from a huddle of mean roofs through which no other building of size, no tower, no steeple, rose to break the ugly sameness. This was Brown Heath.

"It's a rough place," Etruria said as they picked their way. "But don't be afraid, Miss. I'm often passing, and they know me."

Still it was a rough place. The roadway was a cinder-track, and from the alleys and lanes above it open drains wormed their way across the path and into the stream, long grown foul. The air was laden with smoke, coal dust lay everywhere; the most cleanly must have despaired. Men seated, pipe in mouth, on low walls, watched the two go by--not without some rude banter; frowsy women crouching on door-steps and nursing starveling babes raised sullen faces. Lads in clogs made way for them unwillingly. In one place a crowd seethed from a side street and, shouting and struggling, overflowed the roadway before them and threatened to bar their path.

"It's a dog-fight," Etruria said. "They are rare and fond of them, Miss. We'd best get by quickly."

They passed in safety, passed, too, a brawl between two colliers, the air about them thick with oaths, passed a third eddy round two women fighting before a public-house. "The chaps are none so gentle," Etruria said, falling unconsciously into a commoner way of speaking. "They're all for fighting, dogs or men, and after dark I'm not saying we'd be safe. But we'll be over the moor by dusk, Miss."

They came, as she spoke, to a triangular space, sloping with the hill, skirted by houses, and crossed by an open sewer. It was dreary and cinder-covered, but five publics looked upon it and marked it for the centre of Brown Heath. Etruria crossed the triangle to a building a little cleaner than its neighbors; it was the warehouse, she told her mistress, of a sack-maker who had failed. She entered, and her companion followed her.

Mary found herself in a bare barn-like room, having two windows set high in the walls, the light from which fell coldly on a dozen benches ranged one behind the other, but covering only a portion of the floor. On these were seated, when they entered, about twenty persons, mainly women, but including three or four men of the miner class. No attempt had been made to alter the character of the place, and of formality there was as little. The two had barely seated themselves before a lean young man, with a long pale face and large nose, rose from the front bench, and standing before the little congregation, opened his book. He wore shabby black, but neither surplice nor gown.

The service lasted perhaps twenty minutes, and Mary was not much moved by it. The young man's voice was weak, the man himself looked under-fed. She noticed, however, that as the service went on the number in the room grew, and when it closed she found that all the seats were filled, and that there were even a few men--some of them colliers fresh from the pit--standing at the back. Remembering the odd text that the clergyman had given out the week before, she wondered what he would choose to-day, and, faintly amused, she stole a glance at her companion. But Etruria's rapt face was a reproach to her levity.

The young clergyman pushed back the hair from his forehead. His posture was ungainly, he did not know what to do with his hands, he opened his mouth and shut it again. Then with an effort he began. "My text, my friends," he said, "is but one word, 'Love.' Where will you find it in the Scriptures? In every chapter and in every verse. In the dark days of old the order was 'Thou shalt live!' The new order in these days is 'Thou shalt love!'" He began by describing the battle of life in the animal and vegetable world, where all things lived at the cost of others; and he admitted that the struggle for life, for bread, for work, as they saw it around them, resembled that struggle. In moving terms he enlarged on the distress, on the vast numbers lately living on the rates, on the thousands living, where even the rates fell short, on Government aid. He described the fireless homes, the foodless children, the strong men hopeless. And he showed them that others were stricken, that masters suffered, tradesmen were ruined, the country languished. "The worst may be past," he said. "You are working half-time, you are living on half-wages, you are thankful that things are better." Then he told them that for his part he did not presume to say what was at the root of these unhappy conditions, but that of one thing he felt sure--and this was his message to them--that if the law of love, if the golden rule of preferring another to one's self, if the precept of that charity,

Which seeketh not itself to please

Nor for itself hath any care,

But for another gives its ease,

if that were followed by all, then all

Might build a heaven in hell's despair.

And in words more eloquent than he had yet compassed he begged them to set that example of brotherhood, in the certainty that the worst social evils, nay, all evils save pain and death, would be cured by the love that thought for others, that in the master preferred the servant's welfare and in the servant put first his master's interests. Finally he quoted his old text, "Let two work together, for if they fall, one will lift up his fellow!"

It seemed as if he had done. He was silent; his hearers waited. Then with an effort he continued:

"I have a word to say about something which fell from me in this place last week. While I did not venture, unskilled as I am, to say where lies the cause of our distress, I did say that I found it hard to believe that the system which taxes the bread you earn in the sweat of your brow, which takes a disproportionate part from the scanty crust of the widow and from the food of the child, was in accordance with the law of love. I repeat that now; and because I have been told that I dare not say in the pulpit of Riddsley church what I say here, I shall on the first opportunity state my belief there. You may ask why I have not done so; my answer is, that I am there the representative of another, whereas in this voluntary work I am myself more responsible. In saying that I ask you to judge me, as we should judge all, with that charity which believeth no evil."

A moment later Mary, deeply moved, was passing out with the crowd. As she stood, caught in the press by the door, an old man in horn-rimmed glasses, who was waiting there, held out his hand. She was going to take it, when she saw that it was not meant for her, but for the young clergyman who was following at her heels.

"Master, dunno you do it," the old fellow growled. "You'll break your pick, and naught gotten. Naught gotten, that'll serve. Your gaffer'll not abide it, and you'll lose your job!"

"Would you have me take it," the young man answered, "and not do the work, Cluff? Never fear for me."

"Dunno you be rash, master!" the other rejoined, clutching his sleeve and detaining him. "You be sure----"

Mary heard no more. She felt Etruria's hand pressing her arm. "We'd best lose no time," the girl whispered. And she drew Mary onward, across the triangle and into the lane which led to the moor.

"Are we so late?" The sun had set, but it was still light. "We'd best hurry," Etruria persisted, increasing her speed.

Mary looked at her and saw that she was troubled, but at the moment she set this down to the influence of the sermon, and her own mind went back to it. "I am glad you brought me, Etruria," she said. "I shall always be glad that I came."

"We'd best be getting home now," was Etruria's only answer, but this time Mary's ear caught the sound of footsteps behind them, and she turned. The young clergyman was hastening after them.

"Etruria!" he cried.

For a moment Mary fancied that Etruria did not hear. The girl hurried on. But Mary saw no occasion to run away, and she halted. Then Etruria, with a gesture of despair, stopped.

"It is no use," she said.

The young man came up with them. His head was bare, his hat was in his hand, his long plain face was aglow with the haste he had made. He had heard Etruria's words, and "It is of every use," he said.

"This is--my mistress," Etruria said.

"Miss Audley?"

"I am Miss Audley," Mary announced, wondering much.

"I thought that it might be so," he replied. "I have waited for such an occasion. I am Mr. Colet, the curate at Riddsley. Etruria and I love one another," he continued. "We are going to be married, if ever my means allow me to marry."

"No, we are not," the girl rejoined sharply. "Mr. Colet knows my mind," she continued, her eyes turned away. "I have told him many times that I am a servant, the daughter of a servant, in a different class from his, and I'll never be the one to ruin him and be a disgrace to him! I'll never marry him! Never!"

"And I have told Etruria," he replied, "that I will never take that answer. We love one another. It is nothing to me that she is a servant. My work is to serve. I am as poor as it is possible to be, with as poor prospects as it is possible to have. I shall never be anything but what I am, and I shall think myself rich when I have a hundred pounds a year. I who have so little, who look for so little, am I to give up this happiness because Etruria has less? I, too, say, Never!"

Mary, standing between them, did not know what to answer, and it was Etruria who replied. "It is useless," she said. And then, in a tone of honest scorn, "Who ever heard," she cried, "of a clergyman who married a servant? Or who ever heard of good coming of it?"

Mary had an inspiration. "Does Etruria's father know?" she asked.

"He knows and approves," the young man replied, his eyes bent fondly on his mistress.

Mary too looked at Etruria--beautiful, patient, a servant, loved. And she wondered. All these weeks she had been rubbing elbows with this romance, and she had not discerned it! Now, while her sympathies flew to the lover's side, her prejudices rose up against him. They echoed Etruria's words, "Who ever heard of good coming of such a match?" The days had been, as Mary knew, when the chaplain had married the lady's maid. But those days were gone. Meantime the man waited, and she did not know what to say.

"After all," she said at last, "it is for Etruria to decide."

"No, it is for us both to decide," he replied. And then, as if he thought that he had sufficiently stated his case, "I ask your pardon, Miss Audley, for intruding," he continued. "I am keeping you, and as I am going your way that is needless. I have had a message from a sick woman, and I am on my way to see her."

He took permission for granted, and though Etruria's very shoulders forbade him, he moved on beside them. "Conditions are better here than in many places," he said, "but in this village you would see much to sadden you."

"I have seen enough," Mary answered, "to know that."

"Ten years ago there was not a house here. Now there is a population of two thousand, no church, no school, no gentry, no one of the better class. There is a kind of club, a centre of wild talk; better that, perhaps, than apathy."

"Is it in Riddsley parish?" Mary asked. They were nearly clear of the houses, and the slopes of the hill, pale green in the peaceful evening light, began to rise on either side. It was growing dusk, and from the moorland above came the shrill cries of plovers.

"Yes, it is in Riddsley parish," he answered, "but many miles from the town, and as aloof from it--Riddsley is purely agricultural--as black from white. In such places as this--and there are many of them in Staffordshire, as raw, as rough, and as new--there is work for plain men and plain women. In these swarming hives there is no room for any refinement but true refinement. And the Church must learn to do her work with plain tools, or the work will pass into other hands."

"You may cut cheese with an onion knife," Etruria said coldly. "I don't know that people like it."

"I know nothing better than onions in the right place," he replied.

"That's not in cheese," she rejoined, to Mary's amusement.

"The poor get little cheese," he said, "and the main thing is to cut their bread for them. But here I must leave you. My errand is to that cottage."

He pointed to a solitary house, standing a few score paces above the road on the hillside. Mary shook hands with him, but Etruria turned her shoulder resolutely.

"Good-bye, Etruria," he said. And then to Mary, "I hope that I have made a friend?"

"I think you have," she answered. "I am sure that you deserve one."

He colored, raised his hat, and turned away, and the two went on, without looking back; darkness was coming apace, and they were still two miles from home. Mary kept silence, prudently considering how she should deal with the matter, and what she should say to her companion. As it fell out, events removed her difficulty. They had not gone more than two hundred yards, and were still some way below the level of the Chase, when a cry reached them. It came out of the dusk behind them, and might have been the call of a curlew on the moor. But first one, and then the other stood. They turned, and listened, and suddenly Etruria, more anxious or sharper of eye than her mistress, uttered a cry and broke away at a run across the sloping turf towards the solitary cottage. Alarmed, Mary looked intently in that direction, and made out three or four figures struggling before the door of the house. She guessed then that the clergyman was one of them, and that the cry had come from him, and without a thought for herself she set off, running after Etruria as fast as she could.

Twice Etruria screamed as she ran, and Mary echoed the cry. She saw that the man was defending himself against the onset of three or four--she could hear the clatter of sticks on one another. Then she trod on her skirt and fell. When she had got, breathless, to her feet again, the clergyman was down and the men appeared to be raining blows on him. Etruria shrieked once more and the next moment was lost amid the moving figures, the brandished sticks, the struggle.

Mary ran on desperately. She caught sight of the girl on her knees over the fallen man, she saw her fend off more than one blow, she heard more than one blow fall with a sickening thud. She came up to them. With passion that drove out fear, she seized the arm of the nearest and dragged him back.

"You coward!" she cried. "You coward! I am Miss Audley! Do you hear! Leave him! Leave him, I say!"

Her appearance, the surprise, checked the man; her fearlessness, perhaps her name, gave the others pause. They retreated a step. The man she had grasped shook himself free, but did not attempt to strike her. "Oh, d--n the screech-owls!" he cried. "The place is alive with them! Hold your noise, you fools! We'll have the parish on us!"

"I am Miss Audley!" Mary repeated, and in her indignation she advanced on him. "How dare you?" Etruria, still on her knees, continued to shriek.

"You're like to get a wipe over the head, dang you!" the man growled, "whoever you be! Go to---- and mind your own brats! He'll know better now than to preach against them as he gets his living by! You be gone!"

But Mary stood her ground. She declared afterwards that, brutally as the man spoke, the fight had gone out of him. Etruria, on the contrary, maintained that, finding only women before them, the ruffians would have murdered them. Fortunately, while the event hung in the balance, "What is it?" some one shouted from the road below. "What's the matter there?"

"Murder!" cried Etruria shrilly. "Help! Help!"

"Help!" cried Mary. She still kept her face to the men, but for the first time she began to know fear.

Footsteps thudded softly on the turf, figures came into view, climbing the slope. It needed no more. With a volley of oaths the assailants turned tail and made off. In a trice they were round the corner of the house and lost in the dusk.

A moment later two men, equally out of breath and each carrying a gun, reached the spot. "Well!" said the bigger of the two, "What is it?"

He spoke as if he had not come very willingly, but Mary did not notice this. The crisis over, her knees shook, she could barely stand, she could not speak. She pointed to the fallen man, over whom Etruria still crouched, her hair dragged down about her shoulders, her neckband torn, a ghastly blotch on her white cheek.

"Is he dead?" the new-comer asked in a different tone.

"Ay, dead!" Etruria echoed. "Dead!"

Fortunately the curate gave the lie to the word. He groaned, moved, with an effort he raised himself on his elbow. "I'm--all right!" he gasped. "All right!"

Etruria sprang to her feet. She stepped back as if the ground had opened before her.

"I'm not--hurt," Colet added weakly.

But it was evident that he was hurt, even if no bones were broken. When they came to lift him he could not stand, and he seemed to be uncertain where he was. After watching him a moment, "He should see a doctor," said the man who had come up so opportunely. "Petch," he continued, addressing his companion, who wore a gamekeeper's dress, "we must carry him to the trap and get him down to Brown Heath. Who is he, do you know? He looks like a parson."

"He's Mr. Colet of Riddsley," Mary said.

The man turned and looked at her. "Hallo!" he exclaimed. And then in the same tone of surprise, "Miss Audley!" he said. "At this time of night?"

Mary collected herself with an effort. "Yes," she said, "and very fortunately, for if we had not been here the men would have murdered him. As it is, you share the credit of saving him, Lord Audley."

"The credit of saving you is a good deal more to me," he answered gallantly. "I did not think that we should meet after this fashion."

CHAPTER XI: TACT AND TEMPER

He looked at Etruria, and Mary explained who she was.

"I am afraid that she is hurt."

The girl's temple was bruised and there was blood on her cheek; more than one of the blows aimed at her lover had fallen on her. But she said eagerly that it was "Nothing! Nothing!"

"Are you sure, Etruria?" Mary asked with concern.

"It is nothing, indeed, Miss," the girl repeated. She was trying with shaking fingers to put up her hair.

"Then the sooner," Audley rejoined, "we get this--this gentleman to my dogcart, the better. Take his other arm, Petch. Miss Audley, can you carry my gun?--it is not loaded. And you," he continued to Etruria, "if you are able, take Petch's."

They took the guns, and the little procession wound down the path to the road, where they found a dogcart awaiting them, and, peering from the cart, two setters, whining and fretting. The dogs were driven under the seat, and the clergyman, still muttering that he was all right, was lifted in. "Steady him, Petch," Audley said; "and do you drive slowly," he added, to the other man. "You will be at the surgeon's at Brown Heath in twenty minutes. Stay with him, Petch, and send the cart back for me."

"But are you not going?" Mary cried.

"I am not going to leave you in the dark with only your maid," he answered with severity. "One adventure a night is enough, Miss Audley."

She murmured a word or two, but submitted. The struggle had shaken her; she could still see the men's savage faces, still hear the thud of their blows. And she and Etruria had nearly a mile to go before they reached the park.

When they were fairly started, "How did it happen?" he asked.

Mary told the story, but said no word of Etruria's romance.

"Then you were not with him when they set on him?"

"No, we had parted."

"And you went back?"

"Of course we did!"

"It was imprudent," he said, "very imprudent. If we had not come up at that moment you might have been murdered."

"And if we had not gone back, Mr. Colet might have been murdered!" she answered. "What he had done to offend them----"

"I think I can tell you that. He's the curate at Riddsley, isn't he? Who's been preaching up cheap bread and preaching down the farmers?"

"Perhaps so," Mary answered. "He may be. But is he to be murdered for that? From your tone one might think so."

"No," he replied slowly, "he is not to be murdered for it. But whether he is wise to preach cheap bread to starving men, whether he is wise to tell them that they would have it but for this man or that man, this class or that class--is another matter."

She was not convinced--the sermon had keyed her thoughts to a high pitch. But he spoke reasonably, and he had the knack of speaking with authority, and she said no more. And on his side he had no wish to quarrel. He had come down to Riddsley partly to shoot, partly to look into the political situation, but a little--there was no denying it--to learn how Mary Audley fared with her uncle.

For he had thought much of her since they had parted, and much of the fact that she was John Audley's heir. Her beauty, her spirit, her youth, had caught his fancy. He had looked forward to renewing his acquaintance with her, and he was in no mood, now he saw her, to spoil their meeting by a quarrel. He thought Colet, whose doings had been reported to him, a troublesome, pestilent fellow, and he was not sorry that he had got his head broken. But he need not tell her that. Circumstances had favored him in bringing them together and giving him the beau rôle, and he was not going to cross his luck.

So, "Fire is an excellent thing of course," he continued with an air of moderation, "but, believe me, it's not safe amid young trees in a wind. Whatever your views, to express them in all companies may be honest, but is not wise. I have no doubt that a parson is tried. He sees the trouble. He is not always the best judge of the remedy. However, enough of that. We shall agree at least in this, that our meetings are opportune?"

"Most opportune," Mary answered. "And from my point of view very fortunate!"

"There really is a sort of fate in it. What but fate could have brought about our meeting at the Hôtel Lambert? What but fate could have drawn us to the same spot on the Chase to-night?"

There was a tone in his voice that brought the blood to her cheek and warned her to keep to the surface of things. "The chance that men call fate," she answered lightly.

"Or the fate that fools call chance," he urged, half in jest, half in earnest. "We have met by chance once, and once again--with results! The third time--what will the third time bring? I wonder."

"Not a fright like this, I hope!" Mary answered, remaining cheerfully matter of fact. "Or if it does," with a flash of laughter, "I trust that the next time you will come up a few moments earlier!"

"Ungrateful!"

"I?" she replied. "But it was Etruria who was in danger!"

For the peril had left her with a sense of exhilaration, of lightness, of ease. She was pleased to feel that she could hold her own with him, relieved that she was not afraid of him. And she was glad--she was certainly glad--to see him again. If he were inclined to make the most of his advantage, well, a little gallantry was quite in the picture; she was not deceived, and she was not offended. While he on his side, as they walked over the moor, thought of her as a clever little witch who knew her value and could keep her head; and he liked her none the less for it.

When they came at last to the gap in the wall that divided the Chase from the park, a figure, dimly outlined, stood in the breach waiting for them. "Is that you?" a voice asked.

The voice was Basset's, and Mary's spirits sank. She felt that the meeting was ill-timed. "Yes," she answered.

Unluckily, Peter was one of those whose anxiety takes an irritable form. "What in the world has happened?" he asked. "I couldn't believe that you were still out. It's really not safe. Hallo!" breaking off and speaking in a different tone, "is some one with you?"

"Yes," Mary said. They were within touch now and could see one another. "We have had an adventure. Lord Audley was passing, he came to our rescue, and has very kindly seen us home."

"Lord Audley!" Basset was taken by surprise and his tone was much as if he had said, "The devil!"

"By good fortune, Basset," Audley replied. He may have smiled in the darkness--we cannot say. "I was returning from shooting, heard cries for help, and found Miss Audley playing the knight-errant, encircled by prostrate bodies!"

Basset could not frame a word, so great was his surprise, so overwhelming his chagrin. Was this man to spring up at every turn? To cross him on every occasion? To put him in the background perpetually? To intrude even on the peace and fellowship of the Gatehouse? It was intolerable!

When he did not answer, "It was not I who was the knight-errant," Mary said. "It was Etruria. She is a little the worse for it, I fear, and the sooner she is in bed the better. As Mr. Basset is here," she continued, turning to Audley, "we must not take you farther. Your cart is no doubt waiting for you. But you will allow us to thank you again. We are most grateful to you--both Etruria and I."

She spoke more warmly, perhaps she let her hand rest longer in his, to make up for Basset's silence. For that silence provoked her. She had gathered from many things that Basset did not love the other; but to stand mute and churlish on such an occasion, and find no word of acknowledgment--this was too bad.

And Basset knew, he too knew that he ought to thank Audley. But the black dog was on his back, and while he hesitated, the other made his adieux. He said a pleasant word to Etruria, tossed a careless "Good-night" to the other man, turned away, and was gone.

For awhile the three who remained trudged homewards in silence. Then, "What happened to you?" Basset asked grudgingly.

Vexed and indignant, Mary told the story.

"I did not know that you knew Mr. Colet!"

"When a man is being murdered," she retorted, "one does not wait for an introduction."

He was a good fellow, but jealousy was hot within him, and he could not bridle his tongue. "Oh, but murdered?" he said. "Isn't that rather absurd? Who would murder Colet?"

Mary did not deign to reply.

Baffled, he sought for another opening. "I do not know what your uncle will say."

"Because we rescued Mr. Colet? And perhaps saved his life?"

"No, but----"

"Or because Lord Audley rescued us?"

"He will certainly not be pleased to hear that," he retorted maliciously. He knew that he was misbehaving, but he could not refrain. "If you take my advice you will not mention it."

"I shall tell him the moment I reach the house," she declared.

"You will be very unwise if you do."

"I shall be honest at least! For the rest I would rather not discuss the matter, Mr. Basset. I am a good deal shaken by what we have gone through, and I am very tired."

He muttered humbly that he was sorry--that he only meant----

"Please leave it there," she said. "Enough has been said."

Too late the anger and the spirit died out of the unlucky man, and he would have grovelled before her, he would have done anything to earn his pardon. But Etruria's presence tied his tongue, and gloomy and wretched--oh, why had he not gone farther to meet them, why had he not been the one to rescue her?--he walked on beside them, cursing his unhappy temper. It was dark, the tired girls lagged, Etruria hung heavily on her mistress's arm; he longed to help them. But he did not dare to offer. He knew too well that Mary would reject the offer.

Etruria had her own dreams, and in spite of an aching head was happy. But to Mary, fatigued by the walk, and vexed by Basset's conduct, the way seemed endless. At last the house loomed dark above them, their steps rang hard on the flagged court. The outer door stood ajar, and entering, they found a lamp burning in the hall; but the silence which prevailed, above and below, struck a chill. Silence and an open door go ill together.

Etruria at Mary's bidding went up at once to her room. Basset called angrily for Toft. But no Toft appeared, and Mary, resentment still hot in her, opened the door of the library and went in to see her uncle. She felt that the sooner her story was told the better.

But the library was empty. Lights burned on the several tables, the wood fire smouldered on the hearth, the tall clock ticked in the silence, the old hound flopped his tail. But John Audley was not there.

"Where is my uncle?" she asked, as she stood in the open doorway.

Basset looked over her shoulder. He saw that the room was empty. "He may have gone to look for us."

"And Toft?"

"And Toft, too, I suppose."

"But why should my uncle go to look for us?" she asked, aghast at the thought--he troubled himself so little for others, he lived so completely his own life!

"He might," Basset replied. He stood for a moment, thinking. Then--for the time they had forgotten their quarrel--"You had better get something to eat and go to bed," he said. "I will send Mrs. Toft to you."

She had not the strength to resist. "Very well," she said. "Are you going to look for them?"

"Perhaps Mrs. Toft will know where they are."

She took her candle and went slowly up the narrow winding staircase that led to her room and to Etruria's. As she passed, stair by stair, the curving wainscot of dull wood which so many generations had rubbed, she carried with her the picture of Basset standing in thought in the middle of the hall, his eyes on the doorway that gaped on the night. Then a big man with a genial face usurped his place; and she smiled and sighed.

A moment later she went into Etruria's room to learn how she was, and caught the girl rising from her knees. "Oh, Miss," she said, coloring as she met Mary's eyes, "if we had not been there!"

"And yet--you won't marry him, you foolish girl?"

"Oh no, no!"

"Although you love him!"

"Love him!" Etruria murmured, her face burning. "It is because I love him, Miss, that I will never, never marry him."

Mary wondered. "And yet you love him?" she said, raising the candle so that its light fell on the other's face.

Etruria looked this way and that way, but there was no escape. In a very small voice she said, "Love seeketh not itself to please

Nor for itself hath any care!"

She covered her hot cheeks with her hands. But Mary took away the hands and kissed her.

"Oh, Miss!" Etruria exclaimed.

Mary went out then, but on the threshold of her own room she paused to snuff her candle. "So that is love," she thought. "It's very interesting, and--and rather beautiful!"

CHAPTER XII: THE YEW WALK

Basset had been absent the greater part of the day, and returning at sunset had learned that Miss Audley had not come back from Brown Heath. The servant had hinted alarm--the Chase was lonely, the hour late; and Basset had hurried off without more, not doubting that John Audley was in the house.

Now he was sure that John Audley had been abroad at the time, and he suspected that Toft had known it, and had kept it from him. He stood for a moment in thought, then he crossed the court to Toft's house. Mrs. Toft was cooking something savory in a bonnet before the fire, and the contrast between her warm cheerful kitchen and the stillness of the house from which he came struck him painfully. He told her that her daughter had received a blow on the head, and that Miss Audley needed supper--she had better attend to them.

Mrs. Toft was a stout woman, set by a placid and even temper above small surprises. She looked at the clock, a fork in her hand. "I can't hurry it, Mr. Basset," she said. "You may be Sir Robert Peel himself, but meat's your master and will have its time. A knock on the head?" she continued, with a faint stirring of anxiety. "You don't say so? Lor, Mr. Basset, who'd go to touch Etruria?"

"You'd better go and see."

"But where's Toft?"

Basset's temper gave way at that. "God knows!" he said. "He ought to be here--and he's not!" He went out.

Mrs. Toft stared after him, and by and by she let down her skirt and prepared to go into the house. "On the head?" she ruminated. "Well, 'Truria's a tidy lot of hair! And I will say this, if there's few points a man gives a woman, hair's one of them."

Meanwhile Basset had struck across the court and taken in the darkness the track which led in the direction of the Great House. The breeze, light but of an autumn coldness, swept the upland, whispering through the dying fern, and rustling in the clumps of trees by which he steered his course. He listened more than once, hoping that he might hear approaching footsteps, but he heard none, and presently he came to the yew-trees that masked the entrance to the gardens.

The trees formed a wall of blackness exceeding that of the darkest night, and Basset hesitated before he plunged into it. The growth of a century had long trespassed on the walk, a hundred and fifty yards long, which led through the yew-wood, and had been in its time a stately avenue trimmed to the neatness of a bowling green. Now it was little better than a tunnel, dark even at noon, and at night bristling with a hundred perils. Basset peered into the blackness, listened, hesitated. But he was honestly anxious on John Audley's account, and contenting himself with exclaiming that the man was mad, he began to grope his way along the path.

It was no pleasant task. If he swerved from his course he stumbled over roots, branches swept his cheek, jagged points threatened his eyes, and more than once he found himself in the hedge. Half-way through the wood he came to a circular clearing, some twenty yards across; and here a glimmer of light enabled him to avoid the crumbling stone Butterfly that crouched on its mouldering base in the centre of the clearing--much as a spider crouches in its web. It seemed in that dim light to be the demon of this underworld, a monster, a thing of evil.

The same gleam, however, disclosed the opposite opening, and for another seventy yards he groped his way onward, longing to be clear of the stifling air, and the brooding fancies that dwelt in it, longing to plant his feet on something more solid than this carpet of rotting yew. At last he came to the tall, strait gate, wrought of old iron, that admitted to the pleasance. It was ajar. He passed through it, and with relief he felt the hard walk under his feet, the fresh air on his face. He crossed the walk, and stepping on to the neglected lawn, he halted.

The Great House loomed before him, a hundred yards away. The moon had not risen, but the brightness which goes before its rising lightened the sky behind the monstrous building. It outlined the roof but left the bulk in gloom. No light showed in any part, and it was only the watcher's memory that pictured the quaint casements of the north wing, or filled in the bald rows of unglazed windows, which made of the new portion a death-mask. In that north wing just eighty years before, in a room hung with old Cordovan leather, the fatal house-warming had been held. The duel had been fought at sunrise within a pace or two of the moss-grown Butterfly that Basset had passed; and through the gate of ironwork, wood-smelted and wrought with the arms of Audley, which had opened at his touch, they had carried the dead heir back to his father. Tradition had it that the servant who bore in the old lord's morning draught of cool ale had borne also the tragic news to his bedside.

Basset remembered that the hinges of the gate, seldom as it was used, had not creaked, and he felt sure that he was on the right track. He scanned the dark house, and tried to sift from the soughing of the wind any sound that might inform him.

Presently he moved forward and scrutinized with care the north wing, which abutted on the yew-wood. There lay between the two only a strip of formal garden, once set with rows of birds and beasts cut in yew. Time had turned these to monsters, huge, amorphous, menacing, amidst which rank grass rioted and elder pushed. Even in daylight it seemed as if the ancient trees stretched out arms to embrace and strangle the deserted house.

But the north wing remained as dark as the bulk of the house, and Basset uttered a sigh of relief. Ill-humor began to take the place of misgiving. He called himself a fool for his pains and anticipated with distaste a return through the yew-walk. However, the sooner he undertook the passage the sooner it would be over, and he was turning on his heel when somewhere between him and the old wing a stick snapped.

Under a foot, he fancied; and he waited. In two or three minutes the moon would rise.

Again he caught a faint sound. It resembled the stealthy tread of some one approaching from the north wing, and Basset, peering that way, was striving to probe the darkness, when a gleam of light shot across his eyes. He turned and saw in the main building a bright spark. It vanished. He waited to see it again, and while he waited a second stick snapped. This time the sound was behind him, and near the iron gate.

He had been outflanked, and he had now to choose which he would stalk, the footstep or the light. He chose the latter, the rather as while he stood with his eyes fixed on the house the upper edge of a rising moon peeped above the roof.

He stepped back to the gate, and in the shadow of the trees he waited. Two or three minutes passed. The moon rose clear of the roof, outlining the stately chimneys and gables and flooding with cold light the lower part of the lawn. With the rising of the moon the air grew more chilly. He shivered.

At length a dull sound reached him--the sound of a closing door or a shutter cast back. A minute later he heard the footsteps of some one moving along the walk towards him. The man trod with care, but once he stumbled.

Basset advanced. "Is that you, sir?" he asked.

"D--n!" John Audley replied out of the darkness. He halted, breathing quickly.

"I say d--n, too!" Basset replied. As a rule he was patient with the old man, but to-night his temper failed him.

The other came on. "Why did you follow me?" he asked. "What is the use? What is the use? If you are willing to help me, good! But if not, why do you follow me?"

"To see that you don't come to harm," Basset retorted. "As you certainly will one of these nights if you come here alone."

"Well, I haven't come to harm to-night! On the contrary---- But there, there, man, let us get back."

"The sooner the better," Basset replied. "I nearly put out an eye as I came."

John Audley laughed. "Did you come through the yews in the dark?" he asked.

"Didn't you?"

"No, I brought a lantern." He removed as he spoke the cap of a small bull's-eye lantern and threw its light on the path. "Who's the fool now?"

"Let us get home," Basset snapped.

John Audley locked the iron gate behind them and they started. The light removed their worst difficulties and they reached the open park without mishap. But long before they gained the house the elder man's strength failed, and he was glad to lean on Basset's arm. On that a sense of weakness on the one side and of pity on the other closed their differences. "After all," Audley said wearily, "I don't know what I should have done if you had not come."

"You'd have stayed there!"

"And that would have been--Heavens, what a pity that would have been!" Audley paused and struck his stick on the ground. "I must take care of myself, I must take care of myself! You don't know, Basset, what I----"

"And I don't want to know--here!" Basset replied. "When you are safe at home, you may tell me what you like."

In the courtyard they came on Toft, who was looking out for them with a lantern. "Thank God, you're safe, sir," he said. "I was growing alarmed about you."

"Where were you," Basset asked sharply, "when I came in?" John Audley was too tired to speak.

"I had stepped out at the front to look for the master," Toft replied. "I fancied that he had gone out that way."

Basset did not believe him, but he could not refute the story. "Well, get the brandy," he said, "and bring it to the library. Mr. Audley has been out too long and is tired."

They went into the library and Toft pulled off his master's boots and brought his slippers and the spirit-tray. That done, he lingered, and Basset thought that he was trying to divine from the old man's looks whether the journey had been fruitful.

In the end, however, the man had to go, and Audley leant forward to speak.

"Wait!" Basset muttered. "He is coming back."

"How do you know?"

Basset raised his hand. The door opened. Toft came in. "I forgot to take your boots, sir," he said.

"Well, take them now," his master replied peevishly. When the man had again withdrawn, "How did you know?" he asked, frowning at the fire.

"I saw him go to take your boots--and leave them."

Audley was silent for a time, then "Well," he said, "he has been with me many years and I think he is faithful."

"To his own interests. He dogged you to-night."

"So did you!"

"Yes, but I did not hide! And he did, and hid from me, too, and lied about it. How long he had been watching you, I cannot say, but if you think that you can break through all your habits, sir, and be missing for two hours at night and a man as shrewd as Toft suspect nothing, you are mistaken. Of course he wonders. The next time he thinks it over. The third time he follows you. Presently whatever you know he will know."

"Confound him!" Audley turned to the table and jerked some brandy into a glass. Then, "You haven't asked yet," he said, "what I've done."

"If I am to choose," Basset replied, "I would rather not know. You know my views."

"I know that you didn't think I should do it? Well, I've done it!"

"Do you mean that--you've found the evidence?"

"Is it likely?" the other replied petulantly. "No, but I've been in the Muniment Room. It is fifty years since I heard my father describe its position, but I could have gone to it blindfold! I was a boy then, and the name--he was telling a story of the old lord--took my fancy. I listened. In time the thing faded, but one day when I was at the lawyer's and some one mentioned the Muniment Room, the story came back to me so clearly, that I could almost repeat my father's words."

"And you've been in the room?"

"I've been in it. Why not? A door two inches thick and studded with iron, and a lock that one out of any dozen big keys would open!" He rubbed his calves in his satisfaction. "In twenty minutes I was inside."

"And it was empty?"

"It was empty," the other agreed, with a cunning smile. "As bare as a board. A little whitewashed room, just as my father described it!"

"They had removed the papers?"

"To the bank, or to London, or to Stubbs's. The place was as clean as a platter! Not a length of green tape or an end of parchment was left!"

"Then what have you gained?" Basset asked.

Audley looked slyly at him, his head on one side. "Ay, what?" he said. "But I'll tell you my father's story. At one time the part of the room under the stairs was crumbling and the rats got in. The steward told the old lord and he went to see it. 'Brick it up!' he said. The steward objected that there would not be room--the place was full; there were boxes everywhere, some under the stairs. The old lord tapped one of the boxes with his gold-headed cane. 'What's in these!' he asked. 'Old papers,' the steward explained. 'Of no use, my lord, but curious; old leases for lives, and terriers.' 'Terriers?' cried the old lord. 'Then, by G--d, brick 'em up with the rats!' And that day at dinner he told my father the story and chuckled over it."

"And that's what you've had in your mind all this time?" Basset said. "Do you think it was done?"

"The old lord bricked up many a pipe of port, and I think that he would do it for the jest's sake. And"-- John Audley turned and looked in his companion's face--"the part under the stairs is bricked up, and the room is as square and as flush as the family vault--and very like it. The old lord," he added sardonically, "knows what it is to be bricked up himself now."

"And still there may be nothing there to help you."

Audley rose from his chair. "Don't say it!" he cried passionately. "Or I'll say that there's no right in the world, no law, no providence, no God! Don't dare to say it!" he continued, his cheeks trembling with excitement. "If I believed that I should go mad! But it is there! It is there! Do you think that it was for naught I heard that story? That it was for naught I remembered it, for naught I've carried the story in my mind all these years? No, they are there, the papers that will give me mine and give it to Mary after me! They are there! And you must help me to get them."

"I cannot do it, sir," Basset replied firmly. "I don't think that you understand what you ask. To break into Audley's house like any common burglar, to dig down his wall, to steal his deeds----"

John Audley shook his fist in the young man's face. "His house!" he shrieked. "His wall! His deeds! No, fool, but my house, my wall, my deeds! my deeds! If the papers are there all's mine! All! And I am but taking my own! Can't you see that? Can't you see it? Have I no right to take what is my own?"

"But if the papers are not there?" Basset replied gravely. "No, sir, if you will take my advice you will tell your story, apply to the court, and let the court examine the documents. That's the straightforward course."

John Audley flung out his arms. "Man!" he cried. "Don't you know that as long as he is in possession he can sit on his deeds, and no power on earth can force him to show them?"

Basset drew in his breath. "If that is so," he said, "it is hard. Very hard! But to go by night and break into his house--sticks in my gizzard, sir. I'm sorry, but that is the way I look at it. The man's here too. I saw him this evening. The fancy might have taken him to visit the house, and he might have found you there?"

Audley's color faded, he seemed to shrink into himself. "Where did you see him?" he faltered.

Basset told the story. "I don't suppose that the girls were really in danger," he continued, "but they thought so, and Audley came to the rescue and brought them as far as the park gap."

The other took out his silk handkerchief and wiped his brow. "As near as that," he muttered.

"Ay, and if he had found you at the house, he might have guessed your purpose."

John Audley held out a hand trembling with passion. "I would have killed him!" he cried. "I would have killed him--before he should have had what is there!"

"Exactly," Basset replied. "And that is why I will have nothing to do with the matter! It's too risky, sir. If you take my advice you will give it up."

Audley did not answer. He sat awhile, his shoulders bowed, his eyes fixed on the hearth, while the other wondered for the hundredth time if he were sane. At length, "What is he doing here?" the old man asked in a lifeless tone. The passion had died out of him.

"Shooting, I suppose. But there was some talk in Riddsley of his coming down to stir up old Mottisfont."

"What about?"

"Against the corn-law repeal, I suppose."

Audley nodded. But after a while, "That's a pretext," he said. "And so is the shooting. He has followed the girl."

Basset started. "Followed Mary!" he exclaimed.

"What else? I have looked for it from the first. I've pressed you to come to an understanding with her for that reason. Why the devil can't you? If you leave it much longer you'll be too late! Too late! And, by G--d, I'll never forgive you!" with a fresh spirt of passion. "Never! Never, man!"

"I've not said that I meant to do it."

"You've not said!" Audley replied contemptuously. "Do you think that I don't know that she's all the world to you? Do you think that I've no eyes? Do you think that when you sit there watching her from behind your book by the hour together, I have not my sight? Man, I'm not a fool! And I tell you that if you're not to lose her you must speak! You must speak! Stand by another month, wait a little longer, and Philip Audley will put in his oar, and I'll not give that for your chances!" He snapped his fingers.

"Why should he put in his oar?" Basset asked sullenly. His face had turned a dull red.

John Audley shrugged his shoulders. "Do you think that she is without attractions?"

"But Audley lives in another world."

"The more likely to have attractions for her!"

"But surely he'll look for--for something more," Basset stammered.

"For a rich wife? For an alliance, as the saying is? And sleep ill of nights? And have bad dreams? No, he is no fool, if you are. He sees that if he marries the girl he makes himself safe. He makes himself safe! After me, it lies between them."

"I take it that he does think himself safe."

"Not he!" Audley replied. He was stooping over the ashes, warming his hands, but at that he jumped up. "Not he! he knows better than you! And fears! And sleeps ill of nights, d--n him! And dreams! But there, I must not excite myself. I must not excite myself. Only, if he once begins, he'll be no laggard in love as you are! He'll not sit puling and peeping and looking at the back of her head by the hour together! He'll be up and at her--I know what that big jowl means! And she'll be in his arms in half the time that you've taken to count her eyelashes!" He turned in a fresh fit of fury and seized his candle. "In his arms, I tell you, fool, while you are counting her eyelashes. Well, lose her, lose her, and I never want to see you again, or her! Never! I'll curse you both!"

He stumbled to the door and went out, a queer, gibbering, shaking figure; and Basset had no doubt at such moments that he was mad. But on this occasion he was afraid--he was very much afraid, as he sat pondering in his chair, that there was method in his madness!

CHAPTER XIII: PETER PAUPER

The impression which the events of the evening had made on Mary's mind was still lively when she awoke next day. It was not less clear, because like the feminine letter of the 'forties, crossed and recrossed, it had stamped itself in two layers on her mind, of which the earlier was the more vivid.

The solitude in which her days had of late been spent had left her peculiarly open to new ideas, while the quiet and wholesome life of the Gatehouse had prepared her to answer any call which those ideas might make upon her. Rescued from penury, lifted above anxiety about bed and board, no longer exposed to the panic-fears which in Paris had beset even her courageous nature, Mary had for a while been content simply to rest. She had taken the sunshine, the beauty, the ease and indolence of her life as a convalescent accepts idleness, without scruple or question.

But this could not last. She was young, nature soon rallied in her, and she had seen things and done things during the last two years which forbade her to accept such a limited horizon as satisfied most of the women of that day. Unlike them, she had viewed the world from more than one standpoint; through the grille of a convent school, from the grimy windows of a back-street in Paris; again, as it moved beneath the painted ceilings of a French salon. And now, as it presented itself in this retired house.

Therefore she could not view things as those saw them whose standpoint had never shifted. She had suffered, she still had twinges--for who, with her experience, could be sure that the path would continue easy? And so to her Mr. Colet's sermon had made a strong appeal.

It left the word which Mr. Colet had taken for his text sounding in her ears. Borne upward on the eloquence which earnestness had lent to the young preacher, she looked down on a world in torment, a world holding up piteous hands, craving, itself in ignorance, the help of those who held the secret, and whose will might make that secret sufficient to save. Love! To do to others as she would have others do to her! With every day, with every hour, with every minute to do something for others! Always to give, never to take! Above all to give herself, to do her part in that preference of others to self, which could alone right these mighty wrongs, could find work for the idle, food for the hungry, roofs for the homeless, knowledge for the blind, healing for the sick! Which could save all this world in torment, and could

"Build a Heaven in Hell's despair!"

It was a beautiful vision, and in this her first glimpse of it, Mary's fancy was not chilled by the hard light of experience. It seemed so plain that if the workman had his master's profit at heart, and the master were as anxious for the weal of his men, the interests of the two would be one. Equally plain it seemed that if they who grew the food aimed at feeding the greatest number, and they who ate had the same desire to reward the grower, if every man shrank from taking advantage of other men, if the learned lived to spread their knowledge, and the strong to help the weak, if no man wronged his neighbor, but

"Each for another gave his ease,"

then it seemed equally plain that love would indeed be lord of all!

Later, she might discover that it takes two to make a bargain; that charity does bless him who gives but not always him who takes; even, that cheap bread might be a dear advantage--that at least it might have its drawbacks.

But for the moment it was enough for Mary that the vision was beautiful and, as a theory, true. So that, gazing upward at the faded dimity of her tester, she longed to play her part in it. That world in torment, those countless hands stretched upward in appeal, that murmur of infinite pain, the cry of the hungry, of the widow, of men sitting by tireless hearths, of children dying in mill and mine--the picture wrought on her so strongly, that she could not rest. She rose, and though the hoar frost was white on the grass and the fog of an autumn morning still curtained the view, she began to dress.

Perhaps the chill of the cold water in which she washed sobered her. At any rate, with the comb in one hand and her hair in the other, she drifted down another line of thought. Lord Audley--how strange was the chance which had again brought them together! How much she owed him, with what kindness had he seen to her comfort, how masterfully had he arranged matters for her on the boat. And then she smiled. She recalled Basset's ill-humor, or his--jealousy. At the thought of what the word implied, Mary colored.

There could be nothing in the notion, yet she probed her own feelings. Certainly she liked Lord Audley. If he was not handsome, he had that air of strength and power which impresses women; and he had ease and charm, and the look of fashion which has its weight with even the most sensible of her sex. He had all these and he was a man, and she admired him and was grateful to him. And yesterday she might have thought that her feeling for him was love.

But this morning she had gained a higher notion of love. She had learned from Etruria how near to that pattern of love which Mr. Colet preached the love of man and woman could rise. She had a new conception of its strength and its power to expel what was selfish or petty. She had seen it in its noblest form in Etruria, and she knew that her feeling for Lord Audley was not in the same world with Etruria's feeling for the curate. She laughed at the notion.

"Poor Etruria!" she meditated. "Or should it be, happy Etruria? Who knows? I only know that I am heart-whole!"

And she knotted up her hair and, Diana-like, went out into the pure biting air of the morning, along the green rides hoary with dew and fringed with bracken, under the oak trees from which the wood-pigeons broke in startled flight.

But if the energy of her thoughts carried her out, fatigue soon brought her to a pause. The evening's excitement, the strain of the adventure had not left her, young as she was, unscathed. The springs of enthusiasm waned with her strength, and presently she felt jaded. She perceived that she would have done better had she rested longer; and too late the charms of bed appealed to her.

She was at the breakfast table when Basset--he, too, had had a restless night and many thoughts--came down. He saw that she was pale and that there were shadows under her eyes, and the man's tenderness went out to her. He longed, he longed above everything to put himself right with her; and on the impulse of the moment, "I want you to know," he said, standing meekly at her elbow, "that I am sorry I lost my temper last evening."

But she was out of sympathy with him. "It is nothing," she said. "We were all tired, I think. Etruria is not down yet."

"But I want to ask your----"

"Oh dear, dear!" she cried, interrupting him with a gesture of impatience. "Don't let us rake it up again. If my uncle has not suffered, there is no harm done. Please let it rest."

But he could not let it rest. He longed to put his neck under her foot, and he did not see that she was in the worst possible mood for his purpose. "Still," he said, "you must let me say----"

"Don't!" she cried. She put her hands to her ears. Then, seeing that she had wounded him, she dropped them and spoke more kindly. "Don't let us make much of little, Mr. Basset. It was all natural enough. You don't like Lord Audley----"

"I don't."

"And you did not understand that we had been terribly frightened, and had good reason to be grateful to him. I am sure that if you had known that, you would have behaved differently. There!" with a smile. "And now that I have made the amende for you, let us have breakfast. Here is your coffee."

He knew that she was holding him off, and all his alarms of the night were quickened. Again and again had John Audley's warning recurred to him and as often he had striven to reject it, but always in vain. And gradually, slowly, it had kindled his resolution, it had fired him to action. Now, the very modesty which had long kept him silent and withheld him from enterprise was changed--as so often happens with diffident man--into rashness. He was as anxious to put his fate to the test as he had before been unwilling.

Presently, "You will not need to tell your uncle about Lord Audley," he said. "I've done it."

"I hope you told him," she answered gravely, "that we were indebted to Lord Audley for our safety."

"You don't trust me?"

"Don't say things like that!" she cried. "It is foolish. I have no doubt that in telling my uncle you meant to relieve me. You have helped me more than once in that way. But----"

"But this is a special occasion?"

She looked at him. "If you wish us to be friends----"

"I don't," he answered roughly. "I don't want to be friends with you."

Then, ambiguous as his words were, she saw where she stood, and she mustered her presence of mind. She rose from her seat. "And I," she said, "am not going to quarrel with you, Mr. Basset. I am going now to learn how Etruria is. And then I shall see my uncle."

She escaped before he could answer.

Once or twice it had crossed her mind that he looked at her with intention; and once reading that look in his eyes she had felt her color rise, and her heart beat more quickly. But the absence on her side of any feeling, except that which a sister might feel for a kind brother, this and the reserve of his manner had nipped the fancy as soon as it budded. And if she had given it a second thought, it had been only to smile at her vanity.

Now she had no doubt of the fact, no doubt that it was jealousy that moved him, and her uppermost, almost her only feeling was vexation. Because they had lived in the same house for five months, because he had been useful and she had been grateful, because they were man and woman, how foolish it was! How absurd! How annoying! She foresaw from it many, many, inconveniences; a breach in their pleasant intercourse, displeasure on her uncle's part, trouble in the house that had been so peaceful--oh, many things. But that which vexed her most was the fear that she had, all unwittingly, encouraged him.

She believed that she had not. But while she talked to Etruria, and later, as she went down the stairs to interview her uncle, she had this weight on her mind. She strove to recall words and looks, and upon the whole she was sure that she could acquit herself, sure that of this evil no part lay at her door. But it was very, very vexatious!

On the threshold of the library she wrested her thoughts back to the present, and paused a moment, considering what she should say to her uncle.

She need not have troubled herself, for he was not there. At the first glance she took the room to be empty; a second showed her Basset. She turned to retire, but too late; he stepped between her and the door and closed it. He was a little paler than usual, and his air of purpose was not to be mistaken.

She stiffened. "I came to see my uncle," she said.

"I am the bearer of a message from him," he answered. "He asked me to say that he considers the matter at an end. He does not wish it to be mentioned again. Of course he does not blame you."

"But, Mr. Basset----"

But he would not let her speak. "That was his message," he continued, "and I am glad to be the messenger because it gives me a chance of speaking to you. Will you sit down?"

"But we have only just parted," she remonstrated, struggling against her fate. "I don't understand what you want----"

"To say? No, I am going to explain it--if you will sit down."

She sat down then with the feeling that she was trapped. And since it was clear that she must go through with it, she was glad that his insistence hardened her heart and dried up the springs of pity.

He went to the fire, stooped and moved the wood. "You won't come nearer?" he said.

"No," she replied. How foolish to trap her like this if he thought to get anything from her!

He turned to her and his face was changed. Under his wistful look she discovered that it was not so easy to be hard, not so easy to maintain her firmness. "You would rather escape?" he said, reading her mind. "I know. But I can't let you escape. You are thinking that I have trapped you? And you are fearing that I am going to make you unhappy for--for half an hour perhaps? I know. And I am fearing that you are going to make me unhappy for--always."

No, she could not retain her hardness. She knew that she was going to feel pity after all. But she would not speak.

"I have only hope," he went on. "There is only one thing I am clinging to. I have read that when a man loves a woman very truly, very deeply, as I love you, Mary"--she started violently, and blushed to the roots of her hair, so sudden was the avowal--"as I love you," he repeated sorrowfully, "I have read that she either hates him or loves him. His love is a fire that either warms her or scorches her, draws her or repels her. I thought of that last night, as I thought of many things, and I was sure, I was confident that you did not hate me."

"Oh no," she answered, unsteadily. "Indeed, indeed, I don't! I am very grateful to you. But the other--I don't think it is true."

"No?" he said, keeping his eyes on her face. "And then, you don't doubt that I love you?"

"No." The flush had faded from her face and left her pale. "I don't doubt that--now."

"It is so true that--you know that you have sometimes called me Peter? Well, I would have given much, very much to call you Mary. But I did not dare. I could not. For I knew that if I did, only once, my voice would betray me, and that I should alarm you before the time! I knew that that one word--that word alone--would set my heart upon my sleeve for all to see. And I did not want to alarm you. I did not want to hurry you. I thought then that I had time, time to make myself known to you, time to prove my devotion, time to win you, Mary. I thought that I could wait. Now, since last night, I am afraid to wait. I doubt, nay I am sure, that I have no time, that I dare not wait."

She did not answer, but the color mounted again to her face.

He turned and knocked the fire together with his foot. Then he took a step towards her. "Tell me," he said, "have I any chance? Any chance at all, Mary?"

She shook her head; but seeing then that he kept his eyes fixed on her and would not take that for an answer, "None," she said as kindly as she could. "I must tell you the truth. It is useless to try to break it. I have never once, not once thought of you but as a friend, Peter."

"But now," he said, "cannot you regard me differently--now! Now that you know? Cannot you begin to think of me as--a lover?"

"No," Mary said frankly and pitifully. "I should not be honest if I said that I could. If I held out hopes. You have been always good to me, kind to me, a dear friend, a brother when I had need of one. And I am grateful, Mr. Basset, honestly, really grateful to you. And fond of you--in that way. But I could not think of you in the way you desire. I know it for certain. I know that there is no chance."

He stood for a moment without speaking, and seeing how stricken he looked, how sad his face, her eyes filled with tears. Then, "Is there any one else?" he asked slowly, his eyes on her face.

She did not answer. She rose to her feet.

"Is there any one else?" he repeated, a new note in his voice. He moved forward a step.

"You have no right to ask that," she said.

"I have every right," he replied. "What?" he continued, moving still nearer to her, his whole bearing changed in a moment by the sting of jealousy. "I am condemned, I am rejected, and I am not to ask why?"

"No," she said.

"But I do ask!" he retorted with a passion which surprised and alarmed her; he was no longer the despondent lover of five minutes before, but a man demanding his rights. "Have you no heart? Have you no feeling for me? Do you not consider what this is to me?"

"I consider," Mary replied with a warmth almost equal to his own, "that if I answered your question I should humiliate myself. No one, no one has a right, sir, to ask that question. And least of all you!"

"And I am to be cast aside, I am to be discarded without a reason?"

That word "discarded" seemed so unjust, and so uncalled for, seeing that she had given him no encouragement, that it stung her to anger. "Without a reason?" she retorted. "I have given you a reason--I do not return your love. That is the only reason that you have a right to know. But if you press me, I will tell you why what you propose is impossible. Because, if I ever love a man I hope, Mr. Basset, that it will be one who has some work in the world, something to do that shall be worth the doing, a man with ambitions above mere trifling, mere groping in the dust of the past for facts that, when known, make no man happier, and no man better, and scarce a man wiser! Do you ever think," she continued, carried away by the remembrance of Mr. Colet's zeal, "of the sorrow and pain that are in the world? Of the vast riddles that are to be solved? Of the work that awaits the wisest and the strongest, and at which all in their degree can help? My uncle is an old man, it is well he should play with the past. I am a girl, it may serve for me. But what do you here?" She pointed to his table, laden with open folios and calf-bound volumes. "You spend a week in proving a Bohun marriage that is nothing to any one. Another, in raking up a blot that is better forgotten! A third in tracing to its source some ancient tag! You move a thousand books--to make one knight! Is that a man's work?"

"At least," he said huskily, "I do no harm."

"No harm?" Mary replied, swept away by her feelings. "Is that enough? Because in this quiet corner, which is home to my uncle and a refuge to me, no call reaches you, is it enough that you do no harm? Is there no good to be done? Think, Mr. Basset! I am ignorant, a woman. But I know that to-day there are great questions calling for an answer, wrongs clamoring to be righted, a people in travail that pleads for ease! I know that there is work in England for men, for all! Work, that if there be any virtue left in ancient blood should summon you as with a trumpet call!"

He did not answer. Twice, early in her attack he had moved as if he would defend himself. Then he had let his chin fall and he had listened with his eyes on the table. And--but she had not seen it--he had more than once shivered under her words as under a lash. For he loved her and she scourged him. He loved her, he desired her, he had put her on a pedestal, and all the time she had been viewing him with the clear merciless eyes of youth, trying him by the standard of her dreams, probing his small pretensions, finding him a potterer in a library--he who in his vanity had raised his eyes to her and sought to be her hero!

It was a cruel lesson, cruelly given; and it wounded him to the heart. So that she, seeing too late that he made no reply, seeing the grayness of his face, and that he did not raise his eyes, had a too-late perception of what she had done, of how cruel she had been, of how much more she had said than she had meant to say. She stood conscience-stricken, remorseful, ashamed.

And then, "Oh, I am sorry!" she cried. "I am sorry! I should not have said that! You meant to honor me and I have hurt you."

He looked up then, but neither the shadow nor the grayness left his face. "Perhaps it was best," he said dully. "I am sure that you meant well."

"I did," she cried. "I did! But I was wrong. Utterly wrong!"

"No," he said, "you were not wrong. The truth was best."

"But perhaps it was not the truth," she replied, anxious at once, miserably anxious to undo what she had done, to unsay what she had said, to tell him that she was conceited, foolish, a mere girl! "I am no judge--after all what do I know of these things? What have I done that I should say anything?"

"I am afraid that what is said is said," he replied. "I have always known that I was no knight-errant. I have never been bold until to-day--and it has not answered," with a sickly smile. "But we understand one another now--and I relieve you."

He passed her on his way to the door, and she thought that he was going to hold it open for her to go out. But when he reached the door he fumbled for the handle, found it as a blind man might find it, and went out himself, without turning his head.

CHAPTER XIV: THE MANCHESTER MEN

Basset knew every path that crossed the Chase, and had traversed them at all seasons, and in all weathers. But when, some hours later, he halted on a scarred and blackened waste that stretched to the horizon on every side, he would have been hard put to it to say how he came to be there. He wore his hat, he carried his stick, but he could not remember how he had become possessed of either.

For a time the shock of disappointment, the numbing sense of loss had dulled his mind. He had walked as in a dream, repeating over and over again that that was what she thought of him--and he had loved her. It was possible that in the interval he had sworn at fate, or shrieked against the curlews, or cursed the inhuman sky that mocked him with its sameness. But he did not think that he had. He felt the life in him too low for such outbursts. He told himself that he was a poor creature, a broken thing, a failure. He loved her, and--and that was what she thought of him.

He sat on the stump of an ancient thorn-tree that had been a landmark on the burnt heath longer than the oldest man could remember, and he began to put together what she had said. He was trifling away his life, picking stray finds from the dust-heap of the past, making no man wiser and no man better, doing nothing for any one! Was she right? The Bohun pedigree, at which he had worked so long? He had been proud of his knowledge of Norman descents, proud of the research which had won that knowledge, proud of his taste for following up recondite facts. Were the knowledge, the research, the taste, all things for which he ought to blush? Certainly, tried by the test, cui bono? they came off but poorly. And perhaps, to sit down at his age, content with such employments, might seem unworthy and beneath him, if there were other calls upon him. But were there other calls?

Time had been when his family had played a great part, not in Staffordshire only but in England; and then doubtless public service had been a tradition with them. But the tradition had waned with their fortunes. In these days he was only a small squire, a little more regarded than the new men about him; but with no ability to push his way in a crowd, no mastery among his fellow-men, one whom character and position alike cast for a silent part.

Of course she knew none of these things, but with the enthusiasm of youth she looked to find in every man the qualities of the leading role. He who seldom raised his voice at Quarter Sessions or on the Grand Jury--to which his birth rather than his possessions called him--she would have had him figure among the great, lead causes, champion the oppressed! It was pitiful, if it had not been absurd!

He walked on by and by, dwelling on the pity of it, a very unhappy man. He thought of the evenings in the library when she had looked over his shoulder, and one lamp had lighted them; of the mornings when the sun had gilded her hair as she bent over the task she was even then criticizing; of afternoons when the spirit of the chase had been theirs, and the sunshine and the flowers had had no charm strong enough to draw them from the pursuit of--alas! something that could make no man better or wiser. He had lost her; and if aught mattered apart from that, she had for ever poisoned the springs of content, muddied the wells of his ordered life.

Beyond doubt she loved the other, for had she not, she would have viewed things differently. Beyond doubt in her love for the other lay the bias that weighted her strictures. And yet, making all allowance for that, there was so much of truth in what she had said, so much that hit the mark, that he could never be the same again, never give himself with pleasure to his former pursuits, never find the old life a thing to satisfy!

And still, like the tolling of a death bell above the city's life, two thoughts beat on his mind again and again, and gave him intolerable pain. That was what she thought of him! And he had lost her! That was what she thought of him! And he had lost her! Her slender gracious figure, her smiling eyes, the glint in her hair, her goodness, her very self--all were for another! All were lost to him!

Presently the day began to draw in, and fagged and hopeless he turned and began to make his way back. His road lay through Brown Heath, the mining village, where in all the taverns and low-browed shops they were beginning to light their candles. He crossed the Triangle, and made his way along the lane, deep in coal-dust and foul with drains, that ran upwards to the Chase. A pit, near at hand, had just turned out its shift, and in the dusk tired men, swinging tins in their hands, were moving by twos and threes along the track. With his bent shoulders and weary gait he was lost among them, he walked one with them; yet here and there an older man espied the difference, recognized him, and greeted him with rough respect. Presently the current slackened; something, he could not see what, dammed the stream. A shrewish voice rose in the darkness before him, and other voices, angry, clamant, protesting, struck in. A few of the men pushed by the trouble, others stood, here and there a man added a taunt to the brawl. In his turn Basset came abreast of the quarrel. He halted.

A farm cart blocked the roadway. Over the tail hung three or four wailing children; into it a couple of sturdy men were trying to lift an old woman, seated in a chair. A dingy beadle and a constable, who formed the escort and looked ill at ease, stood beside the cart, and round it half a score of slatternly women pushed and shrieked and gesticulated. On the group and the whole dreary scene nightfall cast a pallid light.

"What is it?" Basset asked.

"They're shifting Nan Oates to the poorhouse," a man answered. "Her son died of the fever, and there's none to keep her or the little uns. She've done till now, but they'll not give her bite nor sup out of the House--that's the law now't seems. So the House it be!"

"Her'd rather die than go!" cried a girl.

"D--n them and their Bastilles!" exclaimed a younger man. "Are we free men, or are we not?"

"Free men?" shrieked a woman, who had seized the horse's rein and was loudest in her outcry. "No, nor Staffordshire men, nor Englishmen, nor men at all, if you let an old woman that's always lived decent go to their stone jug this way. Give me Stafford Gaol--'tis miles afore it!"

"Ay, you're at home there, Bet!" a voice in the crowd struck in, and the laugh that followed lightened matters.

Basset looked with pity at the old woman. Her head sunk upon her breast, her thin shawl tucked about her shoulders, her gray hair in wisps on her cheeks, she gazed in tearless grief upon the hovel which had been home to her. "Who's to support her," he asked, "if she stays?"

"For the bite and sup there's neighbors," a man answered. "Reverend Colet he said he might do something. But he's been lammed. And there's the rent. The boy's ten, and he made four shilling a week in the pit, but the new law's stopped the young uns working."

"Ay, d--n all new laws!" cried another. "Poor laws and pit laws we're none but the worse for them!"

The men were preparing to move the cart. The woman who held the rein clung to it. "Now, Bet, have a care!" said the constable. "Or you'll go home by Weeping Cross again!"

"Cross? I'll cross you!" the termagant retorted. "Selling up widows' houses is your bread and meat! May the devil, hoof and horn, with his scythe on his back, go through you! If there were three men here, ay, men as you'd call men----"

"Easy, woman, easy!"

"Woman, dang you! You call me woman----"

"Now, let go, Bet! You'll be in trouble else!" some one said.

But she held on, and the crowd were beginning to jostle the men in charge when Basset stepped forward. "Steady, a moment," he said. "Will the guardians let the woman stop if the rent is provided?"

"Who be you, master?" the constable asked. "You'd best let us do our duty."

"Dang it, man," an old fellow interposed, "it's Squire Basset of Blore. Dunno you know him? Keep a civil tongue in your head, will you!"

"Ay," chimed in another, pushing forward with a menacing gesture. "You be careful, Jack! You be Jack in office, but 'twon't always be so! 'Twon't always be so!"

"Mr. Colet knows the old woman?" Basset asked.

"Sure, sir, the curate knows her."

"Well, I'll find the rent," Basset said, addressing the constable, "if you'll let her be. I'll see the overseer about her in the morning."

"So long as she don't come on the rates, sir?"

"She'll not come on the rates for six months," Basset said. "I'll be answerable for so much."

The men had little stomach for their task, and with a good excuse they were willing enough to desist. A woman fetched a stub of a pen and a drop of ink and Basset wrote a word for their satisfaction. While he did so, "O'd Staffordshire! O'd Staffordshire!" a man explained in the background. "Bassets of Blore--they be come from an Abbey and come to a Grange, as the saying is. You never heard of the Bassets of Blore, you be neither from Mixen nor Moor!" In old Stafford talk the rich lands of Cheshire stood for the "mixen" as against the bare heaths of the home county.

In five minutes the business was done, the woman freed, and Basset was trudging away through the gathering darkness. But the incident had done him good. It had lightened his heart. It had changed ever so little the direction of his thoughts. Out of his own trouble he had stretched a hand to another; and although he knew that it was not by stray acts such as this that he could lift himself to Mary's standard, though the battle over the new Poor Law had taught him, and many others, that charity may be the greatest of evils, what he had done seemed to bring him nearer to her. A hardship of the poor, which he might have seen with blind eyes, or viewed from afar as the inevitable result of the stay of outdoor relief, had come home to him. As he plodded across the moor he carried with him a picture of the old woman with her gray hair falling about her wrinkled face, and her hands clasped in hopeless resignation. And he felt that his was not the only trouble in the world.

When he had passed the wall of Beaudelays Park, Basset struck--not far from the Gatehouse--into the road leading down to the Vale, and a couple of hours after dark he plodded into Riddsley. He made for the Audley Arms, a long straggling house on the main street, in one part of two stories, in another of three, with a big bay window at the end. Entering the yard by the archway he ordered a gig to go to the Gatehouse for his portmanteau. Then he turned into the inn, and scribbled a note to John Audley, stating that he was called away, and would explain matters when he wrote again. He sent it by the driver.

It was eight o'clock. "I am afraid, Squire," the landlord said, "that there's no fire upstairs. If you'd not mind our parlor for once, there's no one there and it's snug and warm."

"I'll do that, Musters," he said. He was cold and famished and he was not sorry to avoid the company of his own thoughts. In the parlor, next door to the Snug, he might be alone or listen to the local gossip as he pleased.

Ten minutes later he sat in front of a good plain meal, and for the time the pangs of appetite overcame those of disappointment. About nine the landlord entered on some errand. "I suppose, sir," he said, lingering to see that his guest had all that he wanted, "you've heard this about Mr. Mottisfont?"

"No, Musters, what is it? Get a clean glass and tell me about it."

"He's to resign, sir, I hear. And his son is to stand."

"Why?"

"Along o' this about Sir Robert Peel, I understand. They have it that Sir Robert's going to repeal the corn taxes--some say that he's been for it all through, and some talk about a potato failure. Mr. Mottisfont sees that that'll never do for Riddsley, but he don't want to part from his leader, after following him all these years; so he'll go out and the young gentleman will take his place."

"Do you think it is true about Peel?"

"They're saying it, and Mr. Stubbs, he believes it. But it'll never go down in Riddsley, Squire. We're horn and corn men here, two to one of us. There's just the two small factories on the other side, and most of the hands haven't votes. But here's Mr. Stubbs himself."

The lawyer had looked into the room in passing. Seeing Basset he removed his hat. "Pardon, Squire," he said. "I did not know that you were here."

"Not at all," Basset answered. He knew the lawyer locally, and had seen him often--at arm's length--in the peerage suit. "Will you take a glass of wine with me?"

Stubbs said that he would with pleasure, if he might take it standing--his time was short. The landlord was for withdrawing, but Stubbs detained him. "No, John, with Mr. Basset's leave I've a bone to pick with you," he said. "Who are these men who are staying here?"

Musters's face fell. "Lord, Mr. Stubbs," he said, "have you heard of them?"

"I hear most things," the lawyer answered. "But repealers talking treason at the Audley Arms is a thing I never thought to hear. They must go."

The landlord rubbed his head. "I can't turn 'em out," he said. "They'd have the law of me. His lordship couldn't turn 'em out."

"I don't know about that," Stubbs replied. "He's a good landlord, but he likes his own way."

"But what can I do?" the stout man protested. "When they came I knew no more about them than a china babe. When they began to talk, so glib that no one could answer them, I was more took aback than anybody. Seems like the world's coming to an end with Manchester men coming here."

"Perhaps it is," Basset said.

Stubbs met his eye and took his meaning. Later the lawyer maintained that he had his suspicions from that moment. At the time he only answered, "Not in our day, Mr. Basset. Peel or Repeal, there's no one has attacked the land yet but the land has broken them. And so it will be this time. John, the sooner those two are out of your house the better."

"But, dang me, sir, what am I to do?"

"Put 'em in the horse trough for what I care!" the lawyer replied. "Good-evening, Squire. I hope the Riddsley parliament mayn't disturb you."

The landlord followed him out, after handing something through the hatch, which opened into the Snug. He left the hatch a little ajar when he had done so, and the voices of those who gathered there nightly, as to a club, reached Basset. At first he caught no more than a word here or there, but as the debate grew warm the speakers raised their voices.

"All mighty fine," some one said, laying down the law, "but you're like the rest, you Manchester chaps. You've your eyes on your own rack and manger!"

"I'm not denying it," came the answer in a Lancashire accent, "I'm not saying that cheap bread won't suit us. But it isn't for that----"

"No, no, of course not," the former speaker replied with heavy irony--Basset thought that the voice belonged to Hayward of the Leasows, a pompous old farmer, dubbed behind his back "The Duke." "You don't want low wages i' your mills, of course!"

"Cheap bread doesn't make low wages," the other rejoined. "That's where you mistake, sir. Let me put it to you. You've known wheat high?"

"It was seventy-seven shillings seven years back," the farmer pronounced. "And I ha' known it a hundred shillings a quarter for three years together."

"And I suppose the wages at that time were the highest you've ever known?"

"Well, no," the farmer admitted, "I'm not saying that."

"And seven years ago when wheat was seventy-seven--it is fifty-six now--were wages higher then than now?"

"Well," the Duke answered reluctantly, "I don't know as they were, mister, not to take notice of."

"Think it out for yourself, sir," the other replied. "I don't think you'll find that wages are highest when wheat is highest, nor lowest when wheat is lowest."

The farmer, more weighty than ready, snorted. But another speaker took up the cudgels. "Ay, but one minute," he said. "It's the price of wheat fixes the lowest wages. If it's two pound of bread will keep a man fit to work--just keep him so and no more--it's the price of bread fixes whether the lowest wages is eightpence a day or a shilling a day."

"Well, but----"

"Well, but by G--d, he's got you there!" the Duke cried, and smacked his fat thigh in triumph. "We've some sense i' Riddsley yet. Here's your health and song, Dr. Pepper!" At which there was some laughter.

"Well, sir, I'll not say yes, nor no, to that," the Lancashire man replied, as soon as he could get a hearing. "But, gentlemen, it's not low wages we want. I'll tell you the two things we do want, and why we want cheap bread; first, that your laborers after they have bought bread may have something over to buy our woollens, and our cottons, and your pots. And secondly, if we don't take foreign wheat in payment how are foreigners to pay for our goods?"

But at this half a dozen were up in arms. "How?" cried the Duke, "why wi' money like honest men at home! But there it is! There's the devil's hoof! It's foreign corn you're after! And with foreign corn coming in at forty shillings where'll we be?"

"No wheat will ever be grown at that price," declared the free trader with solemnity, "here or abroad!"

"So you say!" cried Hayward. "But put it at forty-five. We'll be on the rates, and our laborers, where'll they be?"

"I don't like such talk in my house!" said Musters.

"I'd certainly like an answer to that," Pepper the surgeon said. "If the farmers are broke where'll their laborers be but flocking to your mills to put down wages there!"

"The laborers? Well, they're protected now, that's true."

"Lucky for them!" cried two or three.

"They are protected now," the stranger repeated slowly. "And I'll tell you what one of them said to me last year. 'I be protected,' he said, 'and I be starving!'"

"Dang his impudence!" muttered old Hayward. "That's the kind of thing they two Boshams at the Bridge talk. Firebrands they be!"

But the shot had told; no one else spoke.

"That man's wages," the Manchester man continued, "were six shillings a week--it was in Wiltshire. And you are protected too, sir," he continued, turning suddenly on the Duke. "Have you made a fortune, sir, farming?"

"I don't know as I have," the farmer answered sulkily--and in a lower voice, "Dang his impudence again!"

"Why not? Because you are paying a protected rent. Because you pay high for feeding-stuff. Because you pay poor-rates so high you'd be better off paying double wages. There's only one man benefits by the corn-tax, sir, there's only one who is truly protected, and that is the landlord!"

But to several in the room this was treason, and they cried out upon it. "Ay, that's the bottom of it, mister," one roared, "down with the landlords and up with the cotton lords!" "There's your Reform Bill," shouted another, "we've put the beggars on horseback, and none's to ride but them now!" A third protested that cheap bread was a herring drawn across the track. "They're for cheap bread for the poor man, but no votes! Votes would make him as good as them!"

"Anyway," the stranger replied patiently, "it's clear that neither the farmer nor the laborer grows fat on Protection. Your wages are nine shillings----"

"Ten and eleven!" cried two or three.

"And your farmers are smothered in rates. If that's all you get by Protection I'd try another system."

"Anyways, I'll ask you to try it out of my house," Musters said. "I've a good landlord and I'll not hear him abused!"

"Hear! Hear! Musters! Quite right!"

"I've not said an uncivil word," the Manchester man rejoined. "I shall leave your house to-morrow, not an hour before. I'll add only one word, gentlemen. Bread is the staff of life. Isn't it the last thing you should tax?"

"True," Mr. Pepper replied. "But isn't agriculture the staple industry? Isn't it the base on which all other industries stand? Isn't it the mainstay of the best constitution in the world? And wasn't it the land that steadied England, and kept it clear of Bonaparte and Wooden Shoes----"

"Ay, wooden ships against wooden shoes for ever!" broke in old Hayward, in great excitement. "Where were the oaks grown as beat Bony! No, master, protect the oak and protect the wheat, and England'll never lack ships nor meat! Your cotton-printers and ironfounders they're great folks now, great folks, with their brass and their votes, and so they've a mind to upset the gentry. It's the town against the country, and new money against the old acres that have fed us and our fathers before us world without end! But put one of my lads in your mills, and amid your muck, and in twelve months he'd not pitch hay, no not three hours of the day!"

Basset could hear the free trader's chair grate on the sanded floor as he pushed it back. "Well, gentlemen," he said, "I'll not quarrel with you. I wish you all the protection you deserve--and I think Sir Robert will give it you! For us, I'm not saying that we are not thinking of our own interests."

"Devil a doubt of that!" muttered the farmer.

"And some of us may have been cold-shouldered by my lord. But you may take it from me that there's some of us, too, are as anxious to better the poor man's lot--ay, as Lord Ashley himself! That's all! Good-night, gentlemen."

When he was gone, "Gi' me a coal for my pipe, John," said the Duke. "I never heard the like of that in Riddsley. He's a gallus glib chap that!"

"I won't say," said Mr. Pepper cautiously, "that there's nothing in it."

"Plenty in it for the cotton people and the coal people, and the potters. But not for us!"

"But if Sir Robert sees it that way?" queried the surgeon, delicately.

"Then if Sir Robert were member for Riddsley," Hayward answered stubbornly, "he'd get his notice to quit, Dr. Pepper! You may bet your hat on that!"

"There's one got a lesson last night," a new-comer chimed in. "Parson Colet got so beaten on the moor he's in bed I am told. He's been speaking free these last two months, and I thought he'd get it. Three lads from your part I am told, Hayward."

"Well, well!" the farmer replied with philosophy. "There's good in Colet, and maybe it'll be a lesson to him! Anyway, good or bad, he's going."

"Going?" cried two or three, speaking at once.

"I met Rector not two hours back. He'd a letter from Colet saying he was going to preach the same rubbish here as he's fed 'em with at Brown Heath--cheap bread and the rest of it. Rector's been to him--he wouldn't budge, and he got his notice to quit right straight. Rector was fit to burst when I saw him."

"Colet be a born fool!" cried Musters. "Who's like to employ him after that? Wheat is tithe and the parsons are as fond of their tithe as any man. You may look a long way before you'll find a parson that's a repealer."

"Serves Colet right!" said one. "But I'm sorry for him all the same. There's worse men than the Reverend Colet."

Basset could never say afterwards what moved him at this point, but whatever it was he got up and went out. The boots was lounging at the door of the inn. He asked the man where Mr. Colet lodged, and learning that it was in Stream Street, near the Maypole, he turned that way.

CHAPTER XV: STRANGE BEDFELLOWS

Had any one told Basset, even that morning, that before night he would seek the advice of the Riddsley curate, he would have met the suggestion with unmeasured scorn. Probably he had not since his college days spent an hour in intimate talk with a man so far from him in fortune and position, and so unlike him in those things which bring men together. Nor in the act of approaching Colet--under the impulse of a few casual words and a sudden thought--was he able to understand or to justify himself.

But when he rose to his feet after an hour spent beside the curate's dingy hearth--over the barber's shop in Stream Street--he did not need to justify the step. He had said little but he had heard much. Colet's tongue had been loosened by the sacrifice he had made, and inspired by that love of his kind which takes refuge in the most unlikely shapes, he had poured forth at length his beliefs and his aspirations. And Basset, whose world had tottered since morning, for whom common things had lost their poise and life its wonted aspect, began to think that he had found in the other's aims a new standpoint and the offer of a new beginning.

The dip candles, which had been many times snuffed, were burning low when the two rose. The curate, whose pale cheeks matched his bandaged head, had a last word to say. "Of the need I am sure," he repeated, as Basset's eye sought the cheap clock on the mantelpiece. "If I have not proved that, the fault, sir, is mine. But the means--they are a question for you; almost any man may see them more clearly than I do. By votes, it may be, and so through the people working out their own betterment. Or by social measures, as Lord Ashley thinks, through the classes that are fitted by education to judge for all. Or by the wider spread, as I hold, of self-sacrifice by all for all--to me, the ideal. But of one thing I am convinced; that this tax upon the commonest food, which takes so much more in proportion from the poor than from the rich, is wrong. Certainly wrong, Mr. Basset,--unless the gain and the loss can be equally spread. That's another matter."

"I will not say any more now," Basset answered cautiously, "than that I am inclined to your view. But for yourself, are there not others who will not pay so dearly for maintaining it?"

A redness spread over the curate's long horse-face. "No, Mr. Basset," he rejoined, "if I left my duty to others I should pay still more dearly. I am my own man. I will remain so."

"But what will you do when you leave here?" Basset inquired, casting his eyes round the shabby room. He did not see it as he had seen it on his entrance. He discerned that, small as it was, and shabby as it was, it might be a man's home. "I fear that there are few incumbents who hold your views."

"There are absentees," Colet replied with a smile, "who are not so particular; and in the north there are a few who think as I think. I shall not starve."

"I have an old house on the Derbyshire border twenty miles from here," Basset said. "A servant and his wife keep it, and during some months of the year I live there. It is an out-of-the-way place, Mr. Colet, but it is at your service--if you don't get work?"

The curate seemed to shrink into himself. "I couldn't trespass on you," he said.

"I hope you will," Basset replied. "In the meantime, who was the man you quoted a few minutes ago?"

"Francis Place. He is a good man though not as we"--he touched his threadbare cloth--"count goodness. He is something of a Socialist, something of a Chartist--he might frighten you, Mr. Basset. But he has the love of the people in him."

"I will see him."

"He has been a tailor."

That hit Basset fairly in the face. "Good heavens!" he said. "A tailor?"

"Yes," Colet replied, smiling. "But a very uncommon tailor. Let me tell you why I quoted him. Because, though he is not a Christian, he has ideals. He aims higher than he can shoot, while the aims of the Manchester League, though I agree with them upon the corn-tax, seem to me to be bounded by the material and warped by their own interests."

Basset nodded. "You have thought a good deal on these things," he said.

"I live among the poor. I have them always before me."

"And I have thought so little that I need time. You must think no worse of me if I wait a while. And now, good-night."

But the other did not take the hand held out to him. He was staring at the candle. "I am not clear that I have been quite frank with you," he said awkwardly. "You have offered me the shelter of your house though I am a stranger, Mr. Basset, and though you must suspect that to harbor me may expose you to remark. Well, I may be tempted to avail myself of your kindness. But I cannot do so unless you know more of my circumstances."

"I know all that is necessary."

"You don't know what I am going to tell you," Colet persisted. "And I think that you should. I am going to marry the daughter of your uncle's servant, Toft."

"Good Lord!" cried Basset. This was a second and more serious blow. It brought him down from the clouds.

"That shocks you, Mr. Basset," the curate continued with dignity, "that I should marry one in her position? Well, I am not called upon to justify it. Why I think her worthy, and more than worthy to share my life, is my business. I only trouble you with the matter because you have made me an offer which you might not have made had you known this."

Basset did not deny the fact. He could not, indeed. His taste, his prejudice, his traditions all had received a blow, all were up in arms; and, for the moment, at any rate he repented of his visit. He felt that in stepping out of the normal round he had made a mistake. He should have foreseen, he should have known that he would meet with such shocks. "You have certainly astonished me," he said after a pause of dismay. "I cannot think the match suitable, Mr. Colet. May I ask if my uncle knows of this?"

"Miss Audley knows of it."

"But--you cannot yourself think it suitable!"

"I have," Colet replied dryly, "or rather I had seventy pounds a year. What girl, born in comfort, gently bred, sheltered from childhood could I ask to share that? How could I, with so little in the present and no prospects, ask a gentlewoman to share my lot?"

Basset did not reply, but he was not convinced. A clergyman to marry a servant, good and refined as Etruria was! It seemed to him to be unseemly, to be altogether wrong.

Colet too was silent a moment. Then, "I am glad I have told you this," he said. "I shall not now trespass on you. On the other hand, I hope that you may still do something--and with your name, you can do much--for the good cause. If rumor goes for anything, many will in the next few months examine the ground on which they stand. It will be much, if what I have said has weight with you."

He spoke with constraint, but he spoke like a man, and Basset owned his equality while he resented it. He felt that he ought to renew his offer of hospitality, but he could not--reserve and shyness had him again in their grip. He muttered something about thinking it over, added a word or two of thanks--which were cut short by the flickering out of the candle--and a minute later he was in the dark deserted street, and walking back to his inn--not over well content with himself, if the truth be told.

Either he should not have gone, he felt, or he should have gone the whole way, sunk his ideas of caste, and carried the thing through. What was it to him if the man was going to marry a servant?

But that was a detail. The main point was that he should not have gone. It had been a foolish impulse--he saw it now--which had taken him to the barber's shop; and one which he might have known that he would repent. He ought to have foreseen that he could not place himself on Colet's level without coming into collision with him; that he could not draw wisdom from him without paying toll.

An impossible person, he thought, a man of ideas quite unlike his own! And yet the man had spoken well and ably, and spoken from experience. He had told the things that he had seen as he passed from house to house, hard, sad facts, the outcome of rising numbers and falling wages, of over-production, of mouths foodless and unwanted. And all made worse, as he maintained, by this tax on bread, that barely touched the rich man's income, yet took a heavy toll from the small wage.

As he recalled some of the things that he had heard, Basset felt his interest revive. Colet had dealt with facts; he had attempted no oratory, he had cast no glamour over them. But he had brought to bear upon them the light of an ideal--the Christian ideal of unselfishness; and his hearer, while he doubted, while he did not admit that the solution was practical, owned its beauty.

For he too, as we know, had had his aspirations, though he had rarely thought of turning them into action. Instead, he had hidden them behind the commonplace; and in this he had matched the times, which were commonplace. For the country lay in the trough of the wave. Neither the fine fury of the generation which had adored the rights of man, nor the splendid endurance which the great war had fostered, nor the lesser ardors of the Reform era, which found its single panacea in votes, touched or ennobled it. Great wealth and great poverty, jostling one another, marked a material age, seeking remedies in material things, despising arms, decrying enthusiasm; an age which felt, but hardly bowed as yet, to the breath of the new spirit.

But Basset--perhaps because the present offered no great prospect to the straitened squire--had had his glimpses of a life higher and finer, devoted to something above the passing whim and the day's indulgence, a life that should not be useless to those who came after him. Was it possible that he now heard the call? Could this be the crusade of which he had idly dreamed? Had the trumpet sounded at the moment of his utmost need?

If only it were so! During the evening he had kept his sorrow at bay as well as he could, distracting his thoughts with passing objects. Now, as the boots ushered him up the close-smelling stairs to the inn's best room, and he stood in his hat and coat, looking on the cold bare aspect and the unfamiliar things--he owned himself desolate. The thought of Mary, of his hopes and plans and of the end of these, returned upon him in an irresistible flood. The waters which he had stemmed all day, though all day they had lapped his lips, overwhelmed him with their bitterness. Mary! He had loved her and she--he knew what she thought of him.

He could not take up the old life. She had made an end of that, the rather as from this time onward the Gatehouse would be closed to him by her presence. And the old house near Wootton where he had been wont to pass part of his time? That hardly met his needs or his aspirations. Unhappy as he was, he could not see himself sitting down in idleness, to brood and to rust in a home so remote, so quiet, so lost among the stony hills that the country said of it,

"Wootton under Weaver

Where God came never!"

No, he could hardly face that. Hitherto he had not been called upon to say what he would do with his life. Now the question was put to him and he had to answer it. He had to answer it. For many minutes he sat on the bed staring before him. And from time to time he sighed.

CHAPTER XVI

It was about a week after this that two men stood on the neglected lawn, contemplating the long blind front of Beaudelays House. With all its grandeur the house lacked the dignity of ruin, for ruin presumes a past, and the larger part of the Great House had no past. The ancient wing that had welcomed brides, and echoed the laughter of children and given back the sullen notes of the passing-bell did not suffice to redeem the whole. By night the house might pass; the silent bulk imposed on the eye. By day it required no effort of fancy to see the scaffold still clinging to the brickwork, or to discern that the grand entrance had never opened to guest or neighbor, that everyday life had never gazed through the blank windows of the long façade.

The house, indeed, was not only dead. It had never lived.

Certainly Nature had done something to shroud the dead. The lawn was knee-deep in weeds, and the evergreens about it had pushed out embracing arms to narrow the vista before the windows. At the lower end of the lawn a paved terrace, the width of the house, promised a freer air, but even here grass sprouted between the flags, and elders labored to uproot the stately balustrade that looked on the lower garden. This garden, once formal, was now a tangle of vegetation, a wilderness amid whose broad walks Venuses slowly turned to Dryads, and classic urns lay in fragments, split by the frosts of some excessive winter. Only the prospect of the Trent Valley and the Derbyshire foot-hills, visible beyond the pleasance, still pleased; and this view was vague and sad and distant. For the Great House, as became its greatness, shunned the public eye, and, lying far back, set a wide stretch of park between its bounds and the verge of the upland.

One of the two men was the owner. The other who bore a bunch of keys was Stubbs. Both had a depressed air. It would have been hard to say which of the two entered more deeply into the sadness of the place.

Presently my lord turned his back on the house. "The view is fine," he said. "The only fine thing about the place," he added bitterly. "Isn't there a sort of Belvedere below the garden?"

"There is, my lord. But I fear that it is out of repair."

"Like everything else! There, don't think I'm blaming you for it, man. You cannot make bricks without straw. But let us look at this Belvedere."

They descended the steps, and passed slowly along the grass-grown walk, now and again stepping aside to avoid the clutch of a straggling rose bough, or the fragments of a broken pillar. They paused to inspect the sundial, a giant Butterfly with closed wings, a replica of the stone monster in the Yew Walk. Lord Audley read the inscription, barely visible through the verdigris that stained the dial-plate:

"Non sine sole volo!"

"Just so!" he said. "A short life and a merry one!"

A few paces farther along the walk they stopped to examine the basin of the great fountain. Cracked from edge to centre, and become a shallow bed of clay and weeds, it was now as unsightly as it had been beautiful in the days when fair women leaning over it had fed the gold fish, or viewed their mirrored faces in its waters.

"The fortunes of the Audleys in a nutshell!" muttered the unlucky owner. And turning on his heel, "Confound it, Stubbs," he cried, "I have had as much of this as I can stand! A little more and I shall go back and cut my throat! It is beginning to rain, too. D--n the Belvedere! Let us go into the house. That cannot be as bad as this."

Without waiting for an answer, or looking behind him, he strode back the way they had come. Stubbs followed in silence, and they regained the lawn.

"I tell you what it is," Audley continued, letting the agent come abreast of him. "You must find some vulgarian to take the place--iron man or cotton man, I don't care who he is, if he has got the cash I You must let it, Stubbs. You must let it! It's a white elephant, it's the d--ndest White Elephant man ever had!"

The lawyer shook his head. "You may be sure, my lord," he said mildly, "I should have advised that long ago, if it were possible. But we couldn't let it in its present state--for a short term; and we have no more power to lease it for a long one than, as your lordship knows, we have power to sell it."

The other swore. At the outset he had scarcely felt his poverty. But he was beginning to feel it. There were moments such as this when his withers were wrung; when the consequence which the title had brought failed to soften the hardships of his lot--a poor peer with a vast house. Had he tried to keep the Great House in repair it would have swallowed the whole income of the peerage--a sum which, as it was, barely sufficed for his needs as a bachelor.

Already Stubbs had hinted that there was one way out--a rich marriage. And Audley had received the hint with the easiness of a man who was in no haste to marry and might, likely enough, marry where money was. But once or twice during the last few days, which they had been spending in a review of the property, my lord had shown irritation. When an old farmer had said to his face, that he must bring home a bride with a good fat chest, "and his lordship would be what his forbears had been," the great man, in place of a laughing answer, had turned glumly away.

Presently the two halted at the door of the north wing. Stubbs unlocked it and pushed it open. They entered an ante-room of moderate size.

"Faugh!" Audley cried. "Open a window! Break one if necessary."

Stubbs succeeded in opening one, and they passed on into the great hall, a room sixty feet long and open to the roof, a gallery running round it. A withdrawing-room of half the length opened at one end, and midway along the inner side a short passage led to a second hall--the servants' hall-- the twin of this. Together they formed an H, and were probably a Jacobean copy of a Henry the Eighth building. A long table, some benches, and a score of massive chairs furnished the room. Between the windows hung a few ragged pictures, and on either side of the farther door a piece of tapestry hung askew.

Audley looked about him. In this room eighty years before the old lord had held his revels. The two hearths had glowed with logs, a hundred wax-lights had shone on silver and glass and the rosy tints of old wine. Guests in satin and velvet, henchmen and led captains, had filled it with laughter and jest, and song. With a foot on the table they had toasted the young king--not stout Farmer George, not the old, mad monarch, but the gay young sovereign. To-day desolation reigned. The windows gray with dirt let in a grisly light. All was bare and cold and rusty--the webs of spiders crossed the very hearths. The old lord, mouldering in his coffin, was not more unlike that Georgian reveller than was the room of to-day unlike the room of eighty years before.

Perhaps the thought struck his descendant. "God! What a charnel-house!" he cried. "To think that men made merry in this room. It's a vault, it's a grave! Let us get away from it. What's through, man?"

They passed into the withdrawing-room, where panels of needlework of Queen Anne's time, gloomy with age, filled the wall spaces, and a few pieces of furniture crouched under shrouds of dust. As they stood gazing two rats leapt from a screen of Cordovan leather that lay in tatters on the floor. The rats paused an instant to stare at the intruders, then fled in panic.

The younger man advanced to one of the panels in the wall. "A hunting scene?" he said. "These may be worth money some day."

The lawyer looked doubtful. "It will be a long day first, I am afraid," he said. "It's funereal stuff at the best, my lord."

"At any rate it is out of reach of the rats," Lord Audley answered. He cast a look of distaste at the shreds of the screen. He touched them with his foot. A third rat sprang out and fled squeaking to covert. "Oh, d--n!" he said. "Let us see something else."

The lawyer led the way upstairs to the ghostly, echoing gallery that ran round the hall. They glanced into the principal guest-room, which was over the drawing-room. Then they went by the short passage of the H to the range of bedrooms over the servants' hall. For the most part they opened one from the other.

"The parents slept in the outer and the young ladies in the inner," Audley said, smiling. "Gad! it tells a tale of the times!"

Stubbs opened the nearest door and recoiled. "Take care, my lord!" he said. "Here are the bats!"

"Faugh! What a smell! Can't you keep them out?"

"We tried years ago--I hate them like poison--but it was of no use. They are in all these upper rooms."

They were. For when Stubbs, humping his shoulders as under a shower, opened a second door, the bats streamed forth in a long silent procession, only to stream back again as silently. In a dusky corner of the second room a cluster, like a huge bunch of grapes, hung to one of the rafters. Now and again a bat detached itself and joined the living current that swept without a sound through the shadowy rooms.

"There's nothing beyond these rooms?"

"No."

"Then let us go down. Rats and bats and rottenness! Non sine sole volo! We may not, but the bats do. Let us go down! Or no! I was forgetting. Where is the Muniment Room?"

"This way, my lord," Stubbs replied, turning with suspicious readiness--the bats were his pet aversion. "I brought a candle and some of the new lucifers. This way, my lord."

He led the way down to a door set in a corner of the ante-room. He unlocked this and they found themselves at the foot of a circular staircase. On the farther side of the stairfoot was another door which led, Stubbs explained, into the servants' quarters. "This turret," he added, "is older even than the wing, and forms no part of the H. It was retained because it supplied a second staircase, and also a short cut from the servants' hall to the entrance. The Muniment Room is over this lobby on the first floor. Allow me to go first, my lord."

The air was close, but not unpleasant, and the stairs were clean. On the first floor a low-browed door, clamped and studded with iron, showed itself. Stubbs halted before it. There was a sputter. A light shone out. "Wonderful invention!" he said. "Electric telegraph not more wonderful, though marvellous invention that, my lord."

"Yes," the other answered dryly. "But--when were you here last, Stubbs?"

"Not for a twelvemonth, my lord."

"Leave your candle?"

"No."

"Then what's that?" The young man pointed to something that lay in the angle between a stair and the wall.

"God bless my soul!" the lawyer cried. "It's a candle."

"And clean. It has not been there a week. Who has been here, my friend?"

Stubbs reflected. "No one with my authority," he said. "But if the devil himself has been here," he continued, stoutly recovering himself, "he can have done no harm. I can prove that in five minutes, my lord--if you will kindly hold the light." He inserted a large key in the lock, and with an effort, he shot back the bolts. He pushed open the door and signed to Lord Audley to enter.

He did so, and Stubbs followed. They stood and looked about them. They were in a whitewashed chamber twelve feet square, clean, bare, empty. The walls gave back the light so that the one candle lit the place perfectly.

"It's as good as air-tight," Stubbs said with pride. "And you see, my lord, we swept it as bare as the palm of my hand. I can answer for it that not a shred of paper or a piece of wax was left."

Audley, gazing about him, seemed satisfied. His face relaxed. "Yes," he said, "you could not overlook anything in a place like this. I'm glad I've seen it."

He was turning to go when a thought struck him. He lowered the light and scanned the floor. "All the same, somebody has been here!" he exclaimed. "There's one of the things you are so pleased with--a lucifer!"

Stubbs stooped and looked. "A lucifer?" he repeated. He picked up the bit of charred wood and examined it. "Now how did that come here? I never used one till six months ago."

My lord frowned. "Who is it?" he asked.

"Some one, I fear, who has had a key made," the agent answered, shaking his head,

"I can see that for myself. But has he learned anything?"

Stubbs stared. "There's nothing to learn, my lord," he said. "You can see that. Whoever he is, he has cracked the nut and found no kernel!"

The young man looked round him again. He nodded. "I suppose so," he said. But he seemed ill at ease and inclined to find fault. He threw the light of the candle this way and that, as if he expected the clean white walls to tell a tale. "What's that?" he asked suddenly. "A crack? Or what?"

Stubbs looked, passed his hand over the mark on the wall, effaced it. "No, my lord, a cobweb," he said. "Nothing."

There was no more to be seen, yet Audley seemed loth to go. At length he turned and went out. Stubbs closed and locked the door behind them, then he took the candle from his lordship and invited him to go down before him. Still the young man hesitated. "I suppose we can learn nothing more?" he said.

"Nothing, my lord," Stubbs answered. "To tell you the truth, I have long thought Mr. John mad, and it is possible that his madness has taken this turn. But I am equally sure that there is nothing for him to discover, if he spends every day of his life here."

"All the same I don't like it," the owner objected. "Whoever has been here has no right here. It is odd that I had some notion of this before we came. You may depend upon it that this was why he fixed himself at the Gatehouse."

"He may have had something of the sort in his mind," Stubbs admitted. "But I don't think so, my lord. More probably, being here and idle, he took to wandering in for lack of something to do."

"And by and by, had a key made and strayed into the Muniment Room! No, that won't do, Stubbs. And frankly there should be closer supervision here. It should not have remained for me to discover this."

He began to descend, leaving Stubbs to digest the remark; who for his part thought honestly that too much was being made of the matter. Probably the intruder was John Audley; the man had a bee in his bonnet, and what more likely than that he should be taken with a craze to haunt the house which he believed was his own? But the agent was too prudent to defend himself while the young man's vexation was fresh. He followed him down in silence, and before many minutes had passed, they were in the open air, and had locked the door behind them.

Clouds hung low on the tops of the trees, mist veiled the view, and a small rain was falling on the wet lawn. Nevertheless the young man moved into the open. "Come this way," he said.

The lawyer turned up the collar of his coat and followed him unwillingly. "Where does he get in?" my lord asked. It seemed as if the longer he dwelt on the matter the less he liked it. "Not by that door--the lock is rusty. The key had shrieked in it. Probably he enters by one of the windows in the new part."

He walked towards the middle of the lawn and Stubbs, thankful that he wore Wellington boots, followed him.

The lawyer thought that he had never seen the house wear so dreary an aspect as it wore under the gray weeping sky. But his lordship was more practical. "These windows look the most likely," he said after a short survey: and he dragged his unwilling attendant to the point he had marked.

A nearer view strengthened his suspicions. On the sill of one of the windows were scratches and stains. "You see?" he said. "It should not have been left to me to discover this! Probably John Audley comes from the Gatehouse by the Yew Walk." He turned to measure the distance with his eye, the distance which divided the spot from the Iron Gate. "That's it," he said, "he comes----"

Then, "Good G--d!" he muttered. "Look! Look!" Stubbs looked. They both looked. Beyond the lawn, on the farther side of the iron grille and clinging to it with both hands, a man stood bareheaded under the rain. Whether he had come uncovered, or his hat had been jerked from him by some movement caused by their appearance, they could not tell; nor how long he had stood thus, gazing at them through the bars. But they could see that his eyes never wavered, that his hands gripped the iron, and the two knew by instinct that in the intensity of his hate, the man was insensible alike to the rain that drenched him, and to the wind that blew out the skirts of his thin black coat.

Even Stubbs held his breath. Even he felt that there was something uncanny and ominous in the appearance. For the gazer was John Audley.

CHAPTER XVII: TO THE RESCUE

Stubbs was the first to collect himself, but a minute elapsed before he spoke. Then, "He must be mad," he cried, "mad, to expose himself to the weather at his age. If I had not seen it, I couldn't believe it!"

"I suppose it is John Audley?"

"Yes." Then raising his voice, "My lord! I don't think I would go to him now!"

But Audley was already striding across the lawn towards the gate. The lawyer hesitated, gave way, and followed him.

They were within twenty paces of the silent watcher when he moved--up to that time he might have been a lay figure. He shook one hand in the air, as if he would beat them off, then he turned and walked stiffly away. Half a dozen steps took him out of sight. The Yew Walk swallowed him.

But, quickly as he vanished, the lawyer had had time to see that he staggered. "I fear, my lord, he is ill," he said. "He will never reach the Gatehouse in that state. I had better follow him."

"Why the devil did he come here?" Audley retorted savagely. The watcher's strange aspect, his face, white against the dark yews, his stillness, his gesture, a something ominous in all, had shaken him. "If he had stopped at home----"

"Still----"

"D--n him, it's his affair!"

"Still we cannot leave him if he has fallen, my lord," Stubbs replied with decision. And without waiting for his employer's assent he tried the gate. It was locked, but in a trice he found the key on his bunch, turned it, and pushed back the gate. Audley noticed that it moved silently on its hinges.

Stubbs, the gate open, began to feel ashamed of his impulse. Probably there was nothing amiss after all. But he had hardly looked along the path before he uttered a cry, and hurrying forward, stooped over a bundle of clothes that lay in the middle of the walk. It was John Audley. Apparently he had tripped over a root and lain where he had fallen.

Stubbs's cry summoned the other, who followed him through the gate, to find him on his knees supporting the old man's head. The sight recalled Audley to his better self. The mottled face, the staring eyes, the helpless limbs shocked him. "Good G--d!" he cried, "you were right, Stubbs! He might have died if we had left him."

"He would have died," Stubbs answered. "As it is--I am not sure." He opened the waistcoat, felt for the beating of the heart, bent his ear to it. "No, I don't think he's gone," he said, "but the heart is feeble, very feeble. We must have brandy! My lord, you are the more active. Will you go to the Gatehouse--there is no nearer place--and get some? And something to carry him home! A hurdle if there is nothing better, and a couple of men?"

"Right!" Audley cried.

"And don't lose a minute, my lord! He's nearly gone."

Audley stripped off his overcoat. "Wrap this about him!" he said. And before the other could answer he had started for the Gatehouse, at a pace which he believed that he could keep up.

Pad, pad, my lord ran under the yew trees, swish, swish across the soaking grass, about the great Butterfly. Pad, pad, again through the gloom under the yews! Not too fast, he told himself-- he was a big man and he must save himself. Now he saw before him the opening into the park, and the light falling on the pale turf. And then, at a point not more than twenty yards short of the open ground, he tripped over a root, tried to recover himself, struck another root, and fell.

The fall shook him, but he was young, and he was quickly on his feet. He paused an instant to brush the dirt from his hands and knees; and it was during that instant that his inbred fear of John Audley, and the certainty that if John Audley died he need fear no more, rose before him.

Yes, if he died--this man who was even now plotting against him--there was an end of that fear! There was an end of uneasiness, of anxiety, of the alarm that assailed him in the small hours, of the forebodings that showed him stripped of title and income and consequence. Stripped of all!

Five seconds passed, and he still stood, engaged with his hands. Five more; it was his knees he was brushing now--and very carefully. Another five--the sweat broke out on his brow though the day was cold. Twenty seconds, twenty-five! His face showed white in the gloom. And still he stood. He glanced behind him. No one could see him.

But the movement discovered the man to himself, and with an oath he broke away. He thrust the damning thought from him, he sprang forward. He ran. In ten strides he was in the open park, and trotting steadily, his elbows to his sides, across the sward. The blessed light was about him, the wind swept past his ears, the cleansing rain whipped his face. Thank God, he had left behind him the heavy air and noisome scent of the yews. He hated them. He would cut them all down some day.

For in a strange way he associated them with the temptation which had assailed him. And he was thankful, most thankful, that he had put that temptation from him--had put it from him, when most men, he thought, would have succumbed to it. Thank God, he had not! The farther he went, indeed, the better he felt. By the time he saw the Gatehouse before him, he was sure that few men, exposed to that temptation, would have overcome it. For if John Audley died what a relief it would be! And he had looked very ill; he had looked like a man at the point of death. The brandy could not reach him under--well, under half an hour. Half an hour was a long time, when a man looked like that. "I'll do my best," he thought. "Then if he dies, well and good. I've always been afraid of him."

He did not spare himself, but he was not in training, and he was well winded when he reached the Gatehouse. A last effort carried him between the Butterflies, and he halted on the flags of the courtyard. A woman, whose skirts were visible, but whose head and shoulders were hidden by an umbrella, was standing in the doorway on his left, speaking to some one in the house. She heard his footsteps and turned.

"Lord Audley!" she exclaimed--for it was Mary Audley. Then with a woman's quickness, "You have come from my uncle?" she cried. "Is he ill?"

Audley nodded. "I am come for some brandy," he gasped.

She did not waste a moment. She sped into the house, and to the dining-room. "I had missed him," she cried over her shoulder. "The man-servant is away. I hoped he might be with him."

In a trice she had opened a cellarette and taken from it a decanter of brandy. Then she saw that he could not carry this at any speed, and she turned to the sideboard and took a wicker flask from a drawer. With a steady hand and without the loss of a minute--he found her presence of mind admirable--she filled this.

As she corked it, Mrs. Toft appeared, wiping her hands on her apron. "Dear, dear, miss," she said, "is the master bad? But it's no wonder when he, that doesn't quit the fire for a week together, goes out like this? And Toft away and all!" She stared at his lordship. Probably she knew him by sight.

"Will you get his bed warmed, Mrs. Toft," Mary answered. She gave Lord Audley the flask. "Please don't lose a moment," she urged. "I am following--oh yes, I am. But you will go faster."

She had not a thought, he saw, for the disorder of her dress, or for her hair dishevelled by the wind, and scarce a thought for him. He decided that he had never seen her to such advantage, but it was no time for compliments, nor was she in the mood for them. Without more he nodded and set off on his return journey--he had not been in the house three minutes. By and by he looked back, and saw that Mary was following on his heels. She had snatched up a sun-bonnet, discarded the umbrella, and, heedless of the rain, was coming after him as swiftly and lightly as Atalanta of the golden apple. "Gad, she's not one of the fainting sort!" he reflected; and also that if he had given way to that d--d temptation he could not have looked her in the face. "As it is," his mind ran, "what are the odds the old boy's not dead when we get there? If he is--I am safe! If he is not, I might do worse than think of her. It would checkmate him finely. More"--he looked again over his shoulder--"she's a fine mover, by Gad, and her figure's perfect! Even that rag on her head don't spoil her!" Whereupon he thought of a certain Lady Adela with whom he was very friendly, who had political connections and would some day have a plum. The comparison was not, in the matter of fineness and figure, to Lady Adela's advantage. Her lines were rather on the Flemish side.

Meanwhile Mary was feeling anything but an Atalanta. Wind and rain and wet grass, loosened hair and swaying skirts do not make for romance. But in her anxiety she gave small thought to these. Her one instinct was to help. With all his oddity her uncle had been kind to her, and she longed to show him that she was grateful. And he was her one relative. She had no one else in the world. He had given her what of home he had, and ease, and a security which she had never known before. Were she to lose him now--the mere fancy spurred her to fresh exertions, and in spite of a pain in her side, in spite of clinging skirts, and shoes that threatened to leave her feet, she pushed on. She was not far behind Audley when he reached the Yew Walk.

She saw him plunge into it, she followed, and was on the scene not many seconds later. When she caught sight of the little group kneeling about the prostrate man, that sense of tragedy, and of the inevitable, which assails at such a time, shook her. The thing always possible, never expected, had happened at last.

Then the coolness which women find in these emergencies returned. She knelt between the men, took the insensible head on her arm, held out her other hand for the cup. "Has he swallowed any?" she asked, taking command of the situation.

"No," Toft answered--and she became aware that the man with Lord Audley was the servant.

She waited for no more, she tilted the cup, and by some knack she succeeded where Toft had failed. A little of the spirit was swallowed. She improvised a pillow and laid the head down on it. "The lower the better," she murmured. She felt the hands and began to rub one. "Rub the other," she said to Toft. "The first thing to do is to get him home! Have you a carriage? How near can you bring it, Lord Audley?"

"We can bring it to the park at the end of the walk," he answered. "My agent has gone to fetch it."

"Will you hasten it?" she replied. "Toft will stay with me. And bring something, please, on which you can carry him to it."

"At once," Audley answered, and he went off in the direction of the Great House.

"I've seen him as bad before, Miss," Toft said. "I found that he had gone out without his hat and I followed him, but I could not trace him at once. I don't think you need feel alarmed."

Certainly the face had lost its mottled look, the eyes were now shut, the limbs lay more naturally. "If he were only at home!" Mary answered. "But every moment he is exposed to the cold is against him. He must be wet through."

She induced the patient to swallow another mouthful of brandy, and with their eyes on his face the two watched for the first gleam of consciousness. It came suddenly. John Audley's eyes opened. He stared at them.

His mind, however, still wandered. "I knew it!" he muttered. "They could not be there and I not know it! But the wall! The wall is thick--thick and----" He was silent again.

The rambling mind is to those who are not wont to deal with it a most uncanny thing, and Mary looked at Toft to see what he made of it. But the servant had eyes only for his master. He was gazing at him with an absorbed face.

"Ay, a thick wall!" the sick man murmured. "They may look and look, they'll not see through it." He was silent a moment, then, "All bare!" he murmured. "All bare!" He chuckled faintly, and tried to raise himself, but sank back. "Fools!" he whispered, "fools, when in ten minutes if they took out a brick----"

The servant cut him short. "Here's his lordship!" he cried. He spoke so sharply that Mary looked up in surprise, wondering what was amiss. Lord Audley was within three or four paces of them--the carpet of yew leaves had deadened his footsteps. "Here's his lordship, sir!" Toft repeated in the same tone, his mouth close to John Audley's ear.

The servant's manner shocked Mary. "Hush, Toft!" she said. "Do you want to startle him?"

"His lordship will startle him," Toft retorted. He looked over his shoulder, and without ceremony he signed to Lord Audley to stand back.

"Bare, quite bare!" John Audley muttered, his mind still far away. "But if they took out--if they took out----"

Toft waved his hand again--waved it wildly.

"All right, I understand," Lord Audley said. He had not at first grasped what was wanted, but the man's repeated gestures enlightened him. He retired to a position where he was out of the sick man's sight.

The servant wiped the sweat from his brow. "He mustn't see him!" he repeated insistently. "Lord! what a turn it gave me. I ask your pardon, Miss," he continued, "but I know the master so well." He cast an uneasy glance over his shoulder. "If the master's eyes lit on him once, only once, when he's in this state, I'd not answer for his life."

Mary reproached herself. "You are quite right, Toft," she said. "I ought to have thought of that myself."

"He must not see any strangers!"

"He shall not. You are quite right."

But Toft was still uneasy. He looked round. Stubbs and a man who had been working in the neighborhood were bringing up a sheep-hurdle, and again the butler's anxiety overcame him. "D--n!" he said: and he rose to his feet. "I think they want to kill him amongst them! Why can't they keep away?"

"Hush! Toft. Why----"

"He mustn't see the lawyer! He must not see him on any account."

Mary nodded. "I will arrange it!" she said. "Only don't excite him. You will do him harm that way if you are not careful. I will speak to them."

She went to meet them and explained, while Stubbs, who had not seen her before, considered her with interest. So this was Miss Audley, Peter Audley's daughter! She told them that she thought it better that her uncle should not find strangers about him when he came to himself. They agreed--it seemed quite natural--and it was arranged that Toft and the man should carry him as far as the carriage, while Mary walked beside him; and that afterwards she and Toft should travel with him. The carriage cushions were placed on the hurdle, and the helpless man was lifted on to them. Toft and the laborer raised their burden, and slowly and heavily, with an occasional stagger, they bore it along the sodden path. Mary saw that the sweat sprang out on Toft's sallow face and that his knees shook under him. Clearly the man was taxing his strength to the utmost, and she felt some concern--she had not given him credit for such fidelity. However, he held out until they reached the carriage.

Babbling a word now and again, John Audley was moved into the vehicle. Mary mounted beside him and supported his head, while Toft climbed to the box, and at a footpace they set off across the sward, the laborer plodding at the tail of the carriage, and Lord Audley and Stubbs following a score of paces behind. The rain had ceased, but the clouds were low and leaden, the trees dripped sadly, and the little procession across the park had a funereal look. To Mary the way seemed long, to Toft still longer. With every moment his head was round. His eyes were now on his master, now jealously cast on those who brought up the rear. But everything comes to an end, and at length they swung into the courtyard, where Mrs. Toft, capable and cool, met them and took a load off Mary's shoulders.

"He's that bad is he?" she said calmly. "Then the sooner he's in his bed the better. 'Truria's warming it. How will we get him up? I could carry him myself if that's all. If Toft'll take his feet, I'll do the rest. No need for another soul to come in!" with a glance at Lord Audley. "But if they would fetch the doctor I'd not say no, Miss."

"I'll ask them to do that," Mary said.

"And don't you worrit, Miss," Mrs. Toft continued, eyeing the sick man judicially. "He's been nigh as bad as this before and been about within the week. There's some as when they wool-gathers, there's no worse sign. But the master he's never all here, nor all there, and like a Broseley butter-pot another touch of the kiln will neither make him nor break him. Now, Toft, wide of the door-post, and steady, man."

Lord Audley and Stubbs had remained outside, but when they saw Mary coming towards them, the young man left Stubbs and went to meet her. "How is he?" he asked.

"Mrs. Toft thinks well of him. She has seen him nearly as ill before, she says. But if he recovers," Mary continued gratefully, "we owe his life to you. Had you not found him he must have died. And if you had lost a moment in bringing the news, I am sure that we should have been too late."

The young man might have given some credit to Stubbs, but he did not; perhaps because time pressed, perhaps because he felt that his virtue in resisting a certain temptation deserved its reward. Instead he looked at Mary with a sympathy so ardent that her eyes fell. "Who would not have done as much?" he said. "If not for him--for you."

"Will you add one kindness then?" she answered. "Will you send Dr. Pepper as quickly as possible?"

"Without the loss of a minute," he said. "But one thing before I go. I cannot come here to inquire, yet I should like to know how he goes on. Will you walk a little way down the Riddsley road at noon to-morrow, and tell me how he fares?"

Mary hesitated. But when he had done so much for them, when he had as good as saved her uncle's life, how could she be churlish? How could she play the prude? "Of course I will," she said frankly. "I hope I shall bring a good report."

"Thank you," he said. "Until to-morrow!"

CHAPTER XVIII: MASKS AND FACES

Cherbuliez opens one of his stories with the remark that if the law of probabilities ruled, the hero and heroine would never have met, seeing that the one lived in Venice and the other seldom left Paris. That in spite of this they fell in with one another was enough to suggest to the lady that Destiny was at work to unite them.

He put into words a thought which has entertained millions of lovers. If in face of the odds of three hundred and sixty-four to one Phyllis shares her birthday with Corydon, if Frederica sprains her ankle and the ready arm belongs to a Frederic, if Mademoiselle has a grain de beauté on the right ear, and Monsieur a plain mole on the left--here is at once matter for reverie, and the heart is given almost before the hands have met.

This was the fourth occasion on which Audley had come to Mary's rescue, and, sensible as she was, she was too thoroughly woman to be proof against the suggestion. On three of the four occasions the odds had been against his appearance. Yet he had come. To-day in particular, as if no pain that threatened her could be indifferent to him, as if no trouble approached her but touched a nerve in him, he had risen from the very ground to help and sustain her.

Could the coldest decline to feel interest in one so strangely linked with her by fortune? Could the most prudent in such a case abstain from day dreams, in which love and service, devotion and constancy, played their parts?

Sic itur ad astra! So men and women begin to love.

She spent the morning between the room in which John Audley was making a slow recovery, and the deserted library which already wore a cold and unused aspect. In the one and the other she felt a restlessness and a disturbance which she was fain to set down to yesterday's alarm. The old interests invited her in vain. Do what she would, she could not keep her mind off the appointment before her. Her eyes grew dreamy, her thoughts strayed, her color came and went. At one moment she would plunge into a thousand attentions to her uncle, at another she opened books only to close them. She looked at the clock--surely the hands were not moving! She looked again--it could not be as late as that! The truth was that Mary was not in love, but she was ready to be in love. She was glad and sorry, grave and gay, without reason; like a stream that dances over the shallows, and rippling and twinkling goes its way through the sunshine, knowing nothing of the deep pool that awaits it.

Presently, acting upon some impulse, she opened a drawer in one of the tables. It contained a portrait in crayons of Peter Basset, which John Audley had shown her. She took out the sketch and set it against a book where the light fell upon it, and she examined it. At first with a smile-- that he should have been so mad as to think what he had thought! And then with a softer look. How hard she had been to him! How unfeeling! Nay, how cruel!

She sat for a long time looking at the portrait. But in fact she had forgotten that it was before her, when the clock, striking the half--hour before noon, surprised her. Then she thrust the portrait back into its drawer, and went with a composed face to put on her hat.

The past summer had been one of the wettest ever known, for rain had fallen on five days out of seven. But to-day it was fine, and as Mary descended the road that led from the house towards Riddsley, a road open to the vale on one side and flanked on the other by a rising slope covered with brushwood, a watery sun was shining. Its rays, aided by the clearness of the air, brought out the colors of stubble and field, flood and coppice, that lay below. And men looking up from toil or pleasure, leaning on spades or pausing before they crossed a stile, saw the Gatehouse transformed to a fairy lodge, gray, clear--cut, glittering, breaking the line of forest trees--saw it as if it had stood in another world.

Mary looked back, looked forward, admired, descended. She had made up her mind that Lord Audley would meet her at a turn near the foot of the hill, where a Cross had once stood, and where the crumbling base and moss-clothed steps still bade travellers rest and be thankful.

He was there, and Mary owned the attraction of the big smiling face and the burly figure, that in a rough, caped riding-coat still kept an air of fashion. He on his side saw coming to meet him, through the pale sunshine, not as yesterday an Atalanta, but a cool Dian, with her hands in a large muff.

"You bring a good report, I hope?" he cried before they met.

"Very good," Mary replied, sparkling a little as she looked at him--was not the sun shining? "My uncle is much better this morning. Dr. Pepper says that it was mainly exertion acting on a weak heart. He expects him to be downstairs in a week and to be himself in a fortnight. But he will have to be more careful in future."

"That is good!"

"He says, too, that if you had not acted so promptly, my uncle must have died."

"Well, he was pretty far gone, I must say."

"So, as he will not thank you himself, you must let me thank you." And Mary held out the hand she had hitherto kept in her muff. She was determined not to be a prude.

He pressed it discreetly. "I am glad," he said. "Very glad. Perhaps after this he may think better of me."

She laughed. "I don't think that there is a chance of it," she said.

"No? Well, I suppose it was foolish, but do you know, I did hope that this might bring us together."

"You may dismiss it," she answered, smiling.

"Ah!" he said. "Then tell me this. How in the world did he come to be there? Without a hat? Without a coat? And so far from the house?"

Mary hesitated. He had turned, they were walking side by side. "I am not sure that I ought to tell you," she said. "What I know I gathered from a word that Mr. Audley let fall when he was rambling. He seems to have had some instinct, some feeling that you were there and to have been forced to learn if it was so."

"But forced? By what?" Lord Audley asked. "I don't understand."

"I don't understand either," Mary answered.

"He could not know that we were there?"

"But he seems to have known."

"Strange," he murmured. "Does he often stray away like that?"

"He does, sometimes," she admitted reluctantly.

"Ah!" Audley was silent a moment. Then, "Well, I am glad he is better," he said in the tone of one who dismisses a subject. "Let us talk of something else--ourselves. Are you aware that this is the fourth time that I have come to your rescue?"

"I know that it is the fourth time that you have been very useful," she admitted. She wished that she had been able to control her color, but though he spoke playfully there was meaning in his voice.

"I, too, have a second sense it seems," he said, almost purring as he looked at her. "Did you by any chance think of me, when you missed your uncle?"

"Not for a moment," she retorted.

"Perhaps--you thought of Mr. Basset?"

"No, nor of Mr. Basset. Had he been at the Gatehouse I might have. But he is away."

"Away, is he? Oh!" He looked at her with a whimsical smile. "Do you know that when he met us the other evening I thought that he was a little out of temper? It was not a continuance of that which took him away, I suppose?"

Mary would have given the world to show an unmoved face at that moment. But she could not. Nor could she feel as angry as she wished. "I thought we were going to talk of ourselves," she said.

"I thought that we were talking of you."

On that, "I am afraid that I must be going back," she said. And she stopped.

"But I am going back with you!"

"Are you? Well, you may come as far as the Cross."

"Oh, hang the Cross!" he answered with a masterfulness of which Mary owned the charm, while she rebelled against it. "I shall come as far as I like! And hang Basset too--if he makes you unhappy!" He laughed. "We'll talk of--what shall we talk of, Mary? Why, we are cousins--does not that entitle me to call you 'Mary'?"

"I would rather you did not," she said, and this time there was no lack of firmness in her tone. She remembered what Basset had said about her name and--and for the moment the other's airiness displeased her.

"But we are cousins."

"Then you can call me cousin," she answered.

He laughed. "Beaten again!" he said.

"And I can call you cousin," she said sedately. "Indeed, I am going to treat you as a cousin. I want you, if not to do, to think of doing something for me. I don't know," nervously, "whether I am asking more than I ought--if so you must forgive me. But it is not for myself."

"You frighten me!" he said. "What is it?"

"It's about Mr. Colet, the curate whom you helped us to save from those men at Brown Heath. He has been shamefully treated. What they did to him might be forgiven--they knew no better. But I hear that because he preaches what is not to everybody's taste, but what thousands and thousands are saying, he is to lose his curacy. And that is his livelihood. It seems most wicked to me, because I am told that no one else will employ him. And what is he to do? He has no friends----"

"He has one eloquent friend."

"Don't laugh at me!" she cried.

"I am not laughing," he answered. He was, in fact, wondering how he should deal with this-- this fad of hers. A little, too, he was wondering what it meant. It could not be that she was in love with Colet. Absurd! He recalled the look of the man. "I am not laughing," he repeated more slowly. "But what do you want me to do?"

"To use your influence for him," Mary explained, "either with the rector to keep him or with some one else to employ him."

"I see."

"He only did what he thought was his duty. And--and because he did it, is he to pay with all he has in the world?"

"It seems a hard case."

"It is more, it is an abominable injustice!" she cried.

"Yes," he said slowly. "It seems so. It certainly seems hard. But let me--don't be angry with me if I put another side." He spoke with careful moderation. "It is my experience that good, easy men, such as I take the rector of Riddsley to be, rarely do a thing which seems cruel, without reason. A clergyman, for instance; he has generally thought out more clearly than you or I what it is right to say in the pulpit; how far it is lawful, and then again how far it is wise to deal with matters of debate. He has considered how far a pronouncement may offend some, and so may render his office less welcome to them. That is one consideration. Probably, too, he has considered that a statement, if events falsify it, will injure him with his poorer parishioners who look up to him as wiser than themselves. Well, when such a man has laid down a rule and finds a younger clergyman bent upon transgressing it, is it unreasonable if he puts his foot down?"

"I had not looked at it in that way."

"And that, perhaps, is not all," he resumed. "You know that a thing may be true, but that it is not always wise to proclaim it. It may be too strong meat. It may be true, for instance, that corn-dealers make an unfair profit out of the poor; but it is not a truth that you would tell a hungry crowd outside the corn-dealer's shop on a Saturday night."

"No," Mary allowed reluctantly. "Perhaps not."

"And again--I have nothing to say against Colet. It is enough for me that he is a friend of yours----"

"I have a reason for being interested in him. I am sure that if you heard him----"

"I might be carried away? Precisely. But is it not possible that he has seen much of one side of this question, much of the poverty for which a cure is sought, without being for that reason fitted to decide what the cure should be?"

Mary nodded. "Have you formed any opinion yourself?" she asked.

But he was too prudent to enter on a discussion. He saw that so far he had impressed her with what he had said, and he was not going to risk the advantage he had gained. "No," he said, "I am weighing the matter at this moment. We are on the verge of a crisis on the Corn Laws, and it is my duty to consider the question carefully. I am doing so. I have hitherto been a believer in the tax. I may change my views, but I shall not do so hastily. As for your friend, I will consider what can be done, but I fear that he has been imprudent."

"Sometimes," she ventured, "imprudence is a virtue."

"And its own reward!" he retorted. They had passed the Cross, they were by this time high on the hill, with one accord they came to a stand. "However, I will think it over," he continued. "I will think it over, and what a cousin may, a cousin shall."

"A cousin may much when he is Lord Audley."

"A poor man in a fine coat! A butterfly in an east wind." He removed his curly-brimmed hat and stood gazing over the prospect, over the wide valley that far and near gleamed with many a sheet of flood-water. "Have you ever thought, Mary, what that means?" he continued with feeling. "To be the shadow of a name! A ghost of the past! To have for home a ruin, and for lands a few poor farms--in place of all that we can see from here! For all this was once ours. To live a poor man among the rich! To have nothing but----"

"Opportunities!" she answered, her voice betraying how deeply she was moved--for she too was an Audley. "For, with all said and done, you start where others end. You have no need to wait for a hearing. Doors stand open to you that others must open. Your name is a passport--is there a Stafford man who does not thrill to it? Surely these things are something. Surely they are much?"

"You would make me think so!" he exclaimed.

"Believe me, they are."

"They would be if I had your enthusiasm!" he answered, moved by her words. "And, by Jove," gazing with admiration at her glowing face, "if I had you by me to spur me on there's no knowing, Mary, what I might not try! And what I might not do!"

Womanlike, she would evade the crisis which she had provoked. "Or fail to do!" she replied. "Perhaps the most worthy would be left undone. But I must go now," she continued. "I have to give my uncle his medicine. I fear I am late already."

"When shall I see you again?" he asked, trying to detain her.

"Some day, I have no doubt. But good-bye now! And don't forget Mr. Colet! Good-bye!"

He stood awhile looking after her, then he turned and went down the hill. By the time he was at the place where he had met her he was glad that she had broken off the interview.

"I might have said too much," he reflected. "She's handsome enough to turn any man's head! And not so cold as she looks. And she spells safety. But there's no hurry--and she's inclined to be kind, or I am mistaken! That clown, Basset, too, has got his dismissal, I fancy, and there's no one else!"

Presently his thoughts took another turn. "What maggots women get into their heads!" he muttered. "That pestilent Colet--I'm glad the rector acted on my hint. But there it is; when a woman meddles with politics she's game for the first spouter she comes across! Fine eyes, too, and the Audley blood! With a little drilling she would hold her own anywhere."

Altogether, he found the walk to the place where he had left his carriage pleasant enough and his thoughts satisfactory. With Mary and safety on one side, and Lady Adela and a plum on the other--it would be odd if he did not bring his wares to a tolerable market.

CHAPTER XIX: THE CORN LAW CRISIS

He had been right in his forecast when he told Mary that a political crisis was at hand. That which had been long whispered, was beginning to be stated openly in club and market-place. The Corn Laws, the support of the country, the mainstay, as so many thought, of the Constitution, were in danger; and behind closed doors, while England listened without, the doctors were met to decide their fate.

Potatoes! The word flew from mouth to mouth that wet autumn, from town to country, from village to village. Potatoes! The thing seemed incredible. That the lordly Corn Laws, the bulwark of the landed interest, the prop of agriculture, that had withstood all attacks for two generations, and maintained themselves alike against high prices and the Corn Law League--that these should go down because a vulgar root like the potato had failed in Ireland--it was a thing passing belief. It couldn't be. With the Conservatives in power, it seemed impossible.

Yet it was certain that the position was grave, if not hopeless. Never since the Reform Bill had there been such meetings of the Cabinet, so frequent, so secret. And strange things were said. Some who had supported Peel yet did not trust him, maintained that this was the natural sequel of his measures, the point to which he had been moving through all the years of his Ministry. Potatoes--bah! Others who still supported him, yet did not trust him, brooded nervously over his action twenty years before, when he had first resisted and then accepted the Catholic claims. Tories and Conservatives alike, wondered what they were there to conserve, if such things were in the wind; they protested, but with growing misgiving, that the thing could not be. While those among them who had seats to save and majorities to guard, met one another with gloomy looks, whispered together in corners and privately asked themselves what they would do--if he did. Happy in these circumstances were those who like Mottisfont, the father, were ready to retire; and still happier those who like Mottisfont, the son, knew the wishes of their constituents and could sing "John Barleycorn, my Joe, John," with no fear of being jilted.

Their anxieties--they were politicians--were mainly personal--and selfish. But there were some, simple people like Mr. Stubbs at Riddsley, who really believed, when these rumors reached them, that the foundations of things were breaking up, and that the world in which they had lived was sinking under their feet. Already in fancy they saw the glare of furnaces fall across the peaceful fields. Already they heard the tall mill jar and quiver where the cosey homestead and the full stackyard sprawled. They saw a weakly race, slaves to the factory bell, overrun the land where the ploughman still whistled at his work and his wife suckled healthy babes. To these men, if the rumors they heard were true, if Peel had indeed sold the pass, it meant the loss of all. It meant the victory of coal and cotton, the ruling of all after the Manchester pattern, the reign of Cash, the Lord, and ten per cent. his profit. It meant the end of the old England they had loved.

Not that Stubbs said this at Riddsley, or anything like it. He smiled and kept silence, as became a man who knew much and was set above common rumor. The landlord of the Audley Arms, the corndealer, the brewer, the saddler went away from him with their fears allayed merely by the way in which he shrugged his shoulders. At the farmers' ordinary he had never been more cheerful. He gave the toast of "Horn and Corn, gentlemen! And when potatoes take their place you may come and tell me!" And he gave it so heartily that the farmers went home, market-peart and rejoicing, laughed at their doubting neighbors, and quoted a hundred things that Lawyer Stubbs had not said.

But a day or two later the lawyer sustained an unpleasant shock. He had been little moved by Lord John's manifesto--the declaration in which the little Whig Leader, seeing that the Government hesitated, had plumped for total repeal. That was in the common course of things. It had heartened him, if anything. It was natural. It would bring the Tories into line and put an end to trimming. But this--this which confronted him one morning when he opened his London paper was different. He read it, he held his breath, he stood aghast a long minute, he swore. After a few minutes he took his hat and the newspaper, and went round to the house in which Lord Audley lived when he was at Riddsley.

It was a handsome Georgian house, built of brick with stone facings, and partly covered with ivy. A wide smooth lawn divided it from the road. The occupant was a curate's widow who lived there with her two sisters and eked out their joint means by letting the first floor to her landlord. For "The Butterflies" was Audley property, and the clergyman's widow was held to derogate in no way by an arrangement which differed widely from a common letting of lodgings. Mrs. Jenkinson was stout, short, and fussy, her sisters were thin, short, and precise, but all three overflowed with words as kindly as their deeds. Good Mrs. Jenkinson, in fact, who never spoke of his lordship behind his back but with distant respect, sometimes forgot in his presence that he was anything but a "dear young man," and when he had a cold, would prescribe a posset or a warming-pan with an insistence which at times amused and more often bored him.

Stubbs found his lordship just risen from a late lunch, and in his excitement, the lawyer forgot his manners. "By G--d, my lord!" he cried, "he's resigned."

Audley looked at him with displeasure. "Who's resigned?" he asked coldly.

"Peel!"

Against that news the young man was not proof. He caught the infection. "Impossible!" he said, rising to his feet.

"It's true! It's in the Morning Post, my lord! He saw the Queen yesterday. She's sending for Lord John. It's black treachery! It's the blackest of treachery! With a majority in the House, with the peers in his pocket, the country quiet, trade improving, everything in his favor, he's sold us-- sold us to Cobden on some d--d pretext of famine in Ireland!"

Audley did not answer at once. He stood deep in thought, his eyes on the floor, his hands in his pockets. At length, "I don't follow it," he said. "How is Russell, who is in a minority, to carry repeal?"

"Peel's promised his support!" Stubbs cried. Like most honest men, he was nothing if not thorough. "You may depend upon it, my lord, he has! He won't deceive me again. I know him through and through, now. He'll take with him Graham and Gladstone and Herbert, his old tail, Radicals at heart every man of them, and he's the biggest!"

"Well," Audley said slowly, "he might have done one thing worse. He might have stayed in and passed repeal himself!"

"Good G--d!" the lawyer cried, "Judas wouldn't have done that! All he could do, he has done. He has let in corn from Canada, cattle from Heaven knows where, he has let in wool. All that he has done. But even he has a limit, my lord! Even he! The man who was returned to support the Corn Laws--to repeal them. Impossible!"

"Well?" Audley said. "There'll be an election, I suppose?"

"The sooner the better," Stubbs answered vengefully. "And we shall see what the country thinks of this. In Riddsley we've been ready for weeks--as you know, my lord. But a General Election? Gad! I only hope they will put up some one here, and we will give them such a beating as they've never had!"

Audley pondered. "I suppose Riddsley is safe," he said.

"As safe as Burton Bridge, my lord!"

The other rattled the money in his pocket. "As long as you give them a lead, Stubbs, I suppose? But if you went over? What then?"

Stubbs opened his eyes. "Went over?" he ejaculated.

"Oh, I don't mean," my lord said airily, "that you're not as staunch as Burton Bridge. But supposing you took the other side--it would make a difference, I suppose?"

"Not a jot!" the lawyer answered sturdily.

"Not even if the two Mottisfonts sided with Peel?"

"If they did the old gentleman would never see Westminster again," Stubbs cried, "nor the young one go there!"

"Or," Audley continued, setting his shoulders against the mantel-shelf, and smiling, "suppose I did? If the Beaudelays interest were cast for repeal? What then?"

"What then?" Stubbs answered. "You'll pardon me, my lord, if I am frank. Then the Beaudelays influence, that has held the borough time out of mind, that returned two members before '32, and has returned one since--there'd be an end of it! It would snap like a rotten stick. The truth is we hold the borough while we go with the stream. In fair weather when it is a question of twenty votes one way or the other, we carry it. And you've the credit, my lord."

Audley moved his shoulders restlessly. "It's all I get by it," he said. "If I could turn the credit into a snug place of two thousand a year, Stubbs--it would be another thing. Do you know," he continued, "I've often wondered why you feel so strongly on the corn-taxes?"

"You asked me that once before, my lord," the agent answered slowly. "All that I can say is that more things than one go to it. Perhaps the best answer I can make is that, like your lordship's influence in the borough, it's part sentiment and part tradition. I have a picture in my mind--it's a picture of an old homestead that my grandfather lived in and died in, and that I visited when I was a boy. That would be about the middle nineties; the French war going, corn high, cattle high, a good horse in the gig and old ale for all comers. There was comfort inside and plenty without; comfort in the great kitchen, with its floor as clean as a pink, and greened in squares with bay leaves, its dresser bright with pewter, its mantel with Toby jugs! There was wealth in the stackyard, with the poultry strutting and scratching, and more in the byres knee-deep in straw, and the big barn where they flailed the wheat! And there were men and maids more than on two farms to-day, some in the house, some in thatched cottages with a run on the common and wood for the getting. I remember, as if they were yesterday, hot summer afternoons when there'd be a stillness on the farm and all drowsed together, the bees, and the calves, and the old sheep-dog, and the only sounds that broke the silence were the cluck of a hen, or the clank of pattens on the dairy-floor, while the sun fell hot on the orchard, where a little boy hunted for damsons! That's what I often see, my lord," Stubbs continued stoutly. "And may Peel protect me, if I ever raise a finger to set mill and furnace, devil's dust and slave-grown cotton, in place of that!"

My lord concealed a yawn. "Very interesting, Stubbs," he said. "Quite a picture! Peace and plenty and old ale! And little Jack Horner sitting in a corner! No, don't go yet, man. I want you." He made a sign to Stubbs to sit down, and settling his shoulders more firmly against the mantel-shelf, he thrust his hands deeper into his trouser-pockets. "I'm not easy in my mind about John Audley," he said. "I'm not sure that he has not found something."

Stubbs stared. "There's nothing to find," he said. "Nothing, my lord! You may be sure of it."

"He goes there."

"It's a craze."

"It's a confoundedly unpleasant one!"

"But harmless, my lord. Really harmless."

The younger man's impatience darkened his face, but he controlled it--a sure sign that he was in earnest. "Tell me this," he said. "What evidence would upset us? You told me once that the claim could be reopened on fresh evidence. On what evidence?"

"I regard the case as closed," Stubbs answered stubbornly. "But if you put the question--" he seemed to reflect--"the point at issue, on which the whole turned, was the legitimacy of your great-grandfather, my lord, Peter Paravicini Audley's son. Mr. John's great-grandfather was Peter Paravicini's younger brother. The other side alleged, but could not produce, a family agreement admitting that the son was illegitimate. Such an agreement, if Peter Paravicini was a party to it, if it was proved, and came from the proper custody, would be an awkward document and might let in the next brother's descendants--that's Mr. John. But in my opinion, its existence is a fairy story, and in its absence, the entry in the register stands good."

"But such a document would be fatal?"

"If it fulfilled the conditions it would be serious," the lawyer admitted. "But it does not exist," he added confidently.

"And yet--I'm not comfortable, Stubbs," Audley rejoined. "I can't get John Audley's face out of my mind. If ever man looked as if he had his enemy by the throat, he looked it; a d--d disinheriting face I thought it! I don't mind telling you," the speaker continued, some disorder in his own looks, "that I awoke at three o'clock this morning, and I saw him as clearly as I see you now, and at that moment I wouldn't have given a thousand pounds for my chance of being Lord Audley this time two years!"

"Liver!" said Stubbs, unmoved. "Liver, my lord, asking your pardon! Nothing else--and the small hours. I've felt like that myself. Still, if you are really uneasy there is always a way out, though it may be impertinent of me to mention it."

"The old way?"

"You might marry Miss Audley. A handsome young lady, if I may presume to say so, of your own blood and name, and no disparagement except in fortune. After Mr. John, she is the next heir, and the match once made would checkmate any action on his part."

"I am afraid I could not afford such a marriage," Audley said coldly. "But I am to you. As for this news--" he flicked the newspaper that lay on the table--"it may be true or it may not. If it is true, it will alter many things. We shall see. If you hear anything fresh let me know."

Stubbs said that he would and took his leave, wondering a little, but having weightier things on his mind. He sought his home by back ways, for he did not wish to meet Dr. Pepper or Bagenal the brewer, or even the saddler, until he had considered what face he would put on Peel's latest move. He felt that his reputation for knowledge and sagacity was at stake.

Meanwhile his employer, left alone, fell to considering, not what face he should put upon the matter, but how he might at this crisis turn the matter and the borough to the best account. Certainly Stubbs was discouraging, but Stubbs was a fool. It was all very well for him; he drew his wages either way. But a man of the world did not cling to the credit of owning a borough for the mere name of the thing. If he were sensible he looked to get something more from it than that. And it was upon occasions such as this that the something more was to be had by those who knew how to go about the business.

Here, in fact, was the moment, if he was the man.

CHAPTER XX: PETER'S RETURN

Not a word or hint of John Audley's illness had come to Basset's ears. At the time of the alarm he had been in London, and it was not until some days later that he took his seat in the morning train to return to Stafford. On his way to town, and for some days after his arrival, he had been buoyed up by plans, nebulous indeed, but sufficient. He came back low in his mind and in poor spirits. The hopes, if not the aspirations, which Colet's enthusiasm had generated in him had died down, and the visit to Francis Place had done nothing to revive them.

Some greatness in the man, a largeness of ideas, an echo of the revolutionary days when the sanest saw visions, Basset was forced to own. But the two stood too far apart, the inspired tailor and the country squire, for sympathy. They were divided by too wide a gulf of breeding and prejudice to come together. Basset was not even a Radical, and his desire to improve things, and to better the world, fell very far short of the passion of humanity which possessed the aged Republican--the man who for half a century had been so forward in all their movements that his fellows had christened him the "Old Postilion."

Nothing but disappointment, therefore, had come of the meeting. The two had parted with a little contempt on the one side, a sense of failure on the other. If a man could serve his neighbors only in fellowship with such, if the cause which for a few hours had promised to fill the void left by an unhappy love, could be supported only by men who held such opinions, then Basset felt that the thing was not for him. For six or seven days he went up and down London at odds with himself and his kind, and ever striving to solve a puzzle, the answer to which evaded him. Was the hope that he might find a mission and found a purpose on Colet's lines, was it just the desire to set the world right that seized on young men fresh from college? And if this were so, if this were all, what was he to do? Whither was he to turn? How was he going to piece together the life which Mary had broken? How was he going to arrange his future so that some thread of purpose might run through it, so that something of effort might still link together the long bede-roll of years?

He found no answer to the riddle. And it was in a gloomy, unsettled mood, ill-content with himself and the world, that he took his seat in the train. Alas, he could not refrain from recalling the May morning on which he had taken his seat in the same train with Mary. How ill had he then appreciated her company, how little had he understood, how little had he prized his good fortune! He who was then free to listen to her voice, to meet her eyes, to follow the changes of her mood from grave to gay! To be to her--all that he could! And that for hours, for days, for weeks!

He swore under his breath and sat back in the shadow of the corner. And a man who entered late, and saw that he kept his eyes shut, fancied that he was ill; and when he muttered a word under his breath, asked him if he spoke.

"No," Basset replied rather curtly. And that he might be alone with his thoughts he took up a newspaper and held it before him. But not a word did he read. After a long interval he looked over the journal and met the other's eyes.

"Surprising news this," the stranger said. He had the look of a soldier, and the bronzed face of one who had lived under warm skies.

Basset murmured that it was.

"The Whigs have a fine opportunity," the other pursued. "But I am not sure that they will use it."

"You are a Whig, perhaps?"

The stranger smiled. "No," he replied. "I am not. I have lived so long abroad that I belong to no party. I am an Englishman."

"Ah?" Basset rejoined, curiosity beginning to stir in him. "That's rather a fine idea."

"Apparently it's a novel one. But it seems natural to me. I have lived for fifteen years in India and I have lost touch with the cant of parties. Out there, we do honestly try to rule for the good of the people; their prosperity is our interest. Here, during the few weeks I have spent in England I see things done, not because they are good, but because they suit a party, or provide a cry, or put the other side in a quandary."

"There's a good deal of that, I suppose."

"Still," the stranger continued, "I know a great man, and I know a fine thing when I see them. And I fancy that I see them here!" He tapped his paper.

"Has Lord John formed his ministry, then?"

"No, I am not sure that he will. I am not thinking of him, I am thinking of Peel."

"Oh! Of Peel?"

"He has done a fine thing! As every man does who puts what is right before what is easy. May I tell you a story of myself?" the Indian continued. "Some years ago in the Afghan war I was unlucky enough to command a small frontier post. My garrison consisted of two companies and six or seven European officers. The day came when I had to choose between two courses. I must either hold my ground until our people advanced, or I must evacuate the post, which had a certain importance--and fall back into safety. The men never dreamed of retiring. The officers were confident that we could hold out. But we were barely supplied for forty days, and in my judgment no reinforcement was possible under seventy. I made my choice, breached the place, and retired. But I tell you, sir, that the days of that retreat, with sullen faces about me, and hardly a man in my company who did not think me a poltroon, were the bitterest of my life. I knew that if the big-wigs agreed with them I was a ruined man, and after ten years service I should go home disgraced. Fortunately the General saw it as I saw it, and all was well. But--" he looked at Basset with a wry smile--"it was a march of ten days to the base, and to-day the sullen looks of those men come back to me in my dreams."

"And you think," Basset said--the other's story had won his respect--"that Peel has found himself in such a position?"

"To compare great issues with small, I do. I suspect that he has gone through an agony--that is hardly too strong a word--such as I went through. My impression is that when he came into office he was in advance of his party. He saw that the distress in the country called for measures which his followers would accept from no one else. He believed that he could carry them with him. Perhaps, even then, he held a repeal of the Corn Laws possible in some remote future; perhaps he did not, I don't know. For suddenly there came on him the fear of this Irish famine-- and forced his hand."

"But don't you think," Basset asked, "that the alarm is premature?" A dozen times he had heard the famine called a flam, a sham, a bite, anything but a reality.

"You have never seen a famine?" the other replied gravely. "You have never had to face the impossibility of creating food where it does not exist, or of bringing it from a distance when there are no roads. I have had that experience. I have seen people die of starvation by hundreds, women, children, babes, when I could do nothing because steps had not been taken in time. God forbid that that should happen in Ireland! If the fear does not outrun the dearth, God help the poor! Now I am told that Peel witnessed a famine in Ireland about '17 or '18, and knows what it is."

"You have had interesting experiences?"

"The experience of every Indian officer. But the burden which rests on us makes us alive to the difficulties of a statesman's position. I see Peel forced--forced suddenly, perhaps, to make a choice; to decide whether he shall do what is right or what is consistent. He must betray his friends, or he must betray his country. And the agony of the decision is the greater if he has it burnt in on his memory that he did this thing once before, that once before he turned his back on his party--and that all the world knows!"

"I see."

"If a man in that position puts self, consistency, reputation all behind him--believe me, he is doing a fine thing."

Basset assented. "But you speak," he added, "as if Sir Robert were going to do the thing himself--instead of merely standing aside for others to do it."

"A distinction without much difference," the other rejoined. "Possibly it will turn out that he is the only man who can do it. If so, he will have a hard row to hoe. He will need the help of every moderate man in the country, if he is not to be beaten. For whether he succeeds or fails, depends not upon the fanatics, but upon the moderate men. I don't know what your opinions are?"

"Well," Basset said frankly, "I am not much of a party-man myself. I am inclined to agree with you, so far."

"Then if you have any influence, use it. Unfortunately, I am out of it for family reasons."

Basset looked at the stranger. "You are not by any chance Colonel Mottisfont?" he said.

"I am. You know my brother? He is member for Riddsley."

"Yes. My name is Basset."

"Of Blore? Indeed. I knew your father. Well, I have not cast my seed on stony ground. Though you are stony enough about Wootton under Weaver."

"True, worse luck. Your brother is retiring, I hear?"

"Yes, he has just horse sense, has Jack. He won't vote against Peel. His lad has less and will take his place and vote old Tory. But there, I mustn't abuse the family."

They had still half an hour to spend together before Basset got out at Stafford. He had time to discover that the soldier was faced by a problem not unlike his own. His service over, he had to consider what he would do. "All I know," the Colonel said breezily, "is that I won't do nothing. Some take to preaching, others to Bath, but neither will suit me. But I'll not drift. I kept from brandy pawnee out there, and I am going to keep from drift here. For you, you're a young man, Basset, and a hundred things are open to you. I am over the top of the hill. But I'll do something."

"You have done something to-day," Basset said. "You have done me good."

Later he had time to think it over during the long journey from Stafford to Blore. He drove by twisting country roads, under the gray walls of Chartley, by Uttoxeter and Rocester. Thence he toiled uphill to the sterile Derbyshire border, the retreat of old families and old houses. He began to think that he had gained some ideas with which he could sympathize, ideas which were at one with Mary Audley's burning desire to help, while they did not clash with old prejudices. If he threw himself into Peel's cause, he would indeed be seen askance by many. He would have to put himself forward after a fashion that gave him the goose-flesh when he thought of it. A landowner, he would have to go against the land. But he would not feel, in his darker moods, that he was the dupe of cranks and fanatics. He saw Peel as Mottisfont had pictured him, as a man putting all behind him except the right; and his heart warmed to the picture. Many would fall away, few would be staunch. From this ship, as from every sinking ship, the rats would flee. But so much the stronger was the call.

The result was that the Peter Basset who descended at the porch of the old gabled house, that sat low and faced east in the valley under Weaver, was a more hopeful man than he who had entered the train at Euston. A purpose, a plan--he had gained these, and the hope that springs from them.

He had barely doffed his driving-coat, however, before his thoughts were swept in another direction. On the hall table lay two letters. He took up one. It was from Colet and written in deep dejection. "The barber was a Tory and had given him short notice. Feeling ran high in the town, and other lodgings were not to be had. The Bishop had supported the rector's action, and he saw no immediate prospect of further work." He did not ask for shelter, but it was plain that he was at his wit's end, and more than a little surprised by the storm which he had raised.

Basset threw down the letter. "He shall come here," he thought. "What is it to me whom he marries?" Many solitary hours spent in the streets of London had gone some way towards widening Peter's outlook.

He took up the second letter. It was from John Audley, and before he had read three lines, he rang the bell and ordered that the post-chaise which had brought him from Stafford should be kept: he would want it in the morning. John Audley wrote that he had been very ill--he was still in bed. He must see Basset. The matter was urgent, he had something to tell him. He hinted that if he did not come quickly it might be too late.

Basset could not refuse to go; summoned after this fashion, he must go. But he tried to believe that he was not glad to go. He tried to believe that the excitement with which he looked forward to the journey had to do with his uncle. It was in vain; he knew that he tricked himself. Or if he did not know this then, his eyes were opened next day, when, after walking up the hill to spare the horses--and a little because he shrank at the last from the meeting--he came in sight of the Gatehouse, and saw Mary Audley standing in the doorway. The longing that gripped him then, the emotion that unmanned him, told him all. It was of Mary he had been thinking, towards Mary he had been travelling, of her work it was that the miles had seemed leagues! He was not cured. He was not in the way to be cured. He was the same love-sick fool whom she had driven from her with contumely an age--it seemed an age, ago.

He bent his head as he approached, that she might not see his face. His knees shook and a tremor ran through him. Why had he come back? Why had he come back to face this anguish?

Then he mastered himself; indeed he took himself the more strongly in hand for the knowledge he had gained. When they met at the door it was Mary, not he, whose color came and went, who spoke awkwardly, and rushed into needless explanations. The man listened with a stony face, and said little, almost nothing.

After the first awkward greeting, "Your room has been airing," she continued, avoiding his eyes. "My uncle has been expecting you for some days. He has asked for you again and again."

He explained that he had been in London--hence the delay; and, further, that he must return to Blore that day. She felt that she was the cause of this, and she colored painfully. But he seemed to be indifferent. He noticed a trifling change in the hall, asked a question or two about his uncle's state, and inquired what had caused his sudden illness.

She told the story, giving details. He nodded. "Yes, I have seen him in a similar attack," he said. "But he gets older. I am afraid it alarmed you?"

She forced herself to describe Lord Audley's part in the matter--and Mr. Stubbs's, and was conscious that she was dragging in Mr. Stubbs more often than was necessary. Basset listened politely, remarked that it was fortunate that Audley had been on the spot, added that he was sure that everything had been done that was right.

When he had gone upstairs to see John Audley she escaped to her room. Her cheeks were burning, and she could have cried. Basset's coldness, his distance, the complete change in his manner all hurt her more than she could say. They brought home to her, painfully home to her what she had done. She had been foolish enough to fling away the friend, when she need only have discarded the lover!

But she must face it out now, the thing was done, and she must put up with it. And by and by, fearing that Basset might suppose that she avoided him, she came down and waited for him in the deserted library. She had waited some minutes, moving restlessly to and fro and wishing the ordeal of luncheon were over, when her eyes fell on the door of the staircase that led up to her uncle's room. It was ajar.

She stared at it, for she knew that she had closed it after Basset had gone up. Now it was ajar. She reflected. The house was still, she could hear no one moving. She went out quickly, crossed the hall, looked into the dining-room. Toft was not there, nor was he in the pantry. She returned to the library, and went softly up the stairs.

So softly that she surprised the man before he could raise his head from the keyhole. He saw that he was detected, and for an instant he scowled at her in the half-light of the narrow passage, uncertain what to do. Mary beckoned to him, and went down before him to the library.

There she turned on him. "Shut the door," she said. "You were listening! Don't deny it. You have acted disgracefully, and it will be my duty to tell Mr. Audley what has happened."

The man, sallow with fear, tried to brave it out.

"You will only make mischief, Miss," he said sullenly. "You'll come near to killing the master."

"Very good!" Mary said, quivering with indignation. "Then instead of telling Mr. Audley I shall tell Mr. Basset. It will be for him to decide whether Mr. Audley shall know. Go now."

But Toft held his ground. "You'll be doing a bad day's work, Miss," he said earnestly. "I want to run straight." He raised his hand to his forehead, which was wet with perspiration. "I swear I do! I want to run straight."

"Straight!" Mary cried in scorn. "And you listen at doors!"

The man made a last attempt to soften her. "For God's sake, be warned, Miss!" he cried. "Don't drive me. If you knew as much as I do----"

"I should not listen to learn the rest!" replied Mary without pity. "That is enough. Please to see that lunch is ready." She pointed to the door. She was not an Audley for nothing.

Toft gave way and went, and she remained alone, perplexed as well as angry. Mrs. Toft and Etruria were good simple folk; she liked them. But Toft had puzzled her from the first. He was so silent, so secretive, he was for ever appearing without warning and vanishing without noise. She had often suspected that he spied on his master.

But she had never caught him in the act, and the certainty that he did so, filled her with dismay. It was fortunate, she thought, that Basset was there, and that she could consult him. And the instant that he appeared, forgetting their quarrel and the strained relations between them, she poured out her story. Toft was ungrateful, treacherous, a danger! With Mr. Audley so helpless, the house so lonely, it frightened her.

It was only when she had run on for some time that Basset's air of detachment struck her. He listened, with his back to the fire, and his eyes bent on the floor, but he did not speak until she had told her story, and expressed her misgivings.

When he did, "I am not surprised," he said. "I've suspected this for some time. But I don't know that anything can be done."

"Do you mean that--you would do nothing?"

"The truth is," he answered, "Toft is pretty far in his master's confidence. And what he does not know he wishes to know. When he knows it, he will find it a mare's nest. The truth--as I see it at any rate--is that your uncle is possessed by a craze. He wants me to help him in it. I cannot. I have told him so, firmly and finally, to-day. Well, I suspect that he will now turn to Toft. I hope not, but he may, and if we report the man's misconduct, it will only precipitate matters and hasten an understanding. That is the position, and if I were you, I should let the matter rest."

"You mean that?" she exclaimed.

"I do."

"But--but I have spoken to Toft!" Her eyes were bright with anger.

He kept his on the floor. It was only by maintaining the distance between them that he could hope to hide what he felt. "Still I would let him be," he repeated. "I do not think that Toft is dangerous. He has surprised one half of a secret, and he wishes to learn the other half. That is all."

"And I am to take no notice?"

"I believe that will be your wisest course."

She was shocked, and she was still more hurt. He pushed her aside, he pushed her out of his confidence, out of her uncle's confidence! His manner, his indifference, his stolidity showed that she had not only killed his fancy for her at a stroke, but that he now disliked her.

And still she protested. "But I must tell my uncle!" she cried.

"I think I would not," he repeated. "But there--" he paused and looked at his watch--"I am afraid that if you are going to give me lunch I must sit down. I've a long journey before me."

Then she saw that no more could be said, and with an effort she repressed her feelings. "Yes," she said, "I was forgetting. You must be hungry."

She led the way to the dining-room, and sat down with him, Toft waiting on them with the impassive ease of the trained man. While they ate, Basset talked of indifferent things, of his journey from town, of the roads, of London, of Colonel Mottisfont--an interesting man whom he had met in the train. And as he talked, and she made lifeless answers, her indignation cooled, and her heart sank.

She could have cried, indeed. She had lost her friend. He was gone to an immense distance. He was willing to leave her to deal with her troubles and difficulties, it might be, with her dangers. In killing his love with cruel words--and how often had she repented, not of the thing, but of the manner!--she had killed every feeling, every liking, that he had entertained for her.

It was clear that this was so, for to the last he maintained his coldness and indifference. When he was gone, when the sound of the chaise-wheels had died in the distance, she felt more lonely than she had ever felt in her life. In her Paris days she had had no reason to blame herself, and all the unturned leaves of life awaited her. Now she had turned over one page, and marred it, she had won a friend and lost him, she had spoiled the picture, which she had not wished to keep!

Her uncle lay upstairs, ready to bear, but hardly welcoming her company. He had his secrets, and she stood outside them. She sat below, enclosed in and menaced by the silence of the house. Yet it was not fear that she felt so much as a sadness, a great depression, a gray despondency. She craved something, she did not know what. She only knew that she was alone--and sad.

She tried to fight against the feeling. She tried to read, to work, even to interest herself in Toft and his mystery. She failed. And at last she gave up the attempt and with her elbows on her knees and her eyes on the fire she fell to musing, the ticking of the tall clock and the fall of the embers the only sounds that broke the stillness of the shadowy room.

CHAPTER XXI: TOFT AT THE BUTTERFLIES

Basset's view of Toft, if it did not hit, came very near the mark. For many years the man had served his master with loyalty, the relations between them being such as were common in days when servants stayed long in a place and held themselves a part of the family. The master had been easy, the man had had no ambitions beyond those of his fellows, and no temptations except those which turned upon the cellar-book.

But a year before Mary Audley's arrival two things had happened. First the curate had fallen in love with Etruria, and the fact had become known to her father, to whom the girl was everything. Her refinement, her beauty, her goodness were his secret delight. And the thought that she might become a lady, that she might sit at the table at which he served had taken hold of the austere man's mind and become a passion. He was ready to do anything and to suffer anything to bring this about. Nor was he deceived when Etruria put the offer aside. She was nothing if not transparent, and he was too fond of her not to see that her happiness was bound up with the man who had stooped to woo her.

He was not blind to the difficulties or to the clergyman's poverty. But he saw that Colet, poor as he was, could raise his daughter in the social scale; and he spent long hours in studying how the marriage might be brought about. He hugged the matter to him, and brooded over it, but he never discovered his thoughts or his hopes either to his wife, or to Etruria.

Then one day the sale of a living happened to be discussed in his presence, and as he went, solemn and silent, round the table he listened. He learned that livings could be bought. He learned that the one in question, with its house and garden and three hundred a year, had fetched a thousand guineas, and from that day Toft's aim was by hook or crook to gain a thousand guineas. He revelled in impossible dreams of buying a living, of giving it to Etruria, and of handing maid and dowry to the fortunate man who was to make her a lady.

There have been more sordid and more selfish ambitions.

But a thousand guineas was a huge sum to the manservant. True, he had saved a hundred and twenty pounds, and for his position in life he held himself a rich man. But a thousand guineas? He turned the matter this way and that, and sometimes he lost hope, and sometimes he pinned his faith to a plan that twenty-four hours showed to be futile. All the time his wife who lay beside him, his daughter who waited on him, his master on whom he waited, were as far from seeing into his mind as if they had lived in another planet.

Then the second thing happened. He surprised, wholly by chance, a secret which gave him a hold over John Audley. Under other circumstances he might have been above using the advantage; as it was, he was tempted. He showed his hand, a sum of four hundred pounds was named; for a week he fancied that he had performed half his task. Then his master explained with a gentle smile that to know and to prove were two things, and that whereas Toft had for a time been able to do both, John Audley had now destroyed the evidence. The master had in fact been too sly for the man, and Toft found himself pretty well where he had been. In the end Audley thought it prudent to give him a hundred pounds, which did but whet his desire and sharpen his wits.

For he had now tasted blood. He had made something by a secret. There might be others to learn. He kept his eyes open, and soon he became aware of his master's disappearances. He tracked him, he played the spy, he discovered that John Audley was searching for something in the Great House. The words that the old man let fall, while half-conscious in the Yew Walk, added to his knowledge, and at the same time scared him. A moment later, and Lord Audley might have known as much as he knew--and perhaps more!

For he did not as yet know all, and it was in the attempt to complete his knowledge that Mary had caught him listening at the door. The blow was a sharp one. He was still so far unspoiled, still so near the old Toft that he could not bear that his wife and daughter should learn the depth to which he had fallen. And John Audley? What would he do, if Mary told him?

Toft could not guess. He knew that his master was barely sane, if he was sane; but he knew also that he was utterly inhuman. John Audley would put him and his family to the door without mercy if that seemed to him the safer course. And that meant an end of all his plans for Etruria, for Colet, for them all.

True, he might use such power as he had. But it was imperfect, and in its use he must come to grips with one who had shown himself his better both in courage and cunning. He had imbibed a strong fear of his master, and he could not without a qualm contemplate a struggle with him.

For a week after his detection by Mary, he went about his work in a fever of anxiety. And nothing happened; it was that which tried him. More than once he was on the point of throwing himself at her feet, of telling her all he knew, of imploring her pardon. It was only her averted eyes and cold tone that held him back.

Such a crisis makes a man either better or worse, and it made Toft worse. At the end of three days a chance word put a fine point on his fears and stung him to action. He might not know enough to face John Audley, but he thought that he knew enough to sell his secret--in the other camp. His lordship was young and probably malleable. He would go to him and strike a bargain.

Arrived at this point the man did not hide from himself that he was going to do a hateful thing. He thought of his wife and her wonder could she know. He thought of Etruria's mild eyes and her goodness. And he shivered. But it was for her. It was for them. Within twenty-four hours he was in Riddsley.

As he passed the Maypole, where Mr. Colet had his lodgings, he noticed that the town wore an unusual aspect. Groups of men stood talking in the doorway, or on the doorsteps. A passing horseman was shouting to a man at a window. Nearer the middle of the town the stir was greater. About the saddler's door, about the steps leading up to the Audley Arms, and round the yard of the inn, knots of men argued and gesticulated. Toft asked the saddler what it was.

"Haven't you heard?"

"No. What's the news?"

"The General Election's off!" The saddler proclaimed it with an inflamed look. "Peel's in again! And damn me, after this," he continued, "there's nothing I won't swallow! He come in in the farming interest, and the hunting interest, and the racing interest, and the gentlemanly interest, that I live by, and you too, Mr. Toft! And it was bad enough when he threw it up! But to go in again and to take our money and do the Radicals' work!" The saddler spat on the brick pavement. "Why, there was never such a thing heard of in the 'varsal world! Never! If Tamworth don't blush for him and his pigs turn pink, I'm d--d, and that's all."

Toft had to ask half a dozen questions before he grasped the position. Gradually he learned that after Peel had resigned the Whigs had tried to form a government; that they had failed, and that now Peel was to come in again, expressly to repeal the Corn Laws. The Corn Laws which he had taken office to support, and to the maintenance of which his party was pledged!

The thing was not much in Toft's way, nor his interest in it great, but as he passed along he caught odds and ends of conversation. "I don't believe a word of it!" cried an angry man. "The Radicals have invented it!" "Like enough!" replied another. "Like enough! There's naught they wouldn't do!" "Well, after all," suggested a third in a milder tone, "cheap bread is something." "What? If you've got no money to buy it? You're a fool! I tell you it'll be the ruin of Riddsley!" "You're right there, Joe!" answered the first speaker. "You're right! There'll be no farmer for miles round'll pay his way!"

At the door of Mr. Stubbs's office three excited clients were clamoring for entrance; an elderly clerk with a high bridge to his nose was withstanding them. Before the Mechanics' Institute the secretary, a superior person of Manchester views, was talking pompously to a little group. "We must take in the whole field," Toft heard him say. "If you'll read Mr. Carlyle's tract on----" Toft lost the rest. The Institute readers belonged mainly to Hatton's Works or Banfield's, and the secretary taught in an evening school. He was darkly suspected of being a teetotaller, but it had never been proved against him.

Toft began to wonder if he had chosen his time well, but he was near The Butterflies and he hardened his heart; to retreat now were to dub himself coward. He told the maid that he came from the Gatehouse, and that he was directed to deliver a letter into his lordship's own hand, and in a moment he found himself mounting the shallow carpeted stairs. In comparison with the Gatehouse, the house was modern, elegant, luxurious, the passages were warm.

When he was ushered in, his lordship, a dressing-gown cast over a chair beside him as if he had just put on his coat, was writing near the fireplace. After an interval that seemed long to Toft, who eyed his heavy massiveness with a certain dismay, he laid down his pen, sat back, and looked at the servant.

"From the Gatehouse?" he asked, after a leisurely survey.

"Yes, my lord," Toft answered respectfully. "I was with Mr. Audley when he was taken ill in the Yew Walk."

"To be sure! I thought I knew your face. You've a letter for me?"

Toft hesitated. "I wished to see you, my lord," he said. The thing was not as easy as he had hoped it would be; the man was more formidable. "On a matter of business."

Audley raised his eyebrows. "Business?" he said. "Isn't it Mr. Stubbs you want to see?"

"No, my lord," Toft answered. But the sweat broke out on his forehead. What if his lordship took a high tone, ordered him out, and reported the matter to his master? Too late it struck Toft that a gentleman might take that line.

"Well, be quick," Audley replied. Then in a different tone, "You don't come from Miss Audley?"

"No, my lord."

"Then what is it?"

Toft turned his hat in his hands. "I have information"--it was with difficulty he could control his voice--"which it is to your lordship's interest to have."

There was a pregnant pause. "Oh!" the young man said at last. "And you come--to sell it?"

Toft nodded, unable to speak. Yet he was getting on as well as could be expected.

"Rather an unusual position, isn't it?"

"Yes, my lord."

"The information should be unusual?"

"It is, my lord." .

Lord Audley smiled. "Well," he answered, "I'll say this, my man. If you are going to sell me a spavined horse, don't! It will not be to your advantage. What's it all about?"

"Mr. Audley's claim, my lord."

Audley had expected this, yet he could not quite mask the effect which the statement made upon him. The thing that he had foreseen and feared, that had haunted him in the small hours and been as it were a death's-head at his feast, was taking shape. But he was quick to recover himself, and "Oh!" said he. "That's it, is it! Don't you know that that's all over, my man?"

"I think not, my lord."

The peer took up a paper-knife and toyed with it. "Well," he said, "what is it? Come, I don't buy a pig in a poke."

"Mr. Audley has found----"

"Found, eh?" raising his eyebrows.

Toft corrected himself. "He has in his power papers that upset your lordship's case. I can still enable you to keep those papers in your hands."

Audley threw down the paper-cutter. "They are certainly worthless," he said. His voice was contemptuous, but there was a hard look in his eyes.

"Mr. Audley thinks otherwise."

"But he has not seen them?"

"He knows what's in them, my lord. He has been searching for them for weeks."

The young man weighed this, and Toft's courage rose, and his confidence. The trumps were in his hand, and though for a moment he had shrunk before the other's heavy jaw he was glad now that he had come; more glad when the big man after a long pause asked quietly, "What do you want?"

"Five hundred pounds, my lord."

The other laughed, and Toft did not like the laugh. "Indeed? Five hundred pounds? That's a good deal of money!"

"The information is worth that, or it is worth nothing."

"I quite agree!" the peer answered lightly. "You're a wit, my man. But that's not saying you've a good case. However, I'll put you to the test. You know where the papers are?"

"I do, my lord."

"Very good. There's a piece of paper. Write on one side the precise place where they lie. I will write on the other a promise to pay £500 if the papers are found in that place, and are of the value you assert. That is a fair offer."

Toft stood irresolute. He thought hard.

My lord pushed the paper across. "Come!" he said; "write! Or I'll write first, if that is your trouble." With decision he seized a quill, held it poised a moment, then he wrote four lines and signed them with a flourish, added the date, and read them to himself. With a grim smile he pushed the paper across to Toft. "There," he said. "What more do you want, my man, than that?"

Toft took the paper and read what was written on it, from the "In consideration of," that began the sentence, to the firm signature "Audley of Beaudelays" that closed it. He did not speak.

"Come! You can't want anything more than that!" my lord said. "You have only to write, read me the secret, and keep the paper until it is redeemed."

"Yes, my lord."

"Then take the pen. Of course the place must be precise. I am not going to pull down Beaudelays House to find a box of papers that I do not believe is there!"

Toft's face was gray, the sweat stood on his lip. "I did not say," he muttered, the paper rustling in his unsteady hand, "that they were in Beaudelays House."

"No?" Audley replied. "Perhaps not. And for the matter of that, it is not a question of saying anything. It is a question of writing. You can write, I suppose?"

Toft did not speak. He could not speak. He had supposed that the power to put his lordship on the scent would be the same as pulling down the fox. When he had said that the papers were in the house, that they were behind a wall, that Mr. Audley knew where they were, he would have earned--he thought--his money!

But he had not known the man with whom he had to deal. And challenged to set down the place where the papers lay, he knew that he could not do it. In the house? Behind a wall? He saw now that that would not do. That would not satisfy the big smiling gentleman who sat opposite him, amused at the dilemma in which he found himself.

He knew that he was cornered, and he lost his countenance and his manners. He swore.

The young man laughed. "The biter bit," he said. "Five hundred pounds you said, didn't you? I wonder whether I ought to send for the constable? Or tell Mr. Audley? That would be wiser perhaps? What do you think you deserve, my man?"

Toft stretched out a shaking arm towards the paper. But my lord was before him. His huge hand fell on it. He tore it across and across, and threw the pieces under the table.

"No," he said, "that won't do! You will write at a venture and if you are right you will claim the money, and if you are wrong you will have this paper to show that I bargained with you. But I never meant to bargain with you, my good rascal. I knew you were a fraud. I knew it from the beginning. And now I've only one thing to say. Either you will tell me freely what you know, and in that case I shall say nothing. Or I report you to your master. That's my last word."

Toft shook from head to foot. He had done a hateful thing, he had been defeated, and exposure threatened him. As far as his master was concerned he could face it. But his wife, his daughter? Who thought him honest, loyal, who thought him a man! Who believed in him! How could he, how would he face them, if this tale were told?

My lord saw the change in him, saw how he shrank, and, smiling, he fancied that he had the man in his grasp, fancied that he would tell what he knew, and tell it for nothing. And twice Toft opened his lips to speak, and twice no words came. For at the last moment, in this strait, what there was of good in him--and there was good--rose up, and had the better; had the better, reinforced perhaps by his hatred of the heavy smiling face that gloated upon him.

For at the last moment, "No, my lord," he said desperately, "I'll not speak. I'm d--d if I do! You may do what you like."

And before his lordship, taken by surprise, could interpose, the servant had turned and made for the door. He was half-way down the stairs before the other had risen from his seat. He had escaped. He was clear for the time, and safe in the road he breathed more freely. But he had gone a hundred yards on his way before he remarked that he was in the open air, or bethought himself to put on his hat.

CHAPTER XXII: MY LORD SPEAKS

For a few moments Audley had certainly hoped that he was going to learn all that Toft knew, and to learn it for nothing. He had been baulked in this. But when he came to think over the matter he was not ill content with himself, nor with his conduct of the interview. He had dealt with the matter with presence of mind, and in the only safe way; and he had taught the man a lesson. "He knows by this time," he reflected, "that if I am a lord, I am not a fool!"

But this mood did not last long, and it was succeeded by one less cheerful. The death's-head had never been wanting at his feast. The family tradition which had come down to him with his blood had never ceased to haunt him, and in the silence of the night he had many a time heard John Audley at work seeking for the means to displace him. Even the great empty house had seemed to mock his pretensions.

But until the last month his fears had been vague and shadowy, and in his busy hours he had laughed at them. He was Lord Audley, he sat, he voted, the doors of White's, of Almack's were open to him. In town he was a personage, in the country a divinity still hedged him, no tradesman spoke to him save hat in hand. Then, lately, the traces which he had found in the Great House had given a shape to his fears; and within the last hour he had learned their solidity. Sane or mad, John Audley was upon his track, bent upon displacing him, bent upon ruining him; and this very day the man might be laying his hand upon the thing he needed.

Audley did not doubt the truth of Toft's story. It confirmed his fears only too well; and the family tradition--that too weighed with him. He sat for a long time staring before him, then, uneasy and restless, he rose and paced the floor. He went to and fro, to and fro, until by-and-by he came to a stand before one of the windows. He drummed with his fingers on the glass. There was one way, certainly. Stubbs had said so, and Stubbs was right. There was one way, if he could make up his mind to the limitations it would impose upon him. If he could make up his mind to be a poor man.

The window at which he stood looked on a road of quiet dignity, a little removed from the common traffic of the town. But the windows, looking sideways, commanded also a more frequented thoroughfare which crossed this street. His thoughts far away and sombrely engaged, the young man watched the stream of passers, as it trickled across the distant opening.

Suddenly his eyes recalled his mind to the present. He started, turned, in three strides he was beside the hearth. He rang the bell twice, the signal for his man. He waited impatiently.

"My hat and coat!" he cried to the servant. "Quick, I'm in a hurry!" Like most men who have known vicissitudes he had a superstitious side, and the figure which he had seen pass across the end of the road had appeared so aptly, so timely, had had so much the air of an answer to his doubts that he took it for an inspiration.

He ran down the stairs, but he knew that his comings and goings were marked, and once outside the house he controlled his impatience. He walked slowly, humming a tune and swaying his cane, and it was a very stately gentleman taking the air and acknowledging with courtesy the respectful salutations of the passers, who came on Mary Audley as she turned from Dr. Pepper's door in the High Street.

He stood. "Miss Audley!" he cried.

Mary was flushed with exercise, ruffled by the wind, travel-stained. But she would have cared little for these things if she could have governed the blood that rose to her cheeks at his sudden appearance. To mask her confusion she rushed into speech.

"You cannot be more surprised than I am," she said. "My uncle is not so well to-day, and in a panic about his medicine. Toft, who should have come in to town to fetch it, was not to be found, so I had to come."

"And you have walked in?"

Smiling, she showed him her boots. "And I am presently going to walk out," she said.

"You will never do it?"

"Before dark? No, perhaps not!" She raised her hand and put back a tress of hair which had strayed from its fellows. "And I shall be tired. But I shall be much surprised if I cannot walk ten miles at a pinch."

"I shall be surprised if you walk ten miles to-day," he retorted. "My plans for you are quite different. Have you got what you came to fetch?"

She had steadied herself, and was by this time at her ease. She made a little grimace. "No," she said. "It will not be ready for quarter of an hour."

He rang Dr. Pepper's bell. An awestruck apprentice, who had watched the interview through the dusty window of the surgery, showed himself.

"Be good enough to send the medicine for Miss Audley to Mrs. Jenkinson's," Audley said. "You understand?"

"Yes, my lord! Certainly, my lord!" She was going to protest. He turned to her, silenced her. "And now I take possession of you," he said, supremely careless what the lad heard. "You are coming to The Butterflies to take tea, or sherry, or whatever you take when you have walked five miles."

"Oh, Lord Audley!"

"And then I am going to drive you as far as the old Cross, and walk up the hill with you--as far as I choose."

"Oh, but I cannot!" Mary cried, coloring charmingly, but whether with pleasure or embarrassment she could not tell. She only knew that his ridiculous way of taking possession of her, the very masterfulness of it, moved her strangely. "I cannot indeed. What would my uncle say?"

"I don't know, and I don't care!" he replied, swinging his walking cane, and smiling as he towered above her.

"He may go hang--for once!"

She hesitated. "It is very good of you," she said. "I confess I did not look forward to the walk back. But----"

"There is no--but," he replied. "And no walk back! It is arranged. It is time--" his eyes dwelt kindly on her as she turned with him--"it is time that some one took it in hand to arrange things for you. Five miles in and five miles out over dirty roads on a winter afternoon--and Miss Audley! No, no! And now--this way, please!"

She yielded, she could not tell why, except that it was difficult to resist him, and not unpleasant to obey him. And after all, why should she not go with him? She had been feeling fagged and tired, depressed, moreover, by her uncle's fears. The low-lying fields, the town, the streets, all dingy under a gray autumn sky, had given her no welcome.

And her thoughts, too, had been dun-colored. She had felt very lonely the last few days, doubtful of the future, without aim, hipped. And now in a moment all seemed changed. She was no longer alone, nor fearful. The streets were no longer dingy nor dreary. There were still pleasant things in the world, kindness, and thought for others, and friendship and--and tea and cake! Was it wonderful that as she walked along beside my lord her spirits rose? That she felt an unaccountable relief, and in the reaction of the moment smiled and sparkled more than her wont? That the muddy brick pavement, the low-browed shops, the leafless trees all seemed brighter than before, and that even the butcher's stall became almost a thing of beauty?

And he responded famously. He swung his stick, he laughed, he was gay. "Don't pretend!" he said. "I see that you were glad enough to meet me!"

"And the tea and cake!" she replied. "After five miles who would not be glad to meet them?"

"Exactly! It is my belief that if I had not met you, you would have fallen by the way. You want some one to look after you, Miss Audley." The name was a caress.

Nor was the pleasure all their own. Great was the excitement of the townsfolk as they passed. "His lordship and a young lady?" cried half Riddsley, running to the windows. "Quick, or you will miss them!" Some wondered who she could be; more had seen her at church and could answer. "Miss Audley? The young lady who had come to live at the Gatehouse? Indeed! You don't say so?" For every soul in Riddsley, over twelve years old, was versed in the Audley history, knew all about the suit, and could tell off the degrees of kindred as easily as they could tell the distance from the Audley Arms to the Portcullis. "Mr. Peter Audley's daughter who lived in Paris? Lady-in-waiting to a Princess. And now walking with his lordship as if she had known him all her life! What would Mr. John say? D'you see how gay he looks! Not a bit what he is when he speaks to us! Wonder whether there's anything in it!" And so on, and so on, with tit-bits from the history of Mary's father, and choice eccentricities from the life of John Audley.

Mrs. Jenkinson's amazement, as she espied them coming up the path to the house, was a thing by itself. It was such that she set her door ajar that she might see them pass through the hall. She was all of a twitter, she said afterwards. And poor Jane and poor Sarah--who were out! What a miss they were having! It was not thrice in the twelve months that his lordship brought a lady to the house.

A greater miss, indeed, it turned out, than she thought. For to her gratification Lord Audley tapped at her door. He pushed it open. "Mrs. Jenkinson," he said pleasantly, "this is my cousin, Miss Audley, who is good enough to take a cup of your excellent tea with me, if you will make it. She has walked in from the Gatehouse."

Mrs. Jenkinson was a combination of an eager, bright-eyed bird and a stout, short lady in dove-colored silk--if such a thing can be imagined; and the soul of good-nature. She took Mary by both hands, beamed upon her, and figuratively took her to her bosom. "A little cake and wine, my dear," she chirruped. "After a long walk! And then tea. To be sure, my dear! I knew your father, Mr. Peter Audley, a dear, good gentleman. You would like to wash your hands? Yes, my dear! Not that you are not--and his lordship will wait for us upstairs. Yes, there's a step. I knew your father, to be sure, to be sure. A new brush, my dear. And now will you let me--not that your sweet face needs any ornament! Yes, I talk too much--but, there, my love, when you are as old--- -"

She was a simple soul, and because her tongue rarely stopped she might have been thought to see nothing. But women, unlike men, can do two things at once, and little escaped her twinkling spectacles. As she told her sister later, "My dear, I saw it was spoons from the first. She sparkled all over, bless her innocent heart! And he, if she had been a duchess, could not have waited on her more elegant--well, elegantly, Sally, if you like, but we can't all talk like you. They thought, the dear creatures, that I saw nothing; but once he said something too low for me to hear and she looked up at him, and her pretty eyes were like stars. And he looked--well, Sally, I could not tell you how he looked!"

"I am not sure that it would be proper," the spinster demurred.

"Ah, well, it was as pretty a thing as you'd wish to see," the good creature ran on, drumming with her fingers on the lap of her silk gown. "And she, bless her, I dare say she was all of a twitter, but she didn't show it. No airs or graces either--but there, an Audley has no need! Why, God bless me, I said something about the Princess and what company she must have seen, and what a change for her, and she up and said--I am sure I loved her for it!--that she had been no more than a governess! My dear, an Audley a governess! I fancied my lord wasn't quite pleased, and very natural! But when a man is spoons----"

"My dear sister!"

"Vulgar? Well, perhaps so, I know I run on, but gentle or simple, they're the same when they're in love! And Jane will be glad to hear that she took two pieces of the sultana and two cups of tea, and he watching every piece she put in her mouth, and she coloring up, once or twice, so that it did my heart good to see them, the pretty dears. Jane will be pleased. And there might have been nothing but seed cake in the house. I shall remember more presently, but I was in such a twitter!"

"What did she call him?" Miss Sarah asked.

"To be sure, my dear, that was what I was going to tell you! I listened, and not a single thing did she call him. But once, when he gave her some cake, I heard him call her Mary, for all the world as if it was a bit of sugar in his mouth. And there came a kind of quiver over her pretty face, and she looked at her plate as much as to say it was a new thing. And I said to myself 'Philip and Mary'--out of the old school-books you know, but who they were I don't remember. But it's my opinion," Mrs. Jenkinson continued, rubbing her nose with the end of her spectacles, "that he had spoken just before they came in, Sally."

"You don't say so?" Sarah cried.

"If you ask me, there was a kind of softness about them both! Law, when I think what you and

Jane missed through going to that stupid Institute! I am sure you'll never forgive yourselves!"

The good lady had not missed much herself, but she was mistaken in thinking that the two had come to an understanding. Indeed when, leaving the warmth of her presence behind them, they drove out of town, with the servant seated with folded arms behind them and Mary snugly tucked in beside my lord, a new constraint began to separate them. The excitement of the meeting had waned, the fillip of the unwonted treat had lost its power. A depression for which she could not account beset Mary as they rolled through the dull outskirts and faced the flat mistridden pastures and the long lines of willows. On his side doubt held him silent. He had found it pleasant to come to the brink, he had not been blind to Mary's smiles and her rare blushes. But the one step farther--that could not be re-trodden, and it was in the nature of the man to hesitate at the last, and to consider if he were getting full value.

So, as they drove through the dusk, now noiselessly over sodden leaves, now drumming along the hard road, the hint of a chill fell between them. Mary's thoughts went forward to the silent house and the lonely rooms, and she chid herself for ingratitude. She had had her pleasure, she had had an unwonted treat. What was wrong with her? What more did she want?

It was nearly dark, and not many words had passed when Lord Audley pulled up the horses at the old Cross. The man leapt down and was going to help Mary to alight, when his master bade him take the box-seat and the reins.

Mary remonstrated. "Oh, don't get down, please!" she cried. "Please! It is nothing to the house from here."

"It is half a mile if it is a yard," he said. "And it is nearly dark. I am going with you." He bade the man walk the horses up and down.

She ventured another protest, but he put it aside. He threw back the rug and lifted her down. For a moment he stamped about and stretched himself. Then "Come, Mary," he said. It was an order.

She knew then what was at hand. And though she had a minute before looked forward with regret to the parting, all her thought now was how she might escape to the Gatehouse. It became a refuge. Her heart, as she started to walk beside him, beat so quickly that she could not speak. She was thankful that it was dark, and that he could not read her agitation in her face.

He did not speak himself for some minutes. Then "Mary," he said abruptly, looking straight before him, "I am rather one for taking than asking, and that stands in my way now. When I've wanted a thing I've generally taken it. Now I want a thing I can't take--without asking. And I feel that I'm not good at the asking. But I want it badly, and I must do the best I can. I love you, Mary. I love you, and I want you for my wife."

She could not find a word. When he went on his tone was lower.

"I'm rather a lonely man," he said. "You didn't know that, or think it? But it is true. And such an hour as we have spent to-day is not mine often. It lies with you to say if I am going to have more of them. I might tell you with truth that I haven't much to offer my wife. That if I am Audley of Beaudelays, I am the poorest Audley that ever was. That my wife will be no great lady, and will step into no golden shoes. The butterflies are moths, Mary, nowadays, and if I am ever to be much she will have to help me. But I will tell no lies, my dear!" He turned to her then and stopped; and perforce, though her knees trembled, she had to stand also, and face him as he looked down at her. "I am not going to pretend that what I have to offer isn't enough. For you are lonely like me; you have no one but John Audley to look to, and I am big enough and strong enough to take care of you. And I will take care of you--if you will let me. If you will say the word, Mary?"

He loomed above her in the darkness. He seemed already to possess her. She tried to think, tried to ask herself if she loved him, if she loved him enough; but the fancy for him which she had had from the beginning, that and his masterfulness swept her irresistibly towards him. She was lonely--more lonely than ever of late, and to whom was she to look? Who else had been as good to her, as kind to her, as thoughtful for her, as he who now wooed her so honestly, who offered her all he had to offer? She hesitated, and he saw that she hesitated.

"Come, we've got to have this out," he said bluntly. And he put his hand on her shoulder. "We stand alone, both of us, you and I. We're the last of the old line, and I want you for my wife, Mary! With you I can do something, with you I believe that I can make something of my life! Without you--but there, if you say no, I won't take it! I won't take it, and I am going to have you, if not to-day, to-morrow, and if not to-morrow, the next day! Make no mistake about that!"

She tried to fence with him. "I have not a penny," she faltered.

"I don't ask you for a penny."

Her instinct was still to escape. "You are Lord Audley," she said, "and I am a poor relation. Won't you--don't you think that you will repent presently!"

"That's my business! If that be all--if there's no one else----"

"No, there's no one else," she admitted. "But----"

"But be hanged!" he cried. "If there's no one else you are mine." And he passed his arm round her.

For a moment she stepped back. "No!" she protested, raising her hands to push him off. "Please--please let me think."

He let her be, for already he knew that he had won; and perhaps in his own mind he was beginning to doubt the wisdom of the step. "My uncle? Have you thought of him?" she asked. "What will he say?"

"I have not thought of him," he cried grandly, "and I am not going to think of him. I am thinking, my dear, only of you. Do you love me?"

She stood silent, gazing at him.

"Don't play with me!" he said. "I've a right to an answer."

"I think I do," she said softly. "Yes--I think--no, wait; that is not all."

"It is all."

"No," between laughing and crying. "You are not giving me time. I want to think. You are carrying me by storm, sir."

"And a good way, too!" he rejoined. Then she did let him take her, and for a few seconds she was in his arms. He crushed her to him, she felt all the world turning. But before he found her lips, the crack of a whip startled them, the creak of a wheel sliding round the corner warned them, she slipped from his arms.

"You little wretch!" he said.

Breathless, hardly knowing what she felt, or what storm shook her, she could not speak. The wagon came creaking past them, the driver clinging to the chain of the slipper. When it was gone by she found her voice. "It shall be as you will," she said, and her tone thrilled him. "But I want to think. It has been so sudden, I am frightened. I am frightened, and--yes, I think I am happy. But please to let me go now. I am safe here--in two minutes I shall be at home."

He tried to keep her, but "Let me go now," she pleaded. "Later it shall be as you wish--always as you wish. But let me go now."

He gave way then. He said a few words while he held her hands, and he said them very well. Then he let her go. Before the dusk hid her she turned and waved her hand, and he waved his. He stood, listening. He heard the sound of her footsteps grow fainter and fainter as she climbed the hill, until they were lost in the rustle of the wind through the undergrowth. At last he turned and trudged down the hill.

"Well, I've done it," he muttered presently. "And Uncle John may find what he likes, damn him! After all, she's handsome enough to turn any man's head, and it makes me safe! But I'll go slow. I'll go slow now. There's no hurry."

CHAPTER XXIII: BLORE UNDER WEAVER

Gratitude and liking, and the worship of strength which is as natural in a woman as the worship of beauty in a man, form no bad imitation of love, and often pass into love as imperceptibly as the brook becomes a river. The morning light brought Mary no repentance. Misgivings she had, as what lover has not, were the truth told. Was her love as perfect as Etruria's, as unselfish, as absorbing? She doubted. But in all honesty she hoped that it might become so; and when she dwelt on the man who had done so much for her, and thought so well for her, who had so much to offer and made so little of the offering, her heart swelled with gratitude, and if she did not love she fancied that she did.

So much was changed for her! She had wondered more than once what would happen to her, if her uncle died. That fear was put from her. Toft--she had been vexed with Toft. How small a matter that seemed now! And Peter Basset? He had been kind to her, and a pang did pierce her heart on his account. But he had recovered very quickly, she reflected. He had shown himself cold enough and distant enough at his last visit! And then she smiled as she thought how differently her new lover had assailed her, with what force, what arrogance, what insistence--and yet with a force and arrogance and insistence to which it was pleasant to yield.

She did not with all this forget that she would be Lady Audley, she, whose past had been so precarious, whose prospects had been so dark, whose fate it might have been to travel through life an obscure teacher! She had not been woman if she had not thought of this; nor if she had failed, when she thought of it, to breathe a prayer for the gallant lover who had found her and saved her, and had held it enough that she was an Audley. He might have chosen far and wide. He had chosen her.

No wonder that Mrs. Toft saw a change in her. "Law, Miss," she remarked, when she came in to remove the breakfast. "One would think a ten-mile walk was the making of you! It's put a color into your cheeks that would shame a June rose! And to be sure," with a glance at the young lady's plate, "not much eaten either!"

"I am not hungry, Mrs. Toft," Mary said meekly. "I drove back to the foot of the hill."

"And I'd like to sort Toft for it! Ifs he who should have gone! He's upstairs now, keeping out of my way, and that grim and gray you'd think he'd seen a ghost! And 'Truria, silly girl, she's all of a quiver this morning. It's 'Mother, let me do this!' and 'Mother, I'll do that!' all because her reverend--not, as I tell her, that aught will ever come of it--has got a roof over his head at last."

"But that's good news! Has Mr. Colet got some work?"

"Not he, the silly man! Nor likely! There's mighty little work for them as go against the gentry. For what he's got he's to thank Mr. Basset."

"Mr. Basset."

"To be sure," Mrs. Toft answered, with a covert glance at the girl, "why not, Miss? Some talk and the wind goes by. There's plenty of those. And some say naught but do--and that's Mr. Basset. He's took in Mr. Colet till he can find a church. Etruria's that up about it, I tell her, smile before breakfast and sweat before night. And so she'll find it, I warrant!"

"It is very good of Mr. Basset," Mary said gravely. And then, "Is that some one knocking, Mrs. Toft?"

"It's well to have young ears!" Mrs. Toft took out the tray, and returned with a letter. "It's for you, Miss," she said. "The postman's late this morning, but cheap's a slow traveller. When a letter was a letter and cost ninepence it came to hand like a gentleman!"

Mary waited to hear no more. She knew the handwriting, and as quickly as she could she escaped from the room. No one with any claim to taste used an envelope in those days, and to open a letter so that no rent might mar its fairness called for a care which she could not exercise in public.

Alone, in her room, she opened it, and her eyes grew serious as they travelled down the page, which bore signs of haste.

"Sweetheart," it began, and she thought that charming, "I do not ask if you reached the Gatehouse safely, for I listened and I must have heard, if harm befel you. I drove home as happy as a king, and grieved only that I had not had that of you which I had a right to have--damn that carter! This troubles me the more as I shall not see you again for a time, and if this does not disappoint you too, you're a deceiver! My plans are altered by to-day's news that Peel returns to office. In any event, I had to go to Seabourne's for Christmas, now I must be there for a meeting to-morrow and go from there to London on the same business. You would not have me desert my post, I am sure? Heaven knows how long I may be kept, possibly a fortnight, possibly more. But the moment I can I shall be with you.

"Write to me at the Brunswick Hôtel, Dover Street. Sweetheart, I am yours, as you, my darling, are

"Philip's.

"P. S.--I must put off any communication to your uncle till I can see him. So for the moment, mum!"

Mary read the letter twice; the first time with eager eyes, the second time more calmly. Nothing was more natural, she told herself, than that her spirits should sink--Philip was gone. The walk with him, the talk which was to bring them nearer, and to make them better known to one another, stood over. The day that was to be so bright was clouded.

But beyond this the letter itself fell a little, a very little, short of her expectations. The beginning was charming! But after that--was it her fancy, or was her lover's tone a little flippant, a little free, a little too easy? Did it lack that tender note of reassurance, that chivalrous thought for her, which she had a right to expect in a first letter? She was not sure.

And as to her uncle. She must, of course, be guided by her lover, his will must be her law now; and it was reasonable that in John Audley's state of health the mode of communication should be carefully weighed. But she longed to be candid, she longed to be open; and in regard to one person she would be open. Basset had let her see that her treatment had cured him. At their last meeting he had been cold, almost unkind; he had left her to deal with Toft as she could. Still she owed him, if any one, the truth, and, were it only to set herself right in her own eyes, she must tell him. If the news did nothing else it would open the way for his return to the Gatehouse, and the telling would enable her to make the amende.

The letter was not written on that day nor the next. But on the fourth day after Audley's departure it arrived at Blore, and lay for an hour on the dusty hall table amid spuds and powder-flasks and old itineraries. There Mr. Colet found it and another letter, and removed the two for safety to the parlor, where litter of a similar kind struggled for the upper hand with piles of books and dog's-eared Quarterlies. The decay of the Bassets dated farther back than the decline of the Audleys, and the gabled house under the shadow of Weaver was little better, if something larger, than a farm-house. There had been a library, but Basset had taken the best books to the Gatehouse. And there were in the closed drawing-room, and in some of the bedrooms, old family portraits, bad for the most part; the best lay in marble in Blore Church. But in the parlor, which was the living-room, hung only paintings of fat oxen and prize sheep; and the garden which ran up to the walls of the house, and in summer was a flood of color, lay in these days dank and lifeless, ebbing away from bee-skips and chicken-coops. The park had been ploughed during the great war, and now pined in thin pasture. The whole of the valley was still Basset land, but undrained in the bottom and light on the slopes, it made no figure in a rent-roll. The present owner had husbanded the place, and paid off charges, and cleared the estate, but he had been able to do no more. The place was a poor man's place, though for miles round men spoke to the owner bareheaded. He was "Basset of Blore," as much a part of Staffordshire as Burton Bridge or the Barbeacon. The memories of the illiterate are long.

He had been walking the hill that morning with a dog and a gun, and between yearnings for the woman he loved, and longings for some plan of life, some object, some aim, he was in a most unhappy mood. At one moment he saw himself growing old, without the energy to help himself or others, still toying with trifles, the last and feeblest of his blood. At another he thought of Mary, and saw her smiling through the flowering hawthorn, or bending over a book with the firelight on her hair. Or again, stung by the lash of her reproaches he tried to harden himself to do something. Should he take the land into his own hands, and drain and fence and breed stock and be of use, were it only as a struggling farmer in his own district? Or should he make that plunge into public life to which Colonel Mottisfont had urged him and from which he shrank as a shivering man shrinks from an icy bath?

For there was the rub. Mary was right. He was a dreamer, a weakling, one in whom the strong pulse that had borne his forbears to the front beat but feebly. He was not equal to the hard facts of life. With what ease had Audley, whenever they had stood foot to foot, put him in the second place, got the better of him, outshone him!

Old Don pointed in vain. His master shot nothing, for he walked for the most part with his eyes on the turf. If he raised them it was to gaze at the hamlet lying below him in the valley, the old house, the ring of buildings and cottages, the church that he loved--and that like the woman he loved, reproached him with his inaction.

About two o'clock he turned homewards. How many more days would he will and not will, and end night by night where he had begun? In the main he was of even temper, but of late small things tried him, and when he entered the parlor and Colet rose at his entrance, he could not check his irritation.

"For heaven's sake, man, sit still!" he cried. "And don't get up every time I come in! And don't look at me like a dog! And don't ask me if I want the book you are reading!"

The curate stared, and muttered an apology. It was true that he did not wear the chain of obligation with grace.

"No, it is I who am sorry!" Basset replied, quickly repenting. "I am a churlish ass! Get up when you like, and say what you like! But if you can, make yourself at home!"

Then he saw the two letters lying on the table. He knew Mary's writing at a glance, and he let it lie, his face twitching. He took up the other, made as if he would open it, then he threw it back again, and took Mary's to the window, where he could read it unwatched.

It was short.

"Dear Mr. Basset," she wrote, "I should be paying you a poor compliment if I pretended that what I am writing will not pain you. But I hope, and since our last meeting, I have reason to believe that that pain will not be lasting.

"My cousin, Lord Audley, has asked me to marry him, and I have consented. Nothing beyond this is fixed, and no announcement will be made until my uncle has recovered his strength. But I feel that I owe it to you to let you know this at once.

"I owe you something more. You crowned your kindness by doing me a great honor. I could not reply in substance otherwise than I did, but for the foolish criticisms of an inexperienced girl, I ask you to believe that I feel deep regret.

"When we meet I hope that we may meet as friends. If I can believe this it will add something to the happiness of my engagement. My uncle is better, but little stronger than when you saw him.

"I am, truly yours,

"Mary Audley."

He stood looking at it for a long time, and only by an effort could he control the emotion that strove to master him. Then his thoughts travelled to the other, the man who had won her, the man who had got the better of him from the first, who had played the Jacob from the moment of their meeting on the steamer; and a passion of jealousy swept him away. He swore aloud.

Mr. Colet leapt in his chair. "Mr. Basset!" he cried. And then, in a different tone, "You have bad news, I fear?"

The other laughed bitterly. "Bad news?" he repeated, and Colet saw that his face was white and that the letter shook in his hand. "The Government's out, and that's bad news. The pig's ill, and that's bad news. Your mother's dead, and that's bad news!"

"Swearing makes no news better," Colet said mildly.

"Not even the pig? If your--if Etruria died, and some one told you that she was dead, you wouldn't swear? You wouldn't curse God?"

"God forbid!" the clergyman cried in horror.

"What would you do then?"

"Try so to live, Mr. Basset, that we might meet again!"

"Rubbish, man!" Basset retorted rudely. "Try instead not to be a prig!"

"If I could be of use?"

"You cannot, nor any one else," Basset answered. "There, say no more. The worst is over. We've played our little part and--what's the odds how we played it?"

"Much when the curtain falls," the poor clergyman ventured.

"Well, I'll go and eat something. Hunger is one more grief!" And Basset went out.

He came back ten minutes later, pale but quiet. "Sorry, Colet," he said. "Very rude, I am afraid! I had bad news, but I am right now. Wasn't there another letter for me?"

He found the letter and read it listlessly. He tossed it across the table to his guest. "News is plentiful to-day," he said.

Colet took the letter and read it. It was from a Mr. Hatton, better known to him than to Basset, and the owner of one of the two small factories in Riddsley. It was an invitation to contest the borough in opposition to young Mottisfont.

"If it were a question, respected sir," Hatton wrote, "of Whigs and Tories we should not approach you. But as the result must depend upon the proportions in which the Tory party splits for and against Sir Robert Peel upon the Corn Laws, we, who are in favor of repeal, recognize the advantage of being represented by a moderate Tory. The adherence to Sir Robert of Sir James Graham in the North and of Lord Lincoln in the Midlands proves that there are landowners who place their country before their rents, and it is in the hope that you, sir, are of the number that we invite you to give us that assistance which your ancient name must afford.

"We are empowered to promise you the support of the Whig party in the borough, conditioned only upon your support of the repeal of the Corn Laws, leaving you free on other points. The Audley influence has been hitherto paramount, but we believe that the time has come to free the borough from the last remnant of the Feudal system.

"A deputation will wait upon you to give you such assurances as you may desire. But as Parliament meets on an early date, and the present member may at once apply for the Chiltern Hundreds, we shall be glad to have your answer before the New Year."

"Well?" Basset asked. "What do you think?"

"It opens a wide door."

"If you wish to have your finger pinched," Basset replied, flippantly, "it does. I don't know that it is an opening to anything else." And as Colet refrained from speaking, "You don't think," he went on, "that it's a way into Parliament? A repealer has as much chance of getting in for Riddsley against the Audley interest as you have of being an archdeacon! Of course the Radicals want a fight if they can find a man fool enough to spend his money. But as for winning, they don't dream of it."

"It is better to lose in some causes than to win in others."

Basset laughed. "Do you know why they have come to me? They think that I shall carry John Audley with me and divide the Audley interest. There's nothing in it, but that's the notion."

"Why look at the seamy side?" Colet objected. "I suppose there always is one, but I don't think that it was at that side Sir Robert looked when he made up his mind to put the country first and his party second! I don't think that it was at that side he looked when he determined to eat his words and pocket his pride, rather than be responsible for famine in Ireland! Believe me, Mr. Basset," the clergyman continued earnestly, "it was no easy change of opinion. Before he came to that resolution, proud, cold man as I am told he is, many a sight and sound must have knocked at the door of his mind; a scene of poverty he passed in his carriage, a passage in some report, a speech through which he seemed to sleep, a begging letter--one by one they pressed the door inwards, till at last, with--it may be with misery, he came to see what he must do!"

"Possibly."

"The call came, he had to answer it. Here is a call to you."

"And do you think," the other retorted, "that I can answer it more cheaply than Sir Robert? So far as I have thought it out, I am with him. But do you think I could do this," he tapped the letter, "without misery--of a different kind it may be? I am not a public man, I have served no apprenticeship to it, I've not addressed a meeting three times in my life, I don't know what I should say or how I should say it. And for Hatton and his friends, they would rub me up a dozen times a day."

"Non sine pulvere!" Mr. Colet murmured.

"Dust enough there'll be! I don't doubt that. And dirt. But there's another thing." He paused, and turning, knocked the fire together. He was nearly a minute about it, while the other waited. "There's another thing," he repeated. "I am not going into this business to pay out a private grudge, and I want to be clear that I am not doing that. And I'm not going into this simply for what I can get out of it. Ambition is a poor stayer with me, a washy chestnut. It would not carry me through, Colet. If I go into this, it will be because I believe in it. It seems as if I were preaching," he continued awkwardly. "But there's nothing but belief will carry me through, and unless I am clear--I'll not start. I'll not start, although I want to make a fresh start badly! Devilish badly, if you'll excuse me!"

"And how will you----"

"Make certain? I don't know. I must fight it out by myself--go up on the hill and think it out. I must believe in the thing, or I must leave it alone!"

"Just so," said Mr. Colet. And prudent for once he said no more.

CHAPTER XXIV: AN AGENT OF THE OLD SCHOOL

It is doubtful if even the great Reform Bill of '32, which shifted the base of power from the upper to the middle class, awoke more bitter feelings that did the volte face of Peel in the winter of '45. Since the days of Pitt no statesman had enjoyed the popularity or wielded the power which had been Sir Robert's when he had taken office four years before. He had been more than the leader of the Tory party; he had been its re-creator. He had been more than the leader of the landed interest; he had been its pride. Men who believed that upon the welfare of that interest rested the stability of the constitution, men with historic names had walked on his right hand and on his left, had borne his train and carried his messages. All things, his origin, his formality, his pride, his quiet domestic life, even his moderation, had been forgiven in the man who had guided the Tories through the bad days, had led them at last to power, and still stood between them and the mutterings of this new industrial England, that hydra-like threatened and perplexed them.

And then--he had betrayed them. Suddenly, some held; in a panic, scared by God knows what bugbear! Coldly and deliberately, said others, spreading his treachery over years, laughing in his sleeve as he led them to the fatal edge. Those who took the former view made faint excuse for him, and perhaps still clung to him. Those who held the latter thought no price too high, no sacrifice too costly, no effort too great, if they could but punish the traitor! If they could but pillory him for all to see.

So, in a moment, in the autumn of '45, as one drop of poison will cloud the fairest water, the face of public life was changed. Bitterness was infused into it, friend was parted from friend and son from father, the oldest alliances were dissolved. Men stood gaping, at a loss whither to turn and whom to trust. Many who had never in all their lives made up their own minds were forced to have an opinion and choose a side; and as that process is to some men as painful as a labor to a woman, the effect was to embitter things farther. How could one who for years past had cursed Cobden in all companies, and in moments of relaxation had drunk to a "Bloody War and a Wet Harvest," turn round and join the Manchester School? It could be done, it was done, but with what a rending of bleeding sinews only the sufferers knew!

Strange to say, few gave weight to Sir Robert's plea of famine in Ireland. Still more strange, when events bore out his alarm, when in the course of a year or two a quarter of a million in that unhappy country died of want, public feeling changed little. Those who had remained with him, stood with him still. Those who had banded themselves against him, held their ground. Only a handful allowed that he was honest, after all. Nor was it until he, who rode his horse like a sack, had died like a demi-god, with a city hanging on his breath, and weeping women filling all the streets about the house, that the traitor became the patriot.

But this is to anticipate. In December of '45, few men believed in famine. Few thought much of dearth. The world was angry, blood was hot, many dreamt of vengeance. Meantime Manchester exulted, and Coal, Iron, Cotton toasted Peel. But even they marvelled that the man who had been chosen to support the Corn Laws had the courage to repeal them!

Upon no one in the whole country did the news fall with more stunning effect than upon poor

Stubbs at Riddsley. He had suspected Peel. He had disliked his measures, and doubted whither he was moving. He had even on the occasion of his resignation predicted that Sir Robert would support the repeal; but he had not thought worse of him than that, and the event left him not uncertain, nor under any stress as to making up his mind, but naked, as it were, in an east wind. He felt older. He owned that his generation was passing. He numbered the friends he had left and found them few. And though he continued to assert that no man had ever pitted himself against the land whom the land had not broken, doubt began to creep into his mind. There were hours when he foresaw the end of the warm farming days, of game and sport, of Horn and Corn, ay, and of the old toast, "The farmer's best friend--the landlord," to which he had replied at many an audit dinner.

One thing remained--the Riddsley election. He found some comfort in that. He drew some pleasure from the thought that Sir Robert might do what he pleased at Tamworth, he might do what he pleased in the Cabinet, in the Commons--there were toadies and turn-coats everywhere; but Riddsley would have none of him! Riddsley would remain faithful! Stubbs steeped himself in the prospect of the election, and in preparations for it. A dozen times a day he thanked his stars that the elder Mottisfont's weakness for Peel had provided this opening for his energies.

Not that even on this ground he was quite happy. There was a little bitter in the cup. He hardly owned it to himself, he did not dream of whispering it to others, but at the bottom of his mind he had ever so faint a doubt of his employer. A hint dropped here, a word there, a veiled question-- he could not say which of these had given him the notion that his lordship hung between two opinions, and even--no wonder that Stubbs dared not whisper it to others--was weighing which would pay him best!

Such a thought was treason, however, and Stubbs buried it and trampled on it, before he went jauntily into the snug little meeting at the Audley Arms, which he had summoned to hear the old member's letter read and to accept the son as a candidate in his father's place. Those whom the agent had called were few and trusty; young Mottisfont himself, the rector and Dr. Pepper, Bagenal the maltster, Hogg the saddler, Musters the landlord, the "Duke" from the Leasows (which was within the borough), and two other tradesmen. Stubbs had no liking for big meetings. He had been bred up to believe that speeches were lost labor, and if they must be made should be made at the Market Ordinary.

At such a gathering as this he was happy. He had the strings in his own hands. The work to be done was at his fingers' ends. At this table he was as great a man as my lord. With young Mottisfont, who was by way of being a Bond Street dandy, solemn, taciturn, and without an opinion of his own, he was not likely to have trouble. The rector was enthusiastic but indolent, Pepper an old friend. The rest were Stubbs's most obedient.

Stubbs read the retiring member's letter, and introduced the candidate. The rector boomed through a few phrases of approbation, Dr. Pepper seconded, the rest cried "Hear! hear!"

"There's little to say," Stubbs went on. "I take it that we are all of one mind, gentlemen, to return Mr. Mottisfont in his father's place?"

"Hear! hear!" from all. "In the old interest?" Stubbs went on, looking round the table. "And on the clear understanding that Mr. Mottisfont is returned to oppose any tampering with the protection of agriculture."

"That is so," said Mr. Mottisfont.

"I will see that that is embodied in Mr. Mottisfont's address," Stubbs continued. "There must be no mistake. These are queer times----"

"Sad times!" said the rector, shaking his head.

"Terrible times!" said the maltster, shaking his.

"Never did I dream I should live to see 'em," said old Hayward. "'Tisn't a month since a chap came on my land, ay, up to my very door, and said things--I'll be damned if I did not think he'd turn the cream sour! And when I cried 'Sam! fetch a pitchfork and rid me of this rubbish----'"

"I know, Hayward," Stubbs said, cutting him short. "I know. You told me about it. You did very well. But to business. It shall be a short address--just that one point. We are all agreed, I think, gentlemen?"

All were agreed.

"I'll see that it is printed in good time," Stubbs continued. "I don't think that we need trouble you further, Mr. Mottisfont. There's a fat-stock sale this day fortnight. Perhaps you'll dine and say a few words? I'll let you know if it is necessary. There'll be no opposition. Hatton will have a meeting at the Institute, but nothing will come of it."

"That's all then, is it?" said the London man, sticking his glass in his eye with a sigh of relief.

"That's all," Stubbs replied. "If you can attend this day fortnight so much the better. The farmers like it, and they've fourteen votes in the borough. Thank you, gentlemen, that's all."

"I think you've forgotten one thing, Mr. Stubbs," said old Hayward, with a twinkle.

"To be sure, I have. Ring the bell, Musters, and send up the two bottles of your '20 port that I ordered and some glasses. A glass of Musters' '20 port, Mr. Mottisfont, won't hurt you this cold day. And we must drink your health. And, Musters, when these gentlemen go down, see that they have what they call for."

The port was sipped, tasted. Mr. Mottisfont's health was drunk, and various compliments were paid to his father. The rector took his two glasses; so did young Mottisfont, who woke up and vowed that he had tasted none better in St. James's Street. "Is it Garland's?" he asked.

"It is, sir," Musters said, much pleased.

"I thought it was--none better!" said young Mottisfont, also pleased. "The old Duke drinks no other."

"Fine tipple! Fine tipple!" said the other "Duke." In the end a third bottle was ordered, of which Musters and old Hayward drank the better part.

At one of these meetings a sad thing had happened. A rash tradesman had proposed his lordship's health. Of course he had been severely snubbed. It had been considered most indecent. But on this occasion no one was so simple as to name my lord, and Stubbs felt with satisfaction that all had passed as it should. So had candidates been chosen as long as he could remember.

But call no man happy until the day closes. As he left the house Bagenal the maltster tacked himself on to him. "I'd a letter from George this morning," he said. George was his son, articled to Mr. Stubbs, and now with Mr. Stubbs's agents in town. "He saw his lordship one day last week."

"Ay, ay. I suppose Master George was in the West End? Wasting his time, Bagenal, I'll be bound."

"I don't know about that. Young fellows like to see things. He went with a lot of chaps to see the crowd outside Sir Robert's. They'd read in a paper that all the nobs were to be seen going in and out. Anyway, he went, and the first person he saw going in was his lordship!"

Mr. Stubbs walked a few yards in silence. Then, "Well, he's no sight to George," he said. "It seems to me they were both wasting their time. I told his lordship he'd do no good. When half the dukes in England have been at Peel, d--n him, it wasn't likely he'd change his course for his lordship! It wasn't to be expected, Bagenal. Did George stop to see him come out?"

"He did. And in a thundering temper my lord looked."

"Ay, ay! Well I told him how it would be."

"They were going in and out like bees, George said."

"Ay, ay."

They parted on that, and the lawyer went into his office. But his face was gloomy. "Ay, like bees!" he muttered. "After the honey! I wonder what he asked for! Whatever it was he couldn't have paid the price! I thought he knew that. I've a good mind--but there, we've held it so long, grandfather, father, and son--I can't afford to give it up."

He turned into his office, but the day was spoiled for him. And the day was not done yet. He had barely sat down before his clerk a thin, gray-haired man, high-nosed, with a look of breeding run to seed, came in, and closed the door behind him. Farthingale was as well known in Riddsley as the Maypole; gossip had it that he was a by-blow of an old name. "I've heard something," he said darkly, "and the sooner you know it the better. They've got a man."

Stubbs shrugged his shoulders. "For repeal in Riddsley?" he said. "You're dreaming."

The clerk smiled. "Well, you'd best be awake," he said. He had been long enough with Stubbs to take a liberty. "Who do you think it is?" he continued, rubbing his chin with the feather-end of a quill.

"Some methodist parson!"

Farthingale shook his head. "Guess again, sir," he said. "You're cold at present. It's a bird of another feather."

"A pretty big fool whoever he is!"

"Mr. Basset of Blore. I have it on good authority."

Stubbs stared. He was silent for a time, thinking hard. "Somebody's fooled you," he said at last, but in a different tone. "He's never shown a sign of coming out."

The clerk looked wise. "It's true," he said. "It cost me four goes of brown brandy at the Portcullis."

"Well, you may score that to me," Stubbs answered. "Basset, eh? Well, he's throwing his money into the gutter if it's true, and he hasn't much to spare. I see Hatton's point. He's not the fool."

"No. He's an old bird is Hatton."

"But I don't see where Squire Basset comes in."

Farthingale looked wiser than ever. "Well," he said, "he may have a score to pay, too. And if he has, there's more ways than one of paying it!"

"What score?"

"Ah, I'm not saying that. Mr. John Audley's may be--against his lordship."

"Umph! If you paid off yours at the Portcullis," Stubbs retorted, losing his temper, "the landlord wouldn't be sorry! Scores are a deal too much in your way, Farthingale!" he continued, severely, forgetting in his annoyance the four goes of brown brandy. "You're too much at home among 'em. Don't bring me cock-and-bull stories like this! I don't believe it. And get to that lease!"

But sure enough Farthingale's story proved to be well founded, for a week later it was known for certain in Riddsley that Mr. Basset of Blore was coming out, and that there would be a fight for the borough.

CHAPTER XXV: MARY IS LONELY

Mary Audley was one of the last to hear the news. Etruria brought it from the town one day in January, when the evenings were beginning to lengthen, and the last hour of daylight was the dreariest of the twenty-four. It had rained, and the oaks in the park were a-drip, the thorn trees stood in tiny pools, the moorland lay stark under a pall of fog. In the vale the Trent was in flood, its pale waters swirling past the willow-stools, creeping over the chilled meadows, and stealing inch by inch up the waterside lanes. Etruria's feet were wet, and she was weary with her trudge through the mud; but when Mary met her on the tiny landing on which their rooms opened, there was a sparkle in the girl's eyes as bright as the red petticoat that showed below her tucked-up gown.

"You didn't forget----" Mary was beginning, and then, "Why, Etruria," she exclaimed, "I believe you have seen Mr. Colet?"

Etruria blushed like the dawn. "Oh no, Miss!" she said. "He's at Blore."

"To be sure! Then what is it?"

"I've heard some news, Miss," Etruria said. "I don't know whether you'll be pleased or not."

"But it is certain that you are!" Mary replied with conviction. "What is it?"

The girl told what she had heard: that there was to be an election at Riddsley in three weeks, and not only an election but a contest, and that the candidate who had come forward to oppose the Corn Laws was no other than Mr. Basset--their Mr. Basset! More, that only the evening before he had held his first meeting at the Institute, and though he had been interrupted and the meeting had been broken up, his short plain speech had made a considerable impression.

"Indeed, Miss," Etruria continued, carried away by the subject, "there was one told me that when he stood up to speak she could see his hand shake, and his face was the color of a piece of paper. But when they began to boo and shout at him, he grew as cool as cool, and the longer they shouted the braver he was, until they saw that if they let him go on he would be getting a hearing! So they put out the lights and stormed the platform, and there was a fine Stafford row, I'm told. Of course," Etruria added simply, "the drink was in them."

Mary hardly knew what her feelings were. "Mr. Basset?" she said at last. "I can hardly believe it."

"Nor could I, Miss, when I first heard it. But it seems they have known it there for ten days and more, and the town is agog with it, everybody taking sides, and some so much against him as never was. It's dreadful to think," Etruria continued, "how misguided men can be. But oh, Miss, I'm thankful he's on the right side, and for taking the burden off the bread! I'm sure it will be returned to him, win or lose. They're farmers' friends here, and they're saying shameful things of him in the market! But there's many a woman will bless him, and the lanes and alleys, they've no votes, but they'll pray for him! Sometimes," Etruria added shyly, "I think it is Mr. Colet has brought him to it."

"Mr. Colet?" Mary repeated--she did not know why she disliked the notion. "Why do you think that?"

"He's been at Blore," Etruria murmured. "Mr. Basset has been so good to him."

"Mr. Basset has a mind of his own," Mary answered sharply. "He is quite capable of forming his own opinion."

"Of course. Miss," Etruria said, abashed. "I should have known that."

"Yes," Mary repeated. "But what was it they were saying of Mr. Basset in the market, Etruria? Not that it matters."

"Well, Miss," Etruria explained, reluctantly. "They were saying it was some grudge Mr. Basset or the Master had against his lordship that brought Mr. Basset out."

"Against Lord Audley?" Mary cried. And she blushed suddenly and vividly. "Why? What has he to do with it?"

"Well, Miss, it's his lordship's seat," Etruria answered naïvely; "what he wishes has always been done in Riddsley. And he's for Mr. Mottisfont."

Mary walked to a window and looked out. "Oh," she said, "I did not know that. But you'd better go now, Etruria, and change your shoes. Your feet must be wet."

Etruria went, and Mary continued to gaze through the window. What strange news! And what a strange situation! The lover whom she had rejected and the lover whom she had taken, pitted against one another! And her words--she could hardly doubt it--the spur which had brought Basset to the post!

So thinking, so pondering, she grew more and more ill at ease. Her sympathies should have been wholly with her betrothed, but they were not. She should have resented Basset's action. She did not. Instead she thought of his shaking hand and his pale face, and of the courage that had grown firmer in the face of opposition; and she found something fine in that, something that appealed to her. And the cause he had adopted? It was the cause to which she naturally inclined. She might be wrong, he might be wrong. Lord Audley knew so much more of these things and looked at them from so enlightened a standpoint, that they must be wrong. And yet--her heart warmed to that cause.

She turned from the window in some trouble, wondering if she were disloyal, wondering why she felt as she did; wondering a little, too, why she had lost the first rapture of her love, and was less happy in it than she had been.

True, she had not seen her lover again, and that might account for it. He had been detained at Lord Seabourne's, and in London; he had been occupied for days together with the crisis. But she had had three letters from him, busy as he was; three amusing letters, full of gossip and sprinkled with anecdotes of the great world. She had opened the first in something of a tremor; but her fingers had soon grown steady, and if she had blushed it had been for her expectation of a vulgar love-letter such as milkmaids prize. She had been silly to suppose that he would write in that strain.

And yet she had felt a degree of disappointment. He might have written with less reserve, she thought; he might have discussed their plans and hopes, he might have let the fire peep somewhere through the chinks. But there, again, what a poor thing she was if her love must be fed with sweetmeats. How weak her trust, how poor her affection, if she could not bear a three weeks' parting! He had come to her, he had chosen her, what more did she want? Did she expect him to put aside the calls and the duties of his station, that he might hang on her apron-strings?

Still, she was not in good spirits, and she felt her loneliness. The house, this gray evening, with the shadows gathering in the corners, weighed on her. Mrs. Toft was far away in her cosey kitchen, Etruria also had gone thither. Toft was with Mr. Audley in the other wing--he had been much with his master of late. So Mary was alone. She was not nervous, but she was depressed. The cold stairs, the austere parlor with its dim portraits, the matted hall, the fireless library--all struck a chill. She remembered other times and other evenings; cosey evenings, when the glow of the wood-fire had vied with the shaded lights, when the three heads had bent over the three tables, when the rustle of turning pages had blended with the snoring of the old hound, when the pursuit of some trifle had sped the pleasant hours. Alas, those evenings were gone, as if they had never been. The house was dull and melancholy.

She might have gone to her uncle, but during the afternoon he had told her that he wished to be alone; he should go to bed betimes. So about seven o'clock she took her meal by herself, and when it was done she felt more at a loss than ever. Presently her thoughts went again to John Audley.

Had she neglected him of late? Had she left him too much to Toft, and let her secret, which she hated to keep secret, come between them? Why should she not, even now, see him before he slept? She could take him the news of Mr. Basset's enterprise. It would serve for an excuse.

Lest her courage should fail she went at once, shivering as she passed through the shadowy library, where a small lamp, burning on a table, did no more than light her to the staircase. She ran up the stairs and was groping for the handle of Mr. Audley's door when the door opened abruptly and Toft stepped out, a candle in his hand. She was so close to him that he all but touched her, and he was, if anything, more startled than she was. He stood gaping at her.

Through the narrow opening she had a glimpse of her uncle, who was on his feet before the fire. He was fully dressed.

That surprised her, for, even before this last attack, he had spent most of his time in his dressing-gown. Still more surprising was Toft's conduct. He shut the door and held it. "The master is going to bed, Miss," he said.

"I see that he is dressed!" she replied. And she looked at Toft in such a way that the man gave way, took his hand from the door, and stood aside. She pushed the door open and went in. Her uncle, standing with his back to her, was huddling on his dressing-gown.

"What is it?" he cried, his face averted. "Who is it?"

"It is only I, sir," she replied. "Mary." She closed the door.

"But I thought I told you that I didn't want you!" he retorted pettishly. "I am going to bed." He turned, having succeeded in girding on his dressing-gown. "Going to bed," he repeated. "Didn't I tell you so?"

"I'm very sorry, sir," she said, "but I had news for you. News that has surprised me. I thought that you would like to hear it."

He looked at her, his furtive eyes giving the lie to his plump face, which sagged more than of old. "News," he muttered, peevishly. "What news? I wish you wouldn't startle me. You ought to remember that--that excitement is bad for me. And you come at this time of night with news! What is it?" He was not looking at her. He seemed to be seeking something. "What is it?"

"It's nothing very terrible," she answered, smiling. "Nothing to alarm you, uncle. Won't you sit down?"

He looked about him like a man driven into a corner. "No, no, I don't want to sit down!" he said. "I ought to be in bed! I ought to be there now."

"Well, I shall not keep you long," she answered, trying to humor his mood, while all the time she was wondering why he was dressed at this time of night, he whom she had not seen dressed for a fortnight. And why had Toft tried to keep her out? "It is only," she continued, "that I heard to-day that there is to be a contest at Riddsley. And that Mr. Basset is to be one of the candidates."

"Is that all?" he said. "News, you said? That's no news! Bigger fool he, unless he does more for himself than he does for his friends! Peter the Hermit become Peter the Great! He'll soon find himself Peter the Piper, who picked a peck of pepper! Hot pepper he'll find it, d--n him!" with sudden spite. "He's no better than the rest! He's all for himself! All for himself!" he repeated, his voice rising in his excitement.

"But----"

"There, don't agitate me!" He wiped his brow with a shaking hand, while his eyes, avoiding hers, continued to look about him as if he sought something. "I knew how it would be. You've no thought for me. You don't remember how weak I am! Hardly able to crawl across the floor, to put one foot before another. And you come chattering! chattering!"

She had thought him odd before, but never so odd as this evening; and she was sorry that she had come. She was going to say what she could and escape, when he began again. "You're the last person who should upset me! The very last!" he babbled. "When it's all for you! It's little good it can do me. And Basset, he'd the ball at his foot, and wouldn't kick it! But I'll show you, I'll show you all!" he continued, gesticulating with a violence that distressed Mary. "Ay, and I'll show him what I am! He thinks he's safe, d--n him! He thinks he's safe! He's spending my money and adding up my balance! He's walking on my land and sleeping in my bed! He's peacocking in my name! But--but----" he stopped, struggling for words. For an instant he turned on her over his shoulder a face distorted by passion.

Thoroughly alarmed, she tried to soothe him. "But I am sure, sir," she said, "Mr. Basset would never----"

"Basset!"

"I'm sure he never dreamt----"

"Basset!" he repeated. "No! but Audley! Lord Audley, Audley of Beaudelays, Audley of nowhere and nothing! And no Audley! no Audley!" he repeated furiously, while again he fought for breath, and again he mastered himself and lowered his tone. "No Audley!" he whispered, pointing a hand at her, "but Jacob, girl! Jacob the supplanter, Jacob the changeling, Jacob the baseborn! And he thinks I lie awake of nights, hundreds of nights, for nothing! He thinks I dream of him--for nothing! He thinks I go out with the bats--for nothing! He thinks I have a canker here! Here!" And he clapped his hand to his breast, a grotesque, yet dreadful figure in his huddled dressing-gown, his flaccid cheeks quivering with rage. "For nothing! But I'll show him! I'll ruin him! I'll----"

His voice, which had risen to a scream, stopped. Toft had opened the door. "Sir! Mr. Audley!" he cried. "For God's sake be calm! For God's sake have a care, sir! And you, Miss," he continued; "you see what you have done! If you'll leave him I'll get him to bed. I'll get him to bed and quiet him--if I can."

Mary was shocked, and yet she felt that she could not go without a word. "Dear uncle," she said, "you wish me to go?"

He had clutched one of the posts of the bed and was supporting himself by it. The fire had died down in him, he was no more now than a feeble, shaking old man. He wiped his brow and his lips. "Yes, go," he whispered. "Go."

"I am very sorry I disturbed you," she said. "I won't do it again. You were right, Toft. Good-night."

The man said "Good-night, Miss." Her uncle said nothing. He had let himself down on the bed, but he still clung to the post. Mary looked at him in sorrow, grieved to leave him in this state. But she had no choice, and she went out and, closing the door behind her, groped her way down the narrow staircase.

It was a little short of ten when she reached the parlor, but she was in no mood for reading. What she had seen had shocked and frightened her. She was sure now that her uncle was not sane; and while she was equally sure that Toft exercised a strong influence over him, she had her misgivings as to that. Something must be done. She must consult some one. Life at the Gatehouse could not go on on this footing. She must see Dr. Pepper.

Unluckily when she had settled this to her mind, and sought her bed, she could not sleep. Long after she had heard Etruria go to her room, long after she had heard the girl's shoes fall--familiar sound!--Mary lay awake, thinking now of her uncle's state and her duty towards him, nor of her own future, that future which seemed for the moment to have lost its brightness. Doubts that the sun dismisses, fears at which daylight laughs, are Giants of Despair in the dark watches. So it was with her. Misgivings which she would not have owned in the daylight, rose up and put on grisly shapes. Her uncle and his madness, her lover and his absence, passed in endless procession through her brain. In vain she tossed and turned, sat up in despair, tried the cooler side of the pillow. She could not rest.

The door creaked. She fancied a step on the staircase, a hand on the latch. Far away in the depths of the house a clock struck. It was three o'clock--only three o'clock! And it would not be light before eight--not much before eight. Oh dear! Oh dear!

And then she slept.

When she awoke it was morning, the light was filtering in through the white dimity curtains, and some one was really at her door. Some one was knocking. She sat up. "What is it?" she cried.

"Can I come in, Miss?"

The voice was Mrs. Toft's, and Mary needed no second warning. She knew in a moment that the woman brought bad news. She sprang out of bed, put on a dressing-gown, and with bare feet she went to the door. She unlocked it. "What is it, Mrs. Toft?" she said.

"Maybe not much," the woman answered cautiously. "I hope not, Miss, but I had to tell you. The Master is missing."

"Missing?" Mary exclaimed, the blood leaving her face. "Impossible! Why, I saw him, I was in his room last evening after nine o'clock."

"Toft was with him up to eleven," Mrs. Toft answered. Her face was grave. "But he's gone now?"

"You mean that he is not in his room!" Mary said. "But have you looked----" and she named places where her uncle might be--places in the house.

"We've looked there," Mrs. Toft answered. "Toft's been everywhere. The Master's not in the house. We're well-nigh sure of that. And the door in the courtyard was open this morning. I am afraid he's gone, Miss."

"In his state and at night? Why, it's----" The girl broke off and took hold of herself. "Very well," she said. "I shall not be more than five minutes. I will come down."

.

CHAPTER XXVI: MISSING

Mary scrambled into her clothes without pausing to do more than knot up her hair. She tried to steady her nerves and to put from her the thought that it was her visit which had upset her uncle. That thought would only flurry her, and she must be cool. In little more than the five minutes that she had named she was in the hall, and found Mrs. Toft waiting for her. The door into the courtyard stood open, the bleak light and raw air of a January morning poured in, but neither of them heeded this. Their eyes met, and Mary saw that the woman, who was usually so placid, was frightened.

"Where is Toft?" Mary asked.

"He's away this ten minutes," Mrs. Toft replied. "He's gone to the Yew Walk, where you found the Master before. But law, Miss, if he's there in this weather!" She lifted up her hands.

Mary controlled herself. "And Etruria?" she asked.

"She's searching outside the house. If she does not find him she is to run over to Petch the keeper, and bring him."

"Quite right," Mary said. "Did Toft take any brandy?"

"He did. Miss. And the big kettle is on, if there is a bath wanted, and I've put a couple of bricks to heat in the oven."

"You're sure you've looked everywhere in the house?"

"As sure as can be, Miss! More by token, I've some coffee ready for you in the parlor."

But Mary said, "Bring it here, Mrs. Toft." And snatching up a shawl and folding it about her, she stepped outside. It was a gray, foggy morning, and the flagged court wore a desolate air. In one corner a crowd of dead leaves were circling in the gusts of wind, in another a little pile of snow had drifted, and between the monsters that flanked the Gateway, the old hound, deaf and crippled, stood peering across the park. Mary fancied that the dog descried Toft returning, and she ran across the court. But no one was in sight. The park with its clumps of dead bracken, its naked trees and gnarled blackthorns, stretched away under a thin sprinkling of snow. Shivering she returned to the hall, where Mrs. Toft awaited her with the coffee.

"Now," Mary said, "tell me about it, please--from the beginning."

"Toft had left Mr. Audley about eleven," Mrs. Toft explained. "The Master had been a bit put out, and that kept him. But he'd settled down, and when Toft left him he was much as usual. It could not have been before eleven," Mrs. Toft continued, rubbing her nose, "for I heard the kitchen clock strike eleven, and I was asleep when Toft came in. The next I remember was finding Toft had got out of bed. 'What is it?' says I. He didn't answer, and I roused up and was going to get a light. But he told me not to make a noise, he'd been woke by hearing a door slam, and thought that some one had crossed the court. He was at the window then, looking out, but we heard nothing, and after a while Toft came back to bed."

"What time was that?"

"I couldn't say, Miss, and I don't suppose Toft could. It was dark and before six, because when I woke again it was on six. But God knows it was a thousand pities we didn't search then, for it's on my mind that it was the poor Master. And if we'd known, Toft would have stopped him."

"Well?" Mary said gravely. "And when did you miss him?"

"Most mornings Etruria'd let me into the house. But this morning she found the door unlocked; howsomever she thought nothing of it, for Toft has a key as well, and since the Master's illness and him coming and going at all hours, he has not always locked the door; so she made no remark. A bit before eight Toft came down--I didn't see him but I heard him--and at eight he took up the Master's cup of tea. Toft makes it in the pantry and takes it up."

Mrs. Toft paused heavily--not without enjoyment.

"Yes," Mary said anxiously, "and then?"

"I suppose it was five minutes after, he came out to me--I was in the kitchen getting our breakfast--and he was shaking all over. I don't know that I ever saw a man more upset. 'He's gone!' he said. 'Law, Toft,' I said. 'What's the matter? Who's gone?' 'The Master!' he said. 'Fiddlesticks!' says I. 'Where should he go?' And with that I went into the house and up to the Master's room. When I saw it was empty you could have knocked me down with a feather! I looked round a bit, and then I went up to Mr. Basset's room that's over, and down again to the library, and so forth. By that time Toft was there, gawpin about. 'He's gone!' he kept saying. I don't know as I ever saw Toft truly upset before."

"And what then?" Mary asked. Twice she had looked through the door, but to no purpose.

"Well," I said, "if he's not here he can't be far! Don't twitter, man, but think! It's my belief he's away sleepwalking or what not, to the place you found him before. On that I gave Toft some brandy and he went off."

"Shouldn't he be back by now?"

"He should, Miss, if he's not found him," Mrs. Toft answered. "But, if he's found him, he couldn't carry him! Toft's not all that strong. And if the Master's lain out long, it's not all the brandy in the world will bring him round!"

Mary shuddered, and moved by a common impulse the two went out and crossed the court. The old hound was still at gaze in the gateway, still staring with purblind eyes down the vistas of the park. "Maybe he sees more than we see," Mrs. Toft muttered. "He'd not stand there, would the old dog, as he's stood twenty minutes, for nothing."

She was right, for the next moment three figures appeared hurrying across the park towards them. It was impossible to mistake Toft's lanky figure. The others were Etruria, with a shawl about her head, and the keeper Petch.

Mary scanned them anxiously. "Have they found him?" she murmured.

"No," Mrs. Toft said. "If they'd found him, one would have stopped with him."

"Of course," Mary said. And heedless of the cold, searching wind that swung their skirts and carried showers of dead leaves sailing past them, they waited until Toft and the others, talking together, came up. Mary saw that, in spite of the pace at which he had walked, Toft's face was colorless. He was almost livid. His daughter wore an anxious look, while the keeper was pleasantly excited.

As soon as the three were within hearing, "You've not found him?" Mary cried.

"No, Miss," Etruria answered.

"Nor any trace?"

"No, Miss. My father has been as far as the iron gate, and found it locked. It was no use going on."

"He could not have walked farther without help," Mrs. Toft said. "If the Master's not between us and the gardens he's not that way."

"Then where is he?" Mary cried, aghast. She looked from one to the other. "Where can he be, Toft?"

Toft raised his hands and let them fall. It was clear that he had given up hope.

But his wife was of different mettle. "That's to be seen," she said briskly. "Anyway, you'll be perished here, Miss, and I don't want another invalid on my hands. We'll go in, if you please."

Mary gave way. They turned to go in, but it was noticeable that as they moved towards the house each, stirred by the same thought, swept the extent of the park with eyes that clung to it, and were loth to leave it. Each hung for a moment, searching this alley or that, fancying a clue in some distant object, or taking a clump of gorse, or a jagged stump for the fallen man. All were harassed by the thought that they might be abandoning him; that in turning their backs on the bald, wintry landscape they might be carrying away with them his last chance.

"'T would take a day to search the park," the keeper muttered. "And a dozen men, I'm afeared, to do it thoroughly."

"Why not take a round yourself!" Mrs. Toft replied. "And if you find nothing be at the house in an hour, Petch, and we'll know better what's to do. The poor gentleman's off his head, I doubt, and there's no saying where he'd wander. But he can't be far, and I'm beginning to think he's in the house after all."

The man agreed willingly, and strode away across the turf. The others entered the hall. Mary was for pausing there, but Mrs. Toft swept them all into the parlor where a good fire was burning. "You'll excuse me, Miss," she said, "but Toft will be the better for this," and without ceremony she poured out a cup of coffee, jerked into it a little brandy from the decanter on the sideboard, and handed it to her husband. "Drink that," she said, "and get your wits together, man! You're no better than a wisp of paper now, and it's only you can help us. Now think! You know him best. Where can he be? Did he say no word last night to give you a clue?"

A little color came back to Toft's face. He sighed and passed his hand across his forehead. "If I'd never left him!" he said. "I never ought to have left him!"

"It's no good going over that!" Mrs. Toft replied impatiently. "He means, Miss, that up to three nights ago he slept in the Master's room. Then when the Master seemed better Toft came back to his bed."

"I ought to have stayed with him," Toft repeated. That seemed the one thought in his mind.

"But where is he?" Mary cried. "Where? Every moment we stand talking--can't you think where he might go? Are there no hiding--places in the house? No secret passages?"

Mrs. Toft raised her hands. "Lord's sake!" she exclaimed. "There's the locked closet in his room where he keeps his papers. I never looked there. It's seldom opened, and----"

She did not finish. With one accord they hurried through the library and up the stairs to the old tapestried room, where Mr. Audley had slept and for the last month had lived. The others had been in it since his disappearance, Mary had not; and she felt a thrill of awe as she passed the threshold. The angular faces, the oblique eyes, of the watchers in the needlework on the wall, that from generation to generation had looked down on marriage and birth and death--what had they seen during the past night? On what had they gazed, she asked herself. Mrs. Toft, less fanciful or more familiar with the room, had no such thoughts. She crossed the floor to a low door which was outlined for those who knew of its existence, by rough cuts in the arras. It led into a closet, contained in one of the turrets.

Mrs. Toft tried the door, shook it, knocked on it. Finally she set her eye to the keyhole. "He's not there," she said. "There's no key in the lock. He'd not take out the key, that's certain."

Mary scanned the disordered room. Books lay in heaps on the deep window-seats, and even on the floor. A table by one of the windows was strewn with papers and letters; on another beside the bed-head stood a tray with night drinks, a pair of candles, an antique hour-glass, a steel pistol. The bedclothes were dragged down, as if the bed had been slept in, and over the rail at the foot, half hidden by the heavy curtains, hung a nightgown. She took this up and found beneath it a pair of slippers and a shoehorn.

"He was dressed then?" she exclaimed.

Toft eyed the things. "Yes, Miss, I've no doubt he was," he said despondently. "His overcoat's gone."

"Then he meant to leave the house?" Mary cried.

"God save us!"

"He's taken his silver flask too," Etruria said in a low voice. She was examining the dressing-table. "And his watch."

"His watch?"

"Yes, Miss."

"But that's odd," Mary said, fixing her eyes on Toft. "Don't you think that's odd? If my uncle had rambled out in some nightmare or--or wandering, would he have taken his flask and his watch, Toft? Are his spectacles there?"

Toft inspected the table, raised the pillow, felt under the bolster. "No, Miss," he said; "he's taken them."

"Ah!" Mary replied; "then I have hope. Wherever he is, he is in his senses. Now, Toft!"--she looked hard at the man--"think again! Surely since he had this in his mind last night he must have let something drop? Some word?"

The man shook his head. "Not that I heard, Miss," he said.

Mary sighed. But Mrs. Toft was less patient. She exploded. "You gaby!" she cried. "Where's your senses? It's to you we're looking, and a poor stick you are in time of trouble! I couldn't have believed it! Find your tongue, Toft, say something! You knew the Master down to his shoe leather. Let's hear what you do think! He couldn't walk far! He couldn't walk a mile without help. Where is he? Where do you think he is?"

Toft's answer silenced them. If one of the mute, staring figures on the walls--that watched as from the boxes of a theatre the living actors--had stepped down, it would hardly have affected them more deeply. The man sat down on the bed, covered his face with his hands, and rocking himself to and fro broke into a passion of weeping. "The poor Master!" he cried between his sobs. "The poor Master!"

Quickly at that Mary's feelings underwent a change. As if she had stood already beside her uncle's grave, sorrow took the place of perplexity. His past kindness dragged at her heart-strings. She forgot that she had never been able to love him, she forgot that behind the man whom she had known she had been ever conscious of another being, vague, shifting, inhuman. She remembered only the help he had given, the home he had offered, the rare hours of sympathy. "Don't, Toft, don't!" she cried, tears in her voice. She touched the man on the shoulder. "Don't give up hope!"

As for Mrs. Toft, surprise silenced her. When she found her voice, "Well," she said, looking round her with a sort of pride, "who'll say after this that Toft's a hard man? Why, if the Master was lying on that bed ready for burial--and we're some way off that, the Lord be thanked!--he couldn't carry on more! But there, let's look now, and weep afterwards! Pull yourself together, Toft, or who's the young lady to depend on? If you take my advice, Miss," she continued, "we'll get out of this room. It always did give me the fantods with them Egyptians staring at me from the walls, and to-day it's worse than a hearse! Now downstairs----"

"You are quite right, Mrs. Toft," Mary said. "We'll go downstairs." She shared to the full Mrs. Toft's distaste for the room. "We're doing no good here, and your husband can follow us when he is himself again. Petch should be back by this time, and we ought to arrange what is to be done outside."

Toft made no demur, and they went down. They found the keeper waiting in the hall. He had made no discovery, and Mary, to whom Toft's breakdown had given fresh energy, took things into her own hands. She gave Petch his orders. He must get together a dozen men, and search the park and every place within a mile of the Gatehouse. He must report by messenger every two hours to the house, and in the meantime he must send a man on horseback to the town for Dr. Pepper.

"And Mr. Basset?" Mrs. Toft murmured.

"I will write a note to Mr. Basset," Mary said, "and the man must send it by post-horses from the Audley Arms. I will write it now." She sat down in the library, cold as the room was, and scrawled three lines, telling Basset that her uncle had disappeared during the night, and that, ill as he was, she feared the worst.

Then, when Petch had gone to get his men together--a task which would take time as there were no farms at hand--she and Mrs. Toft searched the house room by room, while Etruria and her father went again through the outbuildings. But the quest was as fruitless as the former search had been.

Mary had known many unhappy days in Paris, days of anxiety, of loneliness, of apprehension, when she had doubted where she would lodge or what she would eat for her next meal. Now she had a source of strength in her engagement and her love, which should have been inexhaustible. But she never forgot the misery of this day, nor ever looked back on it without a shudder. Probably there were moments when she sat down, when she took a tasty meal, when she sought Mrs. Toft in her warm kitchen or talked with Etruria before her own fire. But as she remembered the day, she spent the long hours gazing across the wintry park; now catching a glimpse of the line of beaters as it appeared for a moment crossing a glade, now watching the approach of the messenger who came to tell her that they had found nothing; or again straining her eyes for the arrival of Dr. Pepper, who, had she known it, was at the deathbed of an old patient, ten miles on the farther side of Riddsley.

Now and again a hailstorm swept across the park, and Mrs. Toft came out and scolded her into shelter; or a farmer, whose men had been borrowed, "happened that way," and after a gruff question touched his hat and went off to join the searchers. Once a distant cry seemed to herald a discovery, and she tried to steady her leaping pulses. But nothing came of it except some minutes of anxiety. And once her waiting ear caught the clang of the bell that hung in the hall and she flew through the house to the front door, only to learn that the visitor was the carrier who three times a week called for letters on his way to town. The dreary house with its open doors, its cold draughts, its unusual aspect, the hurried meals, the furtive glances, the hours of suspense and fear--these stamped the day for ever on Mary's memory: as sometimes an hour of loneliness prints itself on the mind of a child who all his life long hears with distaste the clash of wedding bells.

At length the wintry day with its gusts of snow began to draw in. Before four Petch sent in to say that he had beaten the park and also the gardens at the Great House, but had found nothing. Half his men were now searching the slope on either side of the Riddsley road. With the other half he was going to explore, while the light lasted, the fringe of the Chase towards Brown Heath.

That left Mary face to face with the night; with the long hours of darkness, which inaction must render infinitely worse than those of the day. She had visions of the windswept park, the sullen ponds, the frozen moorland; they spread before her fraught with some brooding terror. She had never much marked, she had seldom felt the loneliness of the house. Now it pressed itself upon her, isolated her, menaced her. It made the thought of the night, that lay before her, almost unbearable.

CHAPTER XXVII: A FOOTSTEP IN THE HALL

Mrs. Toft bringing in candles, and looking grave enough herself, noticed the girl's pale face and chid her gently. "I don't believe that you've sat down this blessed day, Miss!" she said. "Nor no more than looked at good food. But tea you shall have and sit down to it, or my name's not Anne Toft! Fretting's no manner of use, and fasting's a poor stick to beat trouble with!"

"But, Mrs. Toft," Mary said, her face piteous, "it's the thought that he may be lying out there, helpless and dying, while we sit here----"

"Steady, Miss! Giving way does no good, and too much mind's worse than none. If he's out there he's gone, poor gentleman, long ago. And Dr. Pepper'll say the same. It's not in reason he should be alive if he's in the open. And, God knows, if he's under cover it's little better."

"But then if he is alive!" Mary cried. "Think of another night!"

"Ay, I know," Mrs. Toft said. "And hard it is! But you've been a model all this blessed day, and it's no time to break down now. Where that dratted doctor is, beats me, though he could do no more than we've done! But there, Mr. Basset will be with us to-morrow, and he'll find the poor gentleman dead or alive! There's some as are more to look at than the Squire, but there's few I'd put before him at a pinch!"

"Where's Toft?" Mary asked.

"He went to join Petch two hours ago," Mrs. Toft explained. "And there again, take Toft. He's a good husband, but there's no one would say he was a man to wear his heart outside. But you saw how hard he took it? I don't know," Mrs. Toft continued thoughtfully, "as I've seen Toft shed a tear these twenty years--no, nor twice since we went to church!"

"You don't think," Mary asked, "that he knows more than he has told us?"

The question took Mrs. Toft aback. "Why, Miss," she said, "you don't mean as you think he was putting on this morning?"

"No," Mary answered. "But is it possible that he knows the worst and does not tell us?"

"And why shouldn't he tell us? It would be strange if he wouldn't tell his own wife? And you that's Mr. Audley's nearest!"

"It's all so strange," Mary pleaded. "My uncle is gone. Where has he gone?"

Mrs. Toft did not answer the question. She could not. And there came an interruption. "That's Petch's voice," she said. "They're back."

The men trooped into the hall. They advanced to the door of the parlor, Petch leading, a man whom Mary did not know next to him, after these a couple of farmers and Toft, in the background a blur of faces vaguely seen.

"We've found something, Miss," Petch said. "At least Tom has. But I'm not sure it lightens things much. He was going home by the Yew Tree Walk and pretty close to the iron gate, when what should he see lying in the middle of the walk but this!"

Petch held out a silver flask.

"It's the Master's, sure enough," Mrs. Toft said.

"Ay," Petch answered. "But the odd thing is, I searched that place before noon, a'most inch by inch, looking for footprints, and I went over it again when we were beating the Yew Tree Walk this afternoon, and I'm danged if that flask was there then!"

"I don't think as you could ha' missed it, Mr. Petch," the finder said, "it was that bright and plain!"

"But isn't the grass long there?" Mary asked. She had already as much mystery as she could bear and wanted no addition to it.

"Not that long," said Tom.

"No, not that long, the lad's right," Petch added. "I warrant I must have seen it."

"That you must, Mr. Petch," a lad in the background said. "I was next man, and I wondered when you'd ha' done that bit."

"But I don't understand," Mary answered. "If it was not there, this morning----"

"I don't understand neither, lady," the keeper rejoined. "But it is on my mind that there's foul play!"

"Oh, but," Mary protested, "who--why should any one hurt my uncle?"

"I can't say as to that," Petch replied, darkly. "I don't know anybody as would. But there's the flask, and flasks don't travel without hands. If he took it out of the house with him----"

"May he not have dropped it--this afternoon?" Mary suggested. "Suppose he wandered that way after you passed?"

The keeper shook his head. "If he had passed that way this afternoon it isn't one but six pairs of eyes would ha' seen him."

There was a murmur of assent. The searchers were keenly enjoying the drama, taking in every change that appeared on the girl's face. They were men into whose lives not much of drama entered.

"But I cannot think that what you say is likely!" Mary protested. She had held her own stoutly through the day, but now with the eyes of all these men upon her she grew bewildered. The rows of faces, the bashful hands twisting caps, the blurred white of smocked frocks--grew and multiplied and became misty. She had to grasp the table to steady herself.

Mrs. Toft saw how it was, and came to the rescue. "What's Toft say about it?" she asked.

"Ay, to be sure, missus," Petch agreed. "I dunno as he's said anything yet."

"I don't think the Master could have passed and not been seen," Toft replied. His tone was low, and in the middle of his speech he shivered. "But I'm not saying that the flask wasn't there this morning. It's a small thing."

"It couldn't have been overlooked, Mr. Toft," the keeper replied firmly. "I speak as I know!"

Again Mrs. Toft intervened. "I'm sure nobody would ha' laid a hand on the Master!" she said. "Nobody in these parts and nobody foreign, as I can fancy. I've no doubt at all the poor gentleman awoke with some maggot in his brain and wandered off, not knowing. The question is, what can we do? The young lady's had a sad day, and it's time she was left to herself."

"There's nothing we can do now," Petch said flatly. "It stands to reason if we've found nothing in the daylight we'll find nothing in the dark. We'll be back at eight in the morning. Whether we'd ought to let his lordship know----"

"Sho!" said Mrs. Toft with scorn. "What's he in it, I'd like to know? But there, you've said what you come to say and it's time we left the young lady to herself."

Mary raised her head. "One moment," she said. "I want to thank you all for what you've done. And for what Petch says about the flask, he's right to speak out, but I can't think any one would touch my uncle. Only--can we do nothing? Nothing more? Nothing at all? If we don't find him to-night----" She broke off, overcome by her feelings.

"I'm afraid not, Miss," Petch said gently. "We'd all be willing, but we don't know where to look. I own I'm fair beat. Still Tom and I'll stay an hour or two with Toft in case of anything happening. Good-night, Miss. You're very welcome, I'm sure."

The others murmured their sympathy as they trooped out into the darkness. Mrs. Toft bustled away for the tea, and Mary was left alone.

Suspense lay heavy on her. She felt that she ought to be doing something and she did not know what to do. Dr. Pepper did not come, the Tofts were but servants. They could not take the onus, they could not share her burden; and Toft was a broken reed. Meanwhile time pressed. Hours, nay, minutes might make all the difference between life and death.

When Etruria came in with Mary's tea she found her mistress bending over the fire in an attitude of painful depression, and she said a few words, trying to impart to her something of her own patience. That patience was a fine thing in Etruria because it was natural. But Mary was of sterner stuff. She had a more lively imagination, and she could not be blind to the issues, or to the value of every moment that passed. Even while she listened to Etruria she saw with the eyes of fancy a hollow amid a clump of trees not far from a pool that she knew. In summer it was a pleasant dell, clothed with mosses and ferns and the flowers of the bog-bean; in winter a dank, sombre hollow. There she saw her uncle lie, amid the decaying leaves, the mud, the rank grass; and the vision was too much for her. What if he were really lying there, while she sat here by the fire? Sat here in this home which he--he had given her, amid the comforts which he had provided!

The thought was horrible, and she turned fiercely on the comforter. "Don't!" she cried. "You don't think! You don't understand! We can't go through the night like this! They must go on looking! Fetch your father! And bring Petch! Bring them here!" she cried.

Etruria went, alarmed by her excitement, but almost as quickly she came back. Toft had gone out with Petch and the other man. They would not be long.

Mary cried out on them, but could do no more than walk the room, and after a time Etruria coaxed her to sit down and eat; and tea and food restored her balance. Still, as she sat and ate she listened--she listened always. And Etruria, taught by experience, let her be and said nothing.

At last, "How long they are!" Mary cried. "What are they doing? Are they never----"

She stopped. The footsteps of two men coming through the hall had reached her ears, and she recognized the tread of one--recognized it with a rush of relief so great, of thankfulness so overwhelming that she was startled and might well have been more than startled, had she been free to think of anything but the lost man. It was Basset's step, and she knew it--she would have known it, she felt, among a hundred! He had come! An instant later he stood in the doorway, booted and travel-stained, his whip in his hand, just as he had dropped from the saddle--and with a face grave indeed, but calm and confident. He seemed to her to bring relief, help, comfort, safety, all in one!

"Oh!" she cried. "You are here! How--how good of you!"

"Not good at all," he answered, advancing to the table and quietly taking off his gloves. "Your messenger met me half-way to Blore. I was coming into Riddsley to a meeting. I had only to ride on. Of course I came."

"But the meeting?" she asked fearfully. Was he only come to go again?

"D--n the meeting!" he answered, moved to anger by the girl's pale face. "Will you give me a cup of tea, Toft? I will hear Miss Audley's account first. Keep Petch and the other man. We shall want them. In twenty minutes I'll talk to you. That will do."

Ah, with what gratitude, with what infinite relief, did Mary hear his tone of authority! He watched Toft out of the room and, alone with her, he looked at her. He saw that her hand shook as she filled the teapot, that her lips quivered, that she tried to speak and could not. And he felt an infinite love and pity, though he drove both out of his voice when he spoke. "Yes, tea first," he said coolly, as he took off his riding coat. "I've had a long journey. You must take another cup with me. You can leave things to me now. Yes, two lumps, please, and not too strong." He knocked together the logs, and warmed his hands, stooping over the fire with his back to her. Then he took his place at the table, and when he had drunk half a cup of tea, "Now," he said, "will you tell me the story from the beginning. And take time. More haste, less speed, you know."

With a calmness that surprised herself, Mary told the tale. She described the first alarm, the hunt through the house, the discoveries in the bedroom, Toft's breakdown, last of all the search through the park and the finding of the flask.

He listened gravely, asking a question now and then. When she had done, "What of Toft?" he inquired. "Not been very active, has he? Not given you much help?"

"No! But how did you guess?" she asked in surprise.

"I'm afraid that Toft knows more than he has told you. For the rest," he looked at her kindly, "I want you to give up the hope of finding your uncle alive. I have none. But I think I can promise you that there has been no suffering. If it turns out as I imagine, he was dead before he was missed. What the doctor expected has happened. That is all."

"I don't understand," she said.

"And I don't want to say more until I know for certain. May I ring for Toft?" She nodded. He rang, and after a pause, during which he stood, silent and waiting, the servant came in. He shot a swift glance at them, and dropped his eyes.

"Tell Petch and the other man to be ready to start with us in five minutes," Basset said. "Let them fetch a hurdle, and do you put a mattress on it. I suppose--you made sure he was dead, Toft, before you left him?"

The man flinched before the sudden question, but he showed less emotion than Mary. Perhaps he had expected it. After a pause, during which Basset did not take his eyes from him, "I made sure," he said in a low voice. "As God sees me, I did! But if you think I raised a hand to him----"

"I don't!" Basset said sternly. "I don't think so badly of you as that. But nothing but frankness can save you now. Is he in the Great House?"

Toft opened his mouth, but he seemed unable to speak. He nodded.

"What about the flask?"

"I dropped it," the man muttered. He turned a shade paler. "I could not bear to think he was lying there. I thought it would lead the search--that way, and they would find him."

"I see. That's enough now. Be ready to start at once."

The man went out. "Good heavens!" Mary cried. She was horror-stricken. "And he has known it all this time! Do you think that he--he had any part----"

"Oh no. He was alone with Mr. Audley when he collapsed, and he lost his head. They were together in the Great House--it was a difficult position--and he did not see his way to explain. He may have seen some advantage in gaining time--I don't know. The first thing to be done is to bring your uncle home. I will see to that. You have borne up nobly--you have done your part. Do you go to bed now."

Something in his tone, and in his thought for her, brought old times to Mary's mind and the blood to her pale cheek. She did not say no, but she would not go to bed. She made Etruria come to her, and the two girls sat in the parlor listening and waiting, moving only when it was necessary to snuff the candles. It was a grim vigil. An hour passed, two hours. At length they caught the first distant murmur, the tread of men who moved slowly and heavily under a burden--there are few who have not at one time or another heard that sound. Little by little the shuffling feet, the subdued orders, the jar of a stumbling bearer, drew nearer, became more clear. A gust of wind swept through the hall, and moaned upwards through the ancient house. The candles on the table flickered. And still the two sat spell-bound, clasping cold hands, as the unseen procession passed over the threshold, and for the last time John Audley came home to sleep amid his books--heedless now of right or claim, or rank or blood.

* * * * *

A few minutes later Basset entered the parlor. His face betrayed his fatigue, and his first act was to go to the sideboard and drink a glass of wine. Mary saw that his hand shook as he raised the glass, and gratitude for what he had done for her brought the tears to her eyes. He stood a moment, leaning in utter weariness against the wall--he had ridden far that day. And Mary had been no woman if she had not drawn comparisons.

Opportunity had served him, and had not served the other. Nor, had her betrothed been here, could he have helped her in this pinch. He could not have taken Basset's place, nor with all the will in the world could he have done what Basset had done.

That was plain. Yet deep down in her there stirred a faint resentment, a complaint hardly acknowledged. Audley was not here, but he might have been. It was his doing that she had not told her uncle, and that John Audley had passed away in ignorance. It was his doing that in her trouble she had had to lean on the other. It was not the first time during the long hours of the day that the thought had come to her; and though she had put it away, as she put it away now, the opening flower of love is delicate--the showers pass but leave their mark.

When Etruria had slipped out, and left them, Basset came forward, and warmed himself at the fire. "Perhaps it is as well you did not go to bed," he said. "You can go now with an easy mind. It was as I thought--he lay on the stairs of the Great House and he had been dead many hours. Dr. Pepper will tell us more to-morrow, but I have no doubt that he died of syncope brought on by exertion. Toft had tried to give him brandy."

Shocked and grieved, yet sensible of relief, she was silent for a time. She had known John Audley less than a year, but he had been good to her in his way and she sorrowed for him. But at least she was freed from the nightmare which had ridden her all day. Or was she? "May I know what took him there?" she asked in a low voice. "And Toft?"

"He believed that there were papers in the Great House, which would prove his claim. It was an obsession. He asked me more than once to go with him and search for them, and I refused. He fell back on Toft. They had begun to search--so Toft tells me--when Mr. Audley was taken ill. Before he could get him down the stairs, the end came. He sank down and died."

With a shudder Mary pictured the scene in the empty house. She saw the light of the lantern fall on the huddled group, as the panic-stricken servant strove to pour brandy between the lips of the dying man; and truly she was thankful that in this strait she had Basset to support her, to assist her, to advise her! "It is very dreadful," she said. "I do not wonder that Toft gave way. But had he--had my uncle--any right to be there?"

"In his opinion, yes. And if the papers were there, they were his papers, the house was his, all was his. In my opinion he was wrong. But if he believed anything, he believed that he was justified in what he did."

"I am glad of that!"

"There must be an inquest, I am afraid," Basset continued. "One or two will know, and one or two more will guess what Mr. Audley's errand was. But Lord Audley will have nothing to gain by moving in it. And if only for your sake--but you must go to bed. Etruria is waiting in the hall. I will send her to you. Good-night."

She stood up. She wished to thank him, she longed to say something, anything, which would convey to him what his coming had been to her. But she could not find words, she was tongue-tied. And Etruria came in.

CHAPTER XXVIII: THE NEWS FROM RIDDSLEY

The business which had taken Audley away on the morrow of his engagement had been no mere pretext. The crisis in political life which Peel's return to office had brought about was one of those upheavals which are of rare promise to the adventurous. The wise foresaw that the party which Sir Robert had led would be riven from top to bottom. Old allies would be flung into opposing camps, and would be reaching out every way for support. New men would be learning their value, and to those who dared, all things might be added. Places, prizes, honors, all might be the reward of those who knew how to choose their side with prudence and to support it with courage. The clubs were like hives of bees. All day long and far into the winter night Pall Mall roared under the wheels of carriages. About the doors of Whitehall Gardens, where Peel lived, men gathered like vultures about the prey. And, lo, in a twinkling and as by magic the Conservative party vanished in a cloud of dust, to reappear a few days later in the guise of Peelites and Protectionists--Siamese twins, who would not live together, and could not live apart.

At such a time it was Audley's first interest to be as near as possible to the hub of things and to place himself in evidence as a man concerned. He had a little influence in the Foreign Office, he had his vote in the House of Lords. And though he did not think that these would suffice, he trusted that, reinforced by the belief that he carried the seat at Riddsley in his pocket, they might be worth something to him.

Unfortunately he could deal with one side only. If Stubbs were right he could pass for the owner of the borough only as long as he opposed Sir Robert. He could return the younger Mottisfont and have the credit of returning him, in the landed interest; but however much it might suit his book--and it was of that book he was thinking as he travelled to Lord Seabourne's--he could not, if Stubbs were right, return a member in the other interest.

Now when a man can sell to one party only, tact is needed if he is to make a good bargain. Audley saw this. But he knew his own qualities and he did not despair. The occasion was unique, and he thought that it would be odd if he could not pluck from the confusion something worth having; some place under the Foreign Office, a minor embassy, a mission, something worth two, or three, or even four thousand a year.

He travelled up to town thinking steadily of the course he would pursue, and telling himself that he must be as cunning as the serpent and as gentle as the dove. He must let no whip cajole him, and no Tory browbeat him. For he had only this to look to now: a rich marriage was no longer among the possibilities. Not that he regretted his decision in that matter as yet, but at times he wondered at it. He told himself that he had been impulsive, and setting this down to the charms of his mistress he gave himself credit for disinterested motives. And then, too, he had made himself safe!

Still there were difficulties in the way of his ambition, which appeared more clearly at Seabourne Castle, where Lady Adela was a fellow-guest, and in London than at Riddsley; difficulties of shrewd whips, who knew the history of the borough by heart, and had figures at their fingers' ends; difficulties of arrogant leaders, who talked of his duty to the land and assumed that duty was its own reward. Above all, there was the difficulty that he could only sell to the party that was out of office and must pay in promises--bills drawn at long dates and for which no discounters could be found. For who could say when the landed interest, made up of stupid bull-headed men like Lord George Bentinck and Stubbs, a party without a leader and with divided counsels, would be in power? They were a mob rather than a party, and like every other mob were ready to sacrifice future prospects to present revenge.

That was a terrible difficulty, and his lordship did not see how he was to get over it. To the Peelites who could pay, cash down, in honors and places, he could not sell. Nor to the Liberals under little Lord John, though to their promises some prospect of office gave value. So that at times he almost despaired. For he had only this to look to now; if he failed in this he would have love and he would have Mary, and he would have safety, but very little besides. If his word had not been given to Mary, he might almost have reconsidered the matter.

The die was cast, however. Yet many a man has believed this, and then one fine morning he has begun to wonder if it is so--the cast was such an unlucky, if not an unfair one! And presently he has seen that at the cost of a little pride, or a little consistency, or what not, he might call the game drawn. That is, he might--if he were not the soul of honor that he is!

By and by under the stress of circumstances his lordship began to consider that point. He did not draw back, he did not propose to draw back; but he thought that he would keep the door behind him ajar. To begin with, he did not overwhelm Mary with letters--his public engagements were so many; and when he wrote he wrote on ordinary matters. His pen ran more glibly on party gossip than on their joint future; he wrote as he might have written to a cousin rather than to his sweetheart. But he told himself that Mary was not versed in love letters, nor very passionate. She would expect no more.

Then one fine morning he had a letter from Stubbs, which told him that there was to be a real contest in Riddsley, that the Horn and Corn platform was to be challenged, and that the assailant was Peter Basset. Stubbs added that the Working Men's Institute was beside itself with joy, that Hatton's and Banfield's hands were solid for repeal, and that the fight would be real, but that the issue was a foregone conclusion.

The news was not altogether unwelcome. The contest gave value to the seat, and increased my lord's claim; on that party, unfortunately, they could only pay in promises. It also tickled my lord's vanity. His rival, unhorsed in the lists of love, had betaken himself, it seemed, to other lists, in which he would as surely be beaten.

"Poor beggar!" Audley thought. "He was always a day late! Always came in second! I don't know that I ever knew anything more like him than this! From the day I first saw him, standing behind John Audley's counsel at the suit, right to this day, he has always been a loser!"

And he smiled as he recalled the poor figure Basset had cut as a squire of dames.

A week later Stubbs wrote again, and this time his news was startling. John Audley was dead. Stubbs wrote in the first alarm of the discovery, word of which had just been brought into the town. He knew no particulars, but thought that his lordship should be among the first to learn the fact. He added a hasty postscript, in which he said that Mr. Basset was proving himself a stronger candidate than either side had expected, and that not only were the brass-workers with him but a few of the smaller fry of tradesmen, caught by his cry of cheap bread. Stubbs closed, however, with the assurance that the landed interest would carry it by a solid majority.

"D--n their impudence!" Lord Audley exclaimed. And after that he gave no further heed to the postscript. As long as the issue was certain, the election was Mottisfont's and Stubbs's affair. As for Basset, the more money he chose to waste the better.

But John Audley's death was news--it was great news! So he was gone at last--the man whom he had always regarded as a menace! Whom he had feared, whose very name had rung mischief in his ears, by whom, during many a sleepless night, he had seen himself ousted from all that he had gained from title, income, lands, position! He was gone at last; and gone with him were the menace, the danger, the night alarms, the whole pile of gloomy fancies which apprehension had built up!

The relief was immense. Audley read the letter twice, and it seemed to him that a weight was lifted from him. John Audley was dead. In his dressing-gown and smoking-cap my lord paced his rooms at the Albany and said again and again, "He's dead! By gad, he's dead!" Later, he could not refrain from the thought that if the death had taken place a few weeks earlier, in that first attack, he would have been under no temptation to make himself safe. As it was--but he did not pursue the thought. He only reflected that he had followed love handsomely!

A day later a third letter came from Stubbs, and one from Mary. The tidings they brought were such that my lord's face fell as he read them, and he swore more than once over them. John Audley, the lawyer wrote, had been found dead in the Great House. He had been found lying on the stairs, a lantern beside him. Stubbs had visited the house the moment the facts became known. He had examined the muniment room and found part of the wall broken down, and in the room two boxes of papers which had been taken from a recess which the breach had disclosed. One of the boxes had been broken open. At present Stubbs could only say that the papers had been disturbed, he could not say whether any were missing. He begged his lordship--he was much disturbed, it was clear--to come down as quickly as possible. In the meantime, he would go through the papers and prepare a report. They appeared to be family documents, old, and not hitherto known to his lordship's advisers.

Audley was still swearing, when his man came in. "Will you wear the black velvet vest, my lord?" he asked, "or the flowered satin?"

"Go to the devil!" his master cried--so furiously that the man fled without more.

When he was gone Audley read the letter again, and came to the conclusion that in making himself safe he had builded more wisely than he knew. For who could say what John Audley had found? Or who, through those papers, had a hold on him? He remembered the manservant's visit, and the thing looked black. Very black. Alive or dead, John Audley threatened him.

Then he felt bitterly angry with Stubbs. There had been the most shocking carelessness. Had he not himself pointed out what was going on? Had he not put it to Stubbs that the place should be guarded? But the lawyer, stubborn in his belief that there were no papers there, had done nothing. Nothing! And this had come of it! This which might spell ruin!

Or, no. Stubbs had indeed done his best to ruin him, but he had saved himself. He turned with relief to Mary's letter.

It was written sadly, and it was rather cold. He noticed this, but her tone did not alarm him, because he set it down to the reserve of his own letters.

He took care to answer this letter, however, by that day's post, and he wrote more affectionately than before--as if her trouble had broken down a reserve natural to him. He wrote with tact, too. He could not attend the funeral; the dead man's feelings towards him forbade that he should. But his agent would attend, and his carriage and servants. When he had written the letter he was satisfied with it: more than satisfied when he had added a phrase implying that their happiness would not long be postponed.

After he had posted the letter he wondered if she would expect him to come to her. It was a lonely house and with death in it--but no, in the circumstances it was not possible. He would go down to The Butterflies next day. That would be the most that could be expected of him. He would be at hand if she needed anything.

But when the next day came he did not go. A letter from a man belonging to the inner circle of politics reached him. The great man, who had been and might be again in the Cabinet, suggested a meeting. Nothing came of the meeting--it was one of those will-of-the-wisps that draw the unwary on until they find themselves committed. But it kept Audley in London, and it was not until the evening of Monday, the day of the funeral, that, chilled and out of temper, after posting the last stage from Stafford, he reached his quarters at The Butterflies, and gave short answers to Mrs. Jenkinson's inquiries after his health.

"Poor dear young man!" she said, when she rejoined her sisters. "He has a kind heart and he feels it. Mr. John was Mr. John, and odd, very odd. But still he was an Audley!"

CHAPTER XXIX: THE AUDLEY BIBLE

Angry with Stubbs as he was--and with some reason--Lord Audley was not the man to bite off his nose to spite his face. He pondered long what he would say to him, and more than once he rehearsed the scene, toning down this phrase and pruning that. For he knew that after all Stubbs was a good agent. He was honest, he thought much and made much of the property, and nothing would be gained by changing him. Then his influence in the borough was such that even if my lord quarrelled with him, Mottisfont would hardly venture to discard him.

For these reasons Audley had no mind to break with his agent. But he did wish to punish him. He did wish to make his displeasure felt. And he wished this the more because he began to suspect that if Stubbs had been less bigoted, he might have carried the borough the way he wished--the way that would pay him best.

Stubbs on his side foresaw an unpleasant quarter of an hour. He had been too easy. He had paid too little heed to John Audley's trespasses, and had let things pass that he should have stopped. Then, too, he had been over-positive that there were no more documents at the Great House. Evil had not come of this, but it might have; and he made up his mind to hear some hard words.

But when he obeyed my lord's summons his reception tried his patience. A bright fire burned in the grate, half a dozen wax candles shed a softened light on the room. The wine stood at Audley's elbow, and his glass was half full. But he did not give Stubbs even two fingers, nor did he ask him to take wine. And his tone was colder than Stubbs had ever known it. He made it plain that he was receiving a servant, and a servant with whom he was displeased.

Still he was Lord Audley, something of divine right survived in him, and Stubbs knew that he had been himself in the wrong. He took the bull by the horns. "You are displeased, my lord," he said, as he took the seat to which the other pointed. "And I admit with some cause. I have been mistaken and, perhaps, a little remiss! But it is the exception, and it will be a lesson to me. I am sorry, my lord," he added frankly. "I can say no more than that."

"And much good that will do us," my lord growled, "in certain events, Mr. Stubbs!"

"At any rate it will be a sharp lesson to me," Stubbs replied. "It has cost Mr. Audley his life."

"He had no right to be there!"

"No, my lord, he had no right to be there. But he would not have been there if I had seen that the place was properly secured. I take all the blame."

"Unfortunately," the other flung at him contemptuously, "you cannot pay the penalty; that may fall upon me. Anyway, it was a d--d silly thing, Mr. Stubbs, to leave the place open, and you see what has come of it."

"I cannot deny it, my lord," Stubbs said patiently. "But I hope that nothing will come of it. I will tell your lordship first what my own observations were. I made a careful examination of the two chests of papers and I came to the conclusion that Mr. Audley had done little more than open the first when he was taken ill. One chest showed some disturbance. The upper layer had been taken out and replaced. The other box had not been opened."

"What if he found what he wanted and searched no further?" Audley asked grimly. "But the point of the matter does not lie there. It lies in another direction, as I should have thought any lawyer would see."

"My lord?"

"Who was with him?" Lord Audley rapped the table with his fingers. "That's the point, sir! Who was with him?"

"I think I have ascertained that," Stubbs replied, less put out than his employer expected. "I have little doubt that his man-servant, a man called Toft, was with him."

"Ha!" the other exclaimed, "I expected that!"

Stubbs raised his eyebrows. "You know him, my lord?"

"I know him for a d--d blackmailing villain!" Audley broke out. Then he remembered himself. He had not told Stubbs of the blackmailing. And, after all, what did it matter? He had made himself safe. Whatever papers he had found, John Audley was dead, and John Audley's heiress was going to be his wife! The danger to him was naught, and the blackmailer was already disarmed. Still he was not going to spare Stubbs by telling him that. Instead, "What did the boxes contain?" he asked ungraciously.

"Nothing of any value when I examined them, my lord. Old surrenders, fines, and recoveries with some ancient terriers. I could find no document among them that related to the title."

"That may be," Audley retorted. "But John Audley expected to find something that related to the title! He knew more than we knew. He knew that those boxes existed, and he knew what he expected to find in them."

"No doubt. And if your lordship had given me a little more time I should have explained before this that he was disappointed in his expectation; nay, more, that it was that disappointment--as I have little doubt--that caused his collapse and death."

"How the devil do you know that?"

"If your lordship will have patience I will explain," Stubbs said, a gleam of malice in his eyes. He rose from his seat and took from a chair beside the door a parcel which he had laid there on his entrance. "I have here that which he found, and that which I don't doubt caused his death."

"The deuce you have!" Audley cried, rising to his feet in his surprise. And he watched with all his eyes while the lawyer slowly untied the tape and spread wide the wrappers. The action disclosed a thick quarto volume bound in blue leather, sprinkled on the sides with silver butterflies, and stamped with the arms of Audley. "Good G--d!" Audley continued, "the Family Bible!"

"Yes, the Family Bible," the lawyer answered, gazing at it complacently, "about which there was so much talk at the opening of the suit. It was identified by a score of references, called for by both sides, sought for high and low, and never produced!"

"And here it is!"

"Here it is. Apparently at some time or other it went out of fashion, was laid aside and lost sight of, and eventually bricked up with a mass of old and valueless papers."

Audley steadied his voice with difficulty. "And what is its effect?" he asked.

"Its effect, my lord, is to corroborate our case in every particular," the lawyer answered proudly. "Its entries form a history of the family for a long period, and amongst them is an entry of the marriage of Peter Paravicini Audley on the date alleged by us; an entry made in the handwriting of his father, and one of eleven made by the same hand. This entry agrees in every particular with the suspected statement in the register which we support, and fully bears out our case."

"And John Audley found that?" my lord cried, after a moment of pregnant silence. He had regained his composure. His eyes were shining.

"Yes, and it killed him," Stubbs said gravely. "Doubtless he came on it at the moment when he thought success was within his grasp, and the shock was too much for him."

"Good Lord! Good Lord! And how did you get it?"

"From Mr. Basset."

"Basset?"

"Who obtained it, I have no doubt, from the man, Toft, either by pressure or purchase."

"The rascal! The d--d rascal! He ought to be prosecuted!"

"Possibly," the lawyer agreed. "But he was only an accomplice, and we could not prosecute him without involving others; without bringing Mr. John's name into it--and he is dead. As a fact, I have passed my word to Mr. Basset that no steps should be taken against him, and I think your lordship will agree with me that I could not do otherwise."

"Still--the man ought to be punished!"

"He ought, but if any one has paid for his silence or for this book, it is not we."

After that there was a little more talk about the Bible, which my lord examined with curiosity, about the singularity of its discovery, about the handwriting of the entries, which the lawyer said he could himself prove. Stubbs was made free of the decanter, and of everything but my lord's mind. For Audley said nothing of his engagement to Mary--the moment was hardly opportune; and nothing--it was too late in the day--of Toft's former exploit. He stood awhile absorbed and dreaming, staring through the haze of the candles. Here at last was final and complete relief. No more fears, no more calculations. Here was an end at last of the feeling that there was a mine under him. Traditions, when they are bred in the bone, die slowly, and many a time he had been hard put to it to resist the belief, so long whispered, that his branch was illegitimate. At last the tradition was dead. There was no more need to play for safety. What he had he had, and no one could take it from him.

And presently the talk passed to the election.

"There's no doubt," Stubbs said, "that Mr. Basset is a stronger candidate than either side expected."

"But he's no politician! He has no experience!"

The lawyer sat forward, with his legs apart and a hand on either knee. "No," he said. "But the truth is, though it is beyond me how a gentleman of his birth can be so misled, he believes what he says--and it goes down!"

"Is he a speaker?"

"He is and he isn't! I slipped in myself one night at the back of one of the new-fangled meetings his precious League has started. I wanted to see, my lord, if any of our people were there. I heard him for ten minutes, and at the start he was so jumpy I thought that he would break down. But when he got going--well, I saw how it was and what took the people. He believes what he says, and he says it plain. The way he painted Peel giving up everything, sacrificing himself, sacrificing his party, sacrificing his reputation, sacrificing all to do what he thought was right--the devil himself wouldn't have known his own!"

"He almost converted you?"

The lawyer laughed disdainfully. "Not a jot!" he said. "But I saw that he would convert some. Not many," Stubbs continued complacently. "There's some that mean to, but will think better of it at the last. And some would but daren't! Two or three may. Still, he's such a candidate as we've not had against us before, my lord. And with cheap bread and the preachings of this plaguy League--I shall be glad when it is over."

Audley rose and poked the fire. "You're not going to tell me," he said, in a voice that was unnaturally even, "that he's going to beat us? You're not going, after all the assurances you've given me----"

"God forbid," Stubbs replied. "No, no, my lord! Mr. Mottisfont will hold the seat! I mean only that it will be a nearer thing--a nearer thing than it has been."

He had no idea that his patron was fighting a new spasm of anger; that the thought that he might, after all, have dealt with Sir Robert, the thought that he might, after all, have bargained with the party in power, was almost too much for the other's self-command. It was too late now, of course. It was too late. But if the contest was to be so close, surely if he had cast his weight on the other side, he might have carried it!

And what if the seat were lost? Then this stubborn, confident fool, who was as bigoted in his faith as the narrowest Leaguer of them all, had done him a deadly injury! My lord bit off an oath, and young as he was, his face wore a very apoplectic look as he turned round, after laying down the poker.

"That reminds me," the lawyer resumed, blandly unconscious of the crisis, and of the other's anger. "I meant to ask your lordship what's to be done about the two Boshams. You remember them, my lord? They've had the small holding by the bridge with the water meadow time out of mind--for seven generations they say. They pay eighteen pounds as joint tenants, and have votes as old freemen."

"What of them?" the other asked impatiently.

"Well, I'm afraid they'll not support us."

"Do you mean that they'll not vote for Mottisfont?"

"I'm afraid not," Stubbs answered. "They're as stubborn as their own pigs! I've spoken to them myself and told them that they've only one thing to expect if they go against their landlord."

"And that is, to go out!" Audley said. "Well, make that quite clear to them, Stubbs, and depend upon it--they'll see differently."

"I'm afraid they won't, my lord, and that is why I trouble you. They voted against the last lord--twice, I am told--and the story goes that he laid his stick about Ben Bosham's shoulders in the street--that would be in '31, I fancy. But he didn't turn them out--they'd been in the holding so long."

"Two votes may have been nothing to him," Audley replied coldly. "They are something to me. They will vote for Mottisfont or they will go, Stubbs. That is flat, and do you see to it. There, I'm tired now," he continued, rising from his seat.

Stubbs rose. "I don't know if your lordship's heard about Mr. John's will!"

"No!" My lord straightened himself. Earlier in the day he had given some thought to this, and had weighed Mary Audley's chances of inheriting what John Audley had. "No!" he said. And he waited.

"He has left the young lady eight thousand pounds."

"Eight thousand!" Audley ejaculated. "Do you mean--he must have had more than that? He wasted a small fortune in that confounded suit. But he must have had--four times that, man!"

"The residue goes to Mr. Basset."

"Basset!" Audley cried, his face flushed with passion. "To Basset?" he repeated. "Good G--d!"

"So I'm told, my lord," the lawyer answered, staggered by the temper in which his employer received the news.

"But Miss Audley was his own niece! Basset? He was no relation to him!"

"They were very old friends."

"That's no reason why he should leave him thirty thousand pounds of Audley money! Money taken straight out of the Audley property! Thirty thousand----"

"Not thirty, my lord," Stubbs ventured. "Not much above twenty, I should say. If you put it----"

"If I put it that you were--something of a fool at times," the angry man cried, "I shouldn't be far wrong! But there, there, never mind! Good-night! Can't you see I'm dead tired and hardly know what I am saying? Come to-morrow! Come at eleven in the morning."

Stubbs hardly knew how to take it. But after a moment's hesitation, he made the best of the apology, muttered something, and got out of the room. On the stairs he relieved his feelings by a word or two. In the street he wondered what had taken the man so suddenly. Surely he had not expected to get the money!

CHAPTER XXX: A FRIEND IN NEED

Basset had obtained the missing Bible very much in the way the lawyer had indicated--partly by purchase and partly by pressure. Shocked as Toft had been by his master's sudden death, he had had the presence of mind to remember that he might make something of what they had discovered could he secrete it; and with every nerve quivering the man had fought down panic until he had hidden the parcel which had caused John Audley's collapse. Then he had given way. He had turned his back on the Great House, and shuddering, clutched at by grisly hands, pursued by phantom feet, he had fled through the night and the Yew Walk, to hide, for the present at least, his part in the tragedy.

Basset, however, had known too much for him, and the servant, shaken by what had happened, had not been able to persist in his denials. But to tell and to give were two things, and it is doubtful whether he would have released his plunder if Basset had not in the last resort disclosed to him Miss Audley's engagement to her cousin.

The change which this news wrought in Toft had astonished Basset. The man had gone down under it as under a blow on the head. The spirit had gone out of him, and he had taken with thankfulness the sum which Basset, as John Audley's representative, had offered him--rather out of pity than because it seemed necessary. He had given up the parcel on the night before the funeral.

The book in his hands, Basset had hastened to be rid of it. Cynically he had told himself that he did so, lest he too might give way to the ignoble impulse to withhold it. Audley was his rival, but that he might have forgiven, as men forgive great wrongs and in time smile on their enemies. But the little wrongs, who can forgive these--the slight, the sneer, the assumption of superiority, the upper hand lightly taken and insolently held?

Not Peter Basset, at a moment when he was being tried almost beyond bearing. For every day, between the finding of the body and the funeral, and often more than once in the day he had to see Mary, he had to advise her, he had--for there was no one else--to explain matters to her, to bear her company. He had to quit this meeting and that Ordinary--for election business stops for no man--and to go to her. He had to find her alone and to see her face light up at his entrance; he had to look back, and to see her watch him as he rode from the door. Nor when he was absent from the Gatehouse was it any better; nay, it was worse. For then he was forced to think of her as alone and sad, he had to picture her brooding over the fire, he had to fancy her at her solitary meals. And alike, with her or away from her, he had to damp down the old passion, as well as the new regret that each day and each hour and every kind look on her part fanned into a flame. Nor was even this all; every day he saw that she grew more grave, daily he saw her color fading, and he did not know what qualms she masked, what nightmares she might be suffering in that empty house--nay, what cause for unhappiness she might be hiding. At last--it was the afternoon before the funeral--he could bear it no longer, and he spoke.

"You ought not to be here!" he said bluntly. "Why doesn't Audley fetch you away?" He was standing before the fire drawing on his gloves as he prepared to leave. The room was full of shadows, for he had chosen a time when she could not see his face.

She tried to fence with him. "I am afraid," she said, "that some formalities will be necessary before he can do that."

"Then why is he not here?" he retorted. "Or why doesn't he send some one to be with you? You ought not to be alone. Mrs. Jenkinson at The Butterflies--she's a good soul--you know her?"

"Yes."

"She'd come at a word. I know it's not my business----"

"Or you would go about it, I am sure," she replied gently, "with as much respect to my wishes as Lord Audley shows."

"Your wishes? But why--why do you wish----"

"Why do I wish to be alone?" she answered. "Because I owe something to my uncle. Because I owe him a little thought and some remembrance. He made my old life for me--would you have me begin the new one before he is in the grave? This was his house--would you have me entertain Lord Audley in it?" She stood up, slender and straight, with the table between them-- and he did not guess that her knees were trembling. "Please to understand," she continued, "that Lord Audley and I are entirely at one in this. We have our lives before us, and it were indeed selfish of us, and ungrateful of me, if we grudged a few days to remembrance. As selfish," she continued bravely--and he did not know that she braced herself anew--"as if I were ever to forget the friend who was his friend, whose kindness has never failed me, whose loyalty has never--" she broke down there. She could not go on.

"Add, too," he said gruffly, "who has robbed you of the greater part of your inheritance! Don't forget that!" He had been explaining the effect of John Audley's will to her. It had been opened that morning.

His roughness helped her to recover herself. "I do not know what you mean by 'inheritance,'" she said. "My uncle has left me the portion his wife brought to him. I am more than satisfied. I am very grateful. My only fear is that, had he known of my engagement, he would not have wished me to have this."

"The will was made before you came to live here," Basset said. "The eight thousand was left to you because you were his brother's child. It was the least he could do for you, and had he made a new will he would doubtless have increased it. But," breaking off, "I must be going." Yet he still stood, and he still tapped the table with the end of his riding-crop. "When is Audley coming?" he asked suddenly. "To-morrow?"

"Yes, to-morrow."

"Well he ought to," he replied, without looking at her. "You should not be here a day longer by yourself. It is not fitting. I shall see you in the morning before we start for the church, but the lawyer will be here and I shall not be able to come again. But I must be sure that there is some one here." He spoke almost harshly, partly to impress her, partly to hide his own feelings; and he did not suspect that she, too, was fighting for calmness; that she was praying that he would go, before she showed more clearly how much the parting tried her--before every kind word, every thoughtful act, every toilsome journey taken on her behalf, rose to her remembrance and swept away the remnants of her self-control.

She had not imagined that she would feel the leave-taking as she did. She could not speak, and she was thankful that it was too dark for him to see her face. Would he never go? And still the slow tap-tap of his whip on the table went on. It seemed to her that she would never forget the sound! And if he touched her----

But he had no thought of touching her.

"Good-night," he said at last. He turned, moved away, lingered. At the door he looked back. "I am going into the library," he said. "The coffin will be closed in the morning."

"Yes, good-night," she muttered, thankful that the thought of the dead man steadied her and gave her power to speak. "I shall see him in the morning."

He closed the door, and she crept blindly to a chair, and covered by the darkness she gave way. She told herself that she was thinking of her uncle. But she knew that she deceived herself. She knew that her uncle had little to do with her tears, or with the feeling of loneliness that overcame her. Once more she had lost her friend--and a friend so good, so kind. Only now did she know his value!

Five minutes later Basset crossed the court in search of his horse. Mrs. Toft's door stood open and a stream of firelight and candlelight poured from it and cut the January fog. She was hard at work, cooking funeral meats with the help of a couple of women; for quietly as John Audley had lived, he could not be buried without some stir. Odd people would come, drawn by the Audley name, squires who boasted some distant connection with the line, a few who had been intimate with him in past days. And the gentry far and wide would send their carriages, and the servants must be fed. Still the preparations jarred on Basset as he crossed the court. He felt the bustle an outrage on the mourning girl he had left, and on his own depression.

Probably Mrs. Toft had set the door open that she might waylay him, for as he went by she came out and stopped him. "Mr. Basset, sir!" she said in a low voice. "Is this true, what Toft tells me? I declare, when I heard it, you could ha' knocked me down with a common dip!" She was wiping her hands on her apron. "That the young lady is to marry his lordship?"

"I believe it is true," Basset said coldly. "But you had better let her take her own time to make it known. Toft should not have told you."

"Never fear, sir, I'll not let on. But, Lord's sakes, who'd ha' thought it? And she'll be my lady! Not that she's not an Audley, and there's small differ, and she'll make none, or I don't know her! Well, indeed, I hope she's wise, but wedding cake, make it as rich as you like, it's soon stale. And for him, I don't know what the Master would have said if he'd known it! I thought things would come out," with a quick look at Basset, "quite otherways! And wished it, too!"

"Thank you, Mrs. Toft," he said quietly.

"Just so, sir, you'll excuse me. Well, it's not many months since the young lady came, and look at the changes! With the old Master dead, and you going in for elections--drat 'em, I say, plaguy things that set folks by the ears--and Mr. Colet gone and 'Truria that unsettled, and Toft for ever wool-gathering, I shall be glad when tomorrow's over and I can sit down and sort things out a bit!"

"Yes, Mrs. Toft."

"And speaking of elections reminds me. You know they two Boshams of the Bridge End, sir?"

"I know them. Yes."

Mrs. Toft sniffed. "They're sort of kin to me, and middling honest as town folks go. But two silly fellows, always meddling and making and gandering with things they'd ought to leave to the gentry! The old lord was soft with them, and so they've a mind now to see who is the stronger, they or his lordship."

"If you mean that they have promised to vote for me----"

"That's it, sir! Vote their living away, they will, and leave 'em alone! Votes are for poor men to make a bit of money by, odd times; but they two Boshams I've no patience with. Sally, Ben's wife, was with me to-day, and the long and the short of it is, Mr. Stubbs has told them that if they vote for you they'll go into the street."

"It's a hard case," Basset said. "But what can I do?"

"Don't ha' their votes. What's two votes to you? For the matter of that," Mrs. Toft continued, thoroughly wound up, "what's all the votes--put together? Bassets and Audleys, Audleys and Bassets were knights of the shire, time never was, as all the country knows! But for this little borough--place it's what your great-grandfather wouldn't ha' touched with a pair of gloves! I'd leave it to the riff-raff that's got money and naught else, and builds Institutes and such like!"

"But you'd like cheap bread?" Basset said, smiling.

"Bread? Law, Mr. Basset, what's elections to do wi' bread? It's not bread they're thinking of, cheap or dear. It's beer! Swim in it they do, more shame to you gentry! I'll be bound to say there's three goes to bed drunk in the town these days for two that goes sober! But there, you speak to they Boshams, Mr. Basset, sir, and put some sense into them!"

"I'm afraid I can't promise," he answered. "I'll see!"

But it was not of the Boshams he thought as he rode down the hill with a tight rein--for between fog and frost the road was treacherous. He was thinking of the man who had been his friend and of whose face, sphinx-like in death, he had taken farewell in the library. And solemn thoughts, thoughts such as at times visit most men, calmed his spirit. The fret of the contest, the strivings of the platform, the rubs of vanity flitted to a distance, they became small things. Even passion lost its fever and love its selfishness; and he thought of Audley with patience and of Mary as he would think of her in years to come, when time had enshrined her, and she was but a memory, one of the things that had shaped his life. He knew, indeed, that this mood would pass; that passion would surge up again, that love would reach out to its object, that memory would awake and wound him, that pain and restlessness would be his for many days. But he knew also--in this hour of clear views--that all these things would have an end, and only the love,

That seeketh not itself to please

Nor of itself hath any care,

would remain with him.

Already it had carried him some way. In the matter of the election, indeed, he might be wrong. He might have entered on it too hastily--often he thought that he had--he might be of fibre too weak for the task. It cost him much to speak, and the occasional failure, the mistake, the rebuff, worried him for hours and even days. Trifles, too, that would not have troubled another, troubled his conscience; side-issues that were false, but that he must not the less support, workers whom he despised and must still use, tools that soiled his hands but were the only tools. Then the vulgar greeting, the tipsy grasp, the friend in the market-place:--

The man who hails you Tom or Jack
And proves by thumps upon your back
How he esteems your merit!
Who's such a friend that one had need
Be very much his friend indeed
To pardon or to bear it!

these humiliated him. But worse, far worse, than all was his unhappy gift of seeing the merits of the other side and of doubting the cause which he had set out to champion. He had fits of lowness when he was tempted to deny that honesty existed anywhere in politics; when Sir Robert Peel no less than Lord George Bentinck--who was coming to the front as the spokesman of the land--Cobden the Radical no less than Lord John Russell, seemed to be bent only on their own advancement, when all, he vowed, were of the School of the Cynics!

But were he right or wrong in his venture--and right or wrong he had small hope of winning-- he would not the less cling to the thing which Mary had given him--the will to make something of his life, the determination that he would leave the world, were it only the few hundred acres that he owned, or the hamlet in which he lived, better than he had found them. The turmoil of the election over, he would devote himself to his property at Blore. There John Audley's twenty thousand pounds opened a wide door. He would build, drain, manure, make roads, re-stock. He would make all things new. From him as from a centre comfort should flow. He saw himself growing old in the middle of his people, a lonely, but not an unhappy man.

As he passed the bridge at Riddsley he thought of the Boshams, and weary as he was, he drew rein at their door. Ben Bosham came out, bare-headed; a short, elderly man with a bald forehead and a dirty complexion, a man who looked like a cobbler rather than the cow-keeper he was.

"Shut your door, Bosham," Basset said. "I want a word with you."

And when the man had done this, he stooped from the saddle and said a few words to him in a low voice.

"Well, I'm dommed!" the other answered, peering up through the darkness. "It be you, Squire, bain't it? But you're not meaning it?"

"I am," Basset replied in a low voice. "I'd not say, vote for him, Bosham. But leave it alone. You're not called upon to ruin yourself."

"But ha' you thought," the man exclaimed, "that our two votes may make the differ? That they may make you or mar you, Squire!"

"Well, I'd rather be marred than see you put out of your place," Basset answered. "Think it over, Bosham."

But Bosham repudiated even thought of it. This vote and his use of it, this defiance of a lord, was, for the time, his very life. "I'll not do it," he declared. "I couldn't do it! Nor I won't!" he repeated. "We're freemen o' Riddsley, and almost the last of the freemen that has votes as freemen! And while free we are, free we'll be, and vote as we choose, Squire! Vote as we choose! I'd not show my face in the town else! Mr. Stubbs may talk as gallus as he likes--and main ashamed of himself he looked yesterday--he may talk as gallus as never was, we'll not bend to no landlord, nor to no golden image!"

"Then there's no more to be said," Basset answered, feeling that he cut a poor figure. "I don't wish you to do anything against your conscience, Bosham, and I'm obliged to you and your brother for your staunchness. I only wanted you to know that I should understand if you stayed away."

"I'd chop my foot off first!" cried the patriot.

After which Basset had no choice but to leave him and to ride on, feeling that he was himself too soft for the business--that he was a round man in a square hole. He wondered what his committee would think of him if they knew, and what Bosham thought of him--who did know. For Bosham seemed to him at this moment a man of principle, a patriot, nay, a very Brutus: whereas, Ben was in truth no better than a small man of large conceit, whose vote was his one road to fame.

CHAPTER XXXI: BEN BOSHAM

It was Tuesday, market-day at Riddsley, and farmers' wives, cackling as loudly as the poultry they carried, elbowed one another on the brick pavements or clustered before the windows of the low-browed shops. Farmers in white great-coats, with huge handkerchiefs about their necks, streamed from the yards of the Packhorse and the Barley Mow, and meeting a friend planted themselves in the roadway as firmly as if they stood in their own pastures. Now and again a young spark, fancying all eyes upon his four-year-old, sidled through the throng with many a "Whoa!" and "Where be'st going, lad?" While on the steps of the Market-Cross and about the long line of carts that rested on their shafts in the open street, hucksters chaffered and house-wives haggled over the rare egg or the keg of salted butter.

The quacking of ducks, the neighing of horses, the singsong of rustic voices filled the streets. It was common talk that the place was as full as at the March Fair. The excitement of the Election had gone abroad, the cry that the land was at stake had brought in some, others had come to see what was afoot. Many a stout tenant was here who at other times left the marketing to his womenfolk; and shrewd glances he cast at the gentry, as he edged past the justices who lounged before the Audley Arms and killed in gossip the interval between the Magistrates' Meeting, at which they had just assisted, and the Ordinary at which they were to support young Mottisfont.

The great men talked loudly and eagerly, were passionate, were in earnest. Occasionally one of the younger of them would step aside to look at a passing hackney, or an older man would speak to a favorite tenant whom he called by his first name. But, for the most part, they clung together, fine upstanding figures, in high-collared riding-coats and top-boots. They were keen to a man; the farmers keen also, but not so keen. For the argument that high wheat meant high rents, and that most of the benefits of protection went to the landlords had got about even in Riddsley. The squires complained that the farmers would only wake up when it was too late!

Still in such a place, and on market-day, four out of five were in the landed interest; four-fifths of the squires, four-fifths of the parsons, almost four-fifths of the tenants; for the laborers, no one asked what they thought of it--they had ten shillings a week and no votes. "Peel--'od rot him!" cried the majority, "might shift as often as his own spinning-jenny! But not they! No Manchester man, and no Tamworth man either, should teach them their business! Who would die if there were no potatoes? It was a flam, a bite, but it wouldn't bamboozle Stafford farmers!"

Meanwhile Stubbs, moving quietly through the throng, spoke with one here and there. He had the same word for all. "Listen to me, John," he would say, his hand on the yeoman's shoulder. "Peel says he's been wrong all these years and is only right now. Then, if you believe him, he's a fool; and if you don't believe him, he's a knave. Not a very good vet., John, eh? Not the vet. for the old gray mare, eh?"

This had a great effect. John went away and repeated it to himself, and presently grasped the dilemma and chuckled over it. Ten minutes later he imparted it, with the air of a Solomon, to the "Duke," who mouthed it and liked it and rolled it off to the first he met. It went the round of the inns and about four o'clock a farmer fresh from the "tap" put it to Stubbs and convinced him; and that night men, travelling home market-peart in the charge of their wives, bore it to many a snug homestead set in orchards of hard cider apples.

Had the issue of the Election lain with the Market, indeed, it had been over. But of the hundred and ninety voters no more than fifteen were farmers, and though the main trade of the town sided with them, the two factories were in opposition; and cheap bread had its charms for the lesser fry. But the free traders were too wise to flaunt their views on market-day, and it was left for little Ben Bosham, whose vote was pretty near his all, to distinguish himself in the matter.

He, too, had been at the tap, and about noon his voice was heard issuing from a group who stood near the Audley Arms. "Be I free, or bain't I?" he bawled. "Answer me that, Mr. Bagenal!"

A knot of farmers had edged him into a corner and were disposed to bait him. A stubby figure in a velveteen coat and drab breeches, his hand on an ash-plant, he held his ground among them, tickled by the attention he excited and fired by his own importance. "Be I free, or bain't I?" he repeated.

"Free?" Bagenal answered contemptuously. "You be free to make a fool of yourself, Ben! I'm thinking you'd ha' us all lay down the ground to lazy pasture and live by milk, as you do!"

"Milk?" ejaculated a stout man of many acres, whose contempt for such traffic was above speech.

"You'll be free to go out of Bridge End," cried a third. "That's what you'll be free to do! And where'll your vote be then, Ben?"

But there Bosham was sure of himself. "That's where you be wrong, Mr. Willet," he retorted with gusto. "My vote dunno come o' my landlord, and in the Bridge End or out of the Bridge End, I've a vote while I've a breath! 'Tain't the landlord's vote, and why'd I give it to he? Free I be--not like you, begging your pardon! Freeman, old freeman, I be, of this borough! Freeman by marriage!"

"Then you be a very rare thing!" Bagenal retorted slyly. "There's many lose their freedom that way, but you be the first I ever heard of that got it!"

"And a hard bargain, too, as I hear," said Willet.

This drew a roar of laughter. The crowd grew thicker and the little man's temper grew short, for his wife was no beauty. He began to see that they were playing with him.

"You leave me alone, Mr. Willet," he said angrily, "and I'll leave you alone!"

"Leave thee alone!" said the farmer who had turned up his nose at milk. "So I would, same as any other lump o' dirt! But yo' don't let us. Yo' set up to know more than your betters! Pity the old lord ain't alive to put his stick about your back!"

"Did it smart, Ben?" cried a lad who had poked himself in between his betters.

"You let me catch you," Ben cried, "and I'll make you smart. You be all a set of slaves! You'd set your thatch afire if squires'd tell you! Set o' slaves, set o' slaves you be!"

"And what be you, Bosham?" said a man who had just joined the group. "Head of the men, bain't you? Cheap bread and high wages, that's your line, ain't it!"

"That's his line, be it?" said the old farmer slowly. "Bit of a rascal it seems yo' be? Don't yo' let me find you in my boosey pasture talking to no men o' mine, or I'll make yo' smart a sight more than his lordship did!"

"Ay, that's Ben's line," said the new-comer.

"You're a liar!" Ben shrieked. "A dommed liar you be! I see you not half an hour agone coming out of Stubbs's office! I know who told you to say that, you varmint! I'll have the law of you!"

"Ben Bosham, the laborers' friend!" the man retorted.

Ben was furious, for he was frightened. There was no feud so bitter in the 'forties as the feud between farmer and laborer. The laborer had no vote, he had lost his common rights, his wood, his cow-feed; he was famished, he was crushed by the new Poor Law, and so he was often in an ugly mood, as singed barns and burning stacks went to show. Bosham knew that he might flout the squires, and at worst be turned out of his holding; but woe betide him if he got the name of the laborers' friend. Moreover, there was just so much truth in the accusation as made it dangerous. Ben and his brother eked out the profits of the dairy by occasional labor, and Ben had sometimes vapored in tap-rooms where he had better have held his tongue. He shrieked furiously, therefore, at the false witness, and even tried to reach him with his ash-plant. "Who be you?" he screamed. "You be a lawyer's pup, you be! You'd ruin me, you would! Let me get a hold of you and I'll put a mark on you! You be lying!"

"I don't know about that," said the big farmer slowly and weightily. "I'm feared yo're a bit of a rascal, Ben."

"Ay, and fine he'll look in front of Stafford Gaol some morning!" said Willet. "At the end of a rope."

On that in a happy moment for Ben, while he gaped for a retort and found none, two carriers' vans, huge wooden vehicles festooned with rabbits and market-baskets and drawn by three horses abreast, lumbered through the crowd and scattered it. In a twinkling Ben was left alone, an angry man, aware that he had cut but a poor figure!

He had been frightened, too, and he resented it. He thirsted for some chance of setting himself right, of proving to others that he was a freeman and not as other men. And in the nick of time he saw a chance--if only he had the courage to rise to it. He saw moving towards him through the press a mail-phaeton and pair. On the box, caped and gloved, the pink of fashion, sat no less a person than his lordship himself. A servant in the well-known livery, a white coat with a blue collar, sat behind him.

The vans which had freed Ben blocked the great man's way, and he was moving at a walk. All heads were bared as he passed, and he was acknowledging the courtesy with his whip when Ben stepped before the horses and lifted his hand. In an instant a hundred eyes were on the man and he knew that he had burned his boats. Bravado was now his only chance.

"My lord," he cried, waving his hat impudently. "I want to know what you be going to do about me?"

My lord hardly caught his words and did not catch his meaning, but he saw that the man was almost under the horses' feet and he checked them. Ben stood aside then but, as the carriage passed him, he laid his hand on the splashboard and walked beside it. He looked up at the great man and in the same impudent tone, "Be you agoing to turn me out, my lord?" he cried. "That's what I want to know."

"I don't understand you," Audley said coldly. He guessed that the man referred to the Election, and what was the use of understrappers like Stubbs if he was to be exposed to this?

"I'm Ben Bosham of the Bridge End, my lord, that's who I be," Ben replied brazenly. "I'm not ashamed of my name. I want to know whether you be agoing to turn me out, and my wife and my child! That's what I want to----"

Then a farmer seized him and dragged him back, and others laid hands on him, though he still shouted. "Dunno be a fool!" cried the farmer, deeply shocked. "Drive on, drive on, my lord! Never heed him. He've had a glass too much!"

"Packhorse beer, my lord," explained a second in stentorian tones--though he knew that Ben was fairly sober. "Ought to be ashamed of himself!" cried a third, and he shook the aggressor. Ben was in a minority of one, and those who held him were inclined to be rough.

Audley waved his whip good-humoredly. "Take care of him!" he said. "Don't hurt him!" And he drove on, outwardly unmoved though inwardly fuming. Still had it ended there little harm would have been done. But word of the brawl outran the carriage and, as it chanced, reached the door of Hatton's Works as the men came out to dinner. Ben Bosham had spoken his mind to his lordship! His lordship had driven over him! The farmers had beaten him! The news passed from one to another like flame, and the hands stood, some two score of them, and hooted my lord loudly, shouting "Shame!" and jeering at him.

Now had Audley been the candidate he would have thought nothing of it. He would have laughed in the men's faces and taken it as part of the day's work; or had he been the old lord, he would have flung a curse at the men and cut at the nearest with his whip--and forgotten it.

But he was not the old lord, times were changed, and the thing angered him. It was in an ill-temper that he drove on along the road that rose by gentle degrees to the Great Chase.

For the matter of that, he had been in a black mood for some time, because he could not make up his mind. Night and morning ambition whispered to him to put the vessel about; to steer the course which experience told him that it behooved a man to steer who was not steeped in romance, nor too greedy for the moment's enjoyment; the course which, beyond all doubt, he would have steered were he now starting!

But he was not starting; and when he thought of shifting the helm he foresaw difficulties. He did not think that he was a soft-hearted man, yet he feared that when it came to the point he would flinch. Besides, he told himself that he was a man of honor; and the change was a little at odds with this. But there again, he reflected that truth was honor and in the end would cause less pain.

Eight thousand pounds was so very small a portion! And for safety, he no longer needed to play for it. John Audley was dead and the Bible was in his hands; his case was beyond cavil or question, while the political situation was such that he saw no opening, no chance of enrichment in that direction. To make Mary, handsome, good, attractive as she was--to make her the wife of a poor peer, of a discontented, dissatisfied man--this, if he could only find it in his heart to tell her the truth, would be a cruel kindness.

As he drove along the road, angry with the wretched Bosham, angry with Stubbs, angry with the fools who had hooted him, he was not sorry to feel his ill-temper increase. He might not find it so difficult to speak to her. A little effort and the thing would be done. Eight thousand pounds? The interest would barely dress her. Whereas, if she had played her cards well and been heir to her uncle's thirty thousand--the case would have been different. After all, the fault lay with her.

He roused the off-horse with a sharp cut, and a moment later discerned at the end of a long, straight piece of road, the moss-clad steps of the old Cross and standing beside them a figure he knew.

He was moved, even while, in his irritation, he was annoyed that she had come to meet him at a place that had recollections for him. It seemed to him that in doing this she was putting an undue, an unfair burden on him.

She waved her hand and he raised his hat. The day was bright and cold, and the east wind had whipped a fine color into her cheeks. Perhaps that, too, was unfair. Perhaps that too was putting an undue burden on him.

CHAPTER XXXII: MARY MAKES A DISCOVERY

But his face was not one to betray his thoughts, and as he drew up beside Mary, horses fretting, polechains jingling, the silver of the harness glittering from a score of points, he made a gallant show. The most eager lover, Apollo himself in the chariot of the sun, had scarcely made a better approach to his mistress, had hardly carried it more finely over a mind open to appearances.

With a very fair show of haste he bade his man take the reins, and as the servant swung himself into the front seat the master sprang to the ground. His hand met Mary's, his curly-brimmed hat was doffed, his eyes smiled into hers. "Well, better late than never!" he said.

"Yes," she answered. But she spoke more soberly than he expected and her face was grave. "You have been a long time away."

That was their meeting. The servant was there; under his eyes it could not be warmer. Whether one or the other had foreseen this need not be asked.

He spoke to the man, who, possessed by a natural curiosity, was all ears. "Keep them moving," he said. "Drive back a mile or two and return." Then to Mary, his hat still in his hand, "A long time away? Longer than I expected, and far longer than I hoped, Mary. Shall we go up the hill a little?"

"I thought you would propose that," she said. "I am so glad that it is fine."

The man had turned the horses. Audley took her hand again and pressed it, looking in her face, telling himself that she grew more handsome every day. Why hadn't she thirty thousand pounds? Aloud he said, "So am I, very glad. Otherwise you could not have met me, and I fancied that you might not wish me to come to the house? Was that so, dear?"

"I think it was," she said. "He has been gone so very short a time. Perhaps it was foolish of me."

"Not at all!" he answered, admiring the purity of her complexion. "It was like you."

"If we had told him, it would have been different."

"On the other hand," he said deftly, as he drew her hand through his arm, "it might have troubled his last days? And now, tell me all, Mary, from the beginning. You have gone through dark days and I have not been--I could not be with you. But I want to share them."

She told the story of John Audley's disappearance, her cheeks growing pale as she described the alarm, the search, the approach of night and her anguish at the thought that her uncle might be lying in some place which they had overlooked! Then she told him of Basset's arrival, of the discovery, of the manner in which Peter had arranged everything and saved her in every way. It seemed to her that to omit this, to say nothing of him, would be as unfair to the one as uncandid to the other.

My lord's comment was cordial, yet it jarred on her. "Well done!" he said. "He was made to be of use, poor chap! If it were any one else I should be jealous of him!" And he laughed, pressing her arm to his side.

She was quivering with the memories which her story had called up, and it was only by an effort that she checked the impulse to withdraw her hand. "Had you been there----"

"I hope I should have done as much," he replied complacently. "But it was impossible."

"Yes," she said. And though she knew that her tone was cold, she could not help it. For many, many times during the last month she had pondered over his long absence and the chill of his letters. Many times she had told herself that he was treating her with scant affection, scant confidence, almost with scant respect. But then again she had reflected that she must be mistaken, that she brought him nothing but herself, and that if he did not love her he would not have sought her. And telling herself that she expected too much of love, too much of her lover, she had schooled herself to be patient, and had resolved that not a word of complaint should pass her lips.

But to assume a warmth which she did not feel was another matter. This was beyond her.

He, for his part, set down her manner to a natural depression. "Poor child!" he said, "you have had a sad time. Well, we must make up for it. As soon as we can make arrangements you must leave that gloomy house where everything reminds you of your uncle and--and we must make a fresh start. Do you know where I am taking you?"

She saw that they had turned off the road and were following a track that scrambled upwards through the scrub that clothed the slope below the Gatehouse. It slanted in the direction of the Great House. "Not to Beaudelays?" she said.

"Yes--to Beaudelays. But don't be afraid. Not to the house."

"Oh no!" she cried. "I don't think I could bear to go there to-day!"

"I know. But I want you to see the gardens. I want you to see what might have been ours, what we might have enjoyed had fortune been more kind to us! Had we been rich, Mary! It is hard to believe that you have never seen even the outside of the Great House."

"I have never been beyond the Iron Gate."

"And all these months within a mile!"

"All these months within a mile. But he did not wish it. It was one of the first things he made me understand."

"Ah! Well, there is an end of that!" And again so matter-of-fact was his tone that she had to struggle against the impulse to withdraw her arm. "Now, if there is any one who has a right to be there, it is you! And I want to be the one to take you there. I want you to see for yourself that it is only fallen grandeur that you are marrying, Mary, the thing that has been, not the thing that is. By G--d! I don't know that there is a creature in the world--certainly there is none in my world-- more to be pitied than a poor peer!"

"That's nothing to me," she said. And, indeed, his words had brought him nearer to her than anything he had said. So that when, taking advantage of the undergrowth which hid them from the road below, he put his arm about her and assisted her in her climb, she yielded readily. "To think," he said, "that you have never seen this place! I wonder that after we parted you did not go the very next morning to visit it!"

"Perhaps I wished to be taken there by you."

"By Jove! Do you know that that is the most lover-like thing you have said."

"I may improve with practice," she rejoined. "Indeed, it is possible," she continued demurely, "that we both need practice!"

She had not a notion that he was in two minds; that one half of him was revelling in the hour, pleased with possession, enjoying her beauty, dwelling on the dainty curves of her figure, while the other uncertain, wavering, was asking continually, "Shall I or shall I not?" But if she did not guess thoughts to which she had no clue he was sharp enough to understand hers. "Ah! you are there, are you?" he said. "Wait! Presently, when we are out of sight of that cursed road----"

"I didn't find fault!"

On that there was a little banter between them, gallant and smiling on his part, playful and defensive on hers, which lasted until they reached a door leading into the lower garden. It was a rusty, damp-stained door, once painted green, and masked by trees somewhat higher than the underwood through which they had climbed. Ivy hung from the wall above it, rank grass grew against it, the air about it was dank, and in summer sent up the smell of wild leeks. Once under-gardeners had used it to come and go, and many a time on moonlit nights maids had stolen through it to meet their lovers in the coppice or on the road.

Audley had brought the key and he set it in the lock and turned it. But he did not open the door. Instead, he turned to Mary with a smile. "This is my surprise," he said. "Shut your eyes and open them when I tell you. I will guide you."

She complied without suspicion, and heard the door squeak on its rusty hinges. Guided by his hand she advanced three or four paces. She heard the door close behind her. He put his arm round her and drew her on. "Now?" she asked, "May I look?"

"Yes, now!" he answered. As he spoke he drew her to him, and, before she knew what to expect, he had crushed her to his breast and was pressing kisses on her face and lips.

She was taken by surprise and so completely, that for a moment she was helpless, without defence. Then the instinctive impulse to resist overcame her, and she struggled fiercely; and, presently, she released herself. "Oh, you shouldn't have done it!" she cried. "You shouldn't have done it!"

"My darling!"

"You--you hurt me!" she panted, her breath coming short and quick. She was as red now as she had for a moment been white. Her lips trembled, and there were tears in her eyes. He thought that he had been too rough with her, and though he did not understand, he stayed his impulse to seize her again. Instead, he stood looking down at her, a little put out.

She tried to smile, tried bravely to pass it off; but she was put to it, he could see, not to burst into tears. "Perhaps I am foolish," she faltered, "but please don't do it again."

"I can't promise--for always," he answered, smiling. But, none the less, he was piqued. What a prude the girl was! What a Sainte-ni-touche! To make such a fuss about a few kisses!

She tried to take the same tone. "I know I am silly," she said, "but you took me by surprise."

"You were very innocent, then, my dear. Still, I'll be good, and next time I will give you warning. Now, don't be afraid, take my arm, and let us----"

"If I could sit down?" she murmured. Then he saw that the color had again left her cheeks.

There was an old wheelbarrow inside the door, half full of dead leaves. He swept it clear, and she sat down on the edge of it. He stood by her, puzzled, and at a loss.

Certainly he had played a trick on her, and he had been a little rough because he had felt her impulse to resist. But she must have known that he would kiss her sooner or later. And she was no child. Her convent days were not of yesterday. She was a woman. He did not understand it.

Alas, she did understand it. It was not her lover's kisses, it was not his passion or his roughness that had shaken Mary. She was not a prude and she was a woman. That which had overwhelmed her was the knowledge, the certainty forced on her by his embrace, that she did not love him! That, however much she might have deluded herself a few weeks earlier, however far she might have let the lure of love mislead her, she did not love this man! And she was betrothed to him, she was promised to him, she was his! On her engagement to him, on her future with him had been based--a moment before--all her plans and all her hopes for the future.

No wonder that the color was struck from her face, that she was shaken to the depths of her being. For, indeed, she knew something more--that she had had her warning and had closed her eyes to it. That evening, when she had heard Basset's step come through the hall, that moment when his presence had lifted the burden of suspense from her, should have made her wise. And for an instant the veil had been lifted, and she had been alarmed. But she reflected that the passing doubt was due to her lover's absence and his coldness; and she had put the doubt from her. When Audley returned all would be well, she would feel as before. She was hipped and lonely and the other was kind to her--that was all!

Now she knew that that was not all. She did not love Audley and she did love some one else. And it was too late. She had misled herself, she had misled the man who loved her, she had misled that other whom she loved. And it was too late!

For a time that was short, yet seemed long to her companion, who stood watching her, she sat lost in thought and unconscious of his presence. At length he could bear it no longer. Pale cheeks and dull eyes had no charm for him! He had not come, he had not met her, for this.

"Come!" he said, "come, Mary, you will catch cold sitting there! One might suppose I was an ogre!"

She smiled wanly. "Oh no!" she said, "It is I--who am foolish. Please forgive me."

"If you would like to go back?"

But her ear detected temper in his tone, and with a newborn fear of him she hastened to appease him. "Oh no!" she said. "You were going to show me the gardens!"

"Such as they are. Well, so you will see what there is to be seen. It is a sorry sight, I can tell you." She rose and, taking her arm, he led her some fifty yards along the alley in which they were, then, turning to the right, he stopped. "There," he said. "What do you think of it?"

They had before them the long, dank, weed-grown walk, broken midway by the cracked fountain and closed at the far end by the broad flight of broken steps that led upward to the terrace and so to the great lawn. When Audley had last stood on this spot the luxuriance of autumn had clothed the neglected beds. A tangle of vegetation, covering every foot of soil with leaf and bloom, had veiled the progress of neglect. Now, as by magic, all was changed. The sun still shone, but coldly and on a bald scene. The roses that had run riot, the spires of hollyhocks that had risen above them, the sunflowers that had struggled with the encroaching elder, nay, the very bindweed that had strangled all alike in its green embrace, were gone, or only reared naked stems to the cold sky. Gone, too, were the Old Man, the Sweet William, the St. John's Wort, the wilderness of humbler growths that had pressed about their feet; and from the bare earth and leafless branches, the fountain and the sundial alone, like mourners over fallen grandeur, lifted gray heads.

There is no garden that has not its sad season, its days of stillness and mourning, but this garden was sordid as well as sad. Its dead lay unburied.

Involuntarily Mary spoke. "Oh, it is terrible!" she cried.

"It is terrible," he answered gloomily.

Then she feared that, preoccupied as she was with other thoughts, she had hurt him. She was trying to think of something to comfort him, when he repeated, "It is terrible! But, d--n it, let us see the rest of it! We've come here for that! Let us see it!"

Together they went slowly along the walk. They came by and by to the sundial. She hung a moment, wishing to read the inscription, but he would not stay. "It's the old story," he said. "We are gay fellows in the sunshine, but in the shadow--we are moths."

He did not explain his meaning. He drew her on. They mounted the wide flight which had once, flanked by urns and nymphs and hot with summer sunshine, echoed the tread of red-heeled shoes and the ring of spurs. Now, elder grew between the shattered steps, weeds clothed them, the nymphs mouldered, lacking arms and heads, the urns gaped.

Mary felt his depression and would have comforted him, but her brain was numbed by the discovery which she had made; she was unable to think, without power to help. She shared, she more than shared, his depression. And it was not until they had surmounted the last flight and stood gazing on the Great House that she found her voice. Then, as the length and vastness of the pile broke upon her, she caught her breath. "Oh," she cried. "It is immense!"

"It's a nightmare," he replied. "That is Beaudelays! That is," with bitterness, "the splendid seat of Philip, fourteenth Lord Audley--and a millstone about his neck! It is well, my dear, that you should see it! It is well that you should know what is before you! You see your home! And what you are marrying--if you think it worth while!"

If she had loved him she would have been strong to comfort him. If she had even fancied that she loved him, she would have known what to answer. As it was, she was dumb; she scarcely took in the significance of his words. Her mind--so much of it as she could divert from herself-- was engaged with the sight before her, with the long rows of blank and boarded windows, the smokeless chimneys, the raw, unfinished air that, after eighty years, betrayed that this had never been a home, had never opened its doors to happy brides, nor heard the voices of children.

At last she spoke. "And this is Beaudelays?" she said.

"This is my home," he replied. "That's the place I've come to own! It's a pleasant possession! It promises a cheerful homecoming, doesn't it?"

"Have you never thought of--of doing anything to it?" she asked timidly.

"Do you mean--have I thought of completing it? Of repairing it?"

"I suppose I meant that," she replied.

"I might as well think," he retorted, "of repairing the Tower of London! All I have in the world wouldn't do it! And I cannot pull it down. If I did, the lawyers first and the housebreakers afterwards, would pull down all I have with it! There is no escape, my dear," he continued slowly. "Once I thought there was. I had my dream. I've stood on this lawn on summer days and I've told myself that I would build it up again, and that the name of Audley should not be lost. But I am a peer, what can I do? I cannot trade, I cannot plead. For a peer there is but one way-- marriage. And there were times when I had visions of repairing the breach--in that way; when I thought that I could set the old name first and my pleasure second; when I dreamed of marrying a great dowry that should restore us to the place we once enjoyed. But--that is over! That is over," he repeated in a sinking voice. "I had to choose between prosperity and happiness; I made my choice. God grant that we may never repent it!"

He sank into silence, waiting for her to speak; he waited with exasperation. She did not, and he looked down at her. Then, "I believe," he said, "that you have not heard a word I have said!"

She glanced up, startled. "I am afraid I have not," she answered meekly. "Please forgive me. I was thinking of my uncle, and wondering where he died."

It was all that Audley could do to check the oath that rose to his lips. For he had spoken with intention; he had given her, as he thought, a lead, an opening; and he had wasted his pains. He could hardly believe that she had not heard. He could almost believe that she was playing with him. But in truth she had barely recovered from the shock of her discovery, and the thing before her eyes--the house--held her attention.

"I believe that you think more of your uncle than of me!" he cried.

"No," she replied, "but he is gone and I have you." She was beginning to be afraid of him; afraid of him, because she felt that she was in fault.

"Yes," he replied. "But you must be more kind to me--or I don't know that you will keep me." She thought that he spoke in jest, and she pressed his arm.

"You don't want to go into the house?"

"Oh no! I could not bear it to-day."

"Then you must not mind if I leave you for a moment. I have to look to something inside. I shall not be more than five minutes. Will you walk up and down?"

She assented, thankful to be alone with her thoughts; and he left her. A burly, stately figure, he passed across the lawn and disappeared round the corner of the old wing where the yew trees grew close to the walls. He let himself into the house. He wished to examine the strong-room for himself and to see what traces were left of the tragedy which had taken place there.

But when he stood inside and felt the icy chill of the house, where each footstep awoke echoes, and a ghostly tread seemed to follow him, he went no farther than the shadowy drawing-room with its mouldering furniture and fallen screen. There, placing himself before an unshuttered pane, he stood some minutes without moving, his hands resting on the head of his cane, his eyes fixed on Mary. The girl was slowly pacing the length of the terrace, her head bent.

Whether the lonely figure, with its suggestion of sadness, made its appeal, or the attraction of a grace that no depression could mar, overcame the dictates of prudence, he hesitated. At last, "I can't do it!" he muttered, "hanged if I can! I suppose I ought not to have kissed her if I meant to do it to-day. No, I can't do it."

And when, half an hour later, he parted from her at the old Cross at the foot of the hill, he had not done it.

CHAPTER XXXIII: THE MEETING AT THE MAYPOLE

Within twenty-four hours there were signs that Bosham's brush with his lordship and the show of feeling outside Hatton's Works had set a sharper edge on the fight. Trifles as these were, the farmers about Riddsley took them up and resented them. The feudal feeling was not quite extinct. Their landlord was still a great man to them, and even those who did not love him believed that he was fighting their battle. An insult to him seemed, in any case, a portent, but that such a poor creature as Bosham--Ben Bosham of the Bridge End--should insult him, went beyond bearing.

Moreover, it was beginning to be whispered that Ben was tampering with the laborers. One heard that he was preaching higher wages in the public houses, another that he was asking Hodge what he got out of dear bread, a third that he was vaporing about commons and enclosures. The farmers growled. The farmers' sons began to talk together outside the village inn. The farmers' wives foresaw rick-burning, maimed cattle, and empty hen coops, and said that they could not sleep in their beds for Ben.

Meanwhile those who, perhaps, knew something of the origin of these rumors, and could size up the Boshams to a pound, were not unwilling to push the matter farther. Men who fancied with Stubbs that repeal of the corn-taxes meant the ruin of the country-side, were too much in earnest to pick and choose. They believed that this was a fight between the wholesome country and the black, sweating town, between the open life of the fields and the tyranny of mill and pit; and that the only aim of the repealer was to lower wages, and so to swell the profits that already enabled him to outshine the lords of the soil. They were prone, therefore, to think that any stick was good enough to beat so bad a dog, and if the stout arms of the farmers could redress the balance, they were in no mood to refuse their help.

Nor were sharpeners wanting on the other side. The methods of the League were brought into play. Women were sent out to sing through the streets of an evening, and the townsfolk ate their muffins to the doleful strains of:

Child, is thy father dead?
Father is gone.
Why did they tax his bread?
God's will be done!

And as there were enthusiasts on this side, too, who saw the work of the Corn Laws in the thin cheeks of children and the coffins of babes, the claims of John Barley-corn, roared from the windows of the Portcullis and the Packhorse, did not seem a convincing answer. A big loaf and a little loaf, carried high through the streets, made a wide appeal to non-voters; and a banner with, "You be taxing, we be starving!" had its success. Then, on the evening of the market-day, a band of Hatton's men, fresh from the Three Tailors, came to blows with a market-peart farmer, and a "hand" was not only knocked down, but locked up. Hatton's and Banfield's men were fired with indignation at this injustice, and Hatton himself said a little more at the Institute than Basset thought prudent.

These things had their effect, and more, perhaps, than was expected. For Stubbs, going back to his office one afternoon, suffered an unpleasant shock. Bosham's impudence had not moved him, nor the jeers of Hatton's men. But this turned out to be another matter. Farthingale, the shabby clerk with the high-bred nose, had news for him which he kept until the office door was locked. And the news was so bad that Stubbs stood aghast.

"What? All nine?" he cried. "Impossible, man! The woman's made a fool of you!"

But Farthingale merely looked at him over his steel-rimmed spectacles. "It's true," he said.

"I'll never believe it!" cried the lawyer.

Farthingale shook his head. "That won't alter it," he said patiently. "It's true."

"Dyas the butcher! Why, he served me for years! For years! I go to him at times now."

"Only for veal," replied the clerk, who knew everything "Pitt, of the sausage shop, and Badger, the tripeman, are in his pocket--buy his offal. With the other six, it's mainly the big loaf--Lake has a sister with seven children, and Thomas a father in the almshouse. Two more have big families, and the women have got hold of them!"

"But they've always voted right!" Stubbs urged, with a sinking heart. "What's taken them?"

"If you ask me," the clerk answered, "I should say it was partly Squire Basset--he talks straight and it takes. And partly the split. When a party splits you can't expect to keep all. I doubted Dyas from the first. He's the head. They were all at his house last night and a prime supper he gave them."

Stubbs groaned. At last, "How much?" he asked.

Farthingale shook his head. "Nix," he said. "You may be shaking Dyas's hand and find it's Hatton's. If you take my advice, you'll leave it alone."

"Well," the lawyer cried, "of all the d--d ingratitude I ever heard of! The money Dyas has had from me!"

Farthingale's lips framed the words "only veal," but no sound came. Devoted as he was to his employer, he was enjoying himself. Election times were meat and drink--especially drink--to him. At such times his normal wage was royally swollen by Election extras, such as: "To addressing one hundred circulars, one guinea. To folding and closing the same, half a guinea. To watering the same, half a guinea. To posting the same, half a guinea." A whole year's score, chalked up behind the door at the Portcullis, vanished as by magic at this season.

And then he loved the importance of it, and the secrecy, and the confidence that was placed in him and might safely be placed. The shabby clerk who had greased many a palm was himself above bribes.

But Stubbs was aghast. Scarcely could he keep panic at bay. He had staked his reputation for sagacity on the result. He had made himself answerable for success, to his lordship, to the candidate, to the party. Not once, but twice, he had declared in secret council that defeat was impossible--impossible! Had he not done so, the contest, which his own side had invited, might have been avoided.

And then, too, his heart was in the matter. He honestly believed that these poor creatures, these weaklings whose defection might cost so much, were voting for the ruin of their children, for the impoverishment of the town. They would live to see the land pass into the hands of men who would live on it, not by it. They would live to see the farmers bankrupt, the country undersold, the town a desert!

The lawyer had counted on a safe majority of twenty-two on a register of a hundred and ninety voters. And twenty-two had seemed a buckler, sufficient against all the shafts and all the spite of fortune. But a majority of four--for that was all that remained if these nine went over--a majority of four was a thing to pale the cheek. Perspiration stood on his brow as he thought of it. His hand shook as he shuffled the papers on his desk, looking for he knew not what. For a moment he could not face even Farthingale, he could not command his eye or his voice.

At last, "Who could get at Dyas?" he muttered.

Farthingale pondered for a time, but shook his head. "No one," he said. "You might try Hayward if you like. They deal."

"What's to be done, then?"

"There's only one way that I can think of," the clerk replied, his eyes on his master's face. "Rattle them! Set the farmers on them! Show them that what they're doing will be taken ill. Show 'em we're in earnest. Badger's a poor creature and Thomas's wife's never off the twitter. I'd try it, if I were you. You'd pull some back."

They talked for a time in low voices and before he went into the Portcullis that night Farthingale ordered a gig to be ready at daylight.

It might have been thought that with this unexpected gain, Basset would be in clover. But he, too, had his troubles and vexations. John Audley's death and Mary's loneliness had made drafts on his time as well as on his heart. For a week he had almost withdrawn from the contest, and when he returned to it it was to find that the extreme men--as is the way of extreme men--had been active. In his address and in his speeches he had declared himself a follower of Peel. He had posed as ready to take off the corn-tax to meet an emergency, but not as convinced that free trade was always and everywhere right. He had striven to keep the question of Irish famine to the front, and had constantly stated that that which moved his mind was the impossibility of taxing food in one part of the country while starvation reigned in another. Above all, he had tried to convey to his hearers his notion of Peel. He had pictured the statesman's dilemma as facts began to coerce him. He had showed that in the same position many would have preferred party to country and consistency to patriotism. He had painted the struggle which had taken place in the proud man's mind. He had praised the decision to which Peel had come, to sacrifice his name, his credit, and his popularity to his country's good.

But when Basset returned to his Committee Room, he found that the men to whom Free Trade was the whole truth, and to whom nothing else was the truth, had stolen a march on him. They had said much which he would not have said. They had set up Cobden where he had set up Peel. To crown all, they had arranged an open-air meeting, and invited a man from Lancashire--whose name was a red rag to the Tories--to speak at it.

Basset was angry, but he could do nothing. He had an equal distaste for the man and the meeting, but his supporters, elated by their prospects, were neither to coax nor hold. For a few hours he thought of retiring. But to do so at the eleventh hour would not only expose him to obloquy and injure the cause, but it would condemn him to an inaction from which he shrank.

For all that he had seen of Mary, and all that he had done for her, had left him only the more restless and more unhappy. To one in such a mood success, which began to seem possible, promised something--a new sphere, new interests, new friends. In the hurly-burly of the House and amid the press of business, the wound that pained him would heal more quickly than in the retirement of Blore; where the evenings would be long and lonely, and many a time Mary's image would sit beside his fire and regret would gnaw at his heart.

The open-air meeting was to be held at the Maypole, in the wide street bordered by quaint cottages, that served the town for a cattle-market. The day turned out to be mild for the season, the meeting was a novelty, and a few minutes before three the Committee began to assemble in strength at the Institute, which stood no more than a hundred yards from the Maypole, but in another street. Hatton was entertaining Brierly, the speaker from Lancashire, and in making him known to the candidate, betrayed a little too plainly that he thought that he had scored a point.

"You'll see something new now, sir," he said, rubbing his hands. "What's wanting, he'll win! He's addressed as many as four thousand persons at one time, Mr. Brierly has!"

"Ay, and not such as are here, Squire," Brierly boomed. He was a tall, bulky man with an immense chin, who moved his whole body when he turned his head. "Not country clods, but Lancashire men! No throwing dust i' their eyes!"

"Still, I hope you'll deal with us gently," Basset said. "Strong meat, Mr. Brierly, is not for babes. We must walk before we can run."

"Nay, but the emptier the stomach, the more need o' meat!" Brierly replied, and he rumbled with laughter. "An' a bellyful I'll give them! Truth's truth and I'm no liar!"

"But to different minds the same words do not convey the same thing," Basset urged.

The man stared over his stiff neck-cloth. "That'ud not go down i' Todmorden," he said. "Nor i' Burnley nor i' Bolton! We're down-right chaps up North, and none for chopping words. Hands off the hands' loaf, is Lancashire gospel, and we're out to preach it! We're out to preach it, and them that clems folk and fats pheasants may make what mouth o'er it they like!"

Fortunately the order to start came at this moment, and Basset had to fall in and move forward with Hatton, the chairman of the day. Banfield followed with the stranger, and the rest of the Committee came on two by two, the smaller men enjoying the company in which they found themselves. So they marched solemnly into the street, a score of Hatton's men forming a guard of honor, and a long tail of the riff-raff of the town falling in behind with orange flags and favors. These at a certain signal set up a shrill cheer, a band struck up "See, the Conquering Hero Comes!" and the sixteen gentlemen marched, some proudly and some shamefacedly, into the wider street, wherein a cart drawn up at the foot of the Maypole awaited them.

On such occasions Englishmen out of uniform do not show well. The daylight streamed without pity on the Committee as they stalked or shambled along in their Sunday clothes, and Basset at least felt the absurdity of the position. With the tail of his eye he discerned that the stranger was taking off a large white hat, alternately to the right and left, in acknowledgment of the cheers of the crowd, while ominous sniggers of laughter mingled here and there with the applause. Banfield's men, with another hundred or so of the town idlers, were gathered about the cart, but of the honest and intelligent voters there were scanty signs.

The crowd greeted the appearance of each of the principals with cheers and a shaft or two of Stafford wit.

"Hooray! Hooray!" shouted Hatton's men as he climbed into the cart.

"Hatton's a great man now!" a bass voice threw in.

"But he's never lost his taste for tripe!" squeaked a shrill treble. The gibe won roars of laughter, and the back of the chairman's neck grew crimson.

"Hurrah for Banfield and the poor man's loaf!" shouted his supporters, as he mounted in his turn.

"It's little of the crumb he'll leave the poor man!" squeaked the treble.

It was the candidate's turn to mount next. "Hooray! Hooray!" shouted the crowd with special fervor. Handkerchiefs were waved from windows, the band played a little more of the Conquering Hero.

As the music ceased, "What's he doing, Tommy, along o' these chaps?" asked the treble voice.

"He's waiting for that there Samaritan, Sammy?" answered the bass.

"Ay, ay? And the wine and oil, Sammy?"

It took the crowd a little time to digest this, but in time they did so, and the gust of laughter that followed covered the appearance of the stranger. He was not to escape, however, for as the noise ceased, "Is this the Samaritan, Sammy?" asked the bass.

"Where's your eyes?" whined the treble. "He's the big loaf! and, lor, ain't he crumby!"

"If I were down there----" the Burnley man began, leaning over the side of the cart.

"He's crusty, too!" cried the wit.

But this was too much for the chairman. "Silence! Silence!" he cried, and, as at a signal, there was a rush, the two interrupters were seized and, surrounded by a gang of hobbledehoys, were hustled down the road, fighting furiously and shouting, "Blues! Blues!"

The chairman made use of the lull to step to the edge of the cart and take off his hat. He looked about him, pompous and important.

"Gentlemen," he began, "free and independent electors of our ancient borough! At a crisis such as this, a crisis the most momentous--the most momentous----" he paused and looked into his hat, "that history has known, when the very staff of life is, one may say, the apple of discord, it is an honor to me to take the chair!"

"The cart you mean!" cried a voice, "you're in the cart!"

The speaker cast a withering glance in the direction whence the voice came, lost his place and, failing to find it, went on in a different strain. "I'm a business man," he said, "you all know that! I'm a business man, and I'm not ashamed of it. I stick to my business and my business to-day----"

"Better go on with it!"

But he was getting set, and he was not to be abashed. "My business to-day," he repeated, "is to ask your attention for the distinguished candidate who seeks your suffrages, and for the--the distinguished gentleman on my left who will presently follow me."

A hollow groan checked him at this point, but he recovered himself. "First, however," he continued, "I propose, with your permission, to say a word on the--the great question of the day-- if I may call it so. It is to the food of the people I refer!"

He paused for cheers, under cover of which Banfield murmured to his neighbor that Hatton was set now for half an hour. He had yet to learn that open-air meetings have their advantages.

"The food of the people!" Hatton repeated, uplifted by the applause. "It is to me a sacred thing! My friends, it is to me the Ark of the Covenant. The bread is the life. It should go straight, untaxed, untouched from the field of the farmer to the house of--of the widow and the orphan!"

"Hear! Hear! Hear! Hear!" Then, "What about the miller?"

"It should go from where it is grown," Hatton repeated, "to where it is needed; from where it is grown to the homes of the poor! And to the man," slipping easily and fatally into his Sunday vein, "that lays his 'and upon it, let him be whom he may, I say with the Book, 'Thou shalt not muzzle the ox that treadeth out the corn!' The Law, ay, and the Prophets----"

"Ay, Hatton's profits! Hands off them!" roared the bass voice.

"Low bread and high profits!" shrieked the treble. "Hatton and thirty per cent!"

A gust of laughter swept all away for a time, and when the speaker could again get a hearing he had lost his thread and his temper. "That's a low insinuation!" he cried, crimson in the face. "A low insinuation! I scorn to answer it!"

"Regular old Puseyite you be," shouted a new tormentor. "Quoting Scripture."

Hatton shook his fist at the crowd. "A low, dirty insinuation!" he cried. "I scorn----"

"You don't scorn the profits!"

"Listen! Silence!" Then, "I shall not say another word! You're not worth it! You're below it! I call on Mr. Brierly of Manchester to propose a resolution."

And casting vengeful glances here and there where he fancied he detected an opponent, he stood back. He began for the first time to think the meeting a mistake. Basset, who had held that opinion from the first, scanned the crowd and had his misgivings.

The man from Manchester, however, had none. He stood forward, a smile on his broad face, his chest thrown forward, a something easy in his air, as became one who had confronted thousands and was not to be put out of countenance by a few hisses. He waited good-humoredly for silence. Nor could he see that, behind the cart, there had been gathering for some time a band of men of a different air from those who faced the platform. These men were still coming up by twos and threes, issuing from side-streets; men clad in homespun and with ruddy faces, men in smocked frocks, men in velveteens; a few with belcher neckerchiefs and slouched felts, whom their mothers would not have known. When Brierly raised his hand and opened his mouth there were over two score of these men--and they were still coming up.

But Brierly was unaware of them, and, complacent and confident of the effect he would produce, he opened his mouth.

"Gentlemen," he began. His voice, strong and musical, reached the edge of the meeting. "Gentlemen, free electors! And I tell you straight no man is free, no man had ought to be free----

"

Boom! and again, Boom! Boom! Not four paces behind him a drum rolled heavily, drowning his voice. He stopped, his mouth open; for an instant surprise held the crowd also. Then laughter swept the meeting and supplied a treble to the drum's persistent bass.

And still the drum went on, Boom! Boom! amid cheers, yells, laughter. Then, as suddenly as it had started, it stopped. More slowly, the hurrahs, yells, laughter, died down, the laughter the last to fail, for not only had the big man's face of surprise tickled the crowd, but the drum had so nicely taken the pitch of his voice that the interruption seemed even to his friends a joke.

He seized the opportunity, but defiance not complacency was now his note. "Gentlemen," he said, "it's funny, but you don't drum me down, let me tell you! You don't drum me down! What I said I'm going to say again, and shame the devil and the landlords! Free men----"

But he did not say it. Boom, boom, rolled the drum, drowning his voice beyond hope. And this time, with the fourth stroke, a couple of fifes struck into a sprightly measure, and the next moment three score lively voices were roaring:

You've here the little Peeler,
Out of place he will not go!
But to keep it, don't he turn about
And jump Jim Crow!
But to keep it see him turn about
And jump Jim Crow!
Turn about, and wheel about
And do just so!
Chorus
The only dance Sir Robert knows
Is Jump Jim Crow!
The only dance Sir Robert knows
Is Jump Jim Crow!

For a verse or two the singers had it their own way. Then the band of the meeting struck in with "See, the Conquering Hero Comes!" and as the airs clashed in discord, the stalwarts of the two parties clashed also in furious struggle. In a twinkling and as by magic the scene changed. Women, children, lads, fled every way, screaming and falling. Shrieks of alarm routed laughter. The crowd swayed stormily, flowed this way, ebbed that way. The clatter of staves on clubs rang above oaths and shouts of defiance, as the Yellows made a rush for the drum. Men were down, men were trampled on, men strove to scale the cart, others strove to descend from it. But to descend from it was to descend into a mêlée of random fists and falling sticks, and the man from Manchester bellowed to stand fast; while Hatton shouted to "clear out these rogues," and Banfield called on his men to charge. Basset alone stood silent, measuring the conflict with his eyes. With an odd exultation he felt his spirits rise to meet the need.

He saw quickly that the orange favors were outnumbered, and were giving way; and almost as quickly that, so far as mischief was meant, it was aimed at the Manchester man. He was a stranger, he was the delegate of the League, he was a marked man. Already there were cries to duck him. Basset tapped Banfield on the shoulder.

"They'll not touch us," he shouted in the man's ear, "but we must get Brierly away. There's Pritchard's house opposite. We must fight our way to it. Pass the word!" Then to Brierly, "Mr. Brierly, we must get you away. There's a gang here means mischief."

"Let them come on!" cried the Manchester man, "I'm not afraid."

"No, but I am," Basset replied. "We're responsible, and we'll not have you hurt here. Down all!" he cried raising his voice, as he saw the band whom he had already marked, pressing up to the cart through the mêlée--they moved with the precision of a disciplined force, and most of their faces were muffled. "Down all!" he shouted. "Yellows to the rescue! Down before they upset us!"

The leaders scrambled out of the cart, some panic-stricken, some enjoying the scuffle. They were only just in time. The Yellows were in flight, amid yells and laughter, and before the last of the platform was over the side, the cart was tipped up by a dozen sturdy arms. Hatton and another were thrown down, but a knot of their men, the last with fight in them, rallied to the call, plucked the two to their feet, and, striking out manfully, covered the rear of the retreating force.

The men with the belcher neckerchiefs pressed on silently, brandishing their clubs, and twice with cries of "Down him! Down him!" made a rush for Brierly, striking at him over the shoulders of his companions. But it was plain that the assailants shrank from coming to blows with the local magnates; and Basset seeing this handed Brierly over to an older man, and himself fell back to cover the retreat.

"Fair play, men," he cried, good humoredly. And he laughed in their faces as he fell back before them. "Fair play! You're too many for us to-day, but wait till the polling-day!"

They hooted him. "Yah! Yah!" they cried. "You'd ruin the land that bred you! You didn't ought to be there!" "Give us that fustian rascal! We'll club him!"

"Who makes cloth o' devil's dust?" yelled another. "Yah! You d--d cotton-spawn!"

Basset laughed in their faces, but he was not sorry when the friendly doorway received his party. The country gang, satisfied with their victory, began to fall back after breaking a dozen panes of glass; and the panting and discomfited Yellows, thronging the passage and pulling their coats into shape, were free to exchange condolences or recriminations as they pleased. More than one had been against the open-air meeting, and Hatton, a sorry figure, hatless, and with a sprained knee, was not likely to hear the end of it. Two or three had black eyes, one had lost two teeth, another his hat, and Brierly his note-book.

But almost before a word had been exchanged, a man pushed his way among them. He had slipped into the house by the back way. "For God's sake, gentlemen," he cried, "get the constable, or there'll be murder!"

"What is it?" asked a dozen voices.

"They've got Ben Bosham, half a hundred of them! They're away to the canal with him. They're that mad with him they'll drown him!"

So far Basset had treated the affair as a joke. But Bosham's plight in the hands of a mob of angry farmers seemed more than a joke. Murder might really be done. He snatched a thick stick from a corner--he had been hitherto unarmed--and raised his voice. "Mr. Banfield," he said, "go to Stubbs and tell him what is doing! He can control them if any one can. And do some of you, gentlemen, come with me! We must get him from them."

"But we're not enough," a man protested.

"The man must not be murdered," Basset replied. "Come, gentlemen, they'll not dare to touch us who know them, and we've the law with us! Come on!"

"Well done, Squire!" cried Brierly. "You're a man!"

"Ay, but I'm not man enough to take you!" Basset retorted. "You stay here, please!"

CHAPTER XXXIV: BY THE CANAL

It was noon on that day, the day of the meeting at Riddsley, and Mary was sitting in the parlor at the Gatehouse. She was stooping over the fire with her eyes on the embers. The old hound lay beside her with his muzzle resting on her shoe, and Mrs. Toft, solidly poised on her feet, on the farther side of the table, rolled her apron about her arms and considered the pair.

"It's given us all a rare shock," she said as she marked the girl's listless pose, "the poor Master's death! That sudden and queer, too! I don't know that I'm better for it, myself, and Toft goes up and down like a toad under a harrow, he's that restless! For 'Truria, she's fairly mazed. Her body's here and her thoughts are lord knows where. Toft, he seems to think something will come of her and her reverend----"

"I hope so," Mary said gently.

"But it's beyond me what Toft thinks these days. I asked him point--blank yesterday, 'Toft,' I says, 'are we going or are we staying?' And, bless the man, he looks at me as if he'd eat me. 'Take time and you'll know,' he says. 'But whose is the house?' I asks, 'and who's to pay us?' 'God knows!' he says, and whiffs out of the room like one of these lucifers!"

"I think that the house is Mr. Basset's," Mary explained, "for the rest of the lease; that's about three years."

"But you'll not be staying, begging your pardon, Miss? I suppose you'll be naming the day soon? The Master's gone and his lordship will be wanting you somewhere else than here."

"Yes, Mrs. Toft," Mary said quietly. "I suppose so."

Mrs. Toft looked for a blush and saw none, and she drew her conclusions. She went on another tack. "There's like to be a fine rumpus in the town to-day," she said comfortably. "The Squire's brought a foreigner down to trim their nails, and there's to be a wagon and speaking and such like foolishness at the Maypole. As if all the speeches of all the fools in Staffordshire would lower the quartern loaf! Anyway, if what Petch says is true, the farmers are that mad there's like to be lives lost!"

Mary stooped and carefully put a piece of wood on the fire.

"And, to be sure, they're a rough lot," Mrs. Toft continued, dropping her apron. "I'm not forgetting what happened to the reverend Colet, and I wish the young master safe out of it. It's all give and no take with him, too much for others and too little for himself! I'm thinking if anybody's hurt he'll be there or thereabouts."

Mary turned. "Is Petch--couldn't Petch go down and----"

"La, Miss," Mrs. Toft answered--the girl's face told her all that she wished to know--"Petch don't dare, with his lordship on the other side! But, all said and done, I'll be bound the young master'll come through. It's a pity, though," she continued thoughtfully, as she began to dust the sideboard, "as people don't know their own minds. There's the Squire, now. He's lived quiet and pleasant all these years and now he must dip his nose into this foolishness, same as if he dipped it into hot worts when Toft's a-brewing! I don't know what's come to him. He goes riding up to Blore these winter nights, twenty miles if it's a furlong, when this house is his! He's more like to take his death that way, if I'm a judge."

"Is he doing that?" Mary asked in a small voice.

"To be sure," Mrs. Toft returned. "What else! Which reminds me, Miss, are those papers to go to the bank to-day?"

"I believe so."

"Well, you're looking that peaky, you'd best take a jaunt with them. Why not? It's a fine day, and if there is a bit of a clash there's none will hurt you. Do you go, Miss, and get a little color in your cheeks. At worst, you'll bring back the news and I'm sure we're that dead-alive and moped a little's a godsend!"

"I think I will go," Mary said.

So when the gig, which was to convey the boxes to the bank, arrived about three, she mounted beside the driver. Here, were it only for an hour, was distraction and a postponement of that need to decide, to choose between two courses, which was crushing her under its weight.

For Mary was very unhappy. That moment which had proved to her that she did not love the man she was to marry and did love another, had stamped itself on her memory, never to be wiped from it. In Audley's company, and for a time after they had parted, the shock had numbed her mind and dulled her feelings. But once alone and free to think, she had grasped all that the discovery meant--to her and to him; and from that moment she had not known an instant of ease.

She saw that she had made a terrible mistake, and one so vital that, if nothing could be done, it must wreck her happiness and another's happiness. And what was she to do? What ought she to do? In a moment of emotion, led astray by that love of love which is natural to women, and something swayed--so she told herself in scorn--by

Those glories of our blood and state,

which to women are not shadows, she had made this mistake, and now, self-tricked, she had only herself to blame if

Sceptre and crown

Were tumbled down

And in the dust were lesser made

Than the poor crooked scythe and spade!

But to see her folly did not avail. What was she to do?

Ought she to tell the truth, however painful it might be, to the man whom she had deceived? Or ought she to go through with it, to do her duty and save him at least from hurt? Either way, she had wrecked her own craft, but she might still hope to save his. Or--might she hope? She was not certain even of this.

What was she to do? Hour after hour she asked herself the question, sometimes looking through the windows with eyes that saw nothing, at others pacing her room in a fever of anxiety. What was she to do? She could not decide. Now she thought one thing, now another. And time was passing. No wonder that she was glad even of the distraction of this journey to Riddsley that at another time had been so dull an adventure! It was, at least, a reprieve, a respite from the burden of decision.

She would not own, even to herself, that she had any other thought in going, or that anxiety had any part in her restlessness. From that side of the battle she turned her eyes with all the strength of her will. Her conduct had been that of a silly girl rather than that of a woman who had seen and suffered; but she was not light--and besides Basset was cured. She was only unfortunate, and desperately unhappy.

As they drove by the old Cross at the foot of the hill she averted her eyes. Surely it must have been in some other life that she had made it the object of a walk, and had told herself that she would never forget it.

Alas, she had been right. She would never forget it!

The man who drove saw that her face matched her mourning, and he left her to her thoughts, so that hardly a word passed between them until they were close upon the outskirts of the town. Then the driver, to whom the dull winter landscape, the lines of willows, and the low water-logged fields, were no novelty, pricked up his ears.

"Dang me!" he said, "they've started! There's a fine rumpus in the town. Do you hear 'em, Miss? That's a band I'm thinking?"

"I hope no one will be hurt."

The man winked at his horse. "None of the right side, Miss," he said slyly. "But it might be a hanging, front o' Stafford gaol, by the roar! I met a tidy lot going in as I came out, a right tidy lot! I'm blest," after listening a moment, "if they're not coming this way!"

"I hope they won't do anything to----"

"La, Miss," the man answered, misreading her anxiety and interrupting her, "they'll never touch us. And for the old nag, he's yeomanry. He'd not start if he met a mile o' funerals!"

Certainly the noise was growing. But the lift of the canal bridge and bank, which crossed the road a hundred yards before them, hid all of the town from them save a couple of church towers, some tiled roofs, and the brick gable of Hatton's Works. The man whipped up his horse.

"Teach they Manchester chaps a trick!" he muttered. "Shouldn't wonder if there'll be work for the crowner out of this! Gee-up, old nag, let's see what's afoot! 'Pears to me," as the shouting grew plainer, "we'll be in at the death yet, Miss!"

Mary winced at the word, but if the man feared that she would refuse to go on, he was mistaken. On the contrary, she looked eagerly to the front as the old horse, urged by the whip, took the rise of the bridge at a canter, and, having reached the crown, relapsed into an absent-minded walk.

"Dang me!" cried the driver, greatly excited, "but they do mean business! It's in knee in neck with 'em! Never thought it would come to this. And who is't they've got, Miss?"

Certainly there was something out of the common on foot. Moving to meet the gig, and filling the road from ditch to ditch, appeared a disorderly crowd of two or three hundred persons. Cheering, hooting, and brandishing sticks, they came on at something between a walk and a run, although in the heart of the mass there was a something that now and again checked the movement, and once brought it to a stand. When this happened the crowd eddied and flowed about the object in its centre and presently swept on again with the same hooting and laughter.

But in the laughter, as in the hooting, there was, after each of these pauses, a more savage note. "What is it?" Mary cried, as the driver, scared by the sight, pulled up his horse. "What is it?"

"D--n me," the man replied, forgetting his manners, "if I don't think it's Ben Bosham they've got! It is Ben! And they're for ducking him! It's mortal deep by the bridge there, and s'help me, if it's not ten to one they drown him!"

"Ben Bosham?" Mary repeated. Then she recalled the name. She remembered what Mrs. Toft had said of him--that the man had a wife and would bring her to ruin. The crowd was not fifty yards from them now and was still coming on. To the left a track ran down to the towing-path and the canal, and already the leaders of the mob were swerving in that direction. As they did so--and were once more checked for a moment--Mary espied among them a man's bald head twisting this way and that, as he strove to escape. The man was struggling desperately, his clothes almost torn from his back, but he was helpless in the hands of a knot of stout fellows, and after a brief resistance he was hauled forcibly on. A hundred jeering voices rose about him, and a something cruel in the sound chilled Mary's blood. The dreary scene, the sluggish canal, the flat meadows, the rising mist, all pressed on her mind and deepened the note of tragedy.

But on that she broke the spell. The blood in her spoke. She clutched the driver's arm and shook it. "Go on!" she cried. "Go on! Drive into them!"

The man hesitated--he saw that the crowd was in no jesting mood. But the old horse felt the twitch on the reins and started, and having the slope with him, trotted gently forward as if the road were empty before him. The crowd waved and shouted, and cursed the driver. But the horse, thinking perhaps that this was some new form of parade, only cocked his ears and ambled on till he reached the foremost. Then a man seized the rein, jerked it, and stopped him.

In a moment Mary sprang down, heedless of the fact that she was one woman among a hundred men. She faced the crowd, her eyes bright with indignation. "Let that man go," she cried. "Do you hear? Do you want to murder him?" And, advancing a step, she laid her hand on Ben Bosham's ragged, filthy sleeve--he had been down more than once and been rolled in the mud. "Let him go!" she continued imperiously. "Do you know who I am, you cowards? Let him go!"

"Yah!" shouted the crowd, and drowned her voice and pressed roughly about her, threatened her. One of the foremost asked her what she would do, another cried that she had best make herself scarce! Furious faces surrounded her, fists were shaken at her. But Mary was not daunted. "If you don't let him go, I shall go to Lord Audley!" she said.

"You're a fool meddling in this!" cried a voice. "We're only going to wash the devil!"

"You will let him go!" she replied, facing them all without fear and, advancing a step, she actually plucked the man from the hands that held him. "I am Miss Audley! If you do not let him go----"

"We're only going to wash him, lady," whined one of the men who held him.

"That's all, lady!" chimed in half-a-dozen. "He wants it!"

But Ben was not of that opinion, or he did not value cleanliness. "They're going to drown me!" he spluttered, his eyes wild. All the fight had been knocked out of him. "They're paid to do it!

They'll drown me!"

"And sarve him right!" shouted half-a-dozen at the rear of the crowd. "Sarve him right, the devil!"

"They will not do it!" Mary said firmly. "They'll not lay another hand on you. Get in! Get in here!" And then to the crowd, "For shame!" she cried. "Stand back!"

The man was so shaken that he could not help himself, but she pushed, the driver pulled, and in a trice, before the mob had recovered from its astonishment, Ben was above their heads, on the seat of the gig--a blubbering, ragged, mud-caked figure with a white face and bleeding lips. "Go on!" Mary said in the same tone, and the gig moved forward, the old yeomanry horse tossing its head. She moved on beside it with her hand on the rail.

The mob let them pass, but closed in behind them, and after a pause began to jeer--a little in amusement, a little to cover its defeat. In a moment farce took the place of tragedy; the danger was over. "We'll tell your wife, Ben!" screamed a youth, and the crowd laughed and followed. Other wits took their turn. "You'll want a new coat for the wedding, Ben!" cried one. And now and again amid the laughter a sterner note survived. "We'll ha' you yet, Ben!" a man would cry. "You're not out of the wood yet, Ben!"

Mary's face burned, but she stuck to her post, plodding on beside the gig, and after this fashion the queer procession, heralded by a score of urchins crying the news, entered the streets of the town. On either side women thronged the doorways and steps, and while some cried, "Bravo, Miss!" others laughed and called to their neighbors to come out and see the sight. And still the crowd clung to the rear of the gig, and hooted and laughed and pretended to make forays on it.

Mary had hoped to shake them off, but as they persisted in following and no relief came--for Basset and his rescue party had gone to the canal by another road--she saw nothing for it but to go on to Lord Audley's. With a curt word she made the man turn that way.

The crowd still attended, curious, amused. It had doubled its numbers, nay, had trebled them. There were friends as well as foes among them now, some of Hatton's men, some of Banfield's, yellow favors as well as blue. If Mary had known it, she might have set Ben down and not a hand would have been laid upon him. Even the leaders of the riot were now thankful that they had not carried the matter farther. Enough had been done.

But Mary did not know this. She thought that the man was still in peril. She did not dream of leaving him. And it was at the head of a crowd of three or four hundred of the riff-raff of Riddsley that she broke in upon the quiet of the suburban road in which The Butterflies stood. Tumultuously, followed by laughter and hooting and cheers, she swept along it with her train, and came to a halt before the house.

No house was ever more surprised. Mrs. Wilkinson's scared face peered above one blind, her sisters' caps showed above another. Was it an accident? Was it a riot? Was it a Puseyite protest? What was it? Every servant, every neighbor, Lord Audley himself came to the windows.

Mary signed to the driver to help Ben down, and the moment the man's foot touched the ground she grasped his arm. With a burning face, but with her head in the air, she guided his stumbling footsteps through the gate and along the paved walk. They came together to the door.

They went in.

The crowd formed up five deep along the railings, and waited in wondering silence to see what would happen. What would his lordship say? What would his lordship do? This was bringing the election to his doors with a vengeance, and there were not a few of the better sort who saw the fun of the situation.

CHAPTER XXXV: MY LORD SPEAKS OUT

Mary had passed through twenty minutes of tense excitement. The risk had been slight, after the first moment of intervention, but she had not known this, and she was still trembling with indignation, a creature all fire and passion, when the door of The Butterflies opened to admit her. Leaving Ben Bosham on the threshold she lost not a moment, but with her story on her lips, hurried up the stairs, and on the landing came plump upon Lord Audley.

From the window he had seen something of what was afoot below. He had recognized Mary and the tattered Bosham, and he had read the riddle, grasped the facts, and cursed the busybody, all within thirty seconds. "D--n it! this passes everything," he had muttered to himself as he turned from the window in disgust. "This is altogether too much!" And he had opened the door-- ready also to open his mind to her!

"What in the world is it?" he asked. He held the door for her to enter. "What has happened? I could not believe my eyes when I saw you in company with that wretched creature!" he continued. "And all the tagrag and bobtail in the place behind you? What is it, Mary?"

She felt the check, and the color, which excitement had brought to her cheeks, faded. But she thought that it was only that he did not understand, and, "That wretched creature, as you call him," she cried, "has just escaped from death. They were going to murder him!"

"Murder him?" Audley repeated. He raised his eyebrows. "Murder him?" coldly. "My dear girl, don't be silly! Don't let yourself be carried away. You've lost your head. And, pardon me for saying it, I am afraid have made a fool of yourself! And of me!"

"But they were going to throw him into the canal!" she protested.

"Going to wash him!" he replied cynically. "And a good thing too! It's a pity they left the job undone. The man is a low, pestilent fellow!" he continued severely, "and obnoxious to me and to all decent people. The idea of bringing him, and that pleasant tail, to my house--my dear girl, it's absurd!"

He made no attempt to soften his tone or suppress his annoyance, and she stared at him in astonishment. Yet she still thought, or she strove to think, that he did not understand, and tried to make the facts clear. "But you don't know what they were like," she protested. "You were not there. They had torn the clothes from his back----"

"I can see that."

"And he was so terrified that it was dreadful to see him! They were handling him brutally, horribly! And then I came up and----"

"And lost your head!" he said. "I dare say you thought all this. But do you know anything about elections?"

"No----"

"Have you ever see an election in progress before?"

"No."

"Just so," he replied dryly. "Well, if you had, you would know that brawls of this kind are common things, the commonest of things at such a time, and that sensible people turn their backs on them. You've chosen to turn the farce into a tragedy, and in doing so you've made yourself ridiculous--and me too!"

"If you had seen them," she said, "I do not think you would speak as you are speaking."

"My dear girl," he replied, and shrugged his shoulders, "I have seen many such things, many. But there is one thing I have never seen, and that is a man killed in an election squabble! The whole thing is childish--silly! The least knowledge of the world--"

"Would have saved me from it?"

"Exactly! Would have saved you from it!" he answered austerely. "And me from a very annoying incident! Peers have nothing to do with elections, as you ought to know; and to bring this mob of all sorts to my door as if the matter touched me, is to compromise me. It is past a joke!"

Mary stared. She was trying to place herself. Certainly this was the room in which she had taken tea, and this was the man who had welcomed her, who had hung over her, whose eyes had paid her homage, who had foreseen her least want, who had lapped her in observance. This was the man and this the room, and there was the chair in which good Mrs. Wilkinson had sat and beamed on her.

But there was a change somewhere; and the change was in the man. Could it mean that he, too, had made a mistake and now recognized it? That he, too, had found that he did not love? But in that case this was not the way to confess an error. His tone, his manner, which held no respect for the woman and no softness for the sweetheart, were far from the tone of one in the wrong. On the contrary, they presented a side of him which had been hitherto hidden from her; a phase of the strength that she had admired, which shocked her even while, as deep calls to deep, it roused her pride. She remembered that she was his betrothed, and that he had wooed her, he had chosen her. And on slight provocation he spoke to her in this strain!

She sought the clue, she fancied that she held it, and from this moment she was on her guard. She was quiet, but there was a smouldering fire in her eyes. "Perhaps I was wrong," she said. "I have had little experience of these things. But are not you, on your side, making too much of this? Too much of a very small, a very natural mistake? Isn't it a trifle after all?"

"Not so much of a trifle as you think!" he retorted. "A man in my position has to follow a certain line of conduct. A girl in yours should be careful to guide herself by my views. Instead, out of a foolish sentimentality, you run directly counter to them! It is too late to consider your relation to me when the harm is done, my dear."

"Perhaps we have neither of us considered the relation quite enough?" she said.

"I am not sure that we have." And again, "I am not sure, Mary, that we have," he repeated more soberly.

She knew what he meant now--knew what was in his mind almost as clearly as if, instead of grasping his conclusion, she had been a party to his reasons. And she closed her lips, a spot of color in each cheek. In other circumstances she would have taken on herself a full, nay, the main share, of the blame. She would have been quick to admit that she, too, had made a mistake, and that no harm was done.

But his manner opened her eyes to many things that had been a puzzle to her. Thought is swift, and in a flash her mind had travelled over the whole course of their engagement, had recalled his long absence, the chill of his letters, the infrequency of his visits; and she saw by that light that this was no sudden shift, but an occasion sought and seized. Therefore she would not help him. She at least had been honest, she at least had been in earnest. She had tricked, not him only, but herself!

She closed her lips and waited, therefore. And he, knowing that he had now burned his boats, had to go on. "I am not sure that we did think enough about it?" he said doggedly. "I have suspected for some time that I acted hastily in--in asking you to be my wife, Mary."

"Indeed?" she said.

"Yes. And what has happened to-day, proving that we look at things so differently, has confirmed my suspicion. It has convinced me--" he looked down at his table, avoiding her eyes, but continued firmly--"that we are not suited to one another. The wife of a man, placed as I am, should have an idea of values, a certain reserve, that comes of a knowledge of the world; above all, no sentimental notions such as lead to mistakes like this." He indicated the street by a gesture. "If I was mistaken a while ago in listening to my feelings rather than to my prudence, if I gave you credit for knowledge which you had had no means of gaining, I wronged you, Mary, and I am sorry for it. But I should be doing you a far greater wrong if I remained silent now."

"Do you mean," she asked in a low voice, "that you wish it to be at an end between us? That you wish to--to throw me over?"

He smiled awry. "That is an unpleasant way of putting it, isn't it?" he said. "However, I am in the wrong, and I have no right to quarrel with a word. I do think that to break off our engagement at once is the best and wisest thing for both of us."

"How long have you felt this?" she asked.

"For some time," he replied, measuring his words, "I have been coming slowly--to that conclusion."

"That I am not fitted to be your wife?"

"If you like to put it so."

Then her anger, hitherto kept under, flamed up. "Then what right," she cried, "if that was in your mind, had you to treat me as you treated me at Beaudelays--in the garden? What right had you to kiss me? Rather, what right had you to insult me? For it was an insult--it was an insult, if you were not going to marry me! Don't you know, sir, that it was vile? That it was unforgivable?"

She had never looked more handsome, never more attractive than at this moment. The day was failing, but the glow of the fire fell on her face, and on her eyes sparkling with anger. He took in the picture, he owned her charm, he even came near to repenting. But it was too late, and "It may have been vile--and you may not forgive it," he answered hardily, "but I'd do it again, my dear, on the same provocation!"

"You would----"

"I would do it again," he repeated coolly. "Don't you know that you are handsome enough to turn any man's head? And what is a kiss after all? We are cousins. If you were not such a prude, I would kiss you now?"

She was furiously angry--or she fancied that she was. But it may be that, deep down in her woman's mind, she was not truly angry. And, indeed, how could she be angry when in her heart a little bird was beginning to sing--was telling her that she was free, that presently this cloud would be behind her, and that the sky would be blue? Already the message was making itself heard, already she was finding it hard to keep up appearances, to frown upon him and play her part.

Yet she flashed out at him. Was he not going too fast, was he not riding off too lightly? "Oh!" she cried, "You dare to say that! Even while you break off with me!"

But his selfish, masterful nature had now the upper hand. He had eaten his leek and he was anxious to be done with it. "And what then?" he said. "I believe that you know that I am right. I believe that you know that we are not suited to one another."

"And you think I will let you go at a word?"

"I think you will let me go," he said, "because you are not a fool, Mary. You know as well as I do that you might be 'my lady' at too high a price. I'm not the most manageable of men. I'd make a decent husband, all being well. But I'm not meek and I'd make a very unhandy husband malgré moi."

The threat exasperated her. "I know this at least," she retorted, "that I would not marry you now, if you were twenty times my lord! You have behaved meanly, and I believe falsely! Not to-day! You are speaking the truth to-day. But I believe that from the start you had this in your mind, that you foresaw this, and were careful not to commit yourself too publicly! What I don't understand is why you ever asked me to be your wife--at all?"

"Look in the glass!" he answered impudently.

She put that aside. "But I suppose that you had a reason!" she returned. "That you loved me, that you felt for me anything worthy of the name of love is impossible! For the rest, let me tell you this! If I ever felt thankful for anything I am thankful for the chance that brought me to your house to-day--and brought me to the truth!"

"Anything more to say?" he asked flippantly. The way she was taking it suited him better than if she had wept and appealed. And then she was so confoundedly good-looking in her tantrums!

"Nothing more," she said. "I think that we understand one another now. At any rate, I understand you. Perhaps you will kindly see if I can leave the house without annoyance."

He looked into the street. Dusk had fallen, the lamplighter was going his rounds. Of the crowd that had attended Mary to the house no more than a handful remained; the nipping air, the attractions of free beer, the sound of the muffin-bell, had drawn away the rest. The driver of the gig was moving to and fro, now looking disconsolately at the windows, now beating his fingers on his chest.

"I think you can leave with safety," Audley said with irony. "I will see you downstairs."

"I will not trouble you," she answered.

"But, surely, we may still be friends?"

She looked him in the face. "We need not be enemies," she answered. "And, perhaps, some day I may be able to think more kindly of you. If that day comes I will tell you. Good-bye." She went out without touching his hand. She went down the stairs.

She drove through the dusky, dimly-lighted streets in a kind of dream, seeing all things through a pleasant haze. The bank was closed and to deliver up her papers she had to go into the bank-house. The glimpse she had of the cheerful parlor, of the manager's wife, of his two children playing the Royal Game of Goose at a round table, enchanted her. Presently she was driving again through the darkling streets, passing the Maypole, passing the quaint, low-browed shops, lit only by an oil lamp or a couple of candles. The Audley Arms, the Packhorse, the Portcullis, were all alight and buzzing with the voices of those who fought their battles over again or laid bets on this candidate or that. What the speaker had said to Lawyer Stubbs and what Lawyer Stubbs had said to the speaker, what the "Duke" thought, who would have to pay for the damage, and the odds the stout farmer would give that wheat wouldn't be forty shillings a quarter this day twelvemonth if the Repeal passed--scraps of these and the like poured from the doorways as she drove by.

All fell in delightfully with her mood and filled her with a sense of well-being. Even when the streets lay behind her, and the driver hunched his shoulders to meet the damp night-fog and the dreary stretch that lay beyond the canal-bridge, Mary found the darkness pleasant and the chill no more than bracing. For what were that night, that chill beside the numbing grip from which she had just--oh, thing miraculous!--escaped! Beside the fetters that had been lifted from her within the last hour! O foolish girl, O ineffable idiot, to have ever fancied that she loved that man!

No, for her it was a charming night! The owl that, far away towards the Great House, hooted dolefully above the woods--no nightingale had been more tuneful. Ben Bosham--she laughed, thinking of his plight--blessings on his bare, bald head and his ragged shoulders! The old horse plodding on, with the hill that mounts to the Gatehouse sadly on his mind--he should have oats, if oats there were in the Gatehouse stables! He should have oats in plenty, or what he would if oats failed!

"What do you give him when he's tired?" she asked.

"Well," the driver replied with diplomacy, "times a quart of ale, Miss. He'll take it like a Christian."

"Then a quart of ale he shall have to-night!" she said with a happy laugh. "And you shall have one, too, Simonds."

Her mood held to the end, so that before she was out of her wraps, Mrs. Toft was aware of the change in her. "Why, Miss," she said, "you look like another creature! It isn't the bank, I'll be bound, has put that color in your cheeks!"

"No!" Mary answered, "I've had an adventure, Mrs. Toft. And briefly she told the tale of Ben Bosham's plight and of her gallant rescue. She began herself to see the comic side of it.

"He always was a fool, was Ben!" Mrs. Toft commented. "And that," she continued shrewdly, "was how you come to see his lordship was it, Miss?"

"How did you know I saw him?" Mary asked in surprise. "But you're right, I did." Then, as she entered the parlor, "Perhaps I'd better tell you, Mrs. Toft," she said, "that the engagement between my cousin and myself is at an end. You were one of the very few who knew of it, and so I tell you."

Mrs. Toft showed no surprise. "Indeed, Miss," she answered, stooping to the hearth to light the candles with a piece of wood. "Well, one thing's certain, and many a time my mother's drummed it into me, 'Better a plain shoe than one that pinches!' And again, 'Better live at the bottom of the hill than the top,' she'd say. 'You see less but you believe more.'"

Neither she nor Mary saw Toft. But Toft, who had entered the hall a moment before, was within hearing, and Mary's statement, so coolly received by his wife, had an extraordinary effect on the man-servant. He stood an instant, his lank figure motionless. Then he opened the door beside him, slipped out into the chill and the darkness, and silently, but with extravagant gestures, he broke into a dance, now waving his thin arms in the air, now stooping with his hands locked between his knees. Whether he thus found vent for joy or grief was a secret which he kept to himself.

CHAPTER XXXVI: THE RIDDSLEY ELECTION

The riot at Riddsley found its way into the London Press, and gained for the contest a certain amount of notoriety. The Morning Chronicle pointed out that the election had been provoked by the Protectionists in a constituency in Sir Robert's own country; and the writer inferred that, foreseeing defeat, the party of the land were now resorting to violence. The Morning Herald rejoiced that there were still places which would not put up with the incursions of the Manchester League, "the most knavish, pestilent body of men that ever plagued this or any country!" In the House, where the tempest of the Repeal debate already raged, and the air was charged with the stern invective of Disraeli, or pulsed to the cheering of Peel's supporters--even here men discussed the election at Riddsley, considered it a clue to the feeling in the country, and on the one side hardly dared to hope, on the other refused to fear. What? cried the Land Party. Be defeated in an agricultural borough? Never!

For a brief time, then, the contest filled the public eye and presented itself as a thing of more than common interest. Those who knew little weighed the names and the past of the candidates; those behind the scenes whispered of Lord Audley. Whips gave thought to him, and that one to whom his lordship was pledged, wrote graciously, hinting at the pleasant things that might happen if all went well, and the present winter turned to a summer of fruition.

Alas, Audley felt that the Whip's summer, and
The friendly beckon towards Downing Street,
Which a Premier gives to one who wishes
To taste of the Treasury loaves and fishes,

were very remote, whereas, if the other Whip, he who had the honors under his hand and the places in his power, had written so! But that cursed Stubbs had blocked his play in that direction by asserting that it was hopeless, though Audley himself began at this late hour to suspect that it had not been hopeless! That it had been far from hopeless!

In his chagrin my lord tore the Whip's letter across and across, and then prudently gummed it together again and locked it away. Certainly the odds were long that it would never be honored; on the one side stood Peel with four-fifths of his Cabinet and half his party, with all the Whigs, all the Radicals, all the League, and the Big Loaf: on the other stood the landed interest! Just the landed interest led by Lord George Bentinck, handsome and debonair, the darling of the Turf, the owner of Crucifix; but hitherto a silent member, and one at whom, as a leader, the world gaped. Only, behind this Joseph there lurked a Benjamin, one whose barbed shafts were many a time to clear the field. The lists were open, the lances were levelled, the slogan of Free Trade was met by the cry of "The Land and the Constitution!" and while old friendships were torn asunder and old allies cut adrift, town and country, forge and field, met in a furious grapple that promised to be final.

If, amid the dust of such a conflict, the riot at Riddsley obtained a passing notice in London, intense it may be believed was the excitement which it caused in the borough. Hatton and Banfield and their men went about, vowing to take vengeance at the hustings. The mayor went about, swearing in constables. The farmers and their allies went about grinning. Fights took place nightly behind the Packhorse and the Portcullis, while very old ladies, peering over their blinds, talked of the French Revolution, and very young ones thought that the Militia, adequately officered, should be brought into the town.

The spirit of which Basset had given proof was blazoned about; and he gained in another way. He was one of those to whom a spice of danger is a fillip, whom a little peril shakes out of themselves. On the day after the riot he came upon a score of people collected round a Cheap Jack in the market. The man presently closed his patter and his stall, and, on the impulse of the moment, Basset took his place and made the crowd a speech as short as it was simple. He told them that in his opinion it was impossible to keep food out of the country by a tax while Ireland was threatened by famine. Secondly, that the sacrifice which Peel was making of his party, his reputation, and his consistency was warrant that in his view the change was urgently needed. Thirdly, he asked them whether the farmers were so prosperous and the laborers so comfortable that change must be for the worse. But here he came on delicate ground; murmurs arose and some hisses, and he broke off good-humoredly, thanked the crowd, which had grown to a good size, and, stepping down from his barrow, he walked away amid plaudits. The thing was reported, and though the Tories sneered at it as a hole-and-corner meeting, Farthingale held another view. He told Mr. Stubbs that it was a neat thing--very well done.

Stubbs grunted. "Will it change a vote?" he growled.

"Change a----"

"Will it change a vote, man? You heard what I said."

"Lord, no!" the clerk answered. "I never said it would!"

"Then why trouble about it?" Stubbs retorted fretfully. "Get on with those poll-cards! I don't pay you a guinea a day at election time to praise monkey-tricks."

For Stubbs was not happy. He knew, indeed, that the breaking-up of the open-air meeting had been fairly successful. It had brought back two votes to the fold; and he calculated that the seat would be held. But by a majority how narrow, how fallen, how discreditable! He blushed to think of it.

And other things made him unhappy. Those who are politicians by trade are like cardplayers, who play for the game's sake; one game lost, they cut and deal as keenly as before. Behind the politicians, however, are a few to whom the stake is something; and of these was Stubbs. To him, as we know, the Corn-Tax was no mere toll, but the protection of agriculture, the well-head that guarded the pure waters, the fence that saved from smoke and steam, from slag-heap and brickfield, the smiling face of England. For him, the home of his fathers, the land of field and stubble, of plough and pinfold, was at stake; nay, was passing, wasted by men who thought in percentages and saw no farther than the columns of their ledgers. To that England of his memory--whether it had ever existed in fact or no--a hundred associations bound the lawyer; things tender and things true; quaint memories of his first turkey's nest, of the last load of the harvest, of the loosened plough horses straying to the water at the close of day, of the flat paintings of the Durham Ox and the Coke Ram that adorned the farm parlor.

To the men who bade him look up and see that in his Elysium the farmer struggled and the laborer starved, his answer was short. "Better ten shillings and fresh air, than shoddy dust and a pound a week!"

In the country as a whole--and as time went on--he despaired of success. But he found Lord George a leader after his own heart, and many an evening he pored over the long paragraphs of his long-winded speeches. When he heard that the owner of Crucifix had dismissed his trainers, released his jockeys, sold his stud, and turned his back on the turf, he could have wept. Lord George and Stubbs, indeed, were the true country party. For Lord George's sake Stubbs was prepared to taken even the "Jew boy" to his heart.

As to the potato famine, he did not believe a word of it. He called the Premier, "Potato Peel!"

The rains of February are apt to damp enthusiasm, but before eleven o'clock on the nomination day Riddsley was like a hive of bees about to swarm. The throng in the streets was such that Mottisfont could hardly pass through it. He made his entry into the borough on horseback at the head of a hundred mounted farmers wearing blue sashes and favors. Before him reeled a huge banner upheld by eight men and bearing on one side the legend, "The Land and the Constitution," on the other, "Mottisfont the Farmers' Friend!" Behind the horsemen, and surrounded by a guard of laborers in smocked frocks, moved a plough mounted on a wain and drawn by eight farm horses. Flags with "Speed the Plough," "England's Share is England's Fare," and "Peace and Plenty," streamed from it. Three bands of varying degrees of badness found their places where they could, and thumped and blared against one another until the panes rattled in the deafened streets. The butchers, with marrow-bones and cleavers, brought up the rear, and in comparison were tuneful.

Had Basset got his way, he would have dispensed with pomp and walked the hundred yards which separated his quarters at the Swan from the hustings. But he was told that this would never do. What would the landlord of the Swan say, who kept postchaises? And the postboys who looked for a golden tip? And the men who would hand him in and hand him out, and the men who would open the door and shut the door, and the men who would raise the steps and lower the steps, who would all look for the same tip? So, perforce, he drove in state to the Town Hall-- before which the hustings stood--in a barouche and four accompanied by Banfield and Hatton and his agent. The rest of his Committee followed in postchaises. A bodyguard of "hands" escorted them, and they, too, had their bands--of equal badness--and their yellow banners with "Down with the Corn Laws," "Vote for Basset the Poor Man's Friend," and "No Bread Taxes." The great and little loaf pranced in front of him on spears, and if his procession was not quite so fine or so large as his opponent's, it must be admitted that the blackguards of the town showed no preference and that he could boast about an equal number of the tagrag and bobtail.

The left hand of the hustings was allotted to him, the right hand to Mottisfont, and by a little after eleven both parties had crammed and crushed,

With blustering, bullying, and brow-beating,

A little pummelling and maltreating,

And elbowing, jostling and cajoling,

into their places in front of the platform, the bullies and truncheon-men being posted well to the fore, or craftily ranged where the frontiers met. The bands boomed and blared, the men huzzaed, the air shook, the banners waved, every window that looked out upon the seething mob was white with faces, every 'vantage-point was occupied. It was such a day and such a contest as Riddsley had never seen. The eyes of the country, it was felt, were upon it! Fights took place every five minutes, oaths and bets flew like hail over the heads of the crowd, coarse wit met coarser nicknames, and now and again shrieks varied the hubbub as the huge press of people, gathered from miles round, swayed under the impact of some vicious rush.

"Hurrah! Hurrah! Mottisfont for ever! Basset! Basset and the Big Loaf! Basset! Basset! Hurrah! Mottisfont! Hurrah!"

Then, in a short-lived silence, "Ten to one on Mottisfont! Three cheers for the Duke!" and a roar of laughter.

Or a hundred voices would raise

John Barley-corn, my Joe, John!
When we were first acquaint!

but never got beyond the first two lines, either because they were howled down or they knew no more of the words. The Peelites answered with their mournful,

Child, is thy father dead?
Father is gone!
Why did they tax his bread?
God's will be done!

or with the quicker,

Oh, landlords' devil take
Thy own elect I pray!
Who taxed our cake, and took our cake,
And threw our cake away!

On this would ensue a volley of personalities. "What would you be without your starch, Hayward?" "How's your dad, Farthingale?" "Who whopped his wife last Saturday?" "Hurrah! Hurrah! Who said Potatoes?"

For nearly an hour this went on, the blare of the bands, the uproar, the cheering, the abuse never ceasing. Then the town-crier appeared upon the vacant hustings. He rang his bell for silence and for a moment obtained it. On his heels entered, first the mayor and his assistants, then the candidates, the proposers, the seconders. Each, as he made his appearance, was greeted with a storm of groans, cheers, and cat-calls. Each put on to meet it such a show of ease as he could, some smiling, some affecting ignorance. The candidates and their supporters filed to either side, while the flustered mayor took his stand in the middle with the town clerk at his elbow.

Basset, nearly at the end of his troubles, sought comfort in looking beyond the present moment. He feared that he was not likely to win, but he had done his duty, he had made his effort, and soon he would be free to repeat that effort on a smaller stage. Soon, these days, that in horror rivalled the middle passage of the slave trade, would be over, and if he were not elected he would be free to retire to Blore, and to spend days, lonely and sad indeed, but clean, in the improvement of his acres and his people. His eyes dwelt upon the sea of faces, and from time to time he smiled; but his mind was far away. He thought with horror of elections, and with loathing of the sordid round of flattery and handshaking, of bribery and intimidation from which he emerged. Thank God, the morrow would see the end! He would have done his best, and played his part. And it would be over.

What the mayor said and what the town clerk said is of no importance, for no one heard them. The proposers, the seconders, the candidates, all spoke in dumb show. Basset dwelt briefly on the crisis in Ireland, the integrity of Peel, and the doubtful wisdom of taxing that which, to the poorest, was a necessity of life. If bread were cheaper all would have more to spend on other things and the farmer would have a wider market for his meat, his wool, and his cheese. It read well in the local paper.

But one man was heard. This was a man who was not expected to speak, whose creed it had ever been that speeches were useless, and whom tradition almost forbade to speak, for he was an agent. At the last moment, when a seconder for a formal motion was needed, he thrust himself forward to the astonishment of all. The same astonishment stilled the mob as they gazed on the well-known figure. For a minute or two, curiosity and the purpose in the man's face, held even his opponents silent.

The man was Stubbs; and from the moment he showed himself it was plain that he was acting under the stress of great emotion. The very fuglemen forgot to interrupt him. They scented something out of the common.

"I have never spoken on the hustings in my life," he said. "I speak now to warn you. I believe that you, the electors of Riddsley, are going to sell the birthright of health which you have received; and the heritage of freedom which this land has enjoyed for generations and on which the power of Bonaparte broke as on a rock. You think you are going to have cheap bread, and, maybe, you are! But at what a cost! Cheap bread is foreign bread. To you, the laborers, I say that foreign bread means that the fields you till will be laid to grass and you will go to work in Dudley and Walsall and Bury and Bolton, in mills and pits and smoke and dust! And your children will be dwarfed and wizened and puny! Foreign bread means that. And it means that the day will come when war will cut off your bread and you will starve; or the will of the foreigner who feeds you will cut it off--for he will be your master. I say, grow your own bread and eat your own bread, and you will be free men. Eat foreign bread and in time you will be slaves! No land that is fed by another land----"

His last words were lost. Signals from furious principals roused the fuglemen, and he was howled down, and stood back ashamed of the impulse which had moved him and little less astonished than those about him. Young Mottisfont clapped him on the back and affected to make much of him. But even he hardly knew how to take it. Some said that Stubbs had had tears in his eyes, while the opposing agent whispered to his neighbor that the lawyer was breaking and would never handle another contest. Sober men shook their heads; agents should hardly be seen, much less heard!

But Stubbs's words were marked, and when the bad times came thirty years later, aged farmers recalled them and thought over them. Nor were they without fruit at the time. For next morning when the poll opened, Basset's people suffered a shock. Two men on whom he had counted appeared and voted short and sharp for Mottisfont. Basset's agent asked them pleasantly if they were not making a mistake; and then less pleasantly had the Bribery Oath administered to them. But they stuck to their guns, the votes were recorded, and Mottisfont shook hands with them. Later in the day when the two were fuddled they denied that they had voted for Mottisfont. They had voted for old Stubbs--and they would do it again and fight any man who said to the contrary. Their desire in this direction was quickly met, and both, to the indignation of the Tories, were fined five shillings at the next petty sessions.

Whether this start gave the Protectionists a fillip or no, they were in great spirits, and Mottisfont was up and down shaking hands all the morning. At noon the figures as exhibited outside the Mottisfont Committee-room--amid tremendous cheering--were:

Mottisfont . . . 41

Basset 30

though Basset outside his Committee-room claimed one more. Soon after twelve Hatton brought up the two Boshams in his carriage, and Ben, recovered from his fright, flung his hat before him into the booth, danced a war-dance on the steps, and gave three cheers for Basset as he came down. Banfield brought up three more voters in his carriage and thence onward until one o'clock the polling was rapid. The one o'clock board showed:

Mottisfont . . . 60

Basset 57

with seventy votes to poll. The Mottisfont party began to look almost as blue as their favors, but Stubbs, returned to his senses, continued to read his newspaper in a closet behind the Committee-room, as if there were no contest within a hundred miles of Riddsley.

During the next three hours little was done. The poll-clerks sent out for pots of beer, the watchers drowsed, the candidates were invisible--some said that they had gone to dine with the mayor. The bludgeon-men and blackguards went home to sleep off their morning's drink, and to recruit themselves for the orgy of the Chairing. The crowd before the polling booth shrank to a knot of loafing lads and a stray dog. At four Mottisfont still held the lead with 64 to 61.

But as the clock struck four the town awoke. Word went round that a message from Sir Robert Peel would be read outside Basset's Committee-room. Hearers were whipped up, and the message, having been read with much parade, was posted up through the town and as promptly pulled down. Animated by the message, and making as much of it as if it had not been held back for the purpose, the Peelites polled five-and-twenty votes in rapid succession, and at half-past four issued a huge placard with:

Basset 87

Mottisfont . . . 83

Vote for Basset and the Big Loaf!

Basset wins!

Great was the enthusiasm, loud the cheering, vast the stir outside their Committee-room. The Big and the Little Loaf waltzed out on their poles. The placard, mounted as a banner, was entrusted to the two Boshams. The band was ready, a dozen flares were ready, the Committee were ready, all was ready for a last rally which might decide the one or two doubtful voters. All was ready, but where was Mr. Basset? Where was the candidate?

He could not be found, and great was the hubbub, vast the running to and fro. "The Candidate? Where's the Candidate?" One ran to the Swan, another to the polling-booth, a third to his agent's office. He could not be found. All that was known of him or could be learned was that a tall man, who looked like an undertaker, had stopped him near the polling-booth and had kept him in talk for some minutes. From that time he had been seen by no one.

Foul play was talked of, and the search went on, but meantime the procession--the poll closed at half-past six--must start if it was to do any good. It did so, and with its flares, its swaying placard, its running riff-raff, now luridly thrown up by the lights, now lost in shadow, formed the most picturesque scene that the election had witnessed. The absence of the candidate was a drawback, and some shook their heads over it. But the more knowing put their tongues in their cheeks, aware that whether he were there or not, and whether they marched or stayed at home, neither side would be a vote the better!

At half--past five the figures were,

Basset 87

Mottisfont . . . 86

There were still fourteen votes to poll, and on the face of things victory hung in the balance.

But at that hour Stubbs moved. He laid down his newspaper, gave Farthingale an order, took up a slip of paper and his hat, and went by way of the darkest street to The Butterflies. He walked thoughtfully, with his chin on his breast, as if he had no great appetite for the interview before him. By the time he reached the house the poll stood at

Mottisfont . . . 96

Basset 87

And long and loud was the cheering, wild the triumph of the landed interest. The town was fuller than ever, for during the last hour the farmers and their men had trooped in, Brown Heath had sent its colliers, and a crowd filling every yard of space within eye-shot of the polling-booth greeted the news. To hell with Peel! Down with Cobden! Away with the League! Hurrah! Hurrah! Stubbs, had he been there, would have been carried shoulder-high. Old Hayward was lifted and carried, old Musters of the Audley Arms, one or two of the Committee. It was known that four votes only remained unpolled, so that Mottisfont's victory was secure.

At The Butterflies, whither the cheering of the crowd came in gusts that rose and fell by turns, Stubbs nodded to the maid and went up the stairs unannounced. Audley was writing at a side-table facing the room. He looked up eagerly. "Well?" he said, putting down his quill. "Is it over?"

Stubbs laid the slip of paper before him. "It's not over, my lord," he answered soberly. "But that is the result. I am sorry that it is no better."

Audley looked at the paper. "Nine!" he exclaimed. He looked at Stubbs, he looked again at the paper. "Nine? Good G--d, man, you don't mean it? You can't mean it! You don't mean that that is the best we could do?"

"We hold the seat, my lord," Stubbs said.

"Hold the seat!" Audley replied, staring at him with furious eyes. "Hold the seat? But I thought that it was a safe seat? I thought that it was a seat that couldn't be lost! When five, only five, votes would have cast it the other way! Why, man, you cannot have known anything about it! No more about it than the first man in the street!"

"My lord----"

"Not a jot more!" Audley repeated. He had been prepared for something like this, but the certainty that if he had cast his weight on the other side, the side that had sinecures and places and pensions, he would have turned the scale--this was too much for his temper. "Nine!" he rapped out with another oath. "I can only think that the Election has been mismanaged! Grievously, grievously mismanaged, Mr. Stubbs!"

"If your lordship thinks so----"

"I do!" Audley retorted, his certainty that the man before him had thwarted his plans, carrying him farther than he intended. "I do! Nine! Good G--d, man! When you assured me----"

"Whatever I assured your lordship," Stubbs said firmly, "I believed. And--no, my lord, you must allow me to speak now--what I promised would have been borne out--fully borne out by the result in normal times. But I did not allow enough for the split in the party, nor for the wave of madness----"

"As you think it!"

"And surely as your lordship also thinks it!" Stubbs rejoined smartly, "that has swept over the country! In these circumstances it is something to hold the seat, which a return to sanity will certainly assure to us at the next election."

"The next election!" Audley muttered scornfully. For the moment he was too angry to play a part or to drape his feelings.

"But if your lordship is dissatisfied----"

"Dissatisfied? I am d--nably dissatisfied."

"Then your lordship has the power," Stubbs said slowly, "to dispense with my services."

"I know that, sir."

"And if you do not think fit to take that step, my lord----"

"I shall consider it!"

Another word or two and the deed had been done, for both men were too angry to fence. But before that last word was spoken Audley's man entered. He handed a card to his master and waited.

Audley looked at the card longer than was necessary and under cover of the pause regained control of himself. "Who brought this?" he asked.

"A messenger from the Swan, my lord."

"Tell him----" He broke off. Holding out the card for Stubbs to take, "Do you know anything about this?" he asked.

Stubbs returned the card. "No, my lord," he said coldly. "I know nothing."

"Business of great importance to me? D--n his impudence, what business important to me can he have?" Audley muttered. Then, "My compliments to Mr. Basset and I am leaving in the morning, but I shall be at home this evening at nine."

The servant retired. Audley looked askance at his agent. "You'd better be here," he muttered ungraciously. "We can settle what we were talking about later."

"Very good, my lord," Stubbs answered. And nothing more being said, he took himself off.

He was not sorry that they had been interrupted. Much of his income and more of his importance sprang from the Audley agency, but rather than be treated as if he were a servant, he would surrender both--in his way he was a proud man. Still he did not want to give up either; and if time were given he thought that his lordship would think better of the matter.

As he returned to his office, choosing the quiet streets by which he had come, he had a glimpse, through an opening, of the distant Market-place. A sound of cheering, a glare of smoky light, a medley of leaping, running forms, a something uplifted above the crowd, moved across his line of vision. Almost as quickly it vanished, leaving only the reflection of retreating torches. "Hurrah! Hurrah for Mottisfont! Hurrah!" Still the cheering came faintly to his ears.

He sighed. Riddsley had remained faithful-by nine! But he did not deceive himself. It was the writing on the wall. The Corn Laws were doomed, and with them much that he had loved, much that he cherished, much in which he believed.

CHAPTER XXXVII: A TURN OF THE WHEEL

Audley was suspicious and ill at ease. Standing on the hearth-rug with his back to the fire, he fixed the visitor with his eyes, and with secret anxiety asked himself what he wanted. The possibility that Basset came to champion Mary had crossed his mind more than once; if that were so he would soon dispose of him! In the meantime he took civility for his cue, exchanged an easy word or two about the poll and the election, and between times nodded to Stubbs to be seated. Through all, his eyes were watchful and he missed nothing.

"I asked Mr. Stubbs to be here," he said when a minute or two had been spent in this by-play, "as you spoke of business. You don't object?"

"Not at all," Basset replied. His face was grave. "I should tell you at once, Audley," he added, "that my mission is not a pleasant one."

The other raised his eyebrows. "You are sure that it concerns me?"

"It certainly concerns you. Though, as things stand, not very materially. I knew nothing of the matter myself until three o'clock to-day, and at first I doubted if it was my duty to communicate it. But the facts are known to a third person, they may be used to annoy you in the future, and though the task is unpleasant, I decided that I had no option."

Audley set his broad shoulders against the mantel-shelf. "But if the facts don't affect me?" he said.

"In a way they do. Not as they might under other circumstances. That is all."

"And yet you are making our hair stand on end! I confess you puzzle me. Well, let us have it. What is it all about?"

"A little time ago you recovered, if you remember, your Family Bible." "Well? What of that?"

"I have just learned that the man did not hand over all that he had. He kept back--it now appears--certain papers."

"Ah!" Audley's voice was stern. "Well, he has had his chance. This time, I can promise him a warrant will follow."

"Perhaps you will hear me out first?"

"No," was the sharp reply. Audley's temper was getting the better of him. "Last time, my dear fellow, you compounded with him; your motive an excellent one I don't doubt. But if he now thinks to get more money from me--and for other papers--I can promise him that he will see the inside of Stafford gaol. Besides, my good friend, you gave us to understand that he had surrendered all he had."

"I am afraid I did, and I fear I was wrong. Why he deceived me, and has now turned about, I know no more than you do!"

"I think I can enlighten you," the other answered--his fears as well as his temper were aroused. "The rogue is shallow. He thinks to be paid twice. Once by you and once by me. But you can tell him that this time he will be paid in other coin."

"I'm afraid that there is more in it than that," Basset said. "The fact is the papers he now produces, Audley, are of another character."

"Oh! The wind blows in that quarter, does it?" my lord replied. "You don't mean that you've come here--why, d--n it, man," with sudden passion, "either you are very simple, or you are art and part----"

"Steady, steady, my lord," Stubbs said, interposing discreetly. Hitherto he had not spoken. "There's no need to quarrel! I am sure that Mr. Basset's intentions are friendly. It will be better if he just tells us what these documents are which are now put forward. We shall then be able to judge where we stand."

"Go ahead," Audley said, averting his face and sulkily relapsing against the mantel-shelf. "Put your questions! And, for God's sake, let's get to the point!"

"The paper that is pertinent is a deed," Basset explained. "I have the heads of it here. A deed made between Peter Paravicini Audley, your ancestor, the Audley the date of whose marriage has been always in issue--between him on the one side, and his father and two younger brothers on the other."

"What is the date?" Stubbs asked.

"Seventeen hundred and four."

"Very good, Mr. Basset." Stubbs's tone was now as even as he could make it, but an acute listener would have detected a change in it. "Proceed, if you please."

Before Basset could comply, my lord broke in. "What's the use of this? Why the d--l are we going into it?" he cried. "If this man is out for plunder I will make him smart as sure as my name is Audley! And any one who supports him. In the meantime I want to hear no more of it!"

Basset moved in his chair as if he would rise. Stubbs intervened.

"That is one way of looking at it, my lord," he said temperately. "And I'm not saying that it is the wrong way. But I think we had better hear what Mr. Basset has to say. He is probably deceived----"

"He has let himself be used as a catspaw!" Audley cried. His face was flushed and there was an ugly look in his eyes.

"But he means us well, I am sure," the lawyer interposed. "At present I don't see"--he turned and carefully snuffed one of the candles--"I don't see----"

"I think you do!" Basset answered. He had had a long day and he had come on an unpleasant business. His own temper was not too good. "You see this, at any rate, Mr. Stubbs, that such a deed may be of vital import to your client."

"To me?" Audley exclaimed. Was it possible that the thing he had so long feared--and had ceased to fear--was going to befall him? Was it possible that at the eleventh hour, when he had burnt his boats, when he had thought all danger at an end--no, it was impossible! "To me?" he repeated passionately.

"Yes," Basset replied. "Or, rather, it would be of vital import to you in other circumstances."

"In what other circumstances? What do you mean?"

"If you were not about to marry the only person who, with you, is interested."

Audley cut short, by a tremendous effort, the execration that burst from his lips. His face, always too fleshy for his years, swelled till it was purple. Then, and as quickly, the blood ebbed, leaving it gray and flabby. He would have given much, very much at this moment to be able to laugh or to utter a careless word. But he could do neither. The blow had been too sudden, too heavy, too overwhelming. Only in his nightmares had he seen what he saw now!

Meanwhile Stubbs, startled by the half-uttered oath and a little out of his depth--for he had heard nothing of the engagement--intervened. "I think, my lord," he said, "you had better leave this to me. I think you had, indeed. We are quite in the dark and we are not getting forward. Let us have the facts, Mr. Basset. What is the gist of this deed? Or, first, have you seen it?"

"I have."

"And read it?"

"I have."

"It appears to you--I only say it appears--to be genuine?"

"I have no doubt that it is genuine," Basset replied. "It bears the marks of age, and it was found in the chest with the old Bible. If the book is genuine----"

The lawyer raised his hand. "Too fast," he said. "You say it was found! You mean that this man says it was found?"

"Yes."

"Precisely. But there is a difference. Still, we have cleared the ground. Now, what does this deed purport to be?"

Basset produced a slip of paper. "An agreement," he read from it, "between Peter Paravicini Audley and his father and his two younger brothers. After admitting that the entry of the marriage in the register is misleading and that no marriage took place until after the birth of his son, Peter Paravicini undertakes that, in consideration of his father and his brothers taking no action and making no attack upon his wife's reputation, she being their cousin, he will not set up for the said son, or the issue of the said son, any claim to the title or estates."

Audley listened to the description, so clear and so precise, and he recognized that it tallied with the deed which tradition had always held to exist but of which John Audley had been able to give no proof. He heard, he understood; yet while he listened and understood, his mind was working to another end, and viewing with passion the tragedy which fate had prepared for him. Too late! Too late! Had this become known a week, only a week, earlier, how lightly had the blow fallen! How impotently! But he had cut the rope, he had severed the strands once carefully twisted, that bound him to safety! And then the irony, the bitterness, the cruelty of those words of Basset's, "in other circumstances!" They bit into his mind.

Still he suffered in silence, and only his stillness and his unhealthy color betrayed the despair that gripped and benumbed his soul. Stubbs did not look at him; perhaps he was careful not to look at him. The lawyer sat thinking and drumming gently with his fingers on the table. "Just so, just so," he said presently. "On the face of it, the document of which Mr. John Audley tried to give secondary evidence, and which a person fraudulently inclined would of course concoct. That touch of the cousin well brought in!"

"But the lady was his cousin," Basset said.

"All the world knows it," the lawyer retorted coolly, "and use has been made of the knowledge.

But, of course, there are a hundred things to be proved before any weight can be given to this document; its origin, the custody from which it comes, the signatures, the witnesses. Its production by a man who has once endeavored to blackmail is alone suspicious. And the deed itself is at variance with the evidence of the Bible."

"But that variance bears out the deed, which is to secure the younger sons' rights while covering the reputation of the lady."

The lawyer shook his head. "Very clever," he said. "But, frankly, the matter has an ugly look, Mr. Basset."

"Lord Audley says nothing," Basset replied, nettled by the lawyer's phrase.

"And will say nothing," Stubbs rejoined genially, "if he is advised by me. In the circumstances, as I understand them, he is not affected as he might be, but this is still a serious matter. We are not quarrelling with you for coming to us, Mr. Basset. On the contrary. But I would like to know why the man came to you."

"The answer is simple," Basset explained. "I am Mr. Audley's executor. On his account, I am obliged to be interested. The moment I learned this I saw that, be it true or false, I must disclose it to Miss Audley. But I thought it fair to open it to Lord Audley first that he might tell the young lady himself, if he preferred to do so."

Stubbs nodded. "Very proper," he replied. "And where, in the meantime, is this--precious document?"

"I lodged it with Mr. Audley's bankers this afternoon."

Stubbs nodded again. "Also very proper," he said. "Just so."

Basset rose. "I've told you what I know. If there is nothing more?" he said. He looked at Audley, who had turned his back on them and, with his hands in his pockets and one foot on the fender, was gazing into the fire.

"I think that's all," Stubbs hastened to say. "I am sure that his lordship is obliged to you, Mr. Basset, though it is a hundred to one that there is nothing in this."

At that, however, Audley turned about. He had pulled himself together, and his manner was excellent. "I would like to say that for myself," he said frankly, "I owe you many thanks for the straightforward course you have taken, Basset. You must pardon my momentary annoyance. Perhaps you will kindly keep this business to yourself for--shall we say--three days? I will speak myself to my cousin, but I should like to make one or two inquiries first."

Basset agreed willingly. He hated the whole thing and his part in it. It forced him to champion, or to seem to champion, Mary against her betrothed; and so set him in that kind of opposition to his rival which he loathed. It was only after some hesitation that he had determined to see Audley, and now that he had seen him, the sooner he was clear of the matter the happier he would be. So, "Certainly," he repeated, thinking that the other was taking it very well. "And now, as I have had a hard day, I will say good-night."

"Good-night, and believe me," my lord added warmly, "we recognize the friendliness of your action."

Outside, in the darkness of the road, Basset drew a breath of relief. He had had a hard day and he was utterly weary. But he had come now, thank God, to an end of many things; of the canvass he had detested and the contest in which he had been beaten; of his relations with Mary, whom he had lost; of this imbroglio, which he hated; of Riddsley and the Gatehouse and the old life there! He could go to his inn and sleep the clock round. In his bed he would be safe, he would be free from troubles. It seemed to him a refuge. Till the morrow he need think of nothing, and when he came forth again it would be to a new life. Henceforth Blore, his old house and his starved acres must bound his ambitions. With the money which John Audley had left him he would dig and drain and fence and build, and be by turns Talpa the mole and Castor the beaver. In time, as he began to see the fruit of his toil, he would win to some degree of content, and be glad, looking back, that he had made this trial of his powers, this essay towards a wider usefulness. So, in the end, he would come through to peace.

But at this point the current of his thoughts eddied against Toft, and he cursed the man anew. Why had he played these tricks? Why had he kept back this paper? Why had he produced it now and cast on others this unpleasant task?

CHAPTER XXXVIII: TOFT'S LITTLE SURPRISE

Toft had gone into Riddsley on the polling-day, but had returned before the result was known. "What the man was thinking of," his wife declared in wrath, "beats me! To be there hours and hours and come out no wiser than he went, and we waiting to hear--a babe would ha' had more sense! The young master that we've known all our lives, to be in or out, and we to know nothing till morning! It passes patience!"

Mary had her own feelings, but she concealed them. "He must know how it was going when he left?" she said.

"He doesn't know an identical thing!" Mrs. Toft replied. "And all he'd say was, 'There, there, what does it matter?' For all the world as if he spoke to a child! 'What else matters, man?' says I. 'What did you go for?' But there, Miss, he's beyond me these days! I believe he's going like the poor master, that had a bee in his bonnet, God forgive me for saying it! But what'd one not say, and we to wait till morning not knowing whether those plaguy Repealers are in or out!"

"But Mr. Basset is for Repeal," Mary said.

"What matter what he's for, if he's in?" Mrs. Toft replied loftily. "But to wait till morning to know--the man's no better than a numps!"

In the end, it was Mr. Colet who brought the news to the Gatehouse. He brought it to Etruria and so much of moment with it that before noon the election result had been set aside as a trifle, and Mary found herself holding a kind of court in the parlor--Mr. Colet plaintiff, Etruria defendant, Mrs. Toft counsel for the defence. Absence had but strengthened Mr. Colet's affection, and he came determined to come to an understanding with his mistress. He saw his way to making a small income by writing sermons for his more indolent brethren, and, in the meantime, Mr. Basset was giving him food and shelter; in return he was keeping Mr. Basset's accounts, and he was saving a little, a very little, money. But the body of his plea rested not on these counts, but on the political change. Repeal was in the air, repeal was in the country. Vote as Riddsley might, the Corn Laws were doomed. His opinions would no longer be banned; they would soon be the opinions of the majority, and with a little patience he might find a new curacy. When that happened he wished to marry Etruria.

"And why not?" Mary asked.

"I will never marry him to disgrace him," Etruria replied. She stood with bowed head, her hands clasped before her, her beautiful eyes lowered.

"But you love him?" Mary said, blushing at her own words.

"If I did not love him I might marry him," Etruria rejoined. "I am a servant, my father's a servant. I should be wronging him, and he would live to know it."

"To my way o' thinking, 'Truria's right," her mother said. "I never knew good come of such a marriage! He's poor, begging his reverence's pardon, but, poor or rich, his place is there." She pointed to the table. "And 'Truria's place is behind his chair."

"But you forget," Mary said, "that when she is Mr. Colet's wife her place will be by his side."

"And much good that'll do him with the parsons and such like, as are all gleg together! If he's in their black books for preaching too free--and when you come to tithes one parson is as like another as pigs o' the same litter--he'll not better himself by taking such as Etruria, take my word for it, Miss!"

"I will never do it," said Etruria.

"But," Mary protested, "Mr. Colet need not live here, and in another part people will not know what his wife has been. Etruria has good manners and some education, Mrs. Toft, and what she does not know she will learn. She will be judged by what she is. If there is a drawback, it is that such a marriage will divide her from you and from her father. But if you are prepared for that?"

Mrs. Toft rubbed her nose. "We'd be willing if that were all," she said. "She'd come to us sometimes, and there'd be no call for us to go to her."

Mr. Colet looked at Etruria. "If Etruria will come to me," he said, "I will be ashamed neither of her nor her parents."

"Bravely said!" Mary cried.

"But there's more to it than that," Mrs. Toft objected. "A deal more. Mr. Colet nor 'Truria can't live upon air. And it's my opinion that if his reverence gets a curacy, he'll lose it as soon as it's known who his wife is. And he can't dig and he can't beg, and where'll they be with the parsons all sticking to one another as close as wax?"

"He'll not need them!" replied a new speaker, and that speaker was Toft. He had entered silently, none of them had seen him, and the interruption took them aback. "He'll not need them," he repeated, "nor their curacies. He'll not need to dig nor beg. There's changes coming. There's changes coming for more than him, Miss. If Mr. Colet's willing to take my girl she'll not go to him empty-handed."

"I will take her as she stands," Mr. Colet said, his eyes shining. "She knows that."

"Well, you'll take her, sir, asking your pardon, with what I give her," Toft answered. "And that'll be five hundred pounds that I have in hand, and five hundred more that I look to get. Put 'em together and they'll buy what's all one with a living, and you'll be your own rector and may snap your fingers at 'em!"

They stared at the man, while Mrs. Toft, in an awestruck tone, cried, "You're out of your mind, Toft! Five hundred pounds! Whoever heard of the like of us with that much money?"

"Silence, woman," Toft said. "You know naught about it."

"But, Toft," Mary said, "are you in earnest? Do you understand what a large sum of money this is?"

"I have it," the man replied, his sallow cheek reddening. "I have it, and it's for Etruria."

"If this be true," Mr. Colet said slowly, "I don't know what to say, Toft."

"You've said all that is needful, sir," Toft replied. "It's long I've looked forward to this. She's yours, and she'll not come to you empty-handed, and you'll have no need to be ashamed of a wife that brings you a living. We'll not trouble except to see her at odd times in the year. It will be enough for her mother and me that she'll be a lady. She never was like us."

"Hear the man!" cried Mrs. Toft between admiration and protest. "You'd suppose she wasn't our child!"

But Mary went to him and gave him her hand. "That's very fine, Toft," she said. "I believe Etruria will be as happy as she is good, and Mr. Colet will have a wife of whom he may be proud. But Etruria will not be Etruria if she forgets her parents or your gift. Only you are sure that you are not deceiving yourself?"

"There's my bank-book to show for half of it," Toft replied. "The other half is as certain if I live three months!"

"Well, I declare!" Mrs. Toft cried. "If anybody'd told me yesterday that I'd have--'Truria, han't you got a word to say?"

Etruria's answer was to throw her arms round her father's neck. Yet it is doubtful if the moment was as much to her as to the ungainly, grim--visaged man, who looked so ill at ease in her embrace.

The contrast between them was such that Mary hastened to relieve the sufferer. "Etruria will have more to say to Mr. Colet," she said, "than to us. Suppose we leave them to talk it over."

She saw the Tofts out after another word or two, and followed them. "Well, well, well!" said Mrs. Toft, when they stood in the hall. "I'm sure I wish that everybody was as lucky this day--if all's true as Toft tells us."

"There's some in luck that don't know it!" the man said oracularly. And he slid away.

"If he said black was white, I'd believe him after this," his wife exclaimed, "asking your pardon, Miss, for the liberties we've taken! But you'd always a fancy for 'Truria. Anyway, if there's one will be pleased to hear the news, it's the Squire! If I'd some of those nine here that voted against him I'd made their ears burn!"

"But perhaps they thought that Mr. Basset was wrong," Mary said.

"What business had they o' thinking?" Mrs. Toft replied. "They had ought to vote; that's enough for them."

"Well, it does seem a pity," Mary allowed. And then, because she fancied that Mrs. Toft looked at her with meaning, she went upstairs and, putting on her hat and cloak, went out. The day was cold and bright, a sprinkling of snow lay on the ground, and a walk promised her an opportunity of thinking things over. Between the Butterflies, at the entrance to the flagged yard, she hung a moment in doubt, then she set off across the park in the direction of the Great House.

At first her thoughts were busy with Etruria's fortunes and the mysterious windfall which had enriched Toft. How had he come by it? How could he have come by it? And was the man really sane? But soon her mind took another turn. She had strayed this way on the morning after her arrival at the Gatehouse, and, remembering this, she looked across the gray, frost-bitten park, with its rows of leafless trees and its naked vistas. Her mind travelled back to that happy morning, and involuntarily she glanced behind her.

But to-day no one followed her, no one was thinking of her. Basset was gone, gone for good, and it was she who had sent him away. The May morning when he had hurried after her, the May sunshine, gay with the songs of larks and warm with the scents of spring were of the past. To-day she looked on a bare, cold landscape and her thoughts matched it. Yet she had no ground to complain, she told herself, no reason to be unhappy. Things might have been worse, ah, so much worse, she reflected. For a week ago she had been a captive, helpless, netted in her own folly! And now she was free.

Yes, she ought to be happy, being free; and, more than free, independent.

But she must go from here. And for many reasons the thought of going was painful to her. During the nine months which she had spent at the Gatehouse it had become a home. Its panelled rooms, its austerity, its stillness, the ancient woodlands about it were endeared to her by the memory of lamp-lit evenings and long summer days. The very plainness and solitude of the life, which had brought the Tofts and Etruria so near to her, had been a charm. And if her sympathy with her uncle had been imperfect, still he had been her uncle and he had been kind to her.

All this she must leave, and something else which she did not define; which was bound up with it, and which she had come to value when it was too late. She had taken brass for gold, and tin for silver! And now it was too late. So that it was no wonder that when she came to the hawthorn-tree where she had gathered her may that morning, a sob rose in her throat. She knew the tree! She had marked it often. But to-day there was no one to follow her, no one to call her back, no one to say that she should go no farther. Basset was gone, her uncle was dead.

Telling herself that, as she would never see it again, she would go as far as the Great House, she pushed on to the Yew Walk. Its recesses showed dark, the darker for the sprinkling of snow that lay in the park. But it was high noon, there was nothing to fear, and she pursued the path until she came to the crumbling monster that tradition said was a butterfly.

She was still viewing it with awe, thinking now of the duel which had taken place there, now of her uncle's attack, when a bird moved in the copse and she glanced nervously behind her, expecting she knew not what. The dark yews shut her in, and involuntarily she shivered. What if, in this solitary place--and then through the silence the sharp click of the Iron Gate reached her ear.

The stillness and the associations shook her nerves. She heard footsteps and, hardly knowing what she feared, she slipped among the trees and stood half-hidden. A moment passed and a man appeared. He came from the Great House. He crossed the opening slowly, his chin sunk upon his breast, his eyes bent on the path before him. A moment and he was gone, the way she had come, without seeing her.

It was Lord Audley, and foolish as the impulse to hide herself had been, she blessed it. Nothing pleasant, nothing good, could have come of their meeting; and into her thoughts of him had crept so much of distaste that she was glad that she had not met him in this lonely spot. She went on to the Iron Gate, and viewed for a few moments the desolate lawn and the long, gaunt front. Then, reflecting that if she turned back at once she might meet him, she took a side-path through the plantation, and emerged on the park at another point.

She was careful not to reach home until late in the day and then she learned that he had called, that he had waited, and that in the end Toft had seen him; and that he had departed in no good temper. "What Toft said to him," Mrs. Toft reported, "I know no more than the moon, but whatever it was his lordship marched off, Miss, as black as thunder."

After that nothing happened, and of the four at the Gatehouse Etruria alone was content. Mrs.

Toft was uneasy about the future--what were they going to do?--and perplexed by Toft's mysterious fortune--how had he come by it? Toft himself was on the rack, looking for things to happen--and nothing happened. And Mary knew that she must take action. She could not stay at the Gatehouse, she could not remain as the guest either of Basset or of Lord Audley.

But she did not know where to go, and no suggestion reached her. At length she wrote, two days after Lord Audley's visit, to Quebec Street, to the house where she had stayed with her father many years before. It was the only address of the kind that she knew. But she received no answer, and her heart sank. The difficulty, small as it was, harassed her; she had no adviser, and ten times a day, to keep up her spirits, she had tell herself that she was independent, that she had eight thousand pounds, that the whole world was open to her, and that compared with the penniless girl who had lived on the upper floor of the Hôtel Lambert she was fortunate!

But in the Hôtel Lambert she had had work to do, and here she had none!

She thought of taking rooms in Riddsley, but Lord Audley was there and she shrank from meeting him. She would wait another week for the answer from London, and then, if none came, she must decide what she would do. But in her room that night the thought that Basset had abandoned her, that he no longer cared, no longer desired to come near her, broke her down. Of course, he was not to blame. He fancied her still engaged to her cousin and receiving from him all the advice, all the help, all the love, she needed. He fancied her happy and content, in no need of him. And, alas, there was the pinch. She had written to him to tell him of her engagement. She could not write to him to tell him that it was at an end!

And then, by the morrow's post, there came a long letter from Basset, and in the letter the whole astonishing, overwhelming story of the discovery of the document which John Audley had sought so long, and in the end so disastrously.

"No doubt," the writer added, "Lord Audley has made you acquainted with the facts, but I think it my duty as your uncle's executor to lay them before you in detail and also to advise you that in your interest and in view of the change in your position--and in Lord Audley's--which this imports, it is proper that you should have independent advice."

The blood ebbed and left Mary pale; it returned in a flood as with a bounding heart and shaking fingers she read and turned and re-read this letter. At length she grasped its meaning, and truly what astounding, what overwhelming news! What a shift of fortune! What a reversal of expectations! And how strangely, how singularly had all things shaped themselves to bring this about--were it true!

Unable to sit still, unable to control her excitement--and no wonder--she rose and paced the floor. If she were indeed Lady Audley! If this were indeed all hers! This dear house and the Great House! This which had seemed to its possessor so small, so meagre, so cramping an inheritance, but was to her fortune, an old name, a great place, a firm position in the world! A position that offered so many opportunities and so much power for good!

She walked the room with throbbing pulses, the letter now crushed in her hand, now smoothed out that she might assure herself of its meaning, might read again some word or some sentence, might resolve some doubt. Oh, it was a wonderful, it was a marvellous, it was an incredible turn of fortune! And presently her mind began to deal with and to sift the past. And, enlightened, she understood many of the things that had perplexed her, and read many of the riddles that had baffled her. And her cheeks burned, her heart was hot with indignation.

CHAPTER XXXIX: THE DEED OF RENUNCIATION

Basset moved in his chair. He was unhappy and ill at ease. He looked at the fire, he looked askance at Mary. "But do you mean," he said, "that you knew nothing about this until you had my letter?"

"Nothing," Mary answered, "not a word." She, too, found it more easy to look at the fire.

"You must have been very much surprised?"

"I was. It was for that reason that I asked you to bring me the papers--to bring me everything, so that I might see for myself how it was."

"I don't understand why Audley did not tell you. He said he would."

It was the question Mary had foreseen and dreaded. She had slept two nights upon the letter and given a long day's thought to it, and she had made up her mind what she would do and how she would do it. But between the planning and the doing there were passages which she would fain have shunned, fain have omitted, had it been possible; and this was one of them. She saw that there was nothing else for it, however--the thing must be told, and told by her. She tried, and not without success, to command her voice. "He did not tell me," she said. "Indeed I have not seen him. And I ought to say, Mr. Basset, you ought to know in these circumstances--that the engagement between my cousin and myself is at an end."

He may have started--he might well be astonished, in view of the business which brought him there. But he did not speak, and Mary could not tell what effect it had on him. She only knew that the silence seemed age-long, the pause cruel, and that her heart was beating so loudly that it seemed to her that he must hear it. At last, "Do you mean," he asked, his voice muffled and uncertain, "that it is all over between you?"

"It is quite over between us," she answered soberly. "It was a mistake from the beginning."

"When--when did he----"

"Oh, before this arose. Some time before this arose." She spoke lightly, but her cheeks were hot.

"He did not tell me."

"No?"

"No," Basset repeated. He spoke angrily, as if he felt this a grievance, but in no other way could he have masked his emotion. Perhaps he did not mask it altogether, for she was observing him--ah, how keenly was she observing him! "On the contrary, he led me to believe," he continued, "that things were as before between you, and that he would tell you this himself. It was for that reason that I let a week go by before I wrote to you."

"Just so," she said, squeezing her handkerchief into a ball, and telling herself that the worst was over now, the story told, that in another minute this would be done and past. "Just so, I quite understand. At any rate there is no longer any question of that, Mr. Basset. And now," briskly, "may I see this famous deed which is to do so much. You brought it with you, I hope?"

"Yes, I brought it," he answered heavily. He took a packet of papers from his breast-pocket, and it did not escape her--she was cooler now--that his fingers were not as steady as a man's fingers should be. The packet he brought out was tied about with old and faded green ribbon, and bore a docket on the outside. She looked at it with curiosity. That ribbon had been tied by a long-dead hand in the reign of Queen Anne! Those yellowish papers had lain in damp and darkness a hundred and forty years, that in the end they might take John Audley's life! "I brought them from the bank this afternoon," he explained. "They have been in the bank's custody since they were handed to me, and I must return them to the bank to-night."

"Everything depends upon them, I suppose?"

"Everything."

"But I thought that it was a deed--just one paper?" she said.

"The actual instrument is a deed. This one!" He took it from the series as he untied the packet. "The other papers are of value as corroboration. They are letters, original letters, bearing on the preparation of the agreement. They were found all together as they are now, and in the same order. I did not disclose the letters to Audley, or to his lawyer, because I had not then gone through them; nor was it necessary to disclose them. I have since examined them, and they provide ample proof of the genuineness of the deed."

"So that you think...?"

"I do not think that it can be contested. I am sure that it cannot--with success. And if it be admitted, your opponent's case is gone. It was practically common ground in the former suit that if this agreement could be produced and proved his claim fell to the ground. Yours remains. I do not suppose," Basset concluded, "that he will contest it, save as a matter of form."

"I am sorry for him," she said thoughtfully. And almost for the first time her eyes met his. But he was not responsive. He shrugged his shoulders. "He has had it long enough to feel the loss of it," she continued, still bidding for his sympathy. "May I look at that now--the deed?" She held out her hand.

He gave it to her. It was a folded sheet of parchment, yellow with age and not very large, perhaps ten inches square. Three or four seals of green wax on ribbon ends dangled from it. It was written all over in a fine and curious penmanship, its initial letter adorned with a portrait of Queen Anne; altogether a pretty and delicate thing, but small--so small, she thought, to effect so great a change, to carry, to wreck, to make the fortunes of a house!

She handled it gently, almost fearfully, with awe and a little distaste. She turned it, she read the signatures. They were clear but faint. The ink had turned brown.

"Peter Paravicini Audley," she murmured. "He must have signed it sadly, to save his wife, his cousin, a young girl, a girl of my age perhaps! To save her name!" There was a quaver in her voice. Basset moved uncomfortably.

"They are all dead," he said.

"Yes, they are all dead," she agreed. "And their joys and failings, hopes and fears--all dead! It seems a pity that this should live to betray them."

"Not a pity on your account."

"No. You are glad, of course?"

"That you should have your rights?" he said manfully. "Of course I am."

"And you congratulate me?" She rose and held out her hand. Her eyes were shining, there were tears in them, and her face was marvellously soft. "You will be the first, won't you, to congratulate me? You who have done so much for me, you who have been my friend through all? You who have brought me this? You will wish me joy?"

He was deeply moved; how deeply he could not hide from her, and her last doubt faded. He took her hand--his own was cold--but he could not speak. At last, "May you be very happy! It is my one wish, Lady Audley!"

She let his hand fall. "Thank you," she said gently. "I think that I shall be happy. And now--now," in a firmer tone, "will you do something for me, Mr. Basset? It is not much. Will you deal with Toft for me? You told me in your letter that he held my uncle's note for £800, to be paid in the event of the discovery of these papers? And that £300, already paid, might be set off against this?"

"That is so."

"The money should be paid, of course."

"I fear it must be paid."

"Will you see him and tell him that it shall be. I--I am fond of Etruria, but I am not so fond of Toft, and I would rather not--would you see him about this?"

"I quite understand," Basset answered. "Of course I will do it." They had both regained the ordinary plane of feeling and he spoke in his usual tone. "You would like me to see him now?"

"If you please."

He went from the room. There were other things that as executor he must arrange, and when he had dealt with Toft, and not without a hard word or two that went home, had settled that matter, he went round the house and gave the orders he had to give. The light was beginning to fail and shadows to fill the corners, and as he glanced into this room and that and viewed the long-remembered places and saw ghosts and heard the voices of the dead, he knew that he was taking leave of many things, of things that had made up a large part of his life.

And he had other thoughts hardly more cheering. Mary's engagement was broken off. But how? By whom? Had she freed herself? Or had Audley, immemor Divum, and little foreseeing the discovery that trod upon his threshold, freed her? And if so, why? He was in the dark as to this and as to all--her attitude, her thoughts, her feelings. He knew only that while her freedom trebled the moment of the news he had brought, the gifts of fortune which that news laid at her feet, rose insuperable between them and formed a barrier he could not pass.

For he could never woo her now. Whatever dawn of hope crept quivering above the horizon--and she had been kind, ah, in that moment of softness and remembrance she had been kind!--he could never speak now.

The dusk was far advanced and firelight was almost the only light when, after half an hour's absence, he returned to the parlor. Mary was standing before the hearth, her slender figure darkly outlined against the blaze. She held the poker in her hand, and she was stooping forward; and something in her pose, something in the tense atmosphere of the room, drew his gaze--he never knew why--to the table on which he had left the papers. It was bare. He looked round, he could not see them, a cry broke from him. "Mary!"

"They don't burn easily," she said, a quaver of exultation and defiance in her tone. "Parchment is so hard to burn--it burns so slowly, though I made a good fire on purpose!"

"D--n!" he cried, and he was going to seize, he tried to seize her arm. But he saw the next moment that it was useless, he saw that it was too late. "Are you mad? Are you mad?" he cried. Frantically, he went down on his knees, he raked among the embers. But he knew that it was futile, he had known it before he knelt, and he stood up again with a gesture of despair. "My G--d!" he said. "Do you know what you have done? You have destroyed what cannot be replaced! You have ruined your claim! You must have been mad! Mad, to do it!"

"Why, mad? Because I do not wish to be Lady Audley?" she said, facing him calmly, with her hands behind her.

"Mad!" he repeated, bitter self-reproach in his voice. For he felt himself to blame, he felt the full burden of his responsibility. He had left the papers with her, the true value of which she might not have known! And she had done this dreadful, this fatal, this irreparable thing!

She faced his anger without a quiver. "Why, mad!" she repeated. She was quite at her ease now. "Because, having been jilted by my cousin, I do not wish for this common, this vulgar, this poor revenge? Because I will not stoop to the game he plays and has played? Because I will not take from him what is little to me who have not had it, but much, nay all, to him who has?"

"But your uncle?" he cried. He was striving desperately to collect himself, trying to see the thing all round and not only as she saw it, but in its consequences. "Your uncle, whose one aim, whose one object in life----"

"Was to be Lord Audley? Believe me," she replied gently, "he sees more clearly now. And he is dead."

"But there are still--those who come after you?"

"Will they be better, happier, more useful?" she answered. "Will they be less Audleys, with less of ancient blood running in their veins because of what I have done? Because I have refused to rake up this old, pitiful, forgotten stain, this scandal of Queen Elizabeth? No, a thousand times no! And do not think, do not think," she continued more soberly, "that I have acted in haste or on impulse. I have not had this out of my thoughts for a moment since I knew the truth. I have weighed, carefully weighed, the price, and as carefully decided to pay it. My duty? I can do it, I hope, as well in one station as another. For the rest there is only one who will lose by it"--she faced him bravely now--"only one who will have the right to blame me--ever."

"I may have no right----"

"No you have no right at present."

"Still----"

"When you have the right--when you have gained the right, if ever--you may blame me."

Was he deceived? Was it the fact or only his fancy, a mere will-o'-the-wisp inviting him to trouble that led him to imagine that she looked at him queerly? With a mingling of raillery and tenderness, with a tear and a smile, with something in her eyes that he had never seen in them before? With--with--but her face was in shadow, she had her back to the blaze that filled the room with dancing lights, and his thoughts were in a turmoil of confusion. "I wish I knew," he said in a low voice, "what you meant by that?"

"By what?"

"By what you have just said. Did you mean that now that he--now that Audley is out of the way, there was a chance for me?"

"A chance for you?" she repeated. She stared at him in seeming astonishment.

"Don't play with me!" he cried, advancing upon her. "You understand me? You understand me very well! Yes, or no, Mary?"

She did not flinch. "There is no chance for you," she answered slowly, still confronting him. "If there be a second chance for me----"

"Ah!"

"For me, Peter?" And with that her tone told him all, all there was to tell. "If you are willing to take me second-hand," she continued, with a tremulous laugh, "you may take me. I don't deserve it, but I know my own mind now. I have known it since the day my uncle died and I heard your step come through the hall. And if you are still willing?"

He did not answer her, but he took her. He held her to him, his heart too full for anything but a thankfulness beyond speech, while she, shaken out of her composure, trembled between tears and laughter. "Peter! Peter!" she said again and again. And once, "We are the same height, Peter!" and so showed him a new side of her nature which thrilled him with surprise and happiness.

That she brought him no title, no lands, that by her own act she had flung away her inheritance and came to him almost empty-handed was no pain to him, no subject for regret. On the contrary, every word she had said on that, every argument she had used, came home to him now with double force. It had been a poor, it had been a common, it had been a pitiful revenge! It had mingled the sordid with the cup, it had cast the shadow of the Great House on their happiness. In that room in which they had shared their first meal on that far May morning, and where the light of the winter fire now shone on the wainscot, now brought life to the ruffed portraits above it, there was no question of name or fortune, or more or less.

So much so, that when Mrs. Toft came in with the tea she well-nigh dropped the tray in her surprise. As she said afterwards, "The sight of them two as close as chives in a barrel, I declare you might ha' knocked me down with a straw! God bless 'em!"

CHAPTER XL: "LET US MAKE OTHERS THANKFUL"

A man can scarcely harbor a more bitter thought than that he has lost by foul play what fair play would have won for him. This for a week was Lord Audley's mood and position; for masterful as he was he owned the power of Nemesis, he felt the force of tradition, nor, try as he might, could he convince himself that in face of this oft-cited deed his chance of retaining the title and property was anything but desperate. He made the one attempt to see Mary of which we know; and had he seen her he would have done his best to knot again the tie which he had cut. But missing her by a hair's breadth, and confronted by Toft who knew all, he had found even his courage unequal to a second attempt. The spirit in which Mary had faced the breach had shown his plan to be from the first a counsel of despair, and despairing he let her go. In a dark mood he sat down to wait for the next step on the enemy's part, firmly resolved that whatever form it might take he would contest the claim to the bitter end.

And Stubbs was scarcely in happier case. At the time, and face to face with Basset, he had borne up well, but the production of the fateful deed had none the less fallen on him with stunning effect. He appreciated--none better and more clearly now--what the effect of his easiness would have been had Lord Audley not been engaged to his cousin; nor did his negligence appear in a less glaring light because his patron was to escape its worst results. He foresaw that whatever befel he must suffer, and that the agency which his family had so long enjoyed--that, that at any rate was forfeit.

This was enough to make him a most unhappy, a most miserable man. But it did not stand alone. Everything seemed to him to be going wrong. All good things, public and private, seemed to be verging on their end. The world as he had known it for sixty years was crumbling about his ears. It was time that he was gone.

Certainly the days of that Protection with which he believed the welfare of the land to be bound up, were numbered. In the House Lord George and Mr. Disraeli--those strangest of bedfellows!-- might rage, the old Protectionist party might foam, invective and sarcasm, taunt and sneer might rain upon the traitor as he sat with folded arms and hat drawn down to his eyes, rectors might fume and squires swear; the end was certain, and Stubbs saw that it was. Those rascals in the North, they and their greed and smoke, that stained the face of England, would win and were winning. He had saved Riddsley by nine--but to what end? What was one vote among so many? He thought of the nut-brown ale, the teeming stacks, the wagoner's home,

Hard-by, a cottage chimney smokes

From betwixt two aged oaks.

He thought of the sweet cow-stalls, the brook where he had bent his first pin, and he sighed. Half the country folk would be ruined, and Shoddy from Halifax and Brass from Bury would buy their lands and walk in gaiters where better men had foundered. The country would be full of new men--Peels!

Well, it would last his time. But some day there would rise another Buonaparte and they would find Cobden with his calico millennium a poor stay against starvation, his lean and flashy songs a poor substitute for wheat. It was all money now; the kindly feeling, the Christmas dole, the human ties, where father had worked for father and son for son, and the thatch had covered three generations--all these were past and gone. He found one fault, it is true, in the past. He had one regret, as he looked back. The laborers' wage had been too low; they had been left outside the umbrella of Protection. He saw that now; there was the weak point in the case. "That's where they hit us," he said more than once, "the foundation was too narrow." But the knowledge came too late.

Naturally he buried his private mishap--and my lord's--in silence. But his mien was changed. He was an altered, a shaken man. When he passed through the streets, he walked with his chin on his breast, his shoulders bowed. He shunned men's eyes. Then one day Basset entered his office and for a long time was closeted with him.

When he left Stubbs left also, and his bearing was so subtly changed as to impress all who met him; while Farthingale, stepping out in his absence, drank his way through three brown brandies in a silence which grew more portentous with every glass. At The Butterflies, whither the lawyer hastened, Audley met him with moody and repellent eyes, and in the first flush of the news which the lawyer brought refused to believe it. It was not only that the tidings seemed too good to be true, the relief from the nightmare which weighed upon him too great to be readily accepted. But the thing that Mary had done was so far out of his ken and so much beyond his understanding that he could not rise to it, or credit it. Even when he at last took in the truth of the story he put upon it the interpretation that was natural to him.

"It was a forgery!" he cried with an oath. "You may depend upon it, it was a forgery and they discovered it."

But Stubbs would not agree to that. Stubbs was very stout about it, and giving details of his conversation with Basset gradually persuaded his patron. In one way, indeed, the news coming through him wrought a benefit which neither Mary nor Basset had foreseen. It once more commended him to Audley, and by and by healed the breach which had threatened to sever the long connection between the lawyer and Beaudelays. If Stubbs's opinion of my lord could never again be wholly what it had been, if Audley still had hours of soreness when the other's negligence recurred to his mind, at least they were again at one as to the future. They were once more free to look forward to a time when a marriage with Lady Adela, or her like, would rebuild the fortunes of the Great House. Of Audley, whose punishment if short had been severe, one thing at least may be ventured with safety--and beyond this we need not inquire; that to the end his first, last, greatest thought would be--himself!

Late in June, the Corn Laws were repealed. On the same day Sir Robert Peel, in the eyes of some the first, in the eyes of others the last of men, was forced to resign. Thwarted by old friends and abandoned by new ones, he fell by a manœuvre which even his enemies could not defend. Whether he was more to be blamed for blindness than he was to be praised for rectitude, are questions on which party spirit has much to say, nor has history as yet pronounced a final decision. But if his hand gave the victory to the class from which he sprang, he was at least free from the selfishness of that class. He had ideals, he was a man,

He nothing common did nor mean,
Upon that memorable scene,
But bowed his comely head,
Down as upon a bed.

Nor is it possible, even for those who do not agree with him, to think of his dramatic fall without sympathy.

In the same week Basset and Mary were married. They spent their honeymoon after a fashion of their own, for they travelled through the north of England, and beginning with the improvements which Lord Francis Egerton was making along the Manchester Canal, they continued their quiet journey along the inland waterways which formed in the 'forties a link, now forgotten, between the great cities. In this way--somewhat to the disgust of Mary's new maid, whose name was Joséphine--they visited strange things; the famous land-warping upon the Humber, the Doncaster drainage system in Yorkshire, the Horsfall dairies. They brought back to the old gabled house at Blore some ideas which were new even to old Hayward--though the "Duke" would never have admitted this.

"Now that we are not protected, we must bestir ourselves," Basset said on the last evening before their return. "I'll inquire about a seat, if you like," he added reluctantly.

Mary was standing behind him. She put her hand on his shoulder. "You are paying me out, Peter," she said. "I know now that I don't know as much as I thought I knew."

"Which means?" Basset said, smiling.

"That once I thought that nothing could be done without an earthquake. I know now that it can be done with a spade."

"So that where Mary was content with nothing but a gilt coach, Mrs. Basset is content with a nutshell."

"If you are in the nutshell," Mary answered softly, "only--for what we have received, Peter--let us make other people thankful."

"We will try," he answered.

Printed in Great Britain
by Amazon